THE
YEAR *the*
STARS FELL

By

Elizabeth Wehman

Summit Street Publishing

The Year the Stars Fell
Published by Summit Street Publishing
131 West Grand River
Owosso, Michigan 48867

This book is a work of historical fiction based closely on real people and events. Details that cannot be historically verified are purely products of the author's imagination.

ISBN 978-1-7326522-2-4

ISBN 978-1-7326522-3-1 (ebook)

Publishing in the United States by Summit Street Publishing, Owosso, Michigan

Library of Congress Cataloging-in-Publication data
Wehman, Elizabeth
The Year the Stars Fell/Elizabeth Wehman-1st ed. 2020906189
The Newburg Chronicles - 1
Scripture quotations taken from The Holy Bible, New International Version®KJV® Copyright ©1973, 1978, 1984, 2011 by Biblica, Inc.™

Used by permission. All rights reserved worldwide.

Printed in the United States of America
2020
Cover Photo: Emily E. Lawson Photography
Cover Art: Emily E. Lawson
Map Artist: Jim Edward Hill

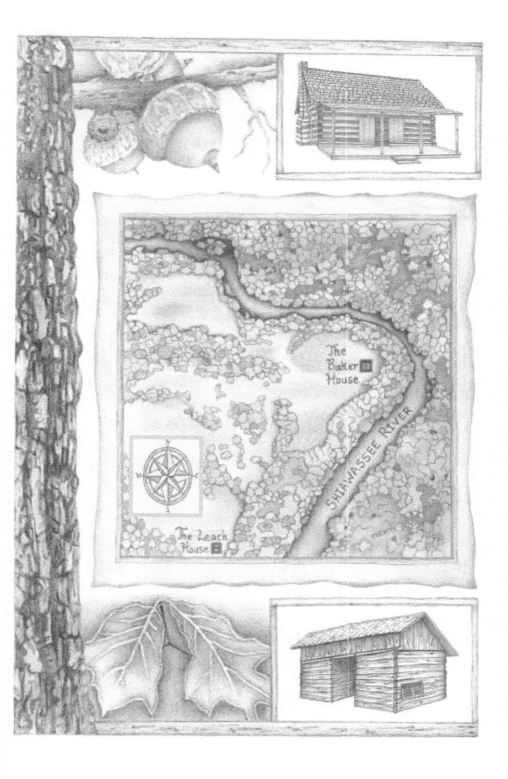

Meadville, Pennsylvania ~ Late March 1833

CHAPTER ONE

"We knew this day was going to come." Betsey Baker-Swain knew her bewildered sister had known their pa's plans since last fall, but her pleading made Betsey's heart ache. "I can't change his mind."

"But Betsey, I can't leave Meadville. I just can't. Not now." Caroline Baker gripped Betsey's shoulders. "Please talk to him." Tears spilled down her younger sibling's cheeks, as she stuttered out the plea amongst heavy shudders. "Please."

Betsey sighed, turning to glance at her husband, Aaron Swain, seated on the wagon behind her. He tried to seem oblivious to Caroline's pleas and cries.

Caroline had run out from her parents' home to greet them as they came up the road. Her shouting had startled the team and Betsey, who'd jumped from the wagon to reach her younger sister, and to find her in such despair.

"Billie is my best friend. We've been close for as long as I can remember. If we leave now, I'll never see him again." Caroline laid her head onto Betsey's shoulder and sobbed.

Betsey wrapped her arms around her sibling. "Hush now. All will be well."

"Headin' to the house, Bit." Aaron snapped the reins to steer the horses toward Betsey's childhood home, veering around the two sisters, leaving them alone on the road.

Betsey pulled Caroline off her shoulder, nudging her chin up with a finger. "I don't think it will make a bit of difference what I say to Pa. Ma had to reason with him even before he and Ambrose left for Michigan Territory last spring." Betsey sighed. "When has he decided to leave?"

Caroline's chin dropped in resignation. "Next week."

Betsey's heart sank. A lump formed in her throat and she fought back tears. "C'mon. Let's get to the house. You don't even have a coat on." Betsey grabbed the hand of her sister who had shrunk back, dragging her feet as though the Pennsylvania clay caked her soles.

Her ma, Sally Baker, always said Pa's lust for adventure was his only sin. Her pa, Hosea Baker, would reply in a whispered tone, but with a twinkle in his eye and a finger pointed heavenward, "God created me to wander as long as He is by my side."

Other sins seemed evident as Betsey came upon her parents arguing in the dining area of her childhood home, while her two youngest sisters were doing their best to gather up the breakfast dishes to wash at the kitchen sink.

Ma retrieved her kerchief from an apron pocket to wipe the tears off her cheeks, and rushed from the room when Betsey interrupted their conversation. Pa's normal looking, sweet disposition was replaced by a stern, squinted expression as he watched Ma scurry into their bedroom and slam the door. Pa sighed and gave Betsey and his other daughters, who had stopped wiping dishes, a hopeful nod, with a forced smile. "It'll be alright, girls. You just watch and see."

Betsey nudged Caroline. "Go help your sisters." Whether out of fear of making the situation more tense, or out of obedience to their older sister, Betsey's sisters took up their towels and commenced finishing up their daily morning chore. But today, singing didn't accompany their work.

Aaron entered the house, and Betsey caught his expression as he assessed the faces around him. Betsey's family rarely greeted guests with the silence that now filled the room. Betsey was embarrassed that he'd walked in and found her family in such turmoil. "Perhaps we best be gettin' on," Betsey said, giving Aaron permission to go outside rather than stay there and watch the uncomfortable scene unfold.

Aaron nodded at his wife. "Yes." Placing his hat back on his head, he walked outside, shutting the heavy door slowly behind him. They needed to continue their trek into town for weekly supplies. The past few days had brought more snow to the hills of Pennsylvania. They didn't want to be caught in an early spring storm before returning home.

Betsey turned back to her pa. "Caroline told me you're ready to leave."

Pa nodded.

It wasn't typical to have her parents in such a discussion, especially in front of her younger sisters. Her parents' 'conversations' had always been reserved for their bedroom, right before bed. As a teenager, Betsey had spent many nights trying hard to decipher their interactions as she'd drift off to sleep. Whenever their conversations got heated, Ma's voice would always be loud enough for Betsey and her sisters to overhear.

Betsey felt it wrong to listen. It was eavesdropping and she knew it. Yet straining to hear would settle her heart. Her parents' love and respect for each other was more evident during their nighttime discussions than any other time; even their tenser conversations would often end in her mother's hushed giggles or soft whispers as Betsey succumbed to blissful sleep.

That's why coming upon her parents in such a deep argument, in the morning and in front of her younger sisters, disillusioned Betsey.

Her pa looked up from his tin plate. It appeared the discussion had even curbed his appetite. Another odd sight. "It's time, Betsey. This shouldn't be a surprise to any of you."

Betsey interrupted her pa. "I know, Pa. But your decision doesn't make it any easier for any of us." Hearing this comment, Caroline dropped her dishtowel and scrambled up the ladder to the sisters' loft bedroom.

Betsey gripped the back of a table chair. Aaron was waiting for her, yet her pa's words held her in place. "There's nothing I can say to change your mind, then?" Even as the words came out of her mouth, she knew her father's answer.

Pa shook his head. "It's time."

Betsey grasped the chair tighter, fighting to think of another plausible appeal. "Why now?"

"Michigan and your brother are waiting for us." Her pa's mournful eyes now seemed to entreat her to help him. It was the same look Ambrose, her older brother, had gotten when he told Pa he wanted to head west himself just the spring before. The look was as if they hated to say their dreams out loud for fear of the retribution that might follow. Yet at the same time, the aim of fulfilling a dream so strong that setting out on a great adventure overrode the cost.

Betsey gulped. "When?"

"Soon. We can't wait much longer. I need to help Ambrose get the crops in. Get the cabin ready before winter hits again. It's March. We need to leave next week. I've put it off long enough."

Betsey's heart fluttered, her breathing intensified. Her parents really were planning to leave her.

"What I found in Michigan made me realize how valuable the property is there. We could be together again. With Ambrose...and the girls. I thought your ma would see it that way, too. Although," tears now formed in his eyes as he looked away from Betsey, "it will entail leaving you and Aaron."

Betsey didn't know what to say. The rattling of the dishes had stopped. Her two youngest sisters stared at her. Their eyes pleaded for Betsey to do something. Say anything to change their pa's mind. Betsey went for a spiritual approach. "I'm sure you've prayed about this, right?"

Pa nodded. "Of course, Bit. Always." Pa fiddled with a fork, stirring the uneaten potatoes around on his plate. "Perhaps you and Aaron...?" He seemed to want to say more, but something held him back.

"We haven't even considered leaving as an option, Pa. Not yet anyway. We just got married last summer. We're trying to make our home here." Despite the fact Betsey had wanted to beg her husband to consider it many times.

"I know." Her pa wiped his face with the cloth napkin. He called for Etta. "Come get this plate for your pa now, would you, Etta?"

Etta came for it. Betsey knew Pa was frustrated over declaring his decision. There was still food on his plate.

"It's not my place to ask you to come with us. I haven't asked Aaron first. You're his wife. I need to remember that you're not my responsibility anymore, but his. But maybe..."

Betsey stood. "I need to go. Aaron will be waiting for me in the wagon. Can you let me talk to him first?"

Pa nodded. "As it should be, Bit." Pa sat back in his chair and folded his arms. "I'll be here if Aaron wants to talk. It's a great opportunity. I know your ma would be greatly comforted to have us all together. She misses Ambrose so much since he left last year. Keep that in mind."

Betsey turned to leave, avoiding any eye contact with her sisters as she closed the door behind her. She knew this day had been coming, but she'd been under the impression it would be later this year, not next week.

Aaron was waiting for her in their wagon. He looked perplexed and worried. Reaching down for her hand, he helped pull her onto the seat beside him, then prodded the horses toward town with a snap of the reins.

Betsey felt tears brim her eyes. She'd left home last August to marry Aaron. She loved him. Leaving the comforts of her childhood home and her family, however, had been hard. To imagine her family not living down the road anymore put a shadow over her heart. The thought of finding the home occupied by someone else, would bring her more grief than she could bear. She buried her cold hand into her husband's pocket and snuggled closer.

He patted her lap. "You okay, Bit?"

Gazing at the sun rising bright in the east, she knew he deserved an answer. Trying to be strong and grown-up, she answered, "I will be." But deep down in her heart, she was far from sure. What would she do without her sisters? Her pa? Tears filled her eyes to think of Ma, especially now.

Aaron was quiet on the way back from town after their morning shopping trip. Betsey wasn't sure how much help he would be, but she decided to ask anyway. "Could you try and talk to Pa? He'll listen to you. He always has. He respects your opinion."

Aaron shook his head. "I don't think anything I can say will change your pa's mind, Bit. He and Ambrose set out for Michigan last year, determined to see what kind of land they could find and a place they could settle in the Michigan Territory. Ambrose was satisfied enough that he stayed through the winter. Alone. Your pa is probably right. It's a good move for them. Didn't you see the price of seed corn today at the store?"

Betsey nodded. The prices on the food she needed seemed awfully high as well. "Would you just talk to him? For me?"

"I don't know, Bit. Your father is awful determined. But I guess I could try." He winked with a smirk that made her heart swell with love for him. "For you."

Betsey knew it would be an uncomfortable conversation for her new husband. If her pa wasn't listening to her ma or to the pleading of her younger sisters, or even to her opinions, he wouldn't listen to Aaron either. *What if her pa knew about her condition?*

"What about?" Aaron leaned in closer to her. "You know. You said you wanted it to be a secret for a while longer."

"I don't know." Betsey knew trying to bribe her pa would never work. He'd told her so many times as she fluttered her eyelashes or planted a kiss on his cheek before asking for something. "I truly don't think even a baby will change Pa's mind. And that's not very Christian-like to try to bribe him with a grandbaby."

Aaron smiled. "I still can't believe it. If I hadn't seen the bump myself, I still don't think I'd know it to be true."

Betsey felt her cheeks grow warm. "Stop it."

Aaron kissed her cheek. "I love to make you blush."

Pulling the wagon up to a railing by her childhood home, Aaron jumped off and tied the horse lead to the post. "I'll go out and see if I can find your pa." Before he left, he helped her down from the wagon.

"I need to talk to Ma. I'll be inside."

Her sisters told Betsey their ma was still in the bedroom as Betsey placed her coat on the back of a chair. She tapped on the door. Ma's voice, with a stern tone, could be heard from behind the door. Betsey hesitated, but knew she needed to see her mother. The frame creaked as Betsey pulled on the rope to open the door to her parents' bedroom.

Ma sat in the corner, her mouth set in a straight line. The only movements were a flourish of looping yarn over knitting needles and the rhythmic back-and-forth motion of the rocker. It was her usual place to hide when she was perplexed or angry. Almost noon, Betsey now wondered if Pa would even see another meal prepared for him.

Her attention raised, Ma's voice changed. "Betsey dear. Oh, my sweet. I'm sorry you had to come up on our argument this morning. I apologize for how I acted."

"No need to apologize to me, Ma. We got you some flour while in town. Etta told me you were out before we left."

Ma nodded. "You might as well keep it for you and Aaron. We won't be using it now." Her mother went back to her knitting.

Betsey crossed the floor to her ma. "He'll change his mind, Ma. He has to. Aaron's out there right now trying to reason with him. Perhaps if another man suggests how foolish his idea of leaving is, he'll come to his senses."

Her ma's sad expression could only mean one thing. Her pa wouldn't be changing his mind. The knitting fell into her lap as she put hands to her face and sobbed. Her body shook.

"It's no use. Your pa is right. We need to move." Her ma wiped the tears off her cheeks with a swipe of her hands. "Find better schools for the girls. Ambrose is waiting."

Betsey knelt by her ma's chair. "But what about me?" Betsey regretted speaking as soon as the words left her mouth. She'd never been very good at holding her emotions in, as exact thoughts rolled off her tongue more than she cared to admit.

"Betsey. Life isn't all about you. You know that."

Betsey did, and she bowed her head in shame. She was a married woman now. She had a life with Aaron. Yet, why did her heart still feel like a little girl's begging her parents not to leave her?

"Ma, we'll work something out. I'll write. We'll keep in touch. Maybe next year Aaron and I can come out for a visit."

Ma lifted Betsey's chin, "All the way to Michigan Territory?" Her ma's years of being a farming wife etched her face. Betsey saw resolution in her expression. Despite her outside demeanor, she'd already resigned herself to Pa's demands.

"It's a long way, but we can come visit."

"You can't just leave. You have a life here. With Aaron. What about his new job?"

Aaron had just started to work as an undersheriff in the county. The job required long hours and was exhausting, but Aaron had told her it was his only chance to be sheriff someday. He'd worked hard to make their house a home. They'd made a good start as newlyweds.

These were all the reasons Betsey had forgone begging Aaron, what she really wanted to do, at the realization of her parents leaving her. Right now, Aaron was outside, probably doing his best to convince Betsey's pa to change his mind. Her mother's next words revealed again what her duty as a wife should be.

"Till death do us part. A woman's job is to stay with her husband and abide by his wishes. It always needs to come before wanting our own way."

Even as the words came out of her mother's mouth, Betsey knew how hard it was for her ma to not only say them, but to believe them, even for herself.

A soft sound outside distracted Betsey's thoughts. Her youngest sister's voice drifted through Ma's bedroom window, which was open just a crack. Jillian was singing a simple hymn, her velvety voice in perfect pitch. *"Prone to wander, Lord, I feel it. Prone to leave the God I love. Here's my heart, oh, take and seal it. Seal it for thy courts above."*

Ma sighed, leaning her head against the back of her rocking chair as she gazed out the window at the blonde girl outside. Jillian's singing, as well as the other girls', always made their ma smile.

"That child's voice is getting stronger and prettier every day." Ma went back to looping yarn around her knitting needles. "I have to be obedient to your pa. If he feels the Lord is tugging us to move west, then we must. I was just sitting here trying very hard to convince God to change his mind, but it seems—God might be on Hosea's side this time."

Betsey leaned into her ma, putting her head in her lap, as she'd done so many times before. Ma stopped knitting and smoothed down Betsey's hair. "You'll be fine, my darling. You're becoming a loving, good wife to Aaron. We'll see each other again, someday. I'm sure of it."

Betsey knew her ma. The right words were coming out of her mouth, but inside, she was fighting for control, too.

As she lifted her head, she knew she needed to act her age and adjust to what next week would mean for Ma, her, and the family. As a young girl all she wanted to do was grow up, get married, and be on her own. Why now did that dream seem to change, as the afternoon sun peeked through a cloud to brighten the room?

Her ma stood. "I need to get on with my day and stop fretting so." She placed her knitting on the chair. "I hope I finish this before we leave."

Betsey focused on the piece of clothing her mother had formed with her knitting needles. The crown twirled in a circle as she'd seen her mother knit a thousand times. This baby's cap was pink. A smile formed on her ma's face, her eyes twinkled. "You might need it soon."

How did her mother know?

CHAPTER TWO

Aaron came into the house, rubbing his hands together and blowing on them. They'd soon head for home and, even though it was a mere two miles, the chilly spring wind still brought tears to his eyes while outside. He shrugged and shook his head. "I tried."

Betsey wasn't sure how much longer she could keep pretending her pa's adventure wasn't shattering her grown-up demeanor. She loved Aaron. More than life itself, but how would she exist without her parents living just minutes from her house? How would their lives change without them? She couldn't bear the agony of thinking about it.

She raised her bonnet and tied the ribbon close under her chin. "We're going home now. When you decide on the day you'll be leaving, will you let us know? I'll come to help you pack."

Her ma nodded, "Thank you, child. We need to spend as much time together this next week as we can." Breathing in deep, tears formed again. "May God grant us strength."

As Aaron opened the door, in walked Jillian continuing to sing. *"Jesus sought me when a stranger, wand'ring from the fold of God. He to rescue me from danger, interposed His precious blood."* Jillian's face was expressive of the promises held in the song. "It's all I can do to keep from bursting into tears."

Aaron helped Betsey into her coat. She buttoned it up and listened to the high soprano voice of her baby sister who smiled up at all of them.

"This is my favorite verse of the song. I love saying Ebenezer." Jillian began again, *"Here I raise my Ebenezer. Here by Thy great help I've come. And I hope, by Thy good pleasure, safely to arrive at home."* Jillian sighed. "Ma, what's 'my Ebenezer' mean?"

"The stone of help. The song relates to Samuel in the Bible. He raised an Ebenezer stone to remind the Israelites of the great victory God had given them. Whenever the Israelites saw the stone, they would remember how He had helped them. And sweet Jillian, thank you for that reminder today."

Jillian's smile was weak, almost forced. "Singing always calms my heart." And with that, she scooted up the ladder to her bedroom. Looking back over her shoulder, she told her ma and Betsey, "I gotta make my bed. It was too cold this morning."

"Betsey, we need to go," Aaron beckoned to her from the door.

Betsey gave her ma a tight hug. "I love you, Ma."

Ma pressed Betsey's cheek to her own and brushed a kiss across it. "God will help me and you, my dear child." Ma touched her cheek with a warm hand. "Keep looking at the Ebenezer and raise it high."

Music always brought their family comfort.

"What did he say?" Betsey couldn't contain her frustration with her pa. He usually listened to reason. Aaron seemed better than anyone to understand him.

Aaron studied her with sensitive eyes but shrugged. "I don't think you really want to know what he said to me."

"What?" Betsey pulled the blanket up over her dress. Her legs were still cold from the trip from town.

"Does it matter?"

"Yes. It does to me." Betsey nodded. "I need to know."

"He talked me into considering going with them."

Betsey stared at the side of her husband's handsome face. He didn't turn back but urged the horses to move faster. "What? What did you say?" For a small moment, hope in spite of this desperate situation appeared possible. Being a newlywed, she was fearful of asking this of Aaron. *A new wife needs to leave and cleave. Right?*

Shaking his head, "I told him I'd think about it, but it was more than likely we wouldn't join them."

Her hope was extinguished like a candle from an abruptly opened door. Venturing into unknown territory sounded daunting, frightening even. She'd heard the stories from others who had family leave them for the Unknown West. Some had left their families who were still awaiting any word of what might have happened to them.

Almost telling himself what he needed to hear, Aaron went on. "Bit, I just got this position in the county. It's a good opportunity for us. I was happy they asked me to be a part of law enforcement here in Crawford County. It's a high honor."

Betsey knew it to be true. They'd just rejoiced over the fact that he'd received the assignment out of five other men wanting the job.

"Your pa loves the sense of adventure. You know that. He says it's how God made him, and I'm not doubting that, but he often puts those he loves in danger because of it. There are wild Indians in Michigan Territory. It's a vast wilderness. Quite unsettled."

Betsey had heard the stories herself.

Aaron continued, "But land is only one dollar and twenty-five cents an acre. That's mighty cheap. Territorial Governor Cass keeps putting all those articles in the newspapers. That's how they enticed Ambrose. We would have a bit more freedom there and could settle fairly close to each other to help one another get started, but Bit, I don't know. It's a risk, and I'm not sure I want to take that risk right now, especially with..."

"What?" Before the word had left her tongue, she knew who he was worried about. Over the last few weeks, her suspicions had been proven, as she felt extreme fatigue, an inability to make it through an entire meal without finding a bucket, and tears welling up at the flick of a horse's tail.

"Babies can be born. Anywhere."

"When do you think the arrival will be?"

"I'm not sure, around harvest time I'm guessing."

Aaron kissed her cheek. "I assume you're correct."

"Did you tell Pa?"

Aaron shook his head, but a smile formed. "I thought that would be something you'd want to tell him."

That was true. She did want to be the one to tell Pa.

Aaron let go of the reins with his right hand, patting her hand beneath the heavy blanket on her lap. "I'm sorry. I don't think even his first grandchild will change his mind."

Aaron had dropped Betsey off at their front door and he was in the barn caring for his horses when his father tapped on the barn door. He motioned for him to come in. "Just taking care of the horses. How are you, Father?"

John Swain lived a mile down the road in the opposite direction of Betsey's parents. "Did you happen to get that seed I needed in town?"

Aaron pointed to the corner of the wagon outside. "I haven't had a chance to bring it inside yet. I didn't realize you were in a hurry to get it, or I would have delivered it to you before unharnessing the horses."

"That's not a problem." Aaron's father waved him off. "Gave me a moment to get out and walk a bit in the spring air. We should be out of the worst of winter now. Warmer days are right around the corner."

Aaron led a horse into a stall. "Just came from seeing Betsey's folks."

"Oh, how are they?"

"They're leaving soon."

John picked up a harness and wiped it off before handing it to Aaron. "For Michigan Territory?"

"Yes."

Aaron sought an expression in his father's eyes. If he had to say out loud the decision he was considering, it would make Aaron feel inept at being a grown, married man. Both stood silent for a moment.

"Well?"

"Well, what?"

"Are you trying to decide to go with them?"

"I know that's what Betsey would like, but with me landing my new job, wouldn't it be silly for us to leave?"

John nodded. "Hosea and Sally leaving isn't a big surprise, is it?"

Aaron hung up a few of the harnesses and began wiping down the rest. "No. Ambrose has been there since last spring. Hosea went with him and found out firsthand what the land was like and whether he wanted to take his womenfolk there or not."

John removed his hat and scratched his head. "It will be awful hard on Betsey to see them go."

Aaron took a deep breath, exhaling slowly. He felt his shoulders relax.

"They've always been close, and from what Hosea has been telling me, the land is good. Perfect soil to grow crops and even a chance for plentiful fruit trees from the way he talks."

"But Father, I'm not a farmer. I want to help enforce the law. Look at the opportunity we've just gotten. What kind of law enforcement could there be in a territory not even settled yet?"

John laughed out loud. "Son, I think you misjudge the hearts of men." He patted his son's shoulder. "I think your recent opportunity to work in the enforcement of our land laws here in Pennsylvania is a great honor. I'm proud to have you a part of it, but Son, you could start on the top if you were to leave here for Michigan Territory. A new settlement needs law enforcement almost as much as here. Right?"

Aaron pulled out a barrel and propped it up to sit down. His father did the same. "You think so?"

His father patted his shoulder again. "I know so. But from what Hosea says, there are nervous, wild Indians and some selfish, contentious newcomers. Perhaps they will need a sheriff sooner rather than later. You could live close to Hosea and Sally and help them build homes and plant crops. It would be a very good opportunity out there for you and Betsey to begin a new life."

Aaron looked down at his hands, "I guess I didn't think of it that way."

"Here, you have to contend with the powers that be that have been in this part of the country for years. But to start off in a new land, where no one knows you as John Swain's son, might be a good idea."

"What are you saying, Father?" Aaron's father had a good reputation in the county, but Aaron knew there had been issues with his new wife. His father had rushed into a marriage after the death of Aaron's mother. Aaron's new stepmother was a gossip. He had many people now angry with him.

"You'll always have me, as a minister, hanging over your head. And most all law enforcement here is settled and has firm people set in place. There," his father pointed in the direction of the Michigan Territory, "you could start your own reputation. Begin anew."

"So you wouldn't mind us leaving you?"

John smirked and shook his head. "I'm not saying it will be easy. But the way I see it, with the opportunities offered in Michigan Territory, if I were your age, I'd take full advantage to get me some good land for cheap and begin again."

"You would?"

"Faster than your stepmother can weave a yarn." Aaron's father stood. "Good for children, too."

"Father, we don't have any yet."

"Even better." His father stood and put his hat back in place. "Your children can be born in a new territory. Betsey would make a great teacher. She could teach them until the schools get settled. If I were you, I'd put considerable prayer into thinking about it. I really would." The two men walked to Aaron's wagon parked outside. Aaron's father threw the sack of seed over his shoulder. "I left the money for this in the house with Betsey."

"Okay." Aaron watched his father start back down the road for home. "Father?" Aaron called out. His father turned back. "I'll miss you."

"Just know, Aaron, we probably won't be far behind. This is a golden time to leave and for a chance to settle in a new place. Start a new homestead. Think long and hard but always know, I'll miss you, too."

Glancing around, considering the horses, barn, and house, Aaron knew he could garner enough money to allow them substantial funds for a trip west. One of his friends from across town had asked about his property just the other day. He'd put off buying his seeds that day in town, hoping the price for it would go down in a week or two. Perhaps he could buy a new team when they reached Michigan Territory. Hosea said a wagon and oxen could be purchased in the new area after they'd gotten off the steamboat. Tickets were cheaper if travelers weren't hauling a team across Lake Erie.

But he'd left out one particular thing about his decision. He knew Betsey wanted to be with her family, but would she want to travel in her condition? His father's words about a new start for he and Betsey made sense, and his father-in-law's persuasive arguments caused him to pause. There was only one way to decide. He began to pray about his heart's attitude, for he knew, it wouldn't be hard to convince Betsey.

Sally packed up as much as she could of the family heirlooms. Hosea had told her that she couldn't take it all, but she'd convinced him to consider one barrel of her favorite heirlooms. She sorted through the baby things of each child. Most weren't in any condition to pass on to grandchildren, especially the girls' dresses. They were threadbare and worn, after going through four daughters.

She carefully folded a pale-blue outfit, once worn by Ambrose, and placed it at the bottom of the barrel. Perhaps Betsey would be blessed with a son. She thought about it more of late, due to Betsey's recent lack of energy, reluctance to eat, and easy tears.

On top of Ambrose's small baby outfit, Sally packed a veil wrapped in paper. Betsey hadn't wanted it for her wedding, but Sally hoped maybe one of her three younger daughters might like it. Such simple choices, but each one caused seeds of bitterness to fill her heart over Hosea's decision. After thirty years, her veil wasn't damaged like so many of her other keepsake clothing items. She'd long lost her wedding dress to rodents and insects, but somehow this small lace apparel had been preserved. She hated to part with it. Lovingly stitched by her grandmother, Sally tucked it into the wrapping paper from whence it came and stored it in what she now deemed her memory barrel. It would be a treasure for her later, holding memories only her heart understood.

So much had happened since the day she'd worn it to marry Hosea. Their wedding had dawned on a new century. They'd married at her family farm in New York, and shortly afterward Hosea had gotten the itch to move the family south to Crawford

County, Pennsylvania. She brought with her two small children, Ambrose and Betsey, and added the last three girls to their family shortly thereafter. Those years of being burdened by little ones seemed like such a long time ago.

Her thoughts were disrupted by the sound of her daughters working on their own packing in the loft above her head. They were giggling and, of course, Jillian's voice echoed off the rafters of their small home. Today she'd decided to sing one of Sally's favorite hymns. It spoke of God's love for animals which was also one of Jillian's loves. Sally would often find her in the barn or backyard, nursing some kind of animal back to health.

Estelle, *Etta* for short, loved music almost as much as Jillian, only in a different way. When frustrated with her chores or sisters, she chose singing to console her soul or settle herself after an argument. Caroline, the oldest of the younger three, wasn't as easily tempted to sing. She would sing, but only after the younger sisters urged. They needed her deeper voice to harmonize. In truth, Caroline could sing perfect pitch, giving her the ability to blend well with her sisters.

A squabble and shout brought Sally out of the bedroom to check on the sisters.

"What's going on up there?" Sally stood at the bottom of the ladder, with both hands on her hips, trying to catch a word or phrase that would hint at what the problem was with the girls. Often, they would shout down immediately who was at fault, but today...there was only silence.

"Jillian, are you aggravating your sisters again?" Sally called up.

All three girls answered, "No, Ma. We're fine."

"Well stop fussing and get to work. Finish packing up your things and get them to the barn for Pa to look over. He needs to start packing the wagon."

A "yes, ma'am" echoed from above.

Sally went for her apron. Her family would soon want their dinner. Today wasn't a day for sorrow nor for the major what-if questions to pose to Hosea. Today was a preparation day. Soon she'd leave what was familiar and venture again with her husband and daughters into the great unknown. The only consolation it would bring—she'd see her son, Ambrose, again.

Making a meal seemed daunting with just bare essentials left. They'd been trying to eat up as much of their stored food from last year's crop as they could, but she also knew much of it would have to be left for the next owner of her home.

Sadness filled her heart as she looked at their kitchen supplies she'd managed to accumulate over the past thirty years. Sorting through each item, she resigned herself to packing only the essentials. She'd regret most of her choices later, but for tonight she had enough pans, not yet packed, to make one more nice meal for her family in their Pennsylvania home.

"I can't believe you said that out loud," whispered Etta with consternation.

Jillian didn't know what else to do but cower in the corner. She'd not minced words with saying how she was really feeling.

"What if Ma heard?" Caroline scolded her younger sister.

"I don't care. I hate to think of us leaving here. I have friends at school, and all Pa wants to do is run away."

Etta turned back to folding her good dress into a small bundle, wrapping it up with the apron that went with it. "I don't want to leave my friends either, but I'm sure we will make new ones in Michigan Territory."

"I don't care what anyone says," Jillian stomped her foot. "I hate Pa for making us leave our home." She couldn't help but say it again. "Why is he making us go?"

"The reverend says that hate is a sin, Jillian. I'm sure you dislike Pa's decision to go west, but that doesn't mean you hate him." Etta said loudly.

Jillian hoped Ma couldn't hear them; Etta always had a hard time whispering.

Caroline shushed them both again. "No one hates Pa. We're just sad."

Jillian left the corner and began putting every hand-me-down outfit her sisters made her wear into the barrel.

"Jillian, we have to share that barrel. You can't take all of those clothes."

"It's only three dresses."

"Three dresses you can no longer wear. You're too big for them. Leave them here." Etta scolded her sister and took out the dresses she'd just placed into the barrel. "Go get your Sunday dress and put it here, on top of mine."

Jillian did what she was told. "I wouldn't be so sad about all of this if we didn't have to leave Betsey."

All the girls sighed now. What would life be like without their big sister? Each girl depended on her in different ways, but leaving her would be hard, especially for Caroline.

"Perhaps Pa will change his mind. At the last minute." Caroline put her Sunday dress on top of Jillian's.

"And leave Ambrose alone with all those Indians? He'd rather die than do that. We all know he loves him the best out of all of us." Etta pressed down on the clothes now filling the barrel.

"He loves us all the same. Stop talking like that." Caroline moved closer to Jillian and gave her a hug and wiped her eyes with the edge of her apron. All Jillian wanted to do was fuss, but she hugged Caroline instead.

"We'll stick together through this. We'll pray Aaron decides to come with us. Everything will be fine. I'm sure of it."

Jillian looked up at her sister, "How can you be so sure?"

"'Cause despite how you feel about Pa, I love and trust him. He knows what's best for us."

The girls' sentiments were interrupted by their mother calling up to them. "Girls, come down here and help get dinner ready for your pa. He's been working hard on getting the wagon ready. He'll be hungry."

Caroline watched her sisters descend the ladder into the bottom portion of their home. She sat down on the edge of her straw tick, putting her face in her hands. She wanted to encourage her sisters to not have hard feelings for Pa and his decision, but her heart was breaking, too. What would she do without Billie? The stories about the strange new territory frightened her.

Betsey had been the only one Caroline had shared her anxiety with about leaving her friend. But he wasn't just a friend. Billie knew it, too.

She'd just have to write him and when he was older, he'd be able to join them in the new territory. That was the only solution. Perhaps she could run into town before they left and talk to him about it.

She wiped her wet cheeks and patted her face. She didn't want Ma or the girls to know how much she hurt. Ma had her own grief. If there was anything to show the family now, it was that she could be mature, strong, and grown-up. Like Betsey. She took a deep breath and descended the ladder.

CHAPTER THREE

Typical days gave way to moving day which arrived sooner than spring. Sally had been so busy sorting and packing there hadn't been enough time to tell her friends goodbye, and of course, her heart ached over leaving Betsey and Aaron. Why hadn't Betsey come to visit more this last week? It wasn't like her.

As she wiped water from the freshly washed skillets, she went outside to attach them to the wagon for the trip north to Erie. The water on her hands nearly froze in the sharp March wind.

Aaron's father, John, was going with them as far as Erie. The wagon they loaded was his. He'd drive it back to Meadville when the Baker family boarded the steamboat for Michigan Territory. Hosea had stored his wagon in Detroit before returning to Pennsylvania for her and their daughters last fall. Their oxen team was stabled there, too.

"I hope the children come to say goodbye before we leave," Sally announced to her husband as he strapped the pans to the side of the wagon. She couldn't possibly leave without telling Betsey goodbye. Tears clouded her vision. She wrapped her shawl tighter.

"Of course they'll come, Sally." Hosea stood back and smacked his hands on his pants. "Do you need every single one of these skillets, Sally?"

"Did you tell them it was today we were leaving?"

Hosea loaded one of the girls' barrels. "They'll be here soon."

Sally glanced into the wagon. Hosea was a master packer. Each journey they'd made as a couple had been a good trip due to Hosea's packing skills. Yet, he'd left a corner of the wagon completely empty.

"What will go here?" Sally pointed to the vacant place.

"I have a few things to put there."

"You were so adamant to not take so many things, yet we have plenty of room for more."

Hosea approached his wife of thirty years. "You're aware of my packing skills. I have a plan."

Sally sighed. Trusting her husband had never been a daily virtue. As much as she tried, Sally knew she needed to stop worrying and trust Hosea. But instead, she still wasn't convinced this was a good idea. Hosea was pushing her to leave the familiar and venture into a place filled with unknowns. Doubts and fear seeped into her heart.

He laughed and caressed her cheek with his cool hand. "Oh, my dear, this will be a good trip. Just wait and see."

A chill coursed through Sally's body. She wasn't sure if it was due to the cold morning or the thought of heading into the strange, new territory. Unsettled land. No neighbors for miles. All of Hosea's stories about his trip the year before didn't satisfy her trepidations.

"I've never been on a boat before. What if one of us becomes ill, like Ambrose did last year?"

"He survived, Sally." Not looking up, Hosea glanced behind each wagon wheel. "Looks like there's enough grease on the wheels to last us on our first leg of the journey."

"How long to Erie?"

"It's only forty miles or so. If God wills, and the weather holds, we should be there in three days. We'll have to purchase tickets and inquire about a schedule for the steamboat."

Caroline came to the wagon, carrying another barrel to load into their soon-to-be-only shelter. "Are Betsey and Aaron coming to tell us goodbye?" Placing the barrel on the back, Hosea answered her in much the same tone as he'd given Sally. "They'll be here."

At that moment, a wagon began to approach their house from the southeast. The rumble could be heard in the distance.

Sally cupped her hand over her eyes to shield against the bright morning sun. "This must be them now." Sally squinted, "but it doesn't look like their wagon."

Caroline looked out through the trees in the same direction. "It isn't Aaron's wagon and those aren't his horses."

Hosea jumped off the back of the wagon after packing the girls' barrels. All three waited on the front porch for the wagon to draw near. Sure enough, John Swain jumped off the front of the wagon. "Brought you something to take on your journey, Sally and Hosea."

Just then, from behind the wagon, came Aaron and Betsey, dressed in warm traveling clothes.

"What is this? What does he mean, something for us to take with us?" Sally searched her daughter's face, "Betsey?"

Betsey's face beamed like the spring sun now rising full on the horizon. "We couldn't let you go alone."

Aaron held a barrel out to Hosea, and Hosea put it in the empty corner of the wagon.

Caroline reacted first by screaming, "Jillian! Etta! Come quick!" She scrambled into the house to retrieve her sisters.

"Oh, my dear God. What blessing are You giving me on this morning?" Sally headed for Betsey who held out her arms to embrace her.

"We're going with you, Ma."

Sally grasped her daughter's shoulders and pulled her into an embrace. "Don't you dare tease me, Betsey Baker-Swain."

Aaron came back and stood beside Betsey. "She isn't teasing, Sally. We've decided to head to the new territory with you. If that's fine with you?"

"Fine?" Sally felt tears spring to her eyes. Joy filled her heart as she clung to Betsey. "Oh, how wonderful. I'm so happy."

Just then Hosea passed by and winked at his daughter. "She didn't have a clue that empty part of the wagon was for your things."

Sally stepped back from her daughter.

Betsey leaned toward her and whispered in her ear, "I couldn't let our new baby be born without a grandma to help raise her."

Sally put her hands to her face, "A baby? Oh Betsey, I knew it."

Hosea slapped Aaron's shoulder, "How wonderful!"

"You said *her*. How do you know it's a girl?" Sally inquired.

"We do have a history of girls in this family." Betsey laughed.

They were going together as a family. Sally couldn't be happier. Perhaps this trip for her family wouldn't be such a disaster after all. As the sun burst brightly and completely above the horizon, Sally thanked God for their bountiful blessings.

"I hope you packed that pink bonnet." Betsey smiled at her mother.

"It's in the memory barrel. Right on top. I had a feeling you'd be needing it soon."

All of Betsey's younger sisters toppled out of the house and rushed down the steps to hug both she and Aaron, who blushed from the attention.

Hosea stopped everyone from hugging and laughing. "Let's get moving, family. Michigan Territory is waiting for us."

Joy filled Betsey's heart to be traveling with her family on this journey. She'd done much to prepare for the journey during the past week. She didn't have as many possessions as her mother, which made her packing easy. Her belongings were much less memorable than her parents', but gathering it into just a few barrels, proved a chore.

Aaron had sold their home quickly before it was time to leave. The friend, who'd offered him money before, had purchased it. The only thing left to sell was their oxen and wagon. Aaron's father had agreed to take their horses.

Hosea took off his hat and gathered Sally into his arms, "Reverend, would you please offer up a word of thanks as well as protection for us this morning?"

Aaron removed his hat just as his father answered, "I'd be more than happy to."

Everyone quieted, and silence came over the group as they stood in a circle, bowing their heads in acknowledgment to Reverend Swain's prayer. Bird chirping filled the air, as a strong, cool wind blew across the gathering of family.

"God...I ask your utmost attention to this dear family as they venture into the unknown. May you guide and protect them. May you give help, health, and success along their journey. May they look to you to meet all their needs. Care for them. Be with them as they cross over the enormous lake by steamboat and as they venture into the new frontier. Protect them from their enemies and get them established before another winter. Thank you for your guidance and protection. Amen."

Hats were replaced as Jillian jumped onto the front porch where she stood and sang into the spring morning. "*O God, our help in ages past. Our hope for years to come. Our shelter from the stormy blast and our eternal home. Under the shadow of Thy throne, Thy saints have dwelt secure. Sufficient is Thine arm alone. And our defense is sure. Oh God, our help in ages past. Our hope for years to come. Be thou our guard while life shall last, and our eternal home.*"

The family nodded and all said amen. Jillian's voice comforted Sally. There were some things that didn't need a barrel, her family's hope and songs.

As the wagon pulled away from their Pennsylvania homestead, Betsey couldn't help but look back. She'd never forget this house of her childhood. Memories flooded back of every moment it took to make it livable and comfortable. Her father had once thought it was the most beautiful place to settle, back when she was a child. He boasted of the terrain and the produce from his crops.

Her father had built the home with his own hands and they'd added three more sisters to the family in the years that followed. She would have never thought they'd leave it behind for a new land, but here they were, pulling away.

Betsey leaned toward Aaron and grasped his hand as he sat on the buckboard's seat. He squeezed her hand back. He was giving up a new job for her, so that she could continue to live close to her parents. She would forever be grateful to him for that sacrifice. She'd chosen a good man to marry.

As they watched the house grow smaller, Betsey's ma commented on the many memories that would always fill their hearts from this home. How Ambrose had learned how to shoot a gun and had shot his first turkey for Thanksgiving their first year there. How Betsey had learned to knit and had made everyone mittens their first winter. Going through each child she reminded them of all they had experienced there.

"Do you think we can make as nice a place in Michigan Territory?" Jillian asked.

Pa tugged on the oxen reins, "You'll love it, Jilly. Wait until you see the stream that flows by our land. It's fresh, clean, and full of amazing fish for us to eat. The crawdads are abundant, and the trees are so large, that it's hard to see where they end and where the sky begins. And the stars," Pa couldn't say enough about the territory he and Ambrose had discovered on their trip the year before. Whenever he lacked words, Pa quoted scripture. "He telleth the number of the stars; He calleth them all by their names."

Betsey couldn't imagine God having names for every star in the sky. If he did that, surely He'd be with them on this trip.

Aaron's father had been following the wagon on a horse. He drew up close beside the wagon. He'd return to Meadville with the old Baker wagon after dropping the family off in Erie. He must have overheard Pa's last comment. "All your excited talk, Hosea. I would love to go with you to see the Michigan Territory as well."

Pa answered, "Perhaps you will join us soon."

The reverend nodded as he slowed his horse to an even trot beside the wagon's oxen. "I pray God allows us the opportunity."

Ambrose had stayed behind in the new country so Pa could return and bring the family back with him. Ambrose was only twenty-four, yet bold and strong enough to live in the new territory alone. They had only received two letters from him after Pa left him. Pa prayed for his safety every night at the supper table, especially since he was living among the Indians in the new land.

"Tell us more about the new territory, Pa." Betsey couldn't wait to hear more about what awaited them. When he'd first returned last November, he'd relayed much about the land but Betsey never tired of hearing about it. Now it seemed much more important to listen.

"It smells of pine. You know, like the pine from the Christmas tree boughs decorating the schoolhouse last year. Remember how I told you that at the Christmas service?"

Everyone nodded.

"But the river is finer than any river you've ever seen."

Pa had told them that Ambrose had decided to stay close to the river. Fur traders were a part of the new land, and by staying close to the river, it provided access to the territory surrounding them without having to cut down trees to form new roads.

"What's the name of the river, Pa?" Jillian giggled as she asked. The name was particularly odd, but they loved saying it out loud.

"Shiawassee! How did I tell you to remember it?"

Jillian laughed out loud. "Shia, wait and see."

Everyone laughed with her.

"That's such a funny sounding, odd name."

Pa pulled back on the reins as the oxen and wagon rumbled over a deep rut in the road. "The Indians named it. '*Shia-*' in Indian means 'winding river,' and *'wassee'* means 'up ahead.' So, it's the winding river that is up ahead."

"Up ahead of what, Pa?" Caroline asked.

"Traders were trying to find a river headed north, and that's how the Indians described it. Follow the Shia—winding river—up ahead—the wassee. Get it?"

"I hope we get to see some Indians," Etta announced.

"Oh, you will, Etta. You will. They might even come into your cabin and eat your food."

"Alright, that's enough Indian talk," commented Ma. "The thought sends shivers up my spine."

It did for Betsey, too. She'd love to see Indians, but from afar. Reports from other settlers going west hadn't always been positive regarding the natives of the land. Pioneers had been killed by Indians. She squeezed Aaron's hand tighter.

"Indians are fine with us until we do something to harm or hurt them, and that's not our purpose for going into Michigan Territory. They are created by God, just like us."

Aaron pointed to something off to the left of the wagon. "Hosea, I think someone is trying to flag us down."

Pa looked to the left and slowed the wagon. "It does appear as if the man is waving at us."

"It's Billie," shouted Caroline who went to the back of the wagon and jumped off.

"Caroline, be a lady!" shouted Ma.

Caroline didn't care. She could see Billie pulling back on the reins of his horse as he skidded to a stop beside the slowly moving wagon.

"Billie!" Her friend jumped off his horse and pulled her into a hug.

"I had to see you before you left."

Caroline stepped back, knowing her entire family was watching them.

"I'll go slow, Caroline. Catch up when you're finished saying goodbye." Pa snapped the oxen to move.

Caroline waved to her pa and the family's wagon continued its trek north.

"I'm glad you came." Caroline didn't know what else to tell the dusty, blonde boy standing beside her.

"I couldn't let you get away without saying goodbye."

"We don't have much time, but please, before we tell each other goodbye, promise me one thing."

Billie nodded.

"Please come and find me. Don't stay away. I promise to not look at another boy in the new territory."

Billie shrugged. "I don't know if I can, but I will try."

"As soon as you turn eighteen." Caroline sighed. They'd both just turned sixteen. Two years would be a long time.

Before she could do anything else, Billie kissed her. She placed her hand over the moist spot on her cheek.

His face flushed crimson as he jumped back up onto his horse and charged back toward Meadville. Caroline stood and watched his horse grow more and more distant before turning into a dot on the horizon. *Would Billie find her?* She clasped her hands over her heart.

Wiping tears now filling her eyes, Caroline realized someone was yelling for her from the family's wagon. Looking toward the voice, she saw Jillian waving her scarf at her from the back of the wagon. She raised her hand to respond. Raising her skirt, she broke into an unladylike run to catch up to the wagon growing more distant from her on the road heading north.

The sway of the wagon intensified with each bump in the road. A settling of their possessions came with each jolt and shake. As the oxen forged ahead, they snorted from the strain in defiant protest.

Betsey thought about the next four days and the long hours they'd spend interacting and what they'd experience in the confines of the simple wagon. She loved her family, but would she start to feel like just a daughter again and not a new wife?

A furrowed brow revealed Ma's worries. There were moments, as of late, when Ma's facial expressions reminded Betsey of her grandmother. They'd had to leave her mother's parents back in New York when they'd moved to Pennsylvania. She remembered how hard that had been on Ma.

Since being married, Betsey saw her ma in a new way. They now shared recipes, housekeeping tips, even long conversations more than they ever had. Chores became less of a burden and more of a joy while working together. Betsey had spent much of the winter alone, but once a week Aaron let her travel to her parents' home to enjoy an afternoon or evening together with them. On the coldest of days, they'd pull chairs up close to the fire to knit or repair torn garments. She treasured those days together and looked forward to them each week.

Now, as they traveled in such a small wagon, quiet evenings with Aaron would be something she'd miss. She hadn't had time to think of that while preparing for the journey during the past few days. Aaron's decision to go with her parents had come as a complete surprise, and together they worked hard to get many of their things sold or given away before leaving Pennsylvania.

Had they made the right decision? Would they all love each other at the end of the trail? As she thought about this, she also imagined a life without her parents and knew in her heart she wouldn't want it any other way.

The journey didn't stop for dinner. Their dried beef and biscuits were eaten among the jolts and shudders of their small wagon. Once dinner was over, Pa announced, "Time to get out women, time to strengthen those leg muscles for the trip ahead."

The day had started off cool, but as the afternoon sun disappeared behind clouds, the air turned chillier and a damp mist hung low.

Pennsylvania spring days were almost always filled with showers. Many days would pass when the sun failed to penetrate the heavy, moist clouds. Today would be one of those days.

Betsey felt more energized to walk, even though a cool rain began to fall. The oxen tugged and lunged to pull the wagon. The walking surface grew slick and made it difficult to keep their steps secure. Pa fought for the next hour or two and soon handed the reins over to Aaron to manage for a time.

Bonnets kept the rain off their faces, but soon their shoulders and backsides grew damp.

"I'm so glad we stitched up our skirts a bit higher last week. If we hadn't of done that, we'd be accumulating much more mud than we are now," Ma exclaimed as she held up her skirt a bit. "But rain. Not sure why I hadn't assumed our travels would include that." Ma's face turned stern.

As their walk continued, their skirts did manage to accumulate a bit of the mud. Their shoes became heavier, too. And to think, this was just the first day.

Aaron seemed determined to keep the oxen on the driest part of the road. Betsey began to wonder what he was thinking as he pushed the team northward. Would he resent her for the trip? Perhaps she should have kept her sadness about her folks leaving to herself. Was he leaving his new job just for her or did he really believe that work in the new territory would suit him better? Step after step, his opinion was all Betsey could think about. If she could talk to him alone, she'd ask him again if he thought this was a good decision. Was it too late for them to change their minds? Did she even want to know the answer?

The longer she walked beside the wagon and the colder she grew, the more doubts and fears weighed on Betsey's heart, similar to how the mud stuck to her shoes, making them heavy. She glanced up at Aaron. He seemed intent on the mission, but had their choice to leave been made in haste? Perhaps they should have taken more time to think it all through.

Betsey felt a warm hand grasp her own. It was Caroline. She smiled at her with a face damp from rain.

"My feet are cold, Betsey. Are yours?"

Betsey nodded. "They're not very happy either."

Caroline squeezed her hand tighter as they negotiated the slippery trail on foot.

"I'm so happy you decided to come with us."

Betsey pulled Caroline closer, wrapping her arm around her sister's wet shoulders. There were six years between her and Caroline. They'd shared a room for years and often sang each other to sleep on cold winter nights. They were the cooks of the family, and kitchen chores kept them close.

"What made you decide to come?"

Betsey smiled. "It wasn't an easy decision. I had planned to stand by the old house and watch you all fade into the distance, and away from me. When I expressed my sadness to Aaron, he seemed to decide for the both of us without me saying much."

"I told Billie to find me. To do everything in his power to come for me, when he turns eighteen."

Betsey took Caroline's hand again. She knew Caroline was having a hard time leaving Billie. "Feelings can change over the years. Perhaps you'll find someone new."

Caroline shook her head. "No. I won't."

Betsey understood her sister's young love. "If God wills you to one day become Billie's wife, it will happen. Billie is a smart young man, and if he loves you that much, he'll do everything in his power to get to you and then you'll have the rest of your lives to be together."

"I hope so." Caroline slipped a bit and Betsey helped right her. "I hope it doesn't rain every single day," Caroline moaned.

"It won't. It seems funny to be out here without a place to call home, doesn't it?" Betsey sighed. "What are you most looking forward to about our new destination?"

"I hope Michigan Territory has nicer teachers than we have here in Meadville."

Betsey tugged on her sister's hand, "Caroline Elizabeth, you should be ashamed of yourself." She also gave her a knowing smile. The transition to a new teacher had been a difficult one from the previous one they'd had when Betsey attended school.

Etta must have overheard their conversation. She scrambled to catch up to her older sisters. "What are you girls talking about?" Etta was never one who liked feeling left out.

Caroline told her, "Teachers!"

Etta spoke her own mind. "I hope there is a better one than Miss Matthews back at the Meadville school. She was so cranky."

"That's just what I said, only Betsey scolded me for saying it."

Betsey gave her sister a serious look. "For all we know, you may have me as a teacher in the new territory. From what Pa says, there isn't even a school started yet."

"Do you think you could be the teacher, Betsey?" Etta clapped her hands. "That would be so wonderful. Miss Matthews always told me I hum too much."

Betsey and Caroline laughed.

"But you do, Etta," Betsey giggled.

"I can't help it. I have music in my soul." Etta stretched out her tongue to catch some raindrops.

"What about the Indians?" Betsey shook off the brim of her bonnet which caught a steady drip that she'd become annoyed by.

"I hope they are all around us. It would be so romantic to have Indians surrounding our new home." Etta stumbled on a large rock on the road.

"Careful," Caroline reached out to steady her sister's walk. "Aren't you afraid to see them?"

"No. God made them, too. In fact, aren't we invading their homes? Seems kind of unfair to me."

Betsey agreed. "Yes, but progress is inevitable. We've been pushing them west for so long, perhaps they're used to it by now."

"I'd be mad if a bunch of people began pushing us from our homes, wouldn't you?" Etta let go of Betsey's hand to take Caroline's instead. She was having a hard time keeping up with the older girl's strides.

"I hope they don't take out their anger on us. We're just coming for the land that the government offered us. They want settlers on the property. You've seen the advertisements Pa has been showing us." Betsey stretched out her hands as if holding a copy of *The Western Star* and pretended to read. "'The land that Governor Lewis Cass organized in 1827 is now available to homestead. Good soil for wheat, corn, and fruit.'"

All the girls nodded at Betsey's statement. Pa had done nothing but talk about the territory of Michigan since the Cass land agreement with the Indians. He said it was the way of the world. Progress was causing the frontier to fill up fast. Being some of the first settlers in a new area of the country brought promise, benefits, and even a better way of living. Why shouldn't everyone feel free to expand and move on to new land?

"It will still be scary to see an Indian in person. Don't you think?" Betsey asked her younger siblings.

They both nodded.

"Miss Matthews had nothing but bad things to tell us in school about Indians. But wouldn't it be wonderful to see a momma carrying a baby on her back though." Etta fell back a bit. "I'm going to go back and walk with Ma and Jillian. You girls walk too fast."

Betsey looked over her shoulder as Etta went back and grasped Ma's hand, who was beginning to show weariness from their walking. Would they all be able to keep this up in the days ahead?

After two hours of walking, all the women climbed up into the wagon to not only relieve their aching feet, but to also get a bit of warmth and protection from the cold rain and damp air. As they did, their dresses dragged much of the mud and dirt into the wagon with them.

Betsey's mother groaned, "I knew our wagon wouldn't stay clean forever, but look at all this dirt. And this is only our first day."

Betsey patted her shoulder, "Not only have we left our homes, but also many of the luxuries of cleanliness as well. As soon as we dry a bit and the rain stops, we'll be able to sweep out the dirt."

Betsey's mother agreed. "I wish it didn't have to rain on our first day."

Hosea turned around. "You girls are mighty good walkers. Walking two hours on the first day will build up your stamina for more. Now take a rest. Aaron and I will manage the wagon for a bit."

"The rain seems to be easing up a bit now." Aaron steered the oxen closer to the edge of the road, trying his best to miss the deep ruts now forming from the heavy rain. With a smile, Betsey tried to reassure him his efforts were worth it, but it seemed he was too busy to notice it.

Betsey's two younger sisters soon bundled together in a heavy blanket near the rear of the wagon. Betsey and her mother brought out their mending. With little light shining in from the front of the wagon, it was harder than they thought it would be to see what they were working on.

"I'm not sure I can do this here. I can't see to thread my needle." Betsey's mother dropped the garment she was just about to try to stitch.

"Here," Betsey held out her free hand, "Let me have a try."

"I have a hard-enough time, if I'm not sitting right next to a lantern."

Betsey leaned closer to the canvas opening for more light and to thread her mother's darning needle. "Just don't poke yourself." Betsey handed her mother's needle back to her.

"I do that whether I'm in a wagon or not," her mother laughed.

Caroline sat close and Betsey patted her hands, now covered up in a blanket, "Sing for us, Caroline."

"What would you like to hear?" Caroline asked.

"Somethin' lively," Pa chimed in. "I need to slap my cold hands on my breeches for a while."

'Fath'r and I went down to camp, along with Captain Good'in. And there we saw the men and girls, as thick as hasty pudd'in. Yandle Doodle, keep it up, Yankee Doodle Dandy. Mind the music and the step and with the girls be handy."

Pa slapped his hands against his knees as a smile broke out on Betsey's ma's face.

Caroline's voice filled the damp interior and reflected off the canvas. *"And there we saw a thousan' men, as rich as Squire David. And when they wasted every day, I wish it could be saved. Yankee Doodle, keep it up, Yankee Doodle Dandy. Mind the music and the step and with the girls be handy."*

Laughter now filled the wagon and almost covered the snorts of the oxen and the screeches of the wagon wheels. Caroline always insisted on changing the boys to girls each time she sang the song.

"Sing another verse, Carrie girl!" Pa had nicknames for each of his girls. Caroline's was Carrie, Betsey's was Bit, and Estelle's nickname was what everyone called her, Etta. To Pa, Jillian was Jilly.

Caroline smiled and continued chirping out the folk song of "Yankee Doodle." Everyone loved to hear her sing. The younger girls napped in the back of the wagon, but if they had been awake, the whole wagon would have been filled with music.

Music had been a part of their family since before Betsey could remember. Their mother had a voice that resembled the birds on a spring morning. She'd sung to them since before each of them had been born. Music was a part of her soul. Pa just loved to hear his girls sing.

When Caroline finished "Yankee Doodle," she continued with "The Rose Tree." It was one of Pa's favorites.

"My days have been so wondrous free, the little birds that fly with careless ease from tree to tree, were but as bless'd as I. Ask gliding waters, if a tear of mine increas'd their stream? Or ask the flying gales, if e'er I lent one sigh to them? But now my former days retire, and I'm by beauty caught. The tender chains of sweet desire, are fix'd upon my thought." Caroline's voice now sounded clear and bright, *"Ye nightingales, ye twisting pines! Ye swains that haunt the grove! Ye gentle echoes, breezy winds! Ye close retreats of love!"*

Betsey sighed, hearing the singing voice of her sister. The rain against the canvas was forgotten as she recalled winter nights sitting by the hearth and listening to her sister's voice echo in their former house. It always brought such contentment and joy to the family. As the younger two girls grew old enough to join in, they accompanied their sister.

Often, travelers or guests coming toward the Baker house would comment on the music that often filtered through the air. Betsey had forgotten how much she missed their singing in the evenings. She could sing, but not as effortlessly or as beautifully as her sister Caroline and the younger two siblings. Music seemed to soothe their souls when distraught or tired, but it also came when hearts were joyful and full of fun.

Oh, how the church, schoolyard, and their Pennsylvania home would be without the singing voices of the Baker sisters. For now, hopefully, it would bring joy to the other travelers they'd find along the way.

Betsey prayed a silent prayer that their music would help sustain them on their trip and help bring spiritual comfort to their new home in the Michigan Territory.

From Meadville to Erie, Pennsylvania

CHAPTER FOUR

The rain continued to pour for the next four days of their journey. When the fourth morning dawned, everyone was wet, cold, tired, and frustrated. The oxen could barely pull the wagon out of the ruts and muck of the Pennsylvania road.

"This is normally a well-traveled road," Pa tried to encourage his family. "We shouldn't be getting stuck every few minutes," yet despite Pa's assurance, the wagon got sucked deep into a rut as the mud held to it like liquid wax to a candlewick.

More than once, Betsey took the reins as her father-in-law, Pa, and Aaron freed a wheel from the clutching mud. The oxen snorted and pawed the ground as they tried to rock the wagon forward. At one point, they were stopped for more than an hour, attempting to unbury a wagon wheel sunk deep into the muddy road. Pa would mount the wagon bench, wiping the sweat from a brow, in spite of the cool temperature.

If only they'd known that spring's arrival would be such a wet one. Even the birds had stopped their morning songs. All the family could hear as they woke each morning was the pattering of rain against the wagon canvas.

Pa, Aaron, and John had to sleep under the wagon on most nights. Their plans of lying by a warm fire only brought a hiss of smoke each night. Guilt now replaced the anxious feelings in Betsey's heart. She hated to think of any of them cold and wet under the wagon, but Aaron was the one doing all of this for her.

They did their best to pick high ground each night, but it just wouldn't stop raining. A grove of trees brought little protection.

The final leg of their journey north to Erie brought one morning of relief; the very last morning before reaching the city, they awoke to silence. All had slept longer than usual due to nothing waking them from their needed slumber. The birds greeted them before the sun rose. By noon, the rain had begun again, but they'd made it to the shoreline of the lake called Erie. It should have taken only three to four days to reach the county seat, but they were headed into day six.

Betsey looked across the great expanse of water. She'd never seen a body of water as large. She could easily see the banks of the opposite side of lakes back at home, but this lake was much wider. Just a hint of land could be seen on the other side. Rain pelted her face as she tried to get a good look.

Pa pointed across the lake. "That's a peninsula you can see there, but past that—lots and lots of water." His eyes twinkled. "They call the peninsula Presque Isle. It was a major fort and safe haven for ships during the War of 1812."

The rest of the family stood mute.

Getting on a steamboat was a frightening thought for everyone except Pa. He'd been on one and raved about how fast it was and how quick the travel had been to Detroit.

Betsey favored solid ground. She couldn't imagine climbing into a wooden boat and traveling far across the water without having the large lake swallow them whole. This time she trembled not from cold, but from true fear. If they couldn't see the shore on the other side of the expanse, what would it feel like to be on a boat in the middle of this huge lake?

"Pa, are you sure it's safe for us to cross this way?" Jillian's tiny voice seemed to echo the thoughts of everyone standing on the shore.

Pa reached out and pulled Jillian closer to him. "Positive. It will be the greatest adventure you've ever had, and someday, Jilly, you'll be able to tell your own family about the experience."

People were everywhere. Betsey had the impression that it would be only them taking a voyage on a boat across the water to their new home, but she was wrong. Wagon after wagon lined the road close to the shore. In the far distance, Betsey could see a city emerging as the morning fog began to lift.

"Is that the county seat, Pa?" She asked while pointing in a direction past the line of wagons.

"Yes. That's Erie." Pa steered the wagon to the side of the road. "Although when Ambrose and I came here last year, we didn't have a line for a steamboat to contend with."

The family looked ahead to the other wagons loaded with people, furniture, and barrels. Some people carried belongings. Other, possible passengers, stood between the wagons and many of those were soaked to the bone. They didn't have wagons to protect them from the spring showers.

"Glad we brought the wagon with us for the ladies," Pa said to Reverend Swain, who had gotten off his horse and now stood beside the wagon. "I need to get back soon, Hosea. How long do you think you'll have to wait?"

Pa shook his head. "No idea. If you stay here with the wagon and the ladies, Aaron and I will head toward the ticket office to get a better idea, time-wise."

Aaron's father nodded, "Be happy to."

Pa slid from the wagon seat, handed John the reins, and motioned for Aaron to follow him. "Might as well get our tickets now and see which steamboat we'll be taking."

Aaron nodded.

"I hate to think how much this will cost us to take a steamboat," Ma commented. "Pa said last year it was about three dollars a person. That will be fifteen dollars for all of us to travel." Ma shook her head, "Lord have mercy! I hope Hosea knows what he's doing."

Betsey thought of Aaron. She hoped her father had warned him about this expense. They'd sold many of their belongings to make the trip, but the thought of spending six dollars so soon brought panic to her heart.

"We might as well eat some dinner while they're gone." Her mother began preparing things for them to eat while they waited.

The wind off the nearby lake penetrated everyone's wet clothing, and as Betsey watched her pa and Aaron return to the wagon, she saw them both shivering from their excursion. It had taken them hours to gain the information they needed and tickets to cross the large lake.

Pa jumped up on the wagon bench as Aaron came to the back of the wagon and climbed aboard.

Aaron's eyes were red and his cheeks pink. "I'm freezing," he whispered to Betsey.

Betsey grabbed a dry blanket from the front of the wagon and wrapped her husband in it.

"I'll get it wet," he murmured to her.

"It's fine," she whispered back. "You won't be any good to me if you're frozen to death." She kissed his cheek.

"How much were the tickets?" Betsey wiped a wisp of hair from her cheek, tucking it behind her ear. The wind off the lake was cold and had turned everyone's cheeks pink.

"We didn't get to the office."

"What?" Betsey wasn't sure she heard Aaron correctly. "What took you so long?"

"The line." Aaron blew into his hands for warmth. "It was too long."

"We didn't have to wait this long last spring," Pa commented as he too blew into his hands. Ma reached for another blanket and placed it over his shoulders.

"What do we do now?" Ma asked, trying to rub warmth into Pa's shoulders.

"The only thing we can do," Pa announced. "Wait our turn."

Erie, Pennsylvania

CHAPTER FIVE

A chorus of birds woke the family the next morning. The sun warmed the earth. Blue skies peeked through a few gray clouds. Aaron and Pa weren't at the fire, just John, who was stoking it with fresh wood.

"I assume Aaron and Hosea have gone for tickets again?" Ma asked.

John nodded.

"Maybe at this early hour, they'll get to the head of the line quicker."

It seemed odd to be living in a wagon at the side of the road, but Betsey was thankful they had something over their heads. Others in line weren't as fortunate.

John appeared to grow more anxious to return home. Betsey knew he'd missed Sunday services with their extra wait time. He seemed to understand the odd situation the family found themselves in, but he appeared agitated. Betsey knew he was expected home much sooner than this.

Betsey's ma seemed to sense his urgency. "I'm sorry we are keeping you longer, John. It wasn't our intention."

John nodded. "Can't be helped. I understand, but I worry about taking the oxen and wagon back over that road by myself. Have to take advantage of the dry weather."

Ma nodded, then gazed toward the horizon for Pa and Aaron.

Just a few minutes later, Aaron and Pa came back to the wagon all smiles.

"We got tickets," Pa announced. He waved pieces of paper in the air. "Five tickets for Detroit. On the steamboat, *Superior.*"

They all cheered.

Aaron smiled at Betsey and handed her his paper. "It's the last boat of the day."

John shouted a hallelujah. "I hate to ask this, but do you think I could leave you here and head for home? With the weather finally breaking, I'd feel better if I left while it's still dry."

Pa nodded. "Can't blame you. Of course. Let's get the wagon unloaded. I think we can manage."

The next hour was hectic, but the family managed to unload all their possessions by the side of the road. They now found themselves among those whom Betsey had felt sorry for just the day before.

Betsey and Aaron said their goodbyes to John as Pa shook his hand. "Thanks so much for helping us on the first part of our journey, John. We appreciate it."

John Swain tipped his hat and tied his horse to the back of the wagon. "I pray the rest of your trip goes well. Please send a letter home as soon as you arrive safely."

Aaron hugged his father. "Goodbye, Father."

Betsey had forgotten the fact that Aaron was leaving his family behind to join hers. Despite her heart being filled with joy at being with her family, more guilt seeped in upon realizing she hadn't considered that fact before now. She went to Aaron and gripped his arm.

"I will write as soon as I can." Aaron waved to his father as the wagon pulled onto the road and bumped along towards the south.

As the family stood on the side of the road watching the wagon disappear, Betsey couldn't help but feel left behind. She wasn't sure if everyone else felt the same way.

Pa clapped his hands and smiled, "Let's keep this fire going, Aaron. It will take a bit of the chill out of the air and Ma can cook us up some food."

"Are you sure this is a good idea, Hosea? Staying here," Ma motioned around them, "On the side of the road. Alone?"

Pa pulled Ma close, "You're not alone, Sally May. We're all here together. It'll be fine."

Throughout the day, Betsey's family inched closer to the city they could only see in the distance the day before. It was hard moving all their belongings along with them, but they managed, by each one carrying certain things assigned to them until they reached the next stopping point. The women carried the smaller barrels as the men hefted the larger ones.

Soon they found themselves closer to the water and on a wooden dock parallel to the lake's edge. The waves beat against the shore in protest from the strong wind blowing in from the west. The temperature had dropped considerably, while they stood at the edge of the Great Lake named Erie.

Betsey thought it was mesmerizing watching wave upon wave roll onto shore and crash against the rock formations along the beach just south of the dock. Almost in synchronization, the rolls followed each other in a repetitive motion. Despite her fear of crossing the lake in nothing but a wooden boat, it somehow brought peace to her soul. Nothing had shown her God's creation better than this large lake stretching out before them.

They'd long ago had to abandon the fire they'd first started, but it seemed at each stopping point, they'd just take over the fire started by earlier travelers in front of them in line. Some families gave up their spot in line to head into town.

Each family appeared eager to board the boat. Some chatted about Michigan Territory. A few groups of passengers said this was just a step in their journey farther west.

Many folks seemed enticed by the newspaper ads about the cheap land awaiting them at their destinations. One old man, with no teeth, couldn't stop chatting with Pa.

"One dollar and twenty-five cents an acre! Can you believe it? Not in my wildest imagination did I ever think I could buy land that cheap. Who wouldn't take advantage of that kind of deal?" He slapped his knee, showing his toothless grin. "You'd be a fool to not get out there and grab you up some."

Pa nodded in agreement and told him a bit about his discovery in the territory of Michigan.

The old man spoke a bit louder. "There's Injuns there, ya know."

Pa nodded again. "I've seen a few."

The old man got closer, but still yelled. "Ya have? What're they like?"

"They keep mostly to themselves." Though Pa did tell him the story of when he and Ambrose had come up on them on the trail to their new property. "They seem like curious fellows," he commented, scratching his head. "They'd rifle through all our belongings and if they came upon food, they'd stand right there and eat it."

"That so?" the old man inquired.

"I think they were just hungry like every other man I know," laughed Pa.

"What would happen after they ate?"

"They'd just disappear into the woods. Several men, but often one man seemed more important than the others. His clothing more ornate, his demeanor authoritative. He would often have another Indian rummage for food in our packs and then he'd reach out and take it from him."

Ma shuddered and pulled her blanket closer around her shoulders. "I don't know why it has to be so cold out here."

Pa's storytelling wasn't helping any of them to believe they'd made the right decision, to head west. Ma's face said it all.

Toward evening, everyone grew tired of lugging possessions closer to a waiting steamboat. Upon a closer view, the boat loomed large and intimidating. Two large black stacks rose from its middle, and it seemed much like some kind of monster floating in the water near the dock. The only thing luring them to board was the thought of having to spend the night outside instead. At least the rain had stopped, and the sun hung bright and huge until it finally sunk on the horizon. The darkness penetrated their comfort; a brisk wind ripped at their garments and overcoats.

Pa grew curious as to why the steamboat didn't seem to be preparing to leave. He approached a sailor, inquiring about a boarding time.

The sailor laughed at Pa. "We don't even know the answer to that, but I did hear one of the captains tell everyone that a strong storm had brewed, and they were holding back a while to see if it would calm a bit before heading out."

Betsey overhead the sailor and Pa's conversation. Pa seemed reluctant to tell Ma, but he did. "We may have to sleep on this dock tonight."

"Sleep on the dock? Hosea, you can't be serious." Ma shivered in the night air.

Betsey scooted closer to Aaron who put his arms around her. He'd finally gotten his clothes dried out, with the help of each fire they came upon throughout the day. Betsey hugged him.

Looking down at her, he whispered, "How are you feeling?"

Betsey had experienced a bit of motion sickness in the wagon on the way here. She blamed it on her changing body. Two things she really longed for were a warm, dry bed, and a long night of sleep. Somewhere.

"We could get a room tonight. We have plenty of money."

Betsey shook her head. "We need to save that. We'll be alright here with the rest of the family. I'd feel horrible to leave them here and go spend a night in a warm bed. I'd be thinking of them out here and probably not sleep a wink."

Aaron nodded. "But you have an excuse. You need to protect your health more."

Betsey turned her face toward his. "I'm fine. Really I am."

Aaron hugged her tighter and kissed the top of her head. Not having had a single day she could take her hair out of its long braid and comb it, she was sure she probably looked worse than she felt. The blackness of the night, along with Aaron's dark hair and clothes, made it hard to see anything but his face.

"Well, we have tickets for this boat. We might as well hunker down for the night and wait until morning." Pa turned to Aaron, "Why don't we take turns sleeping and keeping watch over the womenfolk and our belongings?"

Aaron nodded.

Soon Betsey bundled up and lay close to her sisters and mother. They huddled together for warmth, but the thin blankets covering them couldn't be used as a cushion against the hard, solid wood beneath them. Aaron had propped himself up beside Betsey, leaning on a wooden dock post just above the water.

Pa laughed as he leaned his back against another dock post, "Hopefully this will keep me from taking an unwanted dip in the lake tonight. 'Case I nod off.'"

Ma mumbled something about Pa needing to have some sense knocked into him, but instead of saying it loud enough for Pa to hear, she scolded him for teasing about something so frightening.

Betsey closed her eyes, but the sound of waves crashing on the rocks beneath the dock wasn't helping sleep come easily. Soon she heard Jillian begin to softly sing. It was a new song they'd just sung last year in church.

"Rock of ages, cleft for me. Let me hide myself in Thee. Let the water and the blood, from Thy wounded side which flowed. Be of sin the double cure, save me from wrath and make me pure. Nothing in my hand I bring, simply to Thy cross I cling; Naked, come to Thee for dress; Helpless, look to Thee for grace; Foul, I to the fountain fly; wash me, Savior, or I die."

Betsey heard the small voice grow quiet and then she heard Caroline add to the hymn.

"While I draw this fleeting breath, when my eyes shall close in death. When I rise to worlds unknown and behold Thee on Thy throne. Rock of ages, cleft for me. Let me hide myself in Thee."

Pa murmured, "Amen."

Betsey prayed each one would be protected and could sleep a bit before morning.

The next thing Betsey felt was Aaron shaking her shoulder. "Bit, you need to wake up. We're going to board soon."

Board? What? It took a few moments for Betsey to grow conscious of where she was and why he had said what he did. A drawn-out, high-pitched whistle blew somewhere overhead. The noise startled her and the rest of the family to their feet. The steamboat now chugged steam from its two black stacks, as they stretched themselves awake, shook and folded their blankets from their short night's sleep. Betsey's back ached from the hard dock.

"Where's Pa?" Betsey asked Aaron.

"He's gone to find us a spot on the boat." Aaron handed Betsey her barrel to carry. "Your pa has taken some of the barrels onboard."

The steamboat stacks exploded as the boat seemed to come alive with power. Pa whistled to them from the deck of the large boat. "C'mon. Bring your things. I've found us a good berth and a safe place to put our belongings. Time to head out."

The family hesitated. Not one of them had ever been on such a large boat before. Pa seemed to know everything to do and was waving them aboard with urgency.

Aaron herded the women toward Pa, but the family wasn't alone. A surge of passengers crowded them together on the wooden gangway leading up to Pa and the boat deck. Betsey was sure one of them would lose their footing and take a plunge into the water at either side of the launch. The boat shuddered as dark smoke exploded from the stacks. A foreboding feeling took over her tired, aching body.

Staying together as a family was impossible as they were being pushed and shoved by the other boarding passengers around them. Betsey and Aaron became separated from her ma and sisters. Thankfully, Pa grabbed Ma's hand as soon as she reached him and motioned to Aaron. Betsey's sisters were tucked behind Pa and Aaron, and Betsey followed behind.

The motion of the rocking boat brought more uneasiness. She'd never felt anything like it. Aaron, somewhat unconsciously, pinched her arm as he steered her toward the place to where Pa was leading.

"Come in here. I have a good place for us."

The family followed Pa, who headed toward the stern of the boat and through a hatch, to a large room filled with many other passengers. Betsey tried to adjust her eyes in the faint light. Inside the large passenger section of the boat, the smell of damp wood and mold got Betsey's attention before she could get her eyes adjusted.

Pa took the barrels they were carrying and added them to those already piled up near a corner of the passenger area. Betsey's arms felt relief as Aaron took her barrel and handed it to Pa.

"This is our area. It's every passenger's job to find their place onboard. That's why I came on earlier to find us a good spot." Pa spread blankets on the floor as he did his best to save their place, while other passengers did the same. The room filled quickly with scurrying, anxious travelers and their possessions. Some brought large packs. Others carried heavy barrels. Men boarding alone carried a knapsack, or sometimes just belongings wrapped in a blanket. Everyone tried to find a place to settle in for the passage.

Betsey was certain there wouldn't be enough room for all the passengers streaming through the small hatch. They found themselves smashed together like chicken eggs in a nest, until finally it seemed the flow of those boarding slowed. Now the smells of the boat mingled with the awful odors of sweaty, dirty bodies. Betsey placed her handkerchief over her nose. She'd never been so sensitive to smells.

They all did their best to get comfortable on another hard, wooden surface that would be their seats for the trip. Pa laid his head against a barrel and told everyone he needed a nap. Aaron whispered to Betsey, "I think I slept more than he did last night."

As Betsey lowered herself to the floor and onto a blanket, she felt the swaying motion of the boat intensely. It reminded her of a swing they used to have in the front yard at home. She loved swinging, but with that she'd had control of how high or how long it would go. It was nothing like what she now experienced aboard the stinking, belching smoke, boat.

Cargo shifted, and people murmured, as they did their best to get settled. Crew members shouted demands to the multitude of passengers as well as their shipmates. The heat from the wood-burning furnaces below warmed the deck boards. It did feel good to be warm again, but Betsey could have done without all the smells assaulting her sensitive nose.

"How long will this passage take us, Pa?" Jillian had asked him that question nearly fifteen times before, but her patient pa opened his eyes.

"It will take us one night, plus a day-and-a-half of full travel." His eyes closed again. "Now let me take advantage of this soothing motion and get some shut-eye. You're in charge, Aaron."

Aaron nodded, but his face gradually turned solid-white, in stark contrast to his jet-black hair. He must have been feeling the same as Betsey. "This is gonna take a bit of getting used to."

Often at a time like this Ma would bow her head and pray, which helped her daughters not be so afraid and anxious. Now, Betsey watched as Ma pulled her younger sisters close, and looked around with wide eyes.

All Betsey could think about was how her stomach would not settle from the smells. Until she remembered that none of them knew how to swim.

Steamboat Superior, Lake Erie

CHAPTER SIX

Betsey buried her head deeper into the crook of Aaron's arm to muffle the loud noises from the steamboat's paddle wheel and the furnaces being fueled with wood by the sailors on the deck below them. Every member of her family was feeling the effects of the boat's motion. The rocking sent one after the other, out of the passenger room and out on deck to let loose the contents of their churning bellies.

Aaron seemed the worst. He'd been brave through the first days of their trip, but they were all growing weary. Falling asleep was almost impossible due to the creaks, loud noises, and shuttles of the paddle wheel at the stern of the boat.

Betsey had longed for an end to the swaying motion all afternoon. The swirl of dust circulating on the dirty floor made her sneeze. Soot covered their clothes in a thin layer of dark dust. Aaron's white shirt had turned a dull gray. Her ma sneezed, even after trying to bury her face in her sleeve.

Aaron did his best to doze while leaning against Betsey. It was the only stability they had against the incessant motion. They'd just get settled and another wave of sickness would send Aaron to a nearby pot, or outside, to retch. He had nothing left in his stomach to vomit.

Betsey had loaned him her handkerchief to wipe off his face, so now that smelled bad; he'd apologize every time he gave it back to her.

"Now I have more sympathy for you." Aaron gave her a pitiful glance. Betsey patted his head as he placed it in her lap for comfort.

Her younger sisters and Pa seemed to be the only ones not overcome by seasickness. He'd taken her sisters out on the deck to show them the rolling waves of Lake Erie. They came bounding back, voicing their excitement to Betsey and their ma.

"Oh Ma, you should see the water. It's so blue. It seems to touch the sky." Jillian could barely contain her excitement.

Ma had been trading places with Aaron at the nearby pot. Pa had slept almost the first five hours of their journey, despite the intense noise of the boat. Shouting was a necessity in communicating to each other.

Ma had finally dozed off before supper that night, so Betsey did her best to scrape together a meal for the family from the contents of their carrying bundles. Slivers of dried beef and apples were all she could find that didn't need heat of some kind to be edible. Pa did his best to be sure everyone had water from his wooden canteen.

As darkness descended on the tiny family huddled together for warmth, the motion became more tolerable for all. Each one, tired and weary from the journey, soon fell asleep leaning against one another, and that's where Betsey found herself, as she sat alone with her thoughts. Everyone else seemed to be sleeping peacefully. Even Aaron, now more used to the motion, was asleep and snoring in her ear.

Betsey wondered again if it had been a good idea to take this journey with her parents and sisters. Even now, they would be at their tiny home in Pennsylvania. Of course, as she looked upon the faces of her family, she'd be missing them. But Aaron wouldn't be suffering so, and they'd both be sleeping peacefully in their feathered bed at home.

Was their suffering her fault? Had her complaining forced Aaron's decision? She was a grown woman who needed to focus on being a good wife for her husband and minding her affairs at home. She hadn't begged Aaron to go with her family, but perhaps she didn't need to. Aaron had always been so gracious to her. Whenever she'd asked for something, he'd long for a chance to please her. Had she taken advantage of his kindness?

Through the darkness, Betsey strained to make out each face in the circle their family had formed, oblivious to the sound of the stacks belching and splashing water from the turning paddle. Each face looked weary. The strange sounds were nothing like Betsey had ever endured while trying to sleep.

The battle between staying awake and sleeping had begun to wear on her. She lost focus and her eyes gave in, closing. Then finally, the sounds became soothing enough that she stopped thinking about the ache in her hip, from the hard floor. She could no longer stay awake. She succumbed to sleep.

Aaron startled awake as he felt dampness penetrate his right sleeve, cooling his upper arm. Was he in the rain? Stirring awake more, he focused on the sounds coming from around him. Sailors were screaming at one another, and the motion from the boat grew stronger. His stomach began to gurgle again, and bile started coming up in his throat. He swallowed hard, trying to make it stop. Betsey, still snuggled deep into his left arm, was still sound asleep. He hated to move, but the door had whipped open and a mist began to cover the floor between him and the door. He could hear rain pelting the deck outside.

The dampness made him sneeze. He was just about to move Betsey off his arm so he could get up and shut the door, to keep the wetness from invading their space, when another man across the room beat him to it. As he walked by, Aaron grabbed his arm.

"Be careful."

The man nodded. "I'll close the door." When finished he added, "Looks like it's about dawn."

More rain. Spring rain usually meant melting snowbanks, tillable ground for planting, and warmer temperatures, but traveling in it only brought frustration and fatigue. No one had expected the first days of the trip to turn into such misery. Aaron hadn't felt dry since they'd left Meadville. What he wouldn't give to change into dry clothes. His back felt raw from his damp shirt rubbing on his shoulders each time he moved.

Aaron could hear Hosea stirring on the other side of Betsey. He reached out and touched Aaron's hand.

"Can you see light yet, son?"

With Aaron being closest to the door, he could give him an accurate report. "Not yet, sir."

Hosea patted his shoulder, "Shouldn't be long now."

"The man who just shut the door said it was about sunrise, but it's raining again."

Hosea shook his head, "Of course it is. We sure picked some wet days to begin this journey. Maybe it will get better as we near the shore.

"I hope so."

Betsey began to stir. Her brown hair was tangled on her head, her tight bun now loose, and tendrils of curls edged her face. She sat up with a start.

Aaron patted her arm, "Honey, we're on the steamboat. Remember?"

Betsey sighed, relaxing back against him. He stiffened to cushion her body, despite the ache in his arm from her sleeping against him most of the night.

She closed her eyes again, but then sat up. "I need to wake Ma. I need assistance again."

Betsey and her ma had taken turns helping each other to a nearby place to relieve themselves. All women seemed appalled at the lack of privacy. Aaron felt especially sorry for Betsey who needed to use the bucket more than even her ma. They never went without another woman so they could use their skirts or shawls, they were wearing, to shield the other.

Betsey nudged her ma awake. Each girl leaning against her awoke with her movements. "Let's all go, girls. I need to as well."

As soon as the girls left Aaron and Hosea in their makeshift home on deck, Hosea scooted closer to Aaron. He pointed to a sliver of light now coming from under the door. "Your friend is right. It's almost daybreak."

"How much longer do we have until we get to Detroit?" Aaron asked his father-in-law, who now stood, adjusting his hat.

"We should arrive after dinnertime. But this rain might produce more than just showers. Depends on the winds we have to buck to get there."

Soon the girls reappeared and the daylight infiltrated through the spaced boards above their heads, so at least they could make out faces around them.

Ma distributed food they'd packed for their travels. Aaron turned it down.

Betsey chided him for the refusal.

"I don't want to see any more food until my feet can stand on solid ground again."

She held up Pa's canteen. "Please try and drink something then."

The warm water moistened his lips and he did manage to swallow a few gulps, but he refused any more.

Trickles of water gradually ran toward them from under the door. Moisture filled the air, causing everyone's clothes to grow even damper.

Ma motioned for everyone to eat more food. "It'll grow mold if we don't eat it." Yet Ma packed away most of it as each one declined her offers.

Aaron stood as water crept closer to him from under the door. "It must be pouring out on deck." The noise from the steam engines and paddle wheel drowned out any sound of drops on the ceiling above their berth.

Soon they all had to stand, as water made its way in their direction. Each time the boat tilted their way, rivulets of water, flowing along the deck, were too fast for the family to move away from them. Pa stacked their belongings higher to help protect them from the wet floor.

The boat's pitching grew steeper. Other families' belongings slid closer with each slant of the giant boat.

"The waves must be growing larger," Pa shouted.

Passengers started to cry and yell at each other as they each grasped for support somewhere around them. Looking for something cling to.

The families that had started in the middle of the room now edged closer. Barrels began to fall over and roll around, and into, passengers. Children huddled close to adult family members for protection.

The only thing keeping them from being seasick now was their constant, determined fight to stay upright, and away from, the rolling barrels on deck.

After a couple of hours, the motion began to subside a bit. Children were crying, women were moaning, men were doing their best to keep their family belongings intact. The hatch to the berth slammed open and a sailor stood in the opening.

"Ya'll okay in here?"

A few men claimed I was with, "Yes all is well," but some raised their fists and voices to the sailor merely seeking to find out how everyone was fairing despite the rocking boat.

"When will we be to Detroit?"

"We need water."

"Will this journey ever end?"

The grumbling dissuaded the sailor from asking anything more. He slammed the door shut.

Pa was the first to speak, "Hush now, folks. Hush!"

One man yelled out a curse word at Pa. Pa held up his hands, "Now hold on, folks. I took this journey last spring. It can get rocky and a bit hard to take, but we're almost there. Locate your belongings as best as you can. We'll soon be on solid ground. I promise."

One man stood and shouted at Pa, "How do you know?"

"Like I said, I took this trip. Last spring." Pa's words seemed to ease many fears and frustrations as everyone sought to find their barrels. Many did their best to wring out blankets that once covered the floor under them, now heavy with water, causing the floor to be even more wet and slippery.

A brief glimpse of sun shone through the gaps of wood in the ceiling overhead. The boat's swaying diminished as it seemed the paddle wheel slowed.

A sailor's cry could be heard above the din of the boat's furnaces. He shouted. "Land Ho!"

Detroit, Michigan Territory

CHAPTER SEVEN

Betsey couldn't believe the sight she now saw from the boat deck. Pa had gathered and herded them outside and away from the stinky, wet room. He now pointed toward the west. "Look, can you see it?"

Sure enough, a thin slice of earth could be seen off the bow of the boat.

"That there, my dear family, is Detroit. A little farther to the northwest is our new home."

As they watched, the small sliver turned into a wedge of land. Buildings, which from their vantage point seemed tiny, grew larger on the horizon.

"What's Detroit like?" Ma asked Pa, her red-rimmed eyes now brimming with tears.

Pa reached out and gripped her shoulders. "Well it's not the prettiest part of the territory, but it has one thing we don't have now."

Caroline asked the question they were all thinking. "What Pa?"

Pa tipped his head back, adjusted his hat, and winked. "Solid ground!"

With that comment, Jillian burst into song, *"All other ground is sinking sand."* The families around them turned to listen as Jilly's voice rang out for everyone to hear.

"My hope is built on nothing less, than Jesus' blood and righteousness. I dare not trust the sweetest frame, but wholly lean on Jesus' name."

Others joined in song, *"On Christ the solid rock I stand. All other ground is sinking sand. All other ground is sinking sand."*

All of the passengers and even a few sailors were singing with the Baker sisters and their family. *"When darkness veils His lovely face, I rest in his unchanging grace. In every high and stormy gale, my anchor holds within the veil."*

As the final chorus faded to a murmur, all the families began filing off the deck and back to the large room on the boat to gather belongings. As they did, the sun began to peek out from behind the clouds that had been hovering overhead for the past few days.

Jillian pointed it out and the whole family began to smile. "I think God is happy to see us here."

"That He is." Pa wrapped Jillian in a hug. "That He is."

The rush of passengers getting off the boat was about as bad as when boarding in Erie. Nothing pleased the Baker and Swain families, or their weak legs, more than disembarking the rough, swaying boat to stand on solid ground.

Aaron leaned close to Betsey's ear and said, "If it wouldn't cause a spectacle, I think I would bend down and kiss the earth."

Betsey laughed. As she did, she felt a sudden flutter in her womb. She stopped laughing and touched her belly. She glanced at Aaron as he gave her a quizzical look.

"Is something wrong?"

Betsey waited a moment. "I don't know, but I think the baby just moved. Maybe he wants the rocking motion back."

Aaron enveloped her in an embrace and they both smiled. "Perhaps we have a sailor on the way."

"If a girl can be a sailor? Possibly."

Aaron kissed her forehead. "I don't know, but if she's as beautiful as her ma, her fellow sailors wouldn't get anything done."

It had taken a few steps on the docks surrounding the busy city to realize their legs really did work. But nothing felt as safe and secure as the unmovable ground on which they now stood. Everyone near them must have felt the same way because families were hugging and laughing, the morning's fear now giving way to a successful step on their journey to another home.

One man knelt on shore in thankfulness. Others moved toward the buildings of Detroit to continue their trip inland. Some passengers waited for all their belongings to be unloaded from a cargo portion of the boat.

Pa escorted all of them toward the closest road. It was a slow process as he and Aaron had to keep returning to a nearby dock to gather all the barrels they'd brought with them.

Jillian pointed to some people just lining the shore just north of the dock. "Look Pa, Ma...Indians!"

Pa pulled her hand down. "No need to point, Jilly. You've seen Indians before."

Betsey looked off to where Jillian had pointed.

They'd seen Indians in Pennsylvania, but they seemed much more civilized than these.

"They're just inquisitive and nosy. Easily riled. We need to be careful not to upset them." Pa steered them farther up the hill away from the shoreline.

Etta stood beside her. "I've never seen one dressed like that. Look at that one, he has feathers coming from something on his head." As with the large body of water called Erie and a steamboat ride, this was another first for them—to see the natives of Michigan.

The Indians approached several of the families now leaving the boat, holding out their hands as if to beg for something.

One woman pulled an apple from her pocket and handed it to one. He let out a whoop-like scream, grabbed the fruit, and headed off toward the others. Several Indians then came up beside the woman and held out their hands as well. The woman's husband grabbed her hand and shook his head.

Several Indians swarmed around the man and his family. As she watched the scene unfold, Aaron stiffened beside her, nudging her and her sisters up the bank to a street in the bustling city.

A sailor approached the Indians, shooed them away from the family, and shouted blasphemous words at them. "Don't give them anything. They'll come after the lot of us to get more. Just keep moving, folks."

Trembling, Betsey held tight to Aaron's hand. She shivered and knew it wasn't caused by her damp dress or wet shoes. *Would they ever feel safe among the natives of their new home?* Etta clung to her right hand. Betsey knew that her reaction to situations like this was often mimicked by her little sisters, so she encouraged them to keep moving up the bank.

After a short walk up a fairly steep bank, buildings rose on the horizon as far as she could see. The community of Detroit was bustling and bore no resemblance to Meadville. Dirty buildings, muddy roads, and seagulls dotted the landscape. One bird, with a cackle-like squawk, shuffled toward them on the ground. They'd encountered those in Erie, too, but here they seemed much more plentiful.

Loud saloon music drifted from one edge of town. As they reached the street, wagons of all sorts traveled the dirt road going in both directions. The street was lined with store fronts and businesses. Betsey had never seen so many people in one place. There were men on horseback, women walking through town holding children by the hand, and horses in various locations.

Betsey, Ma, and her sisters stood at the edge of the street while Pa and Aaron gathered all their barrels around them. Pa pointed in the direction of where to head.

"I'll stay here with the belongings," Aaron volunteered.

"Why don't you all stay here? I'm gonna head up a'ways where my wagon and oxen are a'waitn our arrival." Pa kissed Ma's cheek before setting out toward a stable down the street.

They all watched as Pa headed toward several stables a block or so away. A large barn, with double doors, opened out onto the street. A line had begun to form, in front of the building, that included families who had been on the boat with them.

Pa had driven from the new property the fall before, and had paid a large sum to a man to board the oxen and store the wagon, until he could return with his wife and family.

"I think Pa said you can buy an oxen team and wagon there if you'd like." Betsey pulled on her bonnet, tying the straps securely under her chin.

Aaron nodded. Betsey gazed at her handsome husband and thought about having their privacy again. She couldn't wait to spend the night alone with Aaron, in their wagon. She'd missed their private time.

Aaron grabbed her hand, giving her a wide grin, and she realized perhaps he had the same thoughts. His expression made her giggle.

Once at the stable, Pa disappeared through the front door.

The street bustled with an assortment of residents and travelers. Dodging between the crowds and rushing wagons became a bit of a game. Betsey grew thankful they were tucked off the street against an outside stable wall, with all their belongings piled beside them. The last time they'd been around crowds like this was during the Fourth of July celebration in Meadville.

Betsey looked over to see Ma counting barrels.

"Oh Betsey." Ma put her hand to her mouth and let out a small gasp.

Betsey went to her. "What's wrong, Ma?"

"A barrel. I think we're missing a barrel."

Betsey glanced over the barrels that now lined the wall beside them. She couldn't remember which ones were hers and which ones were Ma's. She shrugged. "Which one do you think we lost?"

Ma's frowned. "I don't remember what I packed in which barrel, but we had one that was a darker color than the rest. I don't see it here anywhere."

"I guess that's the chance you have to take, comin' on a trip." Betsey didn't know what else to say.

"I know, I know." Ma counted again, with her finger pointing out each barrel. "What if it contained something important that we'll need in our new home? I tried so hard to pack just the necessities, but if most of what I packed for the kitchen is gone, I'll have to replenish it before we head north."

Each barrel had been tightly closed to ward off insects and to keep water out. Opening one now would be a time-consuming, arduous task. "We'll have to just pray that we have everything we need, Ma. Don't worry."

"I think Pa said we'll have to get a few supplies here to make it to Pontiac. Perhaps we can open the barrels there."

As the women spoke, Pa approached them. "We're all set. You ladies look all set here, I'll go hitch up the wagon and be back soon. Why don't you come with me, Aaron, and you can purchase what you need, too."

Soon Aaron returned, and handed Betsey a bill of sale. "Well, we aren't as rich as we were leaving Meadville, but we now have our own team and wagon. I'm going in now to get it all set up so we can head out soon."

Pa winked at all of them, "As soon as the team is hitched and we load our barrels, we'll get some supplies here and then find us a place to camp tonight. Then we can be on our way." He headed back to the stable.

Betsey handed Aaron back the receipt just as the corral opened up beside them, and Pa led out a team of oxen. Behind him came a large man pulling a wagon out onto the street in front of them.

Pa grinned, waving his hands like he'd just performed a magical act. "There it is, Sally. Our home away from home."

Ma took a deep breath, "It's wonderful, Hosea."

"As soon as I get these oxen hooked up, you can load up the barrels and we'll head into town for more supplies." Pa carefully backed up the work animals and began harnessing them to the wagon.

As Pa and Aaron yoked the team, everyone began loading barrels into the fairly new wagon. Pa had told Ma about purchasing the new wagon right after he and Ambrose had made it to Michigan last year.

"Hosea. We're missing a barrel," Ma exclaimed with frustration.

"Which one?" he asked, as he helped Jillian pick up a heavy one to load.

"I don't know, but didn't we bring more than this?" Ma wiped her hands off on the front of her skirt. The color now resembled a much grayer color than how it had looked back in Pennsylvania. "I hope it isn't the clothing one. I desperately need a clean dress. I hate to be seen in public looking like this."

Pa kissed her forehead. "You're beautiful, but unfortunately it can't be helped now. We'll have to figure it out later."

"But what if it has all my pots and pans we'll need at the new cabin?" Ma squinted into the sun now directly overhead.

Before Pa could answer, Aaron came out of the corral with his own team, and the family got busy helping Betsey and Aaron load their possessions. The barrels all looked alike, so perhaps Ma's barrel was with theirs.

Aaron seemed light-hearted, and the color had returned to his cheeks. "Driving in style now."

Betsey covered her flushed cheeks with her hands. The cool spring air still made her face tingle.

Aaron winked at her and then hollered for Pa's help in getting his oxen hitched up, too.

Shopping in a Detroit store brought tears to Betsey's eyes. She'd never seen so many choices, even back in Meadville. She purchased enough supplies to feed them well until they could reach their next destination. Pa assured them another store awaited them at the halfway point, in case they forgot something. There they would purchase things they'd need to have throughout the coming summer, until they could plant crops and reap a harvest.

It was hard to believe that the wagons they now drove were their only protection against the weather, wild animals, and Indians that inhabited the new frontier, yet they were much better accommodations than they'd had aboard the steamboat.

As they loaded up and prepared to leave the city, they knew the roads would be their next challenge as they appeared to be as rutted and muddy as the ones they'd had to maneuver throughout the first days of their journey north through Pennsylvania. Their only consolation: they now had two strong teams of oxen to pull out any wagons that got stuck.

Similar teams were leaving Detroit in different directions. Many travelers smiled and waved to continue on their journeys into the territory.

During Pa's conversations about the new land, other steamboat passengers asked him for directions. He mentioned a road called, *the Grand River-Pontiac Trail*. This road would lead to locations outside of Detroit where good potential cropland and homesites were plentiful and ready for the take.

As the wagons headed out of town, Betsey noticed her pa stash his rifle underneath the plank seat where Ma now sat. Ma gave Pa the look she'd often give him when she questioned his motives. Pa always had a gun hanging over the mantel at home, and Ma would fuss about it when it wasn't in its rightful place. But out here, Pa's chosen location was probably best.

Betsey overheard Pa tell her ma, "We're headed into regions where this is a necessity more than ever. Trust me, Sally."

Ma sighed, but her tired, red eyes held little hope of believing him.

All three of Betsey's sisters piled onto the back of Pa and Ma's wagon. Their feet dangled off the edge as Aaron pulled up behind them. Their homes-on-wheels now followed a line of others heading out of town. Betsey could hear Jillian's voice singing over the rumbling. Her voice echoed among the woods now enveloping them.

Betsey took Aaron's hand and scooted closer to him. "I can't wait to change out of these clothes tonight. I hope not everything in our barrels is wet. I long for warm, dry stockings and a chance to find my brush."

Aaron squeezed tighter on the reins with his left hand as he gripped Betsey's hand with his right. "Hard to imagine how just a dry shirt could feel so good." Aaron smiled at her.

Betsey had taken off her shoes, thinking that the air might give her feet a chance to dry. They'd been through many challenges in the last several days. Surely, there were better days ahead.

It appeared the baby felt the same way, for again, she felt the baby quiver in her womb. She'd never felt anything as magical.

Michigan Territory

CHAPTER EIGHT

As the oxen labored toward Pontiac, Betsey picked up on a different smell in the forest. It reminded her of the woods at home, yet a distinct scent set it apart. Was it a spice? A bit of musk? The trail ran deep into the thick of large oaks and maples, but the smell of pine was also a strong part of the pleasant aroma.

As they stopped to eat their supper and gather the wagons to spend the night, Betsey asked her father if it was just the pine aroma or something else she smelled.

"This territory is full of pine," he commented. The family gathered around the warm fire to eat. "'Then shall the trees of the wood sing out at the presence of the Lord, because He cometh to judge the earth.'"

"So much timber. I've never seen this many trees, anywhere," Aaron added.

"That's what drew me here. The virgin timber. You know how much I love trees." Pa winked at Ma.

Smiling, she nodded, "You do love trees. I saw maple and oak, but the pine trees stand out, like they were planted here on purpose."

"Much like Pennsylvania. Maple, oak, pine," Pa counted off with his fingers. "We even have some black walnut trees right on our property. There's a blackjack oak on the ridge above the cabin. Can you imagine? It's my favorite tree of all." Pa pointed to Aaron. "Wait until you see the size of the deer here. It'll be a treat to have some Michigan venison for a change. This dried beef is getting old fast." Pa took a bite of his supper and chewed. "Hard for an old man to chew."

Ma slapped Pa's arm, then stood to stir a pot of beans boiling over the fire. "Stop grumbling. You're not old, cause if you are, what does that make me?"

Pa grinned at Ma. "Tarnation woman, you're right. You're not old at all, Sally May." Pa picked up a stick, stirring the fire to life. "We'll need to keep a close eye on the oxen teams tonight. You want the first or second shift, Aaron?"

"I'll take the second, if that's alright?"

"Sure is. I'll try to nap a bit around the fire tonight and then be alert enough for the first watch. Wild wolves are a menace as well as coyotes. They'd love an ox leg to chew on. I'd hate for our first night to be ruined by our oxen bein' kilt."

Aaron nodded.

"Stop, Pa. You're makin' me shake." Jillian cuddled closer to Betsey.

"They don't like scrawny li'l white girls. Not enough meat on their bones."

Everyone laughed, except wide-eyed Jillian and Etta.

Betsey had looked forward to sleeping beside Aaron. She'd already made up a bed from the blankets she'd brought in their barrels. She'd let them air-dry on the trip into the woods from town, hoping they were no longer musty smelling from the steamboat trip.

Etta spoke up, "Pa, the wolves won't bother us, will they?"

"No sugar, as long as I keep the fire going. Anyways, you'll be safe and sound in that wagon of ours and dead asleep before long anyway."

Etta pulled her blanket tighter around her shoulders.

"I think I may hit the wagon much earlier than all of you. As soon as I finish up the dishes from tonight, I'm off to bed."

Betsey agreed with her ma. "I think we'll be heading there ourselves, real soon." *Weary* didn't begin to describe how tired she felt.

As the family sat around the fire, Betsey felt the warmth dissipate the last of the dampness from the boat trip and the previous days of travel. During their traveling today, Betsey had seen evidence of warmer days to come. Bare trees held promises of spring as small buds grew visible on branches. Squirrels had left winter hibernation spots and now jumped from tree to tree and scrambled along the forest floor.

An owl hooted from a nearby location, jerking Betsey from her faraway thoughts. Her younger sisters laughed as they'd all been startled by the sound, too.

"You better all get used to these woodsy sounds. That's a bit like what you'll hear in our new home."

Jillian bounced with excitement. "Tell us again about our property, Pa. What will it be like there?"

Pa sat back, putting his hands behind his head. He sighed, "I've told you many times."

Jillian landed at his knees. "I know, Pa, but tell us again."

"Yes, Hosea. It will help our endurance," exclaimed Ma.

"I've told you about the winding river, which is the best part of our new homestead. But what drew me to the property when I first laid eyes on it was this open, plateau area beside the river. It's a clearing of sorts, right out there in the middle of nowhere. As you'll see, there isn't much between here and there that isn't dotted with every tree you can imagine. That spot was the perfect place to build a cabin. Even the acreage behind the cabin is perfect for some nice crops. And a barn. Ambrose and I decided to build the log home about thirty yards from the river's edge. A right wonderful home for all my girls."

"And the Indians. Are they close?"

"Yes. They're all around us, but they'll leave us alone. For the most part. Sometimes they get hungry and think everyone's food is there for the takin'. God always gives us plenty to share."

"What else?" chimed Etta.

"Well, then there's the trees. Some of the most beautiful trees in the world. They're tall and form canopies of protection around our home. And just like Betsey said, they have this wonderful musky scent of pine. You'll see soon enough."

"How long, Pa? How much longer until we get there?" Jilly hopped onto Pa's lap as he wrapped his arms around her.

"We're going a bit slower with the oxen teams, but it took me five days to get from the new homestead to Detroit when I headed home to get you. So, we'll see. If the weather holds and we don't get much rain, shouldn't be too many days. Hopefully, we'll keep track with my signs at various points along the way."

"That was mighty smart of you, Hosea, to chink out the directions on the trees like that."

Betsey was thrilled that Ma had finally been able to give Pa a compliment. She'd been so stern with him since leaving Meadville.

"It's called blazing. I didn't want to get off-track; you can get right lost in these thick woods, faster than a jackrabbit heading into a hole. We could be wandering for days and end up on the other side of the territory in no time at all."

"How far to Pontiac?" Aaron asked.

"Should be there tomorrow night, Lord willin'. That's where we'll buy some needed supplies to last us most of the summer. Ambrose knows we're comin' if he got the letter I sent him. Maybe he's already ventured there himself." Pa sat up. "His letters made it seem like he'd been mighty lonesome from spending the winter alone. I'm sure he's just as anxious to see us as we are to see him."

Betsey thought of her older brother all alone, enduring last winter all alone. She was sure she couldn't have done that herself. He'd written once saying how high and heavy the snow was there. She was surprised that he'd taken the time to write or even paid the cost to send a letter. He also informed Pa that he'd girdled many of the trees around the property in preparation of building a barn for the oxen as soon the family arrived. This process of cutting down trees had saved Ambrose and Pa when they built their cabin before winter and Pa had to leave.

She couldn't wait until she and Aaron could find a place to start their home. A home for Aaron, her, and the baby.

That night, the families settled into a new mode of shelter. The scent of fresh-cut lumber made Betsey proud that she and Aaron could afford a brand-new wagon. She'd made up a nice bed in the back of the wagon and soon she snuggled close to Aaron, who dozed off far sooner than Betsey would have liked. He'd endured many sleepless nights. Soon Aaron would need to be up to take his early morning shift of watching the oxen, so Betsey cuddled closer. She felt so safe lying beside him.

For the first time on their trip, she felt warm and dry. She'd been able to undo her hair and brush it thoroughly. It felt soft and fresh again, despite it needing a good wash. Aaron loved it when she wore it down at night.

Lying still, she could hear and feel Aaron's heartbeat as well as another tiny flutter in her belly. Betsey felt warmed, comforted, and blessed as she waited a second more to see if the baby would move again.

That's when she heard it. She sat up straight in bed.

Aaron flinched a bit, but quickly went back to snoring. The howl seemed to be just outside their wagon. It pierced the night air, and soon Betsey could hear her mother shushing her younger sisters from the wagon next to theirs. She was sure she could hear Jillian crying.

Betsey had heard wolf howls before, but none so near. Hearing another, Betsey was thankful to know that Pa was out by the fire, watching over everything for them.

Another howl shattered the silence, each one seeming closer than the last. She couldn't help it, she shook Aaron awake.

"Aaron. Aaron! Wake up, please!"

He mumbled something but pulled her back down beside him.

"Go to sleep."

"You have to hear this. It's so close!"

Aaron opened one eye and asked, "What's close?"

"Listen."

They both lay quietly, but all they could hear was the wind rustling through the bare trees.

"I don't hear anything." Aaron wrapped his arm around her tighter. "Go to sleep."

Just then another howl broke through the other night sounds. "He's getting closer."

Aaron did hear that. "It's just a wolf, Bit. You've heard wolves howl before."

"But not this close, Aaron. Are you sure Pa is all right out there by himself?"

"He's fine. Now c'mon. I have to be up sooner than later. Go to sleep. You have to be tired."

"Pa!" Betsey called out to her father.

"Yes, Bit."

"Are you alright? That wolf sounds awful close."

Her father answered, "I know. He does. I've stoked up the fire. We're in the deep woods, Bit. Things will sound louder here. 'The Lord is good, a stronghold in the day of trouble; and He knoweth them that trust in Him.'"

"Do you have your rifle?" Betsey overheard Ma ask from their wagon.

"Right beside me, Sally. Now get some shut-eye."

Betsey nestled down beside Aaron, who wrapped his arm around her shoulders. This was going to take a bit of getting used to.

As Betsey closed her eyes, she heard an owl hooting just above their wagon. The *hoot, hoot, hoot* seemed to lull her to sleep. She prayed for safety for all of them. Pa, and Aaron, as they watched the camp, and her entire family, as they slept. Only a bit of canvas and wood separated them from the wild animals.

Before she knew it, she felt Aaron stirring as Pa tapped on the outside of the wagon.

"Yer turn, Aaron."

Aaron grunted as he sat up and pulled on his boots.

"Be careful, Aaron."

He kissed her forehead. "All will be well, Bit. Get some rest. You need it, as well as the baby."

Betsey knew he was right, but as he left the wagon, she pulled the covers up tight. She knew she'd have to get used to the night sounds in the new territory, but thoughts of a wolf attacking all of them while they slept kept her eyes attentive, and on the canvas flap Aaron had just dropped as he left their wagon.

Maybe if she prayed a bit, it would stop her legs from shaking under the heavy blankets. Since leaving Pennsylvania, she'd prayed without ceasing. It would be a while before she and Aaron could have a home built from the wilderness hardwoods. What if they didn't get it built before winter? Ambrose had said the Michigan snows were harder and deeper than Pennsylvania's. She hated to think of a new baby having to live in a wagon all winter.

Surely her parents wouldn't leave them out in the elements. But thinking of sharing a cabin with her parents, Ambrose, and the girls made Betsey nervous, too. Again, Betsey wondered if they'd made the right decision, to travel here with her parents. But as she thought about their night spent out by the fire and being all together, in the new land, her doubts subsided.

The next time Betsey stirred, light illuminated the canvas covering their wagon. The birds issued their greetings with tweets, chirps, and trills, each in their unique ways. Even a few squirrels chattered to one another in sharp tones.

Ma poked her head into the back of the wagon. "You gonna rise and shine, young lady?"

Betsey pushed the covers off, and brushed her hair up in a neat, tight bun.

Leaving the wagon, she felt stiff and sore. It would take a bit to get used to sleeping every night on hard boards for the next few weeks, but it was better than on the damp deck of a boat.

Betsey came to the fire where breakfast sizzled, sending delicious aromas into the air. Pa had mounted a pole across the fire and a skillet full of breakfast food hung from it, just above the flames. Hot food would be such a treat. She apologized to her mother for sleeping in so late.

"It's fine. Pa and Aaron are checking out the trail ahead to be sure we can maneuver through it with the wagons. Sit here and stir these oats for a few minutes. We'll eat as soon as they get back."

Betsey's sisters piled off the end of the other wagon and Ma held out a brush. "Brush your hair, girls. The snarls from our trip don't have to be permanent."

Soon Aaron and Pa were back, announcing the way was clear as far as they could see.

"It'll be a rough ride, but we'll do our best to maneuver around the ruts left from the previous spring rains," Pa said as he shifted his hat on his head and tousled his hair beneath it. "This trail is a good one and will last until we hit the Pontiac trading post. After that, your guess is as good as mine how the trail will be. My marks on trees should lead us back to our property. When heading directly north last time, Ambrose and I cut down trees to make a new path. Despite that, the going could still get rough for a while. Who knows what winter did to the path."

Ma began scooping out hot food onto tin plates for the family. "It's so desolate here."

"We're new settlers. In fact," Pa sat on a log and waited for everyone to get a plate of their own. "We're not only new, but probably some of the first to settle in this part of the territory. I'm sure others will join us, but for now, it's just our family. Ambrose said he hasn't seen a neighbor yet. But that was before Christmas, when he'd last written us."

As Ma sat down next to Pa, he held out his hand and took off his hat. "Let's thank God for a good night's sleep."

Betsey loved to hear her father pray. He didn't use all the *thee's* and *thou's* like the preacher, but he talked to God like he was talking to a friend. Pa's knowledge of scripture was far beyond anyone she'd ever known. He quoted verses daily, communing with God right out loud. He'd told Betsey many times that when he was a little boy, "it 'twas the only book in the house."

Soon the entire family was placing their plates, that they'd each wiped and dried themselves, back into the bin in Ma and Pa's wagon. They'd use them again later. Pa checked the reins on his oxen, and Aaron checked theirs. Betsey tucked the last of their night gear into the back of the wagon and took her seat beside Aaron. The wagons headed northwest.

Betsey overheard Pa call to her sisters at the back of his wagon. "You girls don't forget to get out and walk. It'll make the time go faster and keep you fit as a fiddle."

All three answered, "Yes, Pa," but soon they were playing a game of sorts, pointing out as many species of birds as they could find. Many were the same as the birds back in Pennsylvania.

"There's a blue jay," giggled Etta as she pointed in one direction.

"Has anyone seen a robin yet?" Jillian asked.

Pa had said that robins were common in these parts, just like back home. Everyone was anxious to see one, as it often heralded a new season.

The forest grew deep and dense. It was hard to spot birds, but they did see a few scurrying rodents.

All four sisters soon gathered behind Aaron and Betsey's wagon, holding hands as they endeavored to get some exercise. A layer of last year's leaves was soft under their feet. Pa was right, it felt good to stretch, and Betsey took deep breaths to smell the scents of the forest around her.

The girls did their best to stay with the wagons, but gradually the wagons were several yards in front of them. Pa had asked them to find kindling for the night's fire, and soon their arms were full of prickly tree branches, which stuck to their dresses and snagged their shawls.

A bug must have crawled up Etta's sleeve, because she dropped her load of branches and began slapping her arm. "Eww, eww!" she uttered as she danced around the pile of branches at her feet.

Everyone laughed. "It's just a bug, Etta. Calm down."

The bug fluttered off Etta's sleeve. She bent down to examine the wood she'd been carrying, a bit more closely, looking for any sign of other insects. "I hate bugs."

"Go put your branches up in the back of our wagon. I think we've gathered plenty for tonight's fire."

Everyone did as Betsey suggested.

"I hope those bugs don't crawl into my bed. I'd hate to have one of those wake me up in the night." Etta looked herself up and down to check for any stray insects that might still be clinging to her skirt or petticoats.

All of them were startled to hear Pa yell to someone from his perch on the front of the wagon. "Hey there. Anyone home?"

Home? Betsey wondered who he was talking to. Surely, they weren't to Pa's cabin yet. She inched her way along the narrow space separating the wagons and up to where Pa and Ma were now stopped. Her sisters followed her.

Sure enough, ahead on their left, was a small cabin. Smoke spewed from the chimney. A small clearing surrounded the tiny building.

The door opened and a man with a heavy beard and scraggly hair appeared. A bit of smoke enveloped him for a moment. "Who's there?"

Pa waved his hat at the man. "Name's Baker. Headed north from here to a clearing of land I settled last year."

The man nodded and waved. "That's odd. I thought I was one of the first in these parts."

"Came last year. With my son. When did you arrive?"

"Last November," the man turned his head and spit.

"Nice to meet ya." Pa tipped his hat to the man. "I'm bringing my family back with me this time."

"I don't got no family." The man held up his hand. "Are you in need of anythin'?"

"No, we're fine for today. But thank ya." Pa smiled and put his hat back on his head as the man disappeared back inside. The door to his cabin slammed shut.

Betsey asked, "Who was that, Pa?"

"Not a clue, Bit."

"I hope all our neighbors won't have a disposition like him, but it was nice of him to ask if we needed anything," Ma added.

"It's called hospitality. Plain old, good-natured hospitality. This won't be the last you'll see or hear of it. Folks along this path, and others, often allow people to spend the night and even feed them if needed. It's what they do to help out a neighbor."

"But we aren't really his neighbor, are we, Pa?" Jillian asked as she picked at a small bug climbing the front of her apron. Etta backed away from her and jumped on the back of Pa's wagon. Jillian wasn't near as scared of bugs as Etta.

"Nope. Our property is still many days northwest of here. Neighbors here know how hard it is to start in a new place and usually offer to help in any way they can. But don't forget," Pa snapped the reins, urging the oxen to trudge forward, "everyone's our neighbor."

The dark, deep woods almost enveloped the small wagons as they continued north along the bumpy trail.

The canopy of tree limbs and branches proved thick, making it hard to see if the sky was blue, or dark with thunderclouds. Occasionally, a tiny bit of opening above would allow them an opportunity to see the color of the sky.

Betsey crawled up and onto the wagon with Aaron, as Jillian and Caroline bounded onto the back of Pa's wagon, in front of them.

Etta called back, "Pa says there's a wagon up ahead. It looks to be abandoned."

Pa slowed his wagon a bit; but Aaron and Betsey couldn't see anything yet. "Pa says it looks like some Indians took what they wanted and left it nearly bare except for a few long sheets of lumber and a heavy yoke.

As Aaron and Betsey finally passed by the oddly shaped, barren wagon, Betsey let her imagination take over as to why someone had left their wagon, to either head back or go on foot deeper into the woods. She hoped they had done it on purpose.

"Someone will be back for that yoke soon, I imagine. It's a good one." Aaron shook the reins to get the oxen to move, and to catch up to Pa's wagon, now a distance ahead of them.

Miles of the thick forest faded away behind the two lumbering wagons, as another small town became visible ahead.

Pa hollered back to Betsey and Aaron, "We'll be stopping here for the night."

As Aaron pulled up beside the Baker wagon, Pa announced that they'd soon be upon the river called Shiawassee. Their new home sat near its banks, a bit north of their current location.

As the wagons maneuvered into the town, travelers of all sorts milled through and amidst the buildings. Wagons, with small fires beside them, circled the outskirts. Men with furs on their backs were coming and going from a small trading hut at the edge of town. Children were playing near the steps of what appeared to be a schoolhouse at the far edge of town.

Pa pointed out a small area, just past town, in which to park their wagons. As Aaron pulled up beside Pa's wagon, they heard Pa say, "This little town is called Pontiac. From here, we'll head north. They tell me a Negro woman named Elizabeth Denison started this part of the town back in 1825. First woman to purchase land here.

She's well known around these parts. Let's get a few more supplies here and then we'll head north to our property."

Pa greeted everyone he met with a tip of his hat and a, "How'd you do?"

Betsey couldn't believe that a woman would be a landowner, let alone here, in a far-away, desolate wilderness. Who would allow a Negro woman to own property? Perhaps this new land they were headed for was a promise of better opportunities.

Ma approached Betsey. "Pa said we should get supplies we'll need to set up a household, here. He said there isn't much but small trading posts beyond this point."

Betsey turned to tell Aaron as he led the oxen to the far side of the road.

He gave her a nod as she approached him. "I heard your pa. Go and watch what your ma buys and buy a little less, of the same, for us."

Aaron handed Betsey a few coins from his pocket.

"I'll stay here with the wagons while everyone heads into town." Aaron had a grip on both sets of reins.

Betsey wished she could have freshened up a bit before heading into civilization again, but it was getting dark and she knew there wasn't time. Putting on her bonnet, she tucked her hair underneath as best as she could.

The wagons headed out again at nightfall; Pa and Aaron decided to camp at the edge of the dense forest, away from the noise and busyness of town. They could build a fire and cook a fresh meal from their purchases.

That night, sleep came easily and quickly for Betsey and Aaron. Being this close to a bustling community, the wolves weren't likely to bother them on this night. Betsey startled when Pa rapped on the wagon early the next morning.

They were all up before dawn, finishing up what was left from last night's meal. Pa said it would be a good day's drive to reach the river that flowed past their new property.

The area around Pontiac appeared swampy. A musky smell lingered in the air. Occasionally, the wagon wheels got stuck in the muck. Betsey was thankful the rain had finally stopped, but the remnants of previous rains still left puddles. The women continued on foot, enjoying a warmer-than-usual spring day. The warmth of the sun prompted them to shed their shawls.

Betsey's sisters were growing tired of the travel, but Pa reminded them that the trip wasn't as bad as some settlers had it. They didn't need to travel for weeks upon weeks like those who headed to the far-western portion of the country. Betsey and the girls discussed this as they trudged behind Aaron's wagon.

"I can't imagine having to do this every day for weeks at a time, can you, Betsey?" Etta commented as she jumped over a small puddle in the middle of the road.

"No. I know I'd grow tired of a journey that far. At least we've had a few warm days in which to dry our clothes and the wagon canvas. Can you imagine never having that opportunity?"

Caroline jumped the same puddle Etta had. "It would be adventurous, even romantic, to go to unknown places like that though, don't you think?"

"I'd be too afraid of the Indians." Jillian wrapped her arms around herself and squeezed tight.

That night, Pa and Aaron took turns guarding the oxen from any possible predators. Pa assured them that their best option was to keep a fire stoked. They had plenty of wood available for the task.

Etta had sneezing fits the next day as they walked behind Pa's wagon through the deep forest.

"I knew someone would be suffering the ill effects of those wet days sooner than later," Ma said.

The only medicine the Bakers had brought with them was castor oil, a vial of peppermint oil, and a bit of rum. Ma didn't want anyone to know about the rum. She'd told Betsey she packed it because it did work well on certain disorders. Ma had also purchased a small bottle of quinine in Pontiac. Betsey wondered if any of the rest of them would get sick from the wet days of travel they'd suffered through. Etta always seemed to get sick quicker than any of the other girls. Ma always said it was because of her small stature. She'd been smaller than all the other girls, from birth.

The deeper into the woods the wagons traveled, the heavier the mist of the morning dew became. Betsey wondered if water surrounded them.

Just before nightfall, Pa hollered back to Aaron, "We're almost to the river."

A delightful aroma hung in the air. It smelled like their house when Ma made maple sugar candy at Christmastime. After a few miles, the scent grew stronger.

And that's when it happened. Pa stopped the wagon sharp. Aaron had been swatting a fly that had landed on his shirt sleeve, but realizing Pa had stopped, he pulled back on the reins of his oxen team just in time to avoid slamming into the back of Pa's wagon. Betsey leaned to her right to see if she could see anything in front of Pa's wagon. She saw nothing unusual. Why had Pa stopped so abruptly?

Aaron asked her, "Can you go up and see?"

Betsey held up her skirt as she slid to the ground. She walked to the right of Pa's wagon to see why he'd stopped. "Pa...?" but before she could say more, she saw why.

Standing in the middle of the road, blocking the trail, was a tall, dark-skinned man wearing nothing but a small cloth over his private parts and what appeared to be an animal hide across his shoulders. His bronze skin gleamed in the late-afternoon sun. His jet-black hair hung in a thick braid over his shoulder.

"An Indian," whispered Betsey.

North of Pontiac, Indian Territory

CHAPTER NINE

Betsey gasped. Her mother motioned to Betsey to get away, but she couldn't move. Without warning, other Indians came out of the woods and surrounded both wagons.

Pa did what he always does in a fearful situation. "'My brethren, count it all joy when ye fall into diverse temptations.'" He then held up his hand in greeting. "Hello."

The Indian who had blocked Pa's wagon walked toward Pa, shouting. A dog close by his side barked a growling warning of its own.

"Hosea, what do they want?" Ma groaned out in whispers.

"Just sit tight. He's Chippewa."

Everyone could clearly hear Pa spouting more scripture as he pulled back on the wagon brake. "'For I was hungry and ye gave me meat, I was thirsty and ye gave me drink, I was a stranger and ye took me in.'"

Pa motioned with his hand that he was getting off the wagon and handed Ma the reins, whispering, "If there's any trouble, kick these oxen into gear and get out of here."

Ma took the reins with shaking hands.

Pa held his hands up to the Indian in front of him. "I come in peace."

The Indian shouted to his companions now getting into the back of both wagons. Betsey could hear her sisters begin to weep.

As she turned to head back to Aaron, an Indian pinned her against Pa's wagon. His gaze was unmoving. At that moment, she wanted nothing more than to crawl up beside Ma, but he had her trapped. The hub of the wagon wheel dug into her back.

He smelled odd. Like a dog recently sprayed by a skunk. Bright-red paint streaks went across his face, and his chin was chiseled and strong. A muscle flexed in his jaw. Dark eyes pierced her own. Her legs began to tremble.

Pa yelled back to Aaron. "Don't move. Just be ready to run if they mean harm."

Betsey couldn't see Aaron or his reaction, but she heard him pull back on the brake, to brace the wagon.

She then heard Pa from the opposite side of the wagon. "Are you hungry? We have food."

Betsey felt like she could soil herself. Despite the cool temperature, she felt a bead of sweat trickle down her neck and into her blouse. The Indian smelled so bad it made her eyes water.

She heard someone rummaging through the wagon and her pa say, "We have flour, sugar...dried beef?"

Betsey could see Indians dashing back into the woods with the bags of flour, sugar, and even some blankets. Bile rose in Betsey's throat. She turned her head to see Indians removing items from their wagon as well. She watched one of her wedding quilts disappear into the woods on the arm of one of the men. She could feel heat on her neck from the Indian's breath.

Pa came around to Betsey's side of the wagon and held out his hand to the Indian leaning closer to Betsey. "Friends." The Indian shook his head.

Relief came over Betsey as the Indian stepped away. She sank to her knees. Kneeling under the wagon, she lost her recently-eaten dinner.

Pa bent over and patted her back. "That was close."

Betsey nearly fainted as Pa reached out to pull her close. "You okay, Bit?"

Wiping her mouth, "What did they want?"

"Food." Pa nodded. "They always come for food or spirits. Often they take firearms, too. Good thing I had those hid out of sight. Traders tell you, just give them what they want. Don't argue or fight for your rights. Works best that way." Pa held out his hand for Betsey to hold so she could stand up.

"They smell really bad," hollered Etta from the back of Pa's wagon.

"By golly, we got through that time."

"What do you mean, Pa?" Betsey gasped.

"Oh nothin' Sugar." Pa patted Ma's arm. "Scoot over, Sally. I'll take the reins now. We need to get movin' before they tell their friends how friendly we are. You get on back with Aaron, Bit."

Betsey edged cautiously toward Aaron, who had released the brake, ready to coax the oxen team on as soon as Pa moved his wagon. She climbed onto the wagon seat beside him and grasped his arm.

"You okay, Bit?"

All Betsey could do was cry as Aaron gave the oxen the command to, "...git up."

"Liquor is sometimes all they want," Pa told everyone later when they stopped for the night beside a different cabin in the woods. "Maybe that's why they took our food, they couldn't find a drop on us."

Betsey caught Ma glancing at her. They did have liquor, if you counted the small bottle of rum in her mother's medicinal bundle.

He told the cabin owner of their experience and the man assured him they'd done a good thing letting the Indians take what they wanted. "They feel it their duty to steal from us in exchange for allowing us to be on their land. Greedy—!" Before he could spew a bad word, he glanced around at Betsey's younger sisters. "Chippewas seem to be the most docile. But I've seen some mean ones, too. Just a day or two ago, I heard them set up a sap-boiling site just south of here. They get territorial about their possessions, yet they get spooked easy."

"That must have been the smell of maple we caught wind of back a'ways," Pa added.

The cabin owner nodded. "Let me know if you folks need anything. I'm headed inside."

"What will we do now, Hosea? They took almost all of our food staples. Should we head back for more?" Ma spooned food onto everyone's plate. "We paid good money for those things. It's sad to think of them carted off by savages."

"Indians believe we are the trespassers. Despite the federal government telling us the land is cheap for the takin', these Indians were here first. They've lived in these parts for hundreds, maybe thousands of years—we're the ones invading their land. How I have it figured is, we gotta be neighborly. That's how God would want us to be. I'd rather they take our food than any of my beautiful girls."

Pa sat down by the fire with his food on his lap. "God will provide. Let's pray for our food."

First, Pa thanked God for the safety of his family and then prayed that they would always do their best to be kind to the Indians who could do them harm. He prayed for protection during the rest of the journey, and for provisions to last until they could purchase or acquire more. Then he thanked God for their meal.

Everyone murmured in unison, "Amen."

"I think," Pa mumbled while eating his food, "We need to be neighborly, but also smart. Before morning, let's put some of the rest of our food in the barrels with our clothes. That way, they'll have to pry the lids off to find anything."

Aaron agreed. "Good idea."

Before bedding down for the night, Aaron and Pa placed some food items into the barrels between layers of clothing and blankets. Settling down for the night, Aaron decided to sit by the fire for a while instead of coming right to bed with Betsey. He seemed more alert and tense than he'd been before this.

"Aaron?" Betsey sat down beside him. "Can you let Pa take the first watch tonight?"

Aaron seemed to study her, waiting for a reason. When she didn't answer him right away he asked, "What's wrong, Bit?"

Betsey couldn't look into his eyes. She looked away. "I don't know, I just want you beside me tonight."

Aaron reached around and squeezed her shoulders. "You're safe, Bit. I won't let anything happen to you."

Betsey stood up to leave. "I know." She tried to be brave, and headed for the wagon. For the first time since being married, she wanted to crawl into the wagon with her ma. Cuddle up beside Caroline.

Betsey lay alone in the wagon. She shivered when a coyote howled a few yards away. She knew her family had ventured into a scary land, but the smell and the dark eyes of the Indian who had pressed her against Pa's wagon caused an even deeper fear to settle in her heart. She'd never forget his eyes. Demanding. Unkind. Neither his smell. Both penetrated her soul. Sleep didn't come until Aaron came to bed.

The next morning, a heavy frost blanketed the ground. Aaron was snoring beside Betsey when Ma gently knocked on the wagon. Betsey's husband rarely slept past dawn; it surprised her he was still asleep.

Birds chirped, tweeted, and sang above the wagons long before the sun peeked through the trees, brightening the trail.

Pa was talking with the owner of the cabin, who patted him on the shoulder and nodded. Despite the journey's dangers, the help provided by other settlers made their way through the untamed wilderness easier.

Back in her usual places the next day, either bouncing atop the wagon seat or walking between the wagons now, Betsey recalled the day before. She could still smell the scent of the man. It was revolting. She knew, in God's eyes, He made all men alike, but she'd never encountered one so menacing. Ma must have sensed her trepidation as they walked the trail. Aaron insisted the women walk between the wagons instead of behind as they had done in the past.

"Bit, you're awful quiet today." Ma grabbed her hand.

"I'm fine." Betsey had reminded herself all morning that they were safe. Pa had even assured her that the Indians were probably miles away from them now, but she couldn't get the Indian's penetrating stare out of her thoughts.

"I was so worried about you yesterday. I felt so helpless sitting just above you as the Indian held you captive." Ma sighed. "I haven't had that kind of fear in a long time."

Betsey didn't know what to say. Tears began filling her eyes, making it hard to see where she was walking.

Her ma seemed to notice. "Bit. We're all safe now."

Betsey wasn't so sure. They were entering a land filled with this kind of danger, and now they were bringing their unborn child into the land, too. What had she been thinking by joining her family into such danger?

"I need to remind myself of what God thinks of the Indians. He loves them as much as He loves me. Their ways are not our ways and I'm sure they feel at a loss as to why strangers are taking over their land. Can you imagine what that must be like for them?"

Betsey wiped her face with her sleeve. Betsey knew her ma's words to be true, but it still didn't replace the terror in her soul.

"The only thing we can do is do our best to repay their evil with God's good."

Betsey knew it would take all she had to remember that and put it into practice. She said a silent prayer for God's protection and repented of her stubborn desire to come with her family, but something had changed in her heart. She felt a fierce desire to protect herself and the child growing in her womb. She needed to be more alert. Another Indian would not put her in such a dangerous situation again.

Betsey had never walked so much in her life. Despite their ordeal the day before, her sisters chatted about the weather and their trip. Soon Etta brought up the topic of the Indians.

"I think the Indians' skin is so pretty, even though they do smell like the dog we had back in Pennsylvania," Etta laughed as she skipped beside her sisters, "just after he had a tussle with a skunk."

Betsey was happy her sisters could laugh off the frightening experience, but she couldn't add anything to the conversation for fear she'd burst into tears again.

"It is a beautiful bronze color, isn't it? They sure do smell funny, though." Jillian stopped to pick up and examine a stone. She loved stones. "The stones are mighty pretty here. Some even have pretty veins of color running through them."

Ma leaned over to see the stone Jillian held up for her. "That is a pretty one, Jillian."

The forest they now ventured through grew dense with trees. It made it hard to see what kind of day it had turned out to be. If a storm were to brew, it would be on top of them before they knew it, with the only warning being the rumble of thunder in the distance or a damp feel to the air.

"Pa said we only have a few days left to travel. He also said we're close to the river our property is on." Caroline began humming as she walked, then stopped. "Do you think we'll see any more Indians?"

Betsey froze, looking over her shoulder and into the woods behind them. "Why do you say that, Caroline?"

"Your pa said the encounter was unusual. Even the settler commented that he'd only heard of a few close calls like that in the past." Ma looked at Betsey as if she wanted to perceive how she was taking in the girls' conversation.

Etta chimed in, "He also said that sweet smell from yesterday was probably from the maple syrup the Indians were making from the abundance of sap."

"Who makes maple syrup?" Jillian dropped her stone.

"The Indians. Pa said it's maple syrup time here. The Indians have places in the woods set up to make the sugary syrup. They hollow out logs and burn the sap over fire, turning it into a sweet mixture they use all year long." Etta walked taller knowing she knew something the rest of her sisters hadn't been told yet.

"I wonder if we can harvest sap, too." Jillian pulled on Betsey's hand as she skipped farther ahead.

Betsey let go of Jillian's hand. Relieved the conversation was changing to food topics, Betsey chimed in, "I can't wait for Ma to make us flapjacks soon."

All the girls chimed in agreement. "I'm getting tired of the hardtack biscuits Ma makes."

Caroline stopped her humming. "We need to be thankful, girls."

Betsey felt bad for complaining in front of her sisters, and she was anxious to talk about something other than Indians.

"How long would it take someone to cross to the Pacific ocean?" Jillian was always eager to change the subject of conversation and for once, Betsey was glad she had.

The girls could hear Pa yell something to them. Fear made Betsey reach for Jillian's hand.

Jillian moaned, "Betsey, that hurts."

Betsey apologized, but felt her body grow tense with fear. She motioned to her sisters to walk closer to Ma.

"What did Pa just holler, Aaron?" Ma turned to ask Betsey's husband.

"I think I heard him say something about the river."

That's when they all heard Pa yell again. "We've made it to the river. Can you hear it?"

Shiawassee River, Michigan Territory

CHAPTER TEN

The roar of the river came and went all afternoon. Sometimes they'd hear what seemed to be water rushing, at other times, a softer ripple. It had to be pretty close, but the thick forest prevented any glimpse.

Pa set the brake on his wagon, jumped off, and patted a large tree beside their path. "See this, family? Here's another mark I put here last fall. All we have to do is follow the chinks in the trees to home."

Aaron smiled at Betsey, "Right smart of your pa to make those marks. The trail ahead seems to be narrowing. I think we're about to leave civilization as we know it behind."

Betsey couldn't imagine the countryside being more desolate than what they'd seen during the past few days. It was hard for her to believe their new home lacked close neighbors, but out here— the only footsteps made were by the Indians, their ancestors, and a few fur traders.

"We're forging a path into uncharted land. Think of that, Bit. We'll be among the first to make our home in this part of the territory. Maybe the baby you're carrying will be the first one born here."

At this possibility, Betsey felt her stomach churn. They were alone and in the depths of the darkest of forests. It made her think of Ambrose. What if something had happened to Ambrose since Pa left him? Her fear of the Indians overtook even her rational thoughts.

Betsey joined Aaron on the wagon seat. She'd had a tiring day. She startled at every single snap of a twig or shout from Pa. It didn't help that she'd gotten little sleep the night before.

As a wagon wheel slipped into a deep rut in the path, Betsey grabbed onto the side of the wagon bench for support. As she did, the baby did a bit of a flip-flop in her womb. She grasped her belly.

"How are you feeling, Bit?" Aaron was doing his best to keep the wagon on level ground, but the trees narrowed the path width, preventing him from bypassing rough patches.

"The baby is protesting a bit," Despite the warm afternoon sun, Betsey shivered as she tightened her grip on the wagon seat.

The next morning, before driving the wagons into what appeared the densest forest yet, Pa and Aaron set out on foot, guns in hand, in hopes of shooting a rabbit or a squirrel for dinner. Not long after, they came back with the largest rabbits Betsey had ever had the honor of skinning and gutting.

Ma helped Betsey with the task, but when Betsey got a whiff of the fresh blood, she immediately had to leave the spot to get a gulp of fresh air. Her stomach was not as queasy as when she first realized she might be with child, but certain smells sent her running for privacy.

On this particular morning, she did indeed lose her breakfast over having to cut the rabbit up. As she wiped her mouth off, Ma headed over to her, patting her on the back. "Let me cook up the meat this time. You haven't had a bad morning in a while."

"I'm sorry, Ma. I haven't been feeling all that well, as of late."

"Nothing to worry about, Betsey. If nothing else, all this walking will help build your strength for the labor ahead." Her ma placed the thin pieces of meat in the skillet sizzling over the fire, and added, "You'll be a good mother."

Betsey's heart ached. Despite what had happened to them during the journey, her love for her ma was strong and it brought her happiness knowing Ma would be able to hold her new grandbaby when her time came.

What would she have done in Pennsylvania when her time came? She needed her ma, now more than ever.

"Now, if you can manage, can you find the plates?"

Another day of walking came and went. Betsey rubbed her arches as she sat on the back of the wagon. The heels on her shoes were beginning to show wear. They hadn't been new, just her well-worn work shoes. Despite her careful steps, the ruts and furrows of the path could easily cause one of them to turn an ankle.

Since Pontiac, the roads were mere paths run over a few times with a wagon. Certain places narrowed so much that Pa had to cut down a sapling or two to squeeze the wagons through. Caroline and Aaron often had to take a scythe to the narrow path to allow the wagons easier access. They'd never been in such a primitive place.

It wasn't long before Pa slammed his wagon to a halt. "Aaron, hold up."

Aaron pulled back on the reins as the oxen snorted to a halt. "What's happening?"

Aaron gave Betsey an apprehensive glance.

At that moment, she knew she needed to make a conscious effort to stop allowing fear to rule her heart. Her parents had raised her to trust God and not allow fear to control her. Taking a deep breath, Betsey pushed her skirt aside and crawled down a wagon wheel. This time, she ventured to Pa's side of the wagon to see what was happening.

She could see Pa ahead. He jerked an ax from its stored place on the side of his wagon. He yelled back to Aaron that he needed to clear a tree off the path.

Ma got down from the wagon to meet Betsey. "Maybe we should prepare an early dinner. Looks like we'll be detained for a bit."

Betsey nodded. Just as she did, she felt a solid kick from the baby. Smiling, she thought of the baby now growing strong in her womb. She'd felt flutters, but never before had she felt this sensation. Stopping to savor the wonder, Caroline nearly bumped into her from behind.

"Betsey, what's wrong?" Etta edged past her by moving bushes out of her way.

"Oh," Betsey shrugged, "nothing." She felt confident that the tiny being in her womb had just kicked her.

Etta folded her arms, "What made you stop so suddenly?" Picking up her skirts, she squealed, "You didn't see a snake, did you?"

"No. No snake." Betsey pushed past her little sister and made her way to Aaron.

"Pa probably needs help, Aaron." Aaron set the brake on the wagon and started to get down. "Hand me the ax, will you, Bit?"

Betsey pried their ax off the side of the wagon and handed it to Aaron.

"Ma and I will start dinner. Are you hungry?"

Aaron placed the reins around the wagon's brake handle and nodded, "I'm always hungry, Bit. You know that."

Betsey touched Aaron's arm, whispering, "I think I just felt the baby kick."

Aaron stood proud, "Must be a boy!"

"That doesn't mean anything. I'm a girl and I kick quite well when I need to."

Aaron laughed, "You're right about that."

Betsey leaned in closer to him, "Maybe it will happen again tonight. Perhaps you can feel it, too."

Beaming, Aaron stood tall. "I hope so."

As Betsey went for the cooking items they normally brought out at dinner time, she thought of the intimate moments she and Aaron had been sharing in their wagon. Snuggled down deep under the covers, Betsey loved Aaron to touch her belly to feel how round it was getting under her otherwise-thick traveling skirt. He would smile every time and tell her how excited he was to become a father.

Caroline followed her to the back of the wagon and must have caught a bit of the conversation she'd had with Aaron. "So, is it true?"

Betsey looked up at her sister, who was grinning. "What?"

"Are you having a baby?"

Betsey knew she couldn't keep the secret, much longer, from her closest sister. Betsey nodded.

Caroline swooned, "Oh how wonderful. A baby." She clasped her hands up in a praying position, "I can't wait. It's been so long since we've been able to enjoy a baby. When?"

"In the fall."

Caroline closed her eyes. "How romantic!"

Betsey laughed, "I'm not sure about that. Having a stomach that often empties its contents the wrong way, having to go behind a bush to relieve myself every fifteen minutes, and being as tired as an old woman—if that's romantic, I consider that to be quite sad."

Caroline laughed. "I can't wait until it's my turn."

"Well," Betsey handed Caroline a skillet, "Let's find you a nice husband first."

Caroline's gushing stopped short, and a scowl appeared. "I'm having a hard time believing that where Pa is taking us will have any eligible bachelors flooding our doorstep anytime soon. Besides that, I only want Billie." With that comment, Caroline turned on her heel to head back up beside Betsey's wagon, to give the skillet to her ma.

Betsey knew this move was going to be hard on the girls. They had many friends they'd had to leave behind, and she knew Caroline was missing her lifelong friend. She knew the friendship had turned into something more romantic, as of late.

Betsey gathered her supplies for dinner and went to her ma's wagon to start preparing it. A beam of sun shifted overhead and flooded the ground around them. They both lifted their faces to see it.

"You sure don't see the sun much here."

Betsey wiped her hands off on a nearby cloth. "It can't seem to penetrate the canopy of trees." Betsey looked up to see the buds on the trees giving way to tiny leaves. "Once the leaves come out, I wonder if the sun will be able to shine through at all."

Caroline, Etta, and Jillian were singing as Betsey approached the back of the wagon where Ma was pulling out the biscuits she'd made the night before.

From behind the wagons came a call, "Hello there!"

The greeting made Betsey jerk alert. She felt her palms grow moist and her heart race. She turned to see who had called out and saw a man covered from head to foot in deer hides. His head was adorned with a fur wreath around his face and his breeches appeared thick and probably warm. He carried a rifle over his right shoulder.

Pa and Aaron were busy and probably hadn't heard the man call to them as they chopped at the tree on their path.

Ma stopped cutting pieces off the leftover rabbit they'd had the night before. "Hello." She wiped her face off with her apron. It had been difficult to look presentable the last few days, especially presentable enough for a stranger.

As he drew near, an odd smell came before the grizzly-looking fellow and at once Betsey covered her mouth with her apron. The scent brought back vivid moments of the Indian encounter. She stepped away from the man.

"That man smells like a skunk, too."

Ma shot Jillian a look of disdain and whispered, "Jillian," even though, by the look on her face, she probably wanted to say the same thing.

"Oh...it's alright, ma'am." The man set down his gun. "I have a skunk musk to me. Better than having to swat mosquitoes every second."

Ma questioned the man, asking the question even on Betsey's mind, "Mosquitoes?"

"Yes'm. Wait until summer draws closer and they hatch. Won't be long." The man stepped away from them. "Not very nice for young ladies to get a whiff. So sorry." The visitor pulled off his hat and wiped the sweat off his brow. "Getting to be warmer these days, gonna have to find me a different kind of hat."

The girls smiled. The hat was nothing like they'd ever seen worn by a human.

"Where ya headed?" the stranger asked.

Betsey went back to doing her ma's job, so she could answer the man now anxious to pick up a conversation with someone.

"Headed north toward the river. My son, Ambrose, lives there and we're coming from Pennsylvania to settle there with him."

"Ambrose? Ambrose Baker?"

Ma's face brightened. "Yes, do you know him?"

"Why yes I do, ma'am. My trading post is just south of his place a bit." The man held out his hand to Ma, "Name's Whitmore Knaggs. Nice to meet ya."

Ma wiped her hand off on her apron and took the man's hand. "My husband told me we're still a bit south of our cabin. What brings you this way?"

"I needed to head to Pontiac for some seed. Ambrose, in fact, was at the trading post last week, asking me if I had any yet. He's been a bit lonesome out here without y'all, but he keeps tellin' me that you'll be a-comin' soon."

"And," Ma smiled, putting her hands on her hips. "Here we are." She pointed toward Betsey and her sisters. "These are my daughters, Betsey, Caroline, Etta and Jillian, sir. They are Ambrose's sisters."

The man nodded their way, "Nice to meet ya. If you don't mind me sayin'...nice to see a few smilin' women around. And such pretty ones, at that. It's been awhile."

The man appeared to be older than Pa by quite a bit. Her sisters giggled at his attention.

"Looks as if the place will be home for many of you's soon enough. My trading post is the main place to come and get your supplies. If I don't have it, I try my darndest to get to Pontiac as much as I can to pick up what the new sett'lers need. I hope to do the same for y'all, too."

Ma nodded. "Thank you. My husband and Betsey's husband are just ahead of our wagon here. A tree has fallen across our path. They're doing their best to get it out of our way."

Whitmore placed his hat back on his balding head and motioned. "Well, let me get on up there and see what I can do to help."

"We'd be so grateful." Ma added, "Please stay and have a bite to eat with us, if you aren't in a hurry."

Picking up his rifle, he leaned it against Pa's wagon, Whitmore nodded, "Much obliged."

With that, the man strode to the front of Pa's wagon and called out to Pa, who welcomed him with a giant hug and greeting, as he would with any friend.

"Fix Whitmore a sandwich, Jillian." Jillian nodded, piling dried beef to another biscuit. "He seems like a nice fellow."

Betsey elbowed Caroline, who was pulling out another cup, for their guest. "Look at that, Caroline. A man. Way out here."

Caroline gave Betsey a poke with her finger. "Hmm, that wasn't exactly the kind of man I was referring to, my dear sister."

Etta giggled.

Caroline gave her a *hush-up* glance.

Whitmore was quite the character. He helped Pa and Aaron with the large tree blocking the path. "Stop by the trading post before heading north. I have a few things Ambrose was asking for," he told Pa. Pa told Whitmore about the trees he'd blazed during his trip south last fall, and how they were doing their best to find and follow them back to Ambrose and the cabin.

"I wondered who made those marks. I've been doing that for years. Ambrose is gonna be so tickled you've arrived. He's been mighty lonesome out here this winter, although for a young whippersnapper, he did right good."

Pa grinned. "Thanks for the update. Been a while since we've made contact with him to know how he was fairin'."

Whitmore ate his biscuit sandwich and even asked for another before pulling out a few green stems from his backpack. He put a stem in his mouth and began chewing on it. The pack seemed loaded and appeared heavier than any of the barrels they'd brought with them. "Sure is good to have you folks here. I know the government is now ready for you to purchase territory. Before long, you won't be alone, I'm sure of that."

Pa told Whitmore he'd decided to purchase nearly six hundred acres near the river, north of Whitmore's trading post.

Whitmore nodded. "That's a mighty fine piece of land. Can't wait to have you all in these parts. All who's here now is Ambrose and a few Indians. Pretty ladies would be much better neighbors than that." When he smiled, the old man's grin revealed missing teeth.

"What is the Indian population? We had a mishap a few days back with some unfriendly ones."

Whitmore scratched his head. "Must have been the chief. He doesn't really seem as willing to let go of the land as others in his tribe. He's just trying to show his authority, to let you know who's boss in these here parts. Sett'lers aren't used to their ways. Just don't try and fight 'em off. You'll lose." Whitmore took another bite of his second sandwich, after spitting out the stem he'd been chewing on. "They are usually just hungry fellows, but occasionally someone has inadvertently pushed onto their private burial grounds or intruded a bit too close, and they will fight back."

"Why do you think they feel it right to steal from people?" Aaron asked.

"They don't consider it stealing. They were here first. Whatever food supply you have on hand, they feel is theirs in the first place. They don't realize you may have purchased it downriver and it's not harvested directly from their land. They haven't quite caught on to how a store works yet. They often come in and steal from me when it is something I've gathered from the land. Honey, corn, walnuts...that sort of thing." Whitmore took a large swig from a metal canteen he'd pulled from his pack. Betsey's keen sense of smell could tell it wasn't water in the man's canteen. "They were here first. So, I guess, they do have a right to what we partake of, off their land. It's their way of keepin' the peace, so to speak."

Pa seemed to understand his point, but Aaron scowled.

Betsey felt a bit more secure after the conversation.

"Well folks, I best be gettin' on. They'll be waitin' for me at the post. I've been gone longer than expected. The rain last night kept me huddled in a cave at the river's edge."

"How close are we to your post?" Pa added, "I thought we had a bit farther to go."

"You're right, Hosea. It's a'ways yet. If this rain doesn't let up, may take you longer than you expected." Whitmore pointed off to the west. "If you were to travel in that direction, you'd be to it in a few days, but best to follow the river and your blazed trail. Road is best closest to the water. My post will be near where you cross the river." The trader took another long swig from his canteen. "Been nice gettin' to know the rest of your family, Hosea. Wish I could be with you when you meet Ambrose. He'll be tickled to death to see y'all again."

Ma then asked about his musky smell. He told her that he'd taken liberty to slather himself liberally before leaving Pontiac. "The mosquitoes are bad closer to summer, but there's also bitin' flies. They're bad this time of year. Seem to bite deeper and the leftover sore they leave, hurts even worse.

"Might early for the mosquitoes yet, but the lotion does help when they do come out. The worst thing we got goin' around these parts. I'd do most anythin' to stop them pesky animals from chewin' into me. Even if it causes a fella to smell like a skunk." Whitmore laughed. "Sorry folks. Gotta be headin' on."

With that comment, Whitmore picked up his heavy pack, thrust his arms through the straps, and pulled it onto his back. He slipped the canteen under his belt and lifted his rifle to his right shoulder. "Nice meetin' you ladies, Aaron." Whitmore situated the heavy fur-lined hat back onto his head.

At that, he made his way past the wagons, whistling the tune the girls had been singing before he came upon them.

"He seems a nice man," Ma said, as she stood to gather up the dinner dishes to wash. "Wish we were closer to the river. I could wash these dishes much quicker."

"We'll see it soon enough. Probably by nightfall, if we're lucky." Pa told Ma as he handed her his plate.

Whitmore had been right. After a long day of fighting through heavy brush and downed trees, the river sound got closer and closer as they moved north.

Despite having walked almost the entire trip, Betsey's ankles hadn't gotten much stronger, and now they ached. She noticed they were a bit swollen.

As the sound of the river drew closer, the canopy of trees overhead grew less dense. When they reached a certain curve in the path, Pa shouted back to their wagon, "We're there. We made it!"

As Aaron urged the oxen along the now muddier trail, Betsey got her first look at the river Pa had told them about over the past few months. It was wider than she had imagined, but they could still see clearly across it, to the other side. The water sparkled as the sun now had full access to light it from above. The banks were covered with brush and weeds instead of the tall, top-heavy trees. The water rushed northward, rippling across rocks or fallen trees strewn throughout the riverbed.

Pa's wagon stopped. Everyone climbed off their seats to make their way to the river's edge. As they did, a large deer lifted his white tail high in the air and darted away into the woods.

"Here she is: The Shiawassee," Pa announced.

"Say it again, Pa." Etta's smile brightened her tired, dirt-smudged cheeks. They'd been practicing saying the name over and over, but for some reason, it was hard to remember the odd Indian pronunciation.

"Shia—wassee." Caroline smiled in the victory of pronouncing it correctly.

"Good job, Carrie. It was Whitmore who told me how to say it proper last year. But we've made it," Pa said as he huddled his family close.

"How much farther to the cabin?" Ma asked.

"Couple days' travel. If the Lord wills and the river doesn't rise." Pa pulled Ma to him and kissed the top of her head.

Pa's description of the water was correct, with all his stories from last fall. It held charm and mystery of what they'd soon see. Their new home.

Shiawassee River, Near Knaggs Bridge

CHAPTER ELEVEN

The river rippled beside them. Bushes, along the banks, contained tiny buds ready to welcome the new season to the territory. A large fish jumped from the river, its sides glimmered in the sunlight from overhead, before it plunged back into the water.

Betsey's sisters removed their thigh-high stockings and began to wade up to their knees into the cold water.

Ma stood on the bank with folded arms, watching their jumps and facial grimaces in reaction to the chilly stream. "You girls will catch your death a'cold out there."

"We can't help it, Ma. I wish I had a bar of soap, too." Etta laughed as she splashed water on her face.

Ma left them all soaking their feet. Soon she returned with a bar of soap in-hand. "Get clean, girls."

Everyone laughed as they washed their faces and hands in the cool stream.

Pa pointed to the river, "Don't venture out too far, girls. It can get deep fairly quick."

Shiny faces surrounded the campfire that night. Everyone was in good spirits after a refreshing cleansing from the same river that flowed beside the property they'd soon call home. As they got into their wagons to sleep that night, they felt rejuvenated and even

128

more interested in the land their pa had been telling them about during the past winter.

Pa and Aaron took time the next morning to catch a few fish for breakfast, and the aroma now drifting from Ma's skillet smelled better than the biscuits and hard tack she'd been fixing since leaving Detroit. The fresh fish brought a new smell to their cooking. Unfortunately, it was one that sent Betsey to the water's edge, mainly for fresh air. She longed for the moment when her stomach wouldn't react to the smells around her. Her mother assured her that it wouldn't be long before she would be able to stand at the cooking fire, for the entire time, without feeling like eating was the last thing she wanted to do.

"We'll dry fish once we reach home, where we can store it for much longer, but for now, we need to eat all the fish we catch. No place to keep it from spoilin'." Pa's request wasn't hard to comply with, for the fish tasted delightful. "We'll have plenty of fish to catch, once we reach the homestead."

Putting the cooking tools back into the wagon and heading out that day, everyone was eager to see Ambrose. It had been almost a year since Ma and the girls had told him goodbye as he and Pa set off for Michigan Territory.

Ma exclaimed over and over her excitement about seeing him soon, "Land, I miss that boy!"

"I knew you were missing him more than you let on," Pa winked at Ma.

The wagon trail took them along the east side of the river that day. Often, they'd catch a glimpse of the wildlife they'd be encountering in the new territory. The deer seemed larger than at home in Pennsylvania. They saw turkeys, raccoons, even a flock of geese, which flew to the river and glided-in with skidding, yet graceful landings. It was fun to watch them. At one moment, they also saw a bear drinking from the river across the bank. It made Betsey a bit nervous to know that they were that close to something so ferocious and dangerous.

Singing voices erupted from Pa's wagon. Jillian was singing, "All Creatures Great and Small," aided by the contralto of Etta's voice, as well as Caroline's. Betsey wanted to add her part in the song, but when she tried to sing, the noisy wagon and shifts in the road made it impossible for her to know if she were on the same word or even the same pitch as her sisters, so she resigned herself to just sit and listen. Oh, how she hoped her baby had the family's musical talents.

There were some moments, out by the nightly fire, that she would feel the baby move more often. The child seemed more active at night. For whatever reason, her walking put him to sleep, but once the day's walking was over, the baby seemed to want to twirl in her womb. It was as if he or she was as excited as the other family members to be near their final destination.

What a feeling it was to have a baby move in her womb! Nothing could compare to it. She lovingly patted her belly and smiled at Aaron each time a small flutter interrupted her talking. He hadn't been able to feel it yet, but Betsey thought it wouldn't be long before the kicks would grow strong enough for others to feel the infant growing within her.

The spring sun grew warmer than when they'd started their journey. Even the daylight stretched a bit longer before darkness settled over the two solitary wagons on the primitive trail.

Buds were giving way to new green growth. This new world seemed to come alive with life. Lush, green leaves would soon emerge from the bursting buds. Pa told them their new home would soon be filled with the many sounds coming from the river, which would include frogs and buzzing, pesky mosquitoes, the ones that Whitmore had told them about.

"They're pesky and annoying little things. Closer to June, you'll wonder how you ever can get anything done with them buzzin' around," Pa told them one night over the campfire. Pa said they'd probably cross the Shiawassee the next morning.

Sure enough, by mid-morning the next day, the two wagons came upon a narrow band of the river. The road sloped down a decline toward the river's edge. They weren't the first people to cross this portion of the river, as a clear trail was evident in visible ruts from earlier wagon wheels.

"This is what folks call the Salt Lick of the Shiawassee. Indians come here to live during the hard winter months. The salt preserves their food. We can cross here, 'cause it isn't as deep as other parts of the river." Pa instructed Aaron on how to handle the oxen team as they crossed the river.

As their wagon made it into the flowing stream, Betsey gripped the edge of her seat and pulled herself closer to Aaron. He put his left arm out but gave her a look that made her scoot away from him. He needed a free arm, not one his wife was clinging to in fear. She chided herself.

The rocks tipped their wagon at different angles as they slowly made their way across. Pa and Ma's wagon cleared the water and was on the bank while Aaron continued urging the oxen on with coaxing commands.

"This ox is determined to go his own way," Aaron grunted as he grasped the reins tighter.

"Which one?"

"The one on the right. He keeps fighting against me." Aaron hollered out a louder command to the team.

When they pulled up onto the far bank of the river, Betsey loosened her grip and relaxed. She hollered out to her pa, "Is that the only place we have to cross?"

Pa nodded, took his hat off, and scratched his forehead. "That's it, Bit. We're ready to head inland a bit again, but not for long."

After they crossed, Pa took time to visit Whitmore's trading post, just off the west bank of the river. After visiting with Whitmore for a bit, he approached Aaron and Betsey's wagon, grinning.

"Don't tell Ma, but Whitmore headed up north to tell Ambrose we were coming."

Soon they were seeing the back of Pa's wagon again as they made their way inland now on the western shore of the Shiawassee.

On the trail the next morning, the girls' singing abruptly stopped. Aaron looked over at Betsey. "Wonder what's going on?"

"They're probably tired of singing."

Just then a shrill shriek from Ma made fear clutch Betsey's heart. She gripped the edge of the wagon seat. They couldn't see beyond Pa's wagon.

"Do you want me to go check?"

Betsey didn't know what to do. She knew someone needed to find out about her ma's outburst, but fear robbed her courage. She could now hear her sisters' squealing. The exclamations didn't seem panicky, but joyful, giving her courage to go and look. Betsey told Aaron, "I'll go. I'm sure it's nothing."

"Sounds like happy shouts to me, too."

Despite Aaron's reassuring words, Betsey walked hesitantly along the side of Pa's wagon, her eyes darting back and forth between the woods alongside the path, and to the front of the wagon.

What was all the commotion? As she reached Pa's wagon seat, she looked up to see her sisters and mother racing toward a man standing in the middle of the road. Betsey couldn't imagine why they were acting as they were, but she cupped her hand over her eyes to shield them from the sun.

Once she focused, she picked up her skirt and began running toward the man, too, whose arms were opened wide. It was Ambrose.

Hosea couldn't help but laugh to see his girls running toward his son. Surprisingly, Sally ran faster and got to Ambrose before their daughters. She abruptly pulled the young man into a hug so tight he was sure Ambrose would topple over. But he didn't, and his sisters came in right behind her to embrace their mother and Ambrose both at the same time. They were a huddle of women with Ambrose right in the middle.

Even from where he sat, Pa noticed that Ambrose had grown. His shoulders broader, he looked strong and solid as he headed toward them with purposeful, confident steps. The young boy he'd left in the woods last fall now appeared a grown man. Hosea could hear his son laughing. Oh, how he'd missed the boy. Soon Ambrose pried himself out of the arms of the women and waved to Hosea, who gave him a broad smile and a wave of his hat.

Nearing the wagon, Sally clung to her son's right arm as each girl tried to grab his other hand. Ambrose planted a kiss on Betsey's cheek. He stood taller than all of them, but the expression on his face was like that of a child on Christmas morning.

When he got within hearing distance, he yelled out to Aaron and Hosea, "I wish all girls greeted me like Ma and my sisters!" Both Pa and Aaron, now standing beside Pa's wagon, laughed.

Hosea hollered out, "Guess our surprise was let out of the bag. Thanks to Whitmore."

As his son drew closer to the wagon, he answered, "I was planning on heading into Pontiac for some supplies and seed. I had been determined to wait for you, but then realized that I needed to prepare myself for spring if you didn't come. Before I left, Whitmore came to visit me. He told me y'all were headed this way."

Hosea chuckled again. "We saw him on the trail. It was good to see him."

Ambrose reached the wagon and held out his hand. "So happy to see y'all! It's been a long winter."

Hosea was sure he saw tears forming in his son's eyes, but they were quickly wiped away with a brush of his shirt sleeve. "Climb aboard, son. We got the entire day to get reacquainted."

Ambrose nodded and sat down beside him on the wagon bench. "Y'all are a sight for sore eyes."

"The last we heard from you was just before Christmas. You sounded like you'd had enough alone time to last you a while."

Ambrose laughed. "I hope you're ready to do some cooking, Ma. I've had enough of my own cooking to last a lifetime."

Ma had gotten behind the wagon bench and now leaned over to place a kiss on Ambrose's cheek. "I'll cook for you tonight, son."

Ambrose smiled. "Boy, I'm sure happy to see you. I'll probably say that a million times before I finally realize I've said it before."

That night by the campfire, Ambrose told his family about the winter he'd spent alone. He told them about the deep snow. "It wasn't long before I realized it was going to be a long winter. I began talking to myself, and even answered myself—a few times." Everyone laughed. "I don't think I ever want to spend a winter like that again. I was thankful Pa and I built the cabin before he'd left, or you might all have had to bury me instead of hug me this morning."

Ambrose began recalling some of the worst days of winter. One late afternoon, he'd gotten stuck out in a snowstorm and couldn't find his way home. An Indian had found him, dug him out of a makeshift snow shelter, and led him back to his home. He said the Indian now stopped into the cabin occasionally to eat with Ambrose. "We can't understand each other's language at all, but somehow we make do."

"Is he scary?" asked Jillian, her eyes as large as her imagination.

"He was at first, and the smell of him comes way before he gets close."

They all nodded. "But he saved my life. I will always be grateful to him."

"Does he have a name?" Aaron asked, as he poked the fire with a stick.

"Whitmore told me his name. He's Chippewa. From what I can make out, his name is Nagamo Nibi. I call him Nibi for short. Whitmore says that *nibi* means 'water.' *Nagamo* means 'singing.' So, his name in English is Singing Water."

"That sounds about right for this area. Is he your age?" Pa seemed much more interested than anyone else in the group to learn more about the Indians.

"A bit older, I do believe. He's helped me more than I care to admit." Ambrose yawned. "I'm mighty tired. I think I'll get to bed a bit early tonight."

"Sleep with us in our wagon, Ambrose." Betsey nodded toward she and Aaron's wagon.

"A bit more room in it than Pa's." Aaron pointed towards the wagon.

"I'll get you a blanket." Betsey rose and headed to the wagon. As they got closer, Ambrose came up beside her.

"I'm so thrilled that you came with the family, Betsey."

"It's so good to see you again, Ambrose."

He gave Betsey a knowing look.

"What?"

"Are you expecting, Betsey? I noticed your pasty white face when helping Ma cook tonight. And—"

"And, what?"

"Your skirt's a bit too tight."

Betsey blushed. Brothers shouldn't talk about these things with sisters, but she and Ambrose had been close through the years. She didn't mind him asking, and nodded.

"That's wonderful news. When?" Ambrose's eyes sparkled.

"Probably in the fall."

Ambrose hugged her. "If no other young, married women come before you, you may end up having the first baby in this area."

Betsey wasn't sure it was something to celebrate. It was exciting to think about it, but at the same time, baby's lives were fragile. Life, especially that of a new baby, should never be taken for granted.

"If the Lord wills it, everything will be fine." Betsey knew this to be true, but saying it out loud triggered an emotion she wasn't expecting. *What if things didn't go well?* Reaching down she patted the little, squirmy soul now forming in her womb. She'd grown attached to the child long before she felt movement, but now she longed to kiss his face. What would happen if she never had that opportunity? They were in a wilderness. Her fear was real.

As if sensing her concerns, Ambrose smiled widely, "It will all be fine." He patted her hand, "If I can live out here all alone for half a year, you'll easily bring a baby into the world."

Betsey prayed he was right.

Ambrose jabbered on the next morning as they traveled the path northward. He sat on the back of Pa's wagon so everyone could hear him. "I think staying this winter all by myself was one of the scariest things I've done yet."

Betsey could see pride on his face. Before Ambrose left, he barely had whiskers to tame. Now he had broadened shoulders, he sat up straighter, and spoke with greater confidence. He'd left Pennsylvania an excited teenager and was now a man talking about adult adventures.

"There was no one to sit down and eat with, or chat with about what had happened throughout my day." Betsey saw tears well up in his eyes, which he wiped dry with the cuff of his sleeve. "It was one of the loneliest times of my life."

"We're here now, son. Don't worry. We'll get a barn up soon, and a house for Aaron and Betsey. We all have each other now." Pa spoke with an air of confident affirmation.

"I'm so happy you and Aaron decided to join the family." Ambrose smiled at Betsey. "But Aaron, what about that new job that was offered?"

Aaron typically only spoke when asked a question. His quiet demeanor was one of the reasons Betsey had loved him to begin with. It made him seem confident and sure of himself. "They'll need a law man here soon enough. Until then, we need to make us a new home, and I think Betsey needs to be close to your folks."

Betsey sat higher on the wagon seat. Aaron did love her. How many husbands would sacrifice a new position to head into the unknown, just so his wife could be with her family?

"Law men will be needed soon. Whitmore says he's seen more people on the road through Pontiac than ever before. He's certain that this summer will bring in more settlers than any of us can imagine." Ambrose took his hat off and slapped it against his knee. "I'm hoping some of them have daughters."

Everyone laughed at that comment. Even though Ambrose was three years older than her, Betsey found it hard to believe that he would also want a wife for himself. She still remembered him as the young man who'd left Pennsylvania, desiring adventure and a chance to make something of himself.

Ambrose stared off into the woods. "There were some hard times too. Not sure if Pa has told you about the mosquitoes, but those critters can torment you to drink. Once it gets warmer, you'll see how miserable they can make a person. As much as I hated the winter, at least they stopped buzzing. They'll go after your blood faster than a buzzard after a fresh animal carcass."

Ma shouted from the wagon seat beside Pa, "What can you do about them?"

"The Indians have some kind of musk rub. Whitmore claims it works pretty good. I don't know quite how to communicate to even Nibi about it. I have no idea how to make something like it."

"I will not wear that stinky stuff." Caroline folded her arms.

"You'll see Caroline. They'll eat you alive. At night, you can close everything off, but somehow they still manage to get into the cabin. They are a force to be reckoned with." Ambrose shook his head. "But ague is another thing we have to endure. Whitmore says it causes you to run to the outhouse and gives you the fever shakes, like you wouldn't believe."

"What causes that?" Betsey asked as she unlaced her boots to ease the tightness of her swollen ankles.

"Not sure. Everyone seems to get it. Whitmore says it's worse in the summer. After a while you just know that it will happen to you at least once a year or so. We could really use a doctor around these parts. Surely, sooner than later."

Betsey's thoughts immediately turned toward the possible complications she might experience delivering a baby and not having a doctor around to help. Yet she needed to remember that babies had been born in worse situations. Glancing at Aaron, he seemed to be having the same thoughts.

Ambrose leaned back. "Pa, I've girdled quite a few trees. I think plenty enough for our barn and a start on Aaron and Betsey's house. They're looking ripe to cut soon. It kept me busy last fall and into the early parts of winter tying and readying them for cutting."

Pa responded, "Good job, son. Might be easier than how we had to cut last year's timber for the cabin."

Ambrose nodded. "I'd planned on getting some seed for early potatoes and peas in Pontiac."

"We bought all of that before leaving Pontiac," said Aaron. "I think we're set for now."

Ma chimed in, "Thankfully, the Indians only took flour, sugar, and some oats from what we'd purchased in Pontiac. They didn't bother stealing the seed potatoes."

"They don't need seed. They've lived off this land without fur trading posts or stores for many a year. They do like to take your food, though. One night, while I was eating supper, a lone Indian walked into the cabin, sat down, and ate my last three potatoes I'd cooked for my own meal. After he was finished, he wiped off his mouth with his shirt sleeve and commenced to lie down on the floor, right in front of the hearth. He was gone by the time I woke up, the next morning."

Jillian's eyes grew wide as she looked to Ambrose seated beside her on the back of the wagon. "Weren't you scared?"

Betsey felt her back stiffen, and she snuggled closer to Aaron.

Ambrose's voice thundered an answer, "Course. Wouldn't you be?"

Jillian nodded, eyes wide.

"The temperature outside that night was near or close to freezin' and I knew he was probably just cold. I think I would have done the same if I'd have found a warm, dry cabin." Ambrose squeezed his baby sister closer to him on the wagon's edge. Jillian leaned her head against Ambrose's shoulder.

"Nibi also taught me how to put nets into the river to catch fish. If it wasn't for him, I'd have been eating potatoes all winter. Fish was one of my main meals during the latter winter months, thanks to him."

"Didn't the river freeze over?" Pa asked from the front of the wagon.

"Oh, it did, but Nibi taught me how to cut a small hole in the ice and how to spear the fish through that hole. It was quite fun."

"You'll have to tell us all about things the Indians have taught you, Ambrose," Ma added.

"I can't say it enough. If it weren't for them, I'm not sure I'd have been here to see you all join me." Ambrose sat up straighter.

"'The Lord is my rock, and my fortress, and my deliverer; my God, my strength, in whom I will trust; my buckler, and the horn of my salvation, and my high tower.'" Pa's voice echoed from the front of his wagon.

Ambrose nodded, "You're right, Pa. He was my rock and fortress through all those cold months."

Caroline, reminded of the hymn, sat down beside Ambrose on the wagon bed and began singing..."*A Mighty Fortress.*"

Instead of joining in, Ambrose just smiled.

First Sight of North Newburg, Michigan Territory

CHAPTER TWELVE

"This it is!" Pa shouted from his wagon seat. "We're home."

Aaron gave Betsey's hand a squeeze. Their new home. Hard to believe it had taken them nearly four weeks of travel to finally arrive at their destination.

Betsey desired nothing more than to cook a full meal over a hearth instead of a blazing campfire. She and Ma had burned more meals than they cared to admit. Open outdoor fires were either intensely hot and scorching or smoky and useless. It either burned their pancakes or made them harder than rocks. Cooking would be so much more convenient and easy over an open hearth fire.

As Betsey and Aaron's wagon reached the spot from where Pa had shouted, they saw what he had been telling them about since his return to Pennsylvania last fall. The banks of the river stretched inland onto a flat clearing. Trees edged the property like a protective shield against the threats of the deep woods past them. They hadn't seen an area, devoid of trees, since leaving Pontiac.

Aaron pulled back on the reins as Pa stopped his wagon in front of them.

Ambrose jumped off Pa's wagon. "We're home."

Pa motioned for Aaron to pull up alongside his wagon. For the first time since Pontiac, there was room for Aaron to do that. Pulling forward into the wide clearing, Betsey saw a small cabin, complete with a chimney and front porch. The dwelling was much smaller than they'd had back in Pennsylvania, but knowing it was Ambrose's home, the one he and Pa had built before he'd returned home, filled Betsey with pride and wonder. She imagined Ma was feeling the same way. They'd heard all about it from Pa's recollections. Now they could see it for themselves.

Ma climbed down from the wagon and headed toward the cabin. Jillian, Caroline, and Etta scampered in the opposite direction, toward the river. Ambrose was already carrying supplies, from the wagons to the tiny cabin.

It was a beautiful area. Ma stood beside a small bush that had just opened fresh leaves to the world.

"I planted your lilac right here by the house," Betsey overheard Pa announce to Ma. "Might not bloom this spring, but give it a year and it will."

Ma had sent it with Pa and Ambrose to plant near her new home. She gushed happily over the one lone plant which had survived the winter and now helped the small cabin feel a bit more like home.

Ma stood on tippy-toes to kiss Pa. "It's a way to remember our place in Pennsylvania." It had been a few weeks since Betsey had seen a bit of affection shown to Pa, by Ma.

Now the real work would begin. Barrels needed to be unloaded and emptied, and the house equipped for a family instead of, just one. As Betsey made her way to the cabin, she had only one concern: how would eight people live in a one-room cabin? Where would they all sleep? How would they set up an efficient way of housekeeping in such a small space? Yet this was their new life. It might not be what she really desired, but they'd do everything they could to make it work. Just like Ambrose had managed to do all winter.

Aaron's face seemed to reveal the same feelings as hers.

Betsey grabbed his hand. "We'll make do."

He nodded.

Before he could say anything, Pa approached them. The sparkle of delight in his eyes gave away his sentiments. "Well, what ya think?"

A gradual smile formed on Aaron's face and he shrugged.

Betsey answered, "It's wonderful, Pa. Just as you said."

"From what Whitmore has told me, Pa, we need to get to the Jackson land office. That's where you purchase land outright," Ambrose said, as Betsey and her sisters began clearing the table after dinner.

"How much, son? What's the land going for?" Pa drank the rest of his hot coffee.

"One dollar and twenty-five cents an acre is what I've been hearing from Whitmore and the settlers who are just south of his post."

Pa hit the table with an opened hand. "By golly! Just like the newspapers reported it to be. Considerably cheaper than back home."

"Whitmore says the land office sends a representative to look over the maps you provide for them. The representative examines the property, by using a compass and maps. We select and pay for the land we want. After we acquire the land, in Jackson, they take the monies and records back to Washington and we get a presidentially-signed patent for our land."

Ambrose slid his plate toward Caroline, who was collecting them to be washed.

"We better get busy and figure out which sections we want. I can't imagine the land settling that fast, but we want to be sure we can get our desired acres."

"We better not wait too long, Pa. Whitmore says he's never seen this many settlers." Ambrose added, "I do believe, Pa, we found just the right spot, though. I can see a whole new town forming here."

Pa's eyes grew wide, "You know, we might have the opportunity to name this area ourselves, see-in's we're some of the first ones here."

"That's what I was thinking." Ambrose smiled.

"We need to stock up on a few supplies, too." Ambrose scooted his chair back and began fumbling for a pipe from a pocket.

"We got quite a few things before we headed north, but yes, we'll need to replenish what the Indians took." Pa watched his son pack his pipe with tobacco.

Everyone was a bit surprised Ambrose was smoking, but he was a man now. Pa commented, "The Indians teach you how to do that, son?"

Ambrose laughed. "I'm tellin' ya Pa, they've taught me a great deal, but this I learnt from Whitmore. He said any man who could live out a winter all alone deserves to know how to smoke a pipe."

Betsey and the others knew Ambrose wasn't the same boy who'd left Pennsylvania, but it was going to take some time watching him behave like a man to convince them that he'd become an adult while they'd been apart.

"I also drink tea." Ambrose laughed, after he inhaled deeply and puffed on the pipe sticking out of his mouth.

"Tea. You have tea?" Ma sat down beside her son. "In that tin over there, Ma. I'd forgotten how much you like tea. I picked it up last time I was in Pontiac. Makes for something else to drink besides water. Speakin' of water, have you told them about the cold spring yet?"

Pa told the family about how they'd found a fresh spring by the river the first time they'd gone out to explore their land, even before choosing the spot on which to build the cabin. Ambrose left the table and went over to a barrel right by the door. "Taste this water. Best water around, if you can keep the mosquitoes out of it."

Ambrose drew a ladle out of the barrel and passed it around the table. Everyone took a sip. "It's mighty sweet, but cold as can be when I first draw it from the spring. It did freeze a bit during the winter months, but all I had to do was chip away at the ice around it and soon the water ran full again. Keeping the mosquitoes out of it, while hauling it up to the cabin, is a bit tricky during the warmer months."

When Betsey took a sip, "It's so cold."

"That's the best part, Bit. It's cool and refreshing especially during the hot summer months." Pa smiled broadly, evidence he was convinced that this land was the best around.

"I'm gettin' mighty tired. How in the world will we all sleep tonight in this tiny cabin, Hosea?" Ma stretched and yawned. It had been a long time since they'd had the chance to get a full night's sleep.

"We'll put Aaron and Betsey in that corner," Pa pointed to the opposite corner, "and you and I will take the bed. The girls can huddle up close to the fire over here."

Ma patted Ambrose on the shoulder. "You'll be sorry, son, that you don't have this cabin all to yourself anymore."

Ambrose puffed smoke out the side of his mouth. "I don't think I'll mind. It's nice to have y'all here. Truly it is. You and Pa are welcome to my bed. We'll make Betsey and Aaron up a tick and put it into the opposite corner. I think we'll all fit just fine."

The next morning, before sunrise, Pa was up stoking the fire in preparation for a new day—their first full day in their new surroundings.

The cabin felt warm, almost stuffy. Betsey heard her mother clamber out of bed. Betsey did the same. As they both emerged from their corners, Betsey's mother pulled her shawl over her nightdress. "Comin' with me, Betsey?"

Betsey nodded, pulling her shawl over her shoulders. One advantage of Pa and Ambrose arrive at the territory first—was she and Ma headed to an already functioning outhouse.

As they stepped out of the cabin, Pa handed them a lantern to light the path. Leaving the cabin, darkness seemed to swallow them whole, except for the tiny glow from the lamp. Ma grasped her hand, as she'd done for years, as they headed down the path. Betsey didn't mind. They'd be doing many ventures and chores together to make this new cabin a true home.

A night owl's hoot interrupted the silence of the early morning. The day dawned chilly. Betsey tightened her shawl around her nightgown. May was days away with a promise of hopefully, warmer temperatures.

"You go first, dear."

Betsey tried to hurry, but the small outhouse made it difficult to maneuver.

When Ma went in, Betsey stood outside, lantern in hand. She held it up to see what she could in the dark morning. Trees towered overhead in the darkness. The horizon brightened, as the sunrise approached, but the night stars clung to the sky as if reluctant to give way to the dawn. Betsey had never seen so many stars in one place. They twinkled and shimmered in the dark sky. They felt so close, as if Betsey could reach up past the lantern's light and touch them. It had been quite a long time since she'd been able to see stars so vividly bright.

When Ma came out of the outhouse, she and Betsey hurried up the path, to the warmth of the cabin.

Once inside, Pa took the lantern from Betsey and placed it back on the table. "Fire started, Sally. You girls can wash up. I'll be back after I check on the oxen."

The small lantern cast shadows on the walls. Betsey did her best to pull off her nightgown and layer-on clothing for the day, in her tiny corner of the cabin. Privacy was now just a luxury. Aaron had left the cabin earlier that morning to help Ambrose with the morning chores and to catch some fish for breakfast.

Her mother spoke softly, "Perhaps we can use the wagon canvas to separate our rooms a bit." It was as if she were reading Betsey's mind.

Betsey answered, "That should work."

"I'm not especially keen of having all us women dress or undress in front of the menfolk."

Betsey's sisters roused upon hearing their mother and Betsey's conversation. They stretched out on their makeshift mats beside the fire.

Ma left her sleeping area, tying her apron as she walked, "Better rise now, girls. Hard enough to move around in this cabin without having to step over you lying near the hearth. Get up and dress, Pa will be back soon. Store your mats and blanket under my bed. The men will be hungry."

The girls did as they were told.

Etta rubbed her eyes, while sitting up. "This floor is as hard as the wagon's."

Ma scolded, "Estelle, that's enough of your grumbling. Get up and do as you're told."

A "yes, Ma" was followed by the rolling of a blanket. Betsey felt bad for the girls. They not only had to sleep on the floor, but they also had to share one blanket. She'd been in their position before and was thankful that she and Aaron had a bed of their own.

As she crossed the floor to help her ma, she felt a solid kick from the baby. Loving the feeling, she rushed to her ma. "Ma, feel him."

Her ma was wiping her hands on her apron. "Is it the baby?"

Betsey placed her ma's hand over the spot where she thought she could feel something.

Ma shook her head, "I'll never get over the joy of feeling a baby move within you." She patted Betsey's belly. "Keep growing strong, little one."

Betsey went over to a barrel sitting by the fire, to look for the utensils needed to prepare breakfast. "Let's have flapjacks this morning, Ma. Surely, now we can serve them before they get too cold."

Ma laughed. "Yes, let's try. But first things first. Where'd the men put my large skillets? Using that tiny one on our journey made it harder than anything to keep food warm for everyone."

Jillian wasn't moving as quickly as the other girls, and after dressing, she came over and placed her head on her mother's arm.

"What's the matter, child?" Ma pulled her away and felt her face. "Jillian, you're burning up."

Etta came from beside the bed, asking Betsey to button the top button on her dress. "She seemed warm all night, Ma. One moment she said she was cold, the next, she kept tossing the blanket back over me."

Jillian's eyes were red. "I need to use the outhouse, and quickly."

Ma took her by the hand. "Come with me. Can you manage without the lantern for a minute, Bit?"

"Yes. I'll try to find a candle or two. I think they're in this barrel." Betsey rolled a barrel closer, to pry off the lid.

As the door shut on her mother and sister, the darkness enveloped them again. The only glow was from the growing fire on the hearth.

"I'll help you look, Bit." Together, Etta and Betsey rummaged through one barrel and then another, hoping to find at least one candle to light. Perhaps they'd used them all on their trip here. A list of chores was beginning to mount. Making candles would need to be near the top.

Ma returned with Jillian, and instead of insisting she help, told her to lie down in she and Pa's bed.

Soon the room was brighter, with a candle on the table, and the fire now blazing on the hearth. Finding a sharp knife required another search, but soon everyone was sitting at the table for breakfast. Even though they were now in a cabin, the breakfast resembled much of the same ingredients they'd had on the road. The only difference was the fresh fish the men had caught that morning and the fact that every pancake made was fresh, hot, and plump. They were even able to eat all at the same time.

Ambrose had made a kitchen table that winter, but there were only two chairs. Pa promised he'd build more in the next few weeks. "We'll make do until we can officially set up household, Sally. Don't you worry."

Bowing their heads, Pa thanked the Lord for their arrival and safety as they'd traveled. He asked for wisdom with decisions and for good health. After saying grace, he looked around. "Where's Jilly?"

Ma pointed toward their bed. "She's caught a fever. At least we've stopped traveling now and she'll have a better chance of getting well faster. I'll open a few more barrels to see if I can find some herbs to help her."

Ambrose put a forkful of pancakes into his mouth and nodded as if to tell everyone he had something to say. Once he swallowed, he said, "It's probably ague, but it's a bit early for that. Maybe she's got grippe." He took a long gulp of his water. "It might last a few days. I've had 'em both."

Ma nodded.

"No doctor to call for around these parts, Ma. We'll have to make do for a few years until we can hire us one."

Ma tsked-tsked as she watched Ambrose put another pancake on his plate, "Land, Ambrose! It's like you haven't eaten in days."

Ambrose grinned, wiping his chin off with his shirt sleeve. "Ma...I haven't eaten this good since I left you in Pennsylvania."

Pa announced, "Well son, it shows."

As Betsey cleaned up after their dinner that day, she thought back to Ambrose's character before he'd left for Michigan Territory. He had a sullen disposition, and Betsey was often the one to calm him down after a particular disagreement with their pa. Now, they were seeing a whole new attitude in their brother. He helped Pa and Aaron with a cheerful temperament.

Jillian called out to Betsey from her bed. "Betsey, I'm so thirsty."

Betsey scooped a bit of water from the barrel near the door and carried it across the wooden floor to her sister, who sat up to drink it. Sweat beaded off her forehead and she'd had to use the chamber pot more than once that morning.

Ma had given her some of the medicine that she had, but sparingly. Perhaps the rest of the family would suffer with the same illness and more would be needed before they'd have a chance to purchase it.

Thankfully, Jillian drank all the water from the ladle, and asked for more. Betsey got another ladleful from the barrel, being careful not to spill any as she carried it to Jillian. Jillian drank it, and leaned back on Ma's quilt.

"I'm so hot, Bit."

Betsey wiped her brow with a cold cloth Ma had placed beside the bed. "I know, Jilly. You look hot. Why don't you unbutton your nightshirt, and I'll wipe down your chest with this cool cloth." Jillian did as her sister asked and soon her eyes shut again.

Betsey hadn't thought about caring for Jillian until Caroline asked her about it, as she placed the lid back on the water barrel. "Are you sure you should be nursing Jilly? What about the baby?"

Betsey shook her head, "God will protect the baby. We're living in too close of quarters to worry about it now." But after Caroline said something, she began to wonder the same thing.

Their cabin was small, only about the size of their parlor back in Pennsylvania. Opposite corners held their makeshift beds from the wagons. The hearth was placed in the southernmost part of the cabin. Ambrose had fashioned it with rocks and mud from the river banks. Betsey had never seen such beautiful rocks. They speckled with all kinds of red, green, and even pink, hues.

The table he made would sit four people. Ma and Pa sat in chairs and the rest of the family sat on barrels. Pa would probably make benches, like they had in Pennsylvania, which would give them plenty of room to sit down for a meal.

Ambrose had installed a wooden plank floor during the winter months. Ma told him how thankful she was not to have to start off with a dirt floor. Making a broom was another item to put on their to-do list, which continued to grow. The summer would be full of making needed household items including another bed, makeshift floor-beds for the girls, and perhaps a cradle for the baby. Ambrose had agreed to sleep in the barn, as soon as they had that finished, at least during the summer months.

He'd also told them about what to expect and what they needed for the winter ahead. April would soon be over, and with

May close at hand, they would need to do their best to get at least one cabin outfitted enough to keep up with the day-to-day housekeeping.

Betsey also had to think about the baby. She needed to stitch up nightgowns as well as nappies before its arrival. She'd have to do that during the late-night hours, by firelight. Would they have their own home built before the baby's arrival?

Betsey stepped out of the musty, stuffy cabin to throw out some dishwater. As she did, she glanced around at their new property. She'd just been so happy to be here and to see Ambrose, she hadn't really taken in the scenery. Now she could.

Brushing the stray tendrils of hair off her forehead, the cool breeze coming from the direction of the river felt refreshing and soothing. The warmth of the cabin felt good during the coolness of the night, but as the temperature grew warmer, it could make the cabin feel uncomfortable during the day. It was sad that poor Jillian had to be cooped up in the cabin on such a bright, sunshiny day.

Walking farther out from the cabin, Betsey took a complete look at the property Pa and Ambrose had selected for the family. The trees were the tallest she'd ever seen. They surrounded the cabin, creating a natural fortress from the outside world. In the deepest parts of the woods, the pines seemed to emit only a portion of sunlight from above. Under certain pines, the ground was covered in a thick blanket of needles, so much so, that low-growing foliage couldn't take root beneath the debris. Still other pine trees had branches brushing the ground, layered with bough upon bough of green.

Intermixed with these pines were basswood, maple, oak, and hemlock, rising into the sky, like nothing Betsey had ever seen.

Marsh grasses sprouted up on the river's banks. Some grasses were so high, it was hard to see the river beyond them.

Betsey heard a stirring in the woods off to her right and watched a tiny family of skunks skirt between the trees and make their way to the riverbank just north of the cabin. She hoped they didn't venture any closer. The thought conjured-up memories of the Indian encounter out on the trail.

Ambrose had told them about the animals that graced their new land. He had relished the deer meat he'd eaten throughout the winter. Large does and bucks he'd shot brought needed meat to the table on many occasions. When he'd gotten his first buck, he was sure that the venison would last him many weeks, until he awoke the next morning to find his deer eaten nigh to the bone. Coyotes and wolves were in abundance here, and if meat wasn't strung high in a tree, it was soon consumed by the other wildlife, before a family could cook and preserve it all.

A fur trader had suggested Ambrose keep the meat high in trees, so after shooting his deer he did exactly what the trader had told him to do, only to later find a bear up in the tree chomping on the carcass. One evening, after a long, but successful deer hunt, Ambrose decided to bring the deer he'd shot into his cabin for safekeeping. That night, amidst the loudest ruckus he's heard yet, Ambrose thought certain that coyotes were going to come into his cabin to feast, if need be. He'd been awake most of the night, and after long hours without sleep, Ambrose ended up tossing the deer carcass out to the coyotes, anyway. They carried away his afternoon's kill and after that experience, he knew he'd need to build a solid door from the leftover cabin-building wood. This grew necessary for not only his safety, but for a chance the meat would last more than just a day.

Betsey shuddered at Ambrose's story. They'd hear the coyotes, and even wolves, howling long into the night, but they also knew the log walls now separated them.

Looking off to the south, Betsey watched Aaron, Pa, and Ambrose survey the trees they were planning to cut for the start of the barn, which would shelter the oxen. They'd worried about their teams most of the night. It would take a solid barn to protect the oxen, and Betsey knew that the three men would be diligent to build the teams shelter as fast as they could. Until then, they'd need to take turns keeping watch at regular intervals throughout the night.

This was new territory and a strange place to start or raise a family. A much different location than the home they'd left behind. Betsey prayed their first harvest would be a good one. The land seemed to hold great potential for gardens and crops, and there was hope, at least, that they would discover new ways to live off its bounty. Yet, Betsey wondered if they'd survive the attempt.

She felt the tiny being squirm in her womb and knew they'd do their best to give their baby a good life here. All they needed to do was survive.

CHAPTER THIRTEEN

Jillian stayed in bed for the next three days. Ma would check on her, and move about the house, doing as many inside-chores as she could, in order to stay near Jillian should she grow worse.

After one particular check of her forehead, she looked up at Betsey with concerned eyes. "This is some fever. Poor girl is burning up. Bring me another blanket from that barrel we opened this morning."

Betsey also fetched a ladle of water from the barrel by the door and brought it over to Ma, along with the blanket tucked under her arm. "Try and see if she'll drink a little more. She hasn't had anything to drink since last night."

Ma did her best to prop Jillian's limp body up, to help her take a drink. The girl could barely lift her head.

"What shall we do without a doctor close by?" Betsey wrung her hands on her apron.

Ma tucked the covers higher and over Jillian's tiny shoulders. "I don't know. I've dreaded this moment since the day we left Pennsylvania. The only thing I know is to try some quinine." Ma went for her medicine bag. "Perhaps a sip will help. Poor child has had the runs for three days now."

Betsey put drops of the medicine into Jillian's water and did her best to get Jillian to drink some before she dozed off to sleep again. Betsey had never felt the head or body of anyone with such a high fever.

Ma warned her, "Bit, you better not get close. That baby doesn't need a sick mother."

Betsey backed off and decided to get busy unpacking more of the barrels. She'd noticed her ma had grown increasingly irritated at things lately. Her attitude toward Pa was changing for the worse instead of the better.

Ambrose had made sturdy shelves at the front, right side of the cabin. Betsey began stocking them with what they'd been able to purchase in Pontiac. After unpacking the barrels, she propped them up along the wall to place items in them for dry storage. Insects like flies, crickets, and pesky mosquitoes would soon emerge with the warmer temperatures. They didn't need them helping themselves to the supplies of flour, sugar, and cornmeal.

Ambrose's stone hearth was a perfect place to bake food for upcoming meals. Each stone was meticulously put into place and surrounded by mortar made from red clay and hardened mud. He'd even cut a piece of basswood to make a small shelf above the fire pit itself.

Ma couldn't stop praising him for his ingenious creations. "I declare, I don't know how Ambrose thought of making this house just how I'd want it to be."

Between checking on Jillian throughout the day and unpacking, the women had a great deal to do before they could serve a good meal. Ambrose had a portion of venison left that he'd recently smoked, so Ma began preparing it for their supper. Betsey set to making at least a small loaf of bread to go with it.

The smells of the musty cabin soon were replaced by the savory scent of fresh meat sizzling over the fire and the aroma of bread plumping near it. "We need to get a cow and some chickens. Fresh milk and eggs will make our meals so much tastier."

Betsey nodded in agreement. What she wouldn't do for a tall glass of milk and some butter. They'd had to leave the door ajar as the warm afternoon sun and the fire heated the cabin.

"Betsey! I know which barrel is missing." Ma went frantically to one barrel and then the next. "It's my memory barrel."

Betsey looked around the room. "Are you sure, Ma? I think we've unpacked all the barrels. What's in the one propped up by your bed?"

Ma went to look in the barrel. Betsey wasn't sure which barrel her ma was calling a memory barrel. She wondered what it contained.

"That one has my extra cloth and sewing items. I can't believe it. The only barrel that contained my memories. Things I have kept for years and treasured. It even had—" Ma sat down. Betsey watched her pull a handkerchief out of her pocket. Her ma was crying.

"Perhaps we've just misplaced it somewhere."

Ma wiped her eyes. "It's just one more thing of Pennsylvania I have to give up."

Betsey sat down beside her ma. "Are you really missing home?"

Her ma stopped crying, wiping her face with her hands. "I don't know why your pa had to bring us way out here. There isn't a neighbor for miles. We have to begin setting up a household all over again. And now we need a doctor. What if Jillian gets worse?"

Betsey put her arm around her ma. "You're good at making us well, Ma. You've always known what to do when we get sick. And yes, we're alone now, but Pa keeps saying the territory is filling up fast. It won't be long before we have neighbors and maybe even a doctor."

"I know. I'm sorry I feel so down. I guess I'm just not as young as I used to be. The trip took more out of me than I thought it would. I'm tired."

"Let me and the girls do more, Ma. You don't have to be the one with all the burdens on your shoulders."

With that comment, her ma smiled a bit. "You're right. I'll try harder. I just wish—"

Betsey waited for her ma to finish her sentence, but she didn't. "What?"

"Oh nothing. Let's keep working." And with that, Ma stood up and checked on Jillian.

Betsey wondered, over the next few hours, what her ma's wish was. Could it be that she'd not wanted to leave Pennsylvania in the first place? What was making her so bitter?

They kept trying their best to work, while keeping an eye on Jillian. "I wonder how bad the mosquitoes will really get, Ma? Every single person we talk to makes it sound like there's a complete outbreak when they begin to hatch."

"It doesn't sound pleasant. Ambrose said he had a hard time keeping them out of his food, even while cooking."

Betsey could imagine their being an annoyance, but she hated to think they'd invade the family's food as well.

They'd sent Etta and Caroline on a mission to gather wood and stack it just outside the door. Ambrose had built a small cradle to hold wood, for easy access. As wood thumped against the outside wall, singing voices accompanied the girls as they worked. Ma had listened to Betsey's advice and added more chores to her sisters' to-do lists. "I hope those girls don't get overwhelmed with all the chores now. We aren't living with certain conveniences anymore."

It did seem as though the chores here far-exceeded their daily duties back in Pennsylvania. Each member of the family often retired each night not because of lack of light, but out of utter exhaustion.

The men had gone to examine the girdled trees, in preparation of building the barn. Aaron had told Betsey that he thought this land was far better than Betsey's pa had described. They'd seen plenty of deer that morning and assured Ma they would kill one soon, to replenish the meat supply for upcoming meals. It's a beautiful place, Betsey. I know we can find an ideal spot for a cabin, he'd told her the night before. It brought her joy to know Aaron was growing fond of the new land, too.

Before Betsey could think anymore about the past night's conversation, Caroline rushed into the cabin, her face ashen and eyes wide. "Ma, you better come outside."

"What's wrong?" Ma rushed from Jillian's bedside.

"Just come see." Caroline grabbed Ma's hand and led her outside. Betsey followed them to the door.

"Look!" Ma and Betsey scanned the north woods, where Caroline pointed at what appeared to be a young boy, standing beside a beautifully dressed Indian woman.

Betsey froze. She knew seeing Indians would be a common occurrence, but her heart hadn't gotten prepared for it. She clung to the door frame, unable to move.

The woman had her hand on the boy's shoulder. When she saw Ma, she pushed the boy toward them as they gathered close to the door. The lad looked at the Indian woman, then bowed his head. He hesitated a moment, then began to shuffle toward them.

Betsey still unable to move from the doorway, "What do you suppose they want, Ma?"

"I can't imagine, but I don't believe that boy is an Indian," Ma answered. "Look at his skin. It's not dark like hers."

"She's so pretty," whispered Caroline.

The woman's jet-black hair hung down, across her shoulders, and her beaded dress flashed against the sun's rays. Her legs and feet were mahogany in color, almost as dark as a rust-colored autumn leaf.

The young boy, probably around the age of six, stepped away from the woman as she said a single word, "*Maajaa.*"

At one point he stopped and seemed to want to return to the woman, but she lifted her hand, and pointed at Ma and the girls. "*Maajaa,*" she demanded in a stern voice.

Soon the boy was within ten feet of them. Ma steered the younger two girls behind her.

"You girls stay close to the door. I'm going to go see what this is all about." As Ma approached the boy, the Indian woman disappeared, like a deer, into the woods.

Betsey gasped. *Was it a trick? How far away was Pa?* Betsey scanned the woods beside the house.

The boy turned one more time as if he wanted to follow the woman, but then turned back towards Ma. Betsey could see tears streaming down his small, dirt-streaked face. His eyes were red as if he'd been crying for longer than just a few minutes. He lifted his arm and wiped his face with the back of a deerskin sleeve.

Ma approached him slowly. "Hello."

The child, now seeming to know he was alone, stood taller.

"What's your name?" Ma asked him.

He stared at Ma.

"Are you lost?"

The boy didn't respond but stood even more erect. He held his chin high, while blinking back tears.

As Ma got closer, he seemed to want to turn and run. Seeming to resign himself to the fate that now awaited him, he stood in front of Ma.

Ma took the boy by the shoulders and led him toward the cabin door where Betsey and her sisters still stood. The smell emitting from the child brought back Betsey's fearful memories of the Indian trail incident.

As Ma led the child into the cabin, Betsey left the doorway and headed around the outside corner of the cabin. She needed Aaron. Pa. Ambrose. At that moment, she realized she'd been holding her breath, and began to gasp for air.

After Betsey had regained her composure, by breathing deeper, she headed out into the field to find the men.

"What did the Indian woman look like?" Ambrose asked her when Betsey told them the story about the boy and the woman.

Betsey tried her best to describe the beautiful woman. "It happened so fast."

"How was she dressed?" Ambrose asked her.

Betsey snuggled tighter to Aaron's side. He must have sensed her fear, for he placed his arm around her shoulders and pulled her close.

"I haven't seen many Indian women yet, but her clothing was more exquisite than what I've noticed other Indian women wearing, especially in Detroit."

"Probably the chief's wife." Ambrose drank a ladleful of water from a nearby bucket.

"Chief?" Pa asked.

"He lives close. I've encountered him quite a bit. He has a dog."

Pa stopped chipping away at a tree stump. "Is he tall, and muscular, and was the dog black with a white muzzle?"

Ambrose nodded, "I think so. Sounds familiar."

"I'm sure it's just a coincidence, but the Indian who stopped us on the road had a dog with him as well."

Betsey felt more fear creep into her soul. If this woman belonged to the same tribe as the Indians who stole from them on the road—Betsey gasped. Everyone looked at her, but continued their conversation.

Ambrose took another long drink of water, wiping his chin with his shirt sleeve. He seemed to sense Betsey's trepidation. "I'm sure it's not the same Indian you saw, but..." Ambrose looked at Betsey, now seeming to understand her concern. "Anyway, the one I'm talking about has a well-dressed wife. I've only been able to see her a few times. She often accompanies the chief as he walks around our land. I've often wondered what she is like, but I've never seen her with a child."

Aaron kissed the top of Betsey's head. "I'll head up to the cabin with Betsey. I'll be sure they're all safe."

Taking Betsey by the hand, he encouraged her to follow him.

Pa added, "We'll all go. We need to rest a spell."

Ambrose pointed to the little boy, now with a clean face, seated beside Caroline at the table. His appetite was big, like Ambrose's, as he picked up his food with his fingers and ate with muffled noises and burps.

"So, he hasn't said a word of English?" Pa asked Ma.

"Not one word. He let me wash his hands and face. Where could he have come from? He isn't Indian. He's white. His face, hands, arms, and legs are dark from the sun, but his torso is as white as yours." Ma cut another slice of bread for Ambrose.

"I'm not sure what it could mean. I'll take him to Whitmore's post tomorrow and ask him about it. He might know more than we do." Ambrose took a large bite of the bread Ma had cut for him.

"Why would an Indian woman have a little white boy, and why would she bring him to us?" Betsey handed another slice of bread to Aaron, who was consuming it almost as fast as Ambrose.

"I don't know, but Whitmore will know. If he doesn't, he speaks Ojibwe. Perhaps he can talk to him for us."

The little boy slept beside Ambrose and the fire that night. He went to sleep quickly after eating as much as Pa and Ambrose during supper. He didn't seem frightened to be with their family. He was a cute lad, yet without manners.

Betsey thought about him as she tried to drift off to sleep beside Aaron, who was snoring as loudly as Pa was at the opposite side of the cabin. The men had been cutting trees for most of three days now. It was hard and dangerous work. Because they had to keep watch over the oxen, each man only got snatches of sleep between their sentinel duties. All were anxious to get the barn finished, so a good night's rest would be more of a guarantee.

What would a tiny boy be doing with an Indian woman? A white boy? Ambrose didn't seem worried about the situation. If Betsey didn't know any better, she was sure the Indian woman wanted them to take the child into their care. But why?

The fear she had surprised her. She'd thought she'd overcome a bit of it. Snuggling closer to Aaron, she realized that it would take her a bit longer to deal with her fear of the natives. Could she ever be comfortable in their presence?

In the middle of the night Betsey startled awake by the creaking of the iron bar which straddled the hearth, from which they hung the Dutch ovens. Hearing further noises by the fireplace made her to sit up straight in bed. Fear ripped through her as she remembered the child sleeping next to Ambrose.

CHAPTER FOURTEEN

Betsey peered out from around the blanket that separated their sleeping areas. Her ma stood in front of a blazing fire, wringing out a rag she'd just lifted from a bucket. She knelt down by Jillian, dabbing her forehead with the damp cloth. Jillian's fever must have gotten worse.

Betsey wondered if she should get out of bed to help, but before she could get her body to cooperate, Aaron reached for her and pulled her close.

Betsey awoke the next morning to find Ma still kneeling over Jillian on the floor. Pushing the covers off her legs, Betsey slipped into her shoes and got out of bed.

"How's Jillian?" Betsey pulled her shawl around her shoulders as she remembered Ma hovering over her little sister in the middle of the night.

"Her fever seems to have subsided a bit this morning."

"Was it bad last night? I saw you up."

"Very high. I've been up with her most of the night."

Betsey knelt beside her sister, still nestled by the fire. Her head was not as hot as it had been the day before.

"I gave her some more medicine during the night. It will probably be wearing off soon and we'll have to give her more, but it does seem to have lessened the fever."

Betsey needed to use the outhouse. Caroline had just risen from her place by the hearth. "Want to head out with me, Caroline?"

Her sister nodded, slipping into her shoes near the door. Betsey grabbed the lantern off the table. She needed to overcome her fear soon. *What if her sisters were to pick up on it and grow fearful as well?*

As the light cast shadows over the room, Betsey noticed the young boy was gone. "Where is he?"

"Who?" Ma seemed oblivious to her fear.

"The boy." Betsey knew she couldn't stand there long and ask questions. Caroline was ready to head out into the morning with her.

Ma looked up from mixing water with the medicine she had. "He went with Ambrose to the trapper's outpost. We need to find out who he is."

Fear was now foremost in her thoughts, about even going to the outhouse. *What if this was all a trap? Would Ambrose run into trouble heading to the outpost?* Scolding herself, Betsey took Caroline's hand and headed out into the cool morning.

Once outside, Caroline tried to let go of Betsey's hand. "Betsey! Why are you holding my hand?"

Betsey couldn't tell her sister it was utter fear that made her still cling to her hand. Instead, she let go and gripped the side of her skirt, praying they wouldn't come upon any Indians on the trail to the outhouse.

Ambrose approached the house on horseback, the boy asleep in front of him. He'd fallen asleep shortly after leaving Whitmore at the trading post. It had taken most of the day to get there and return. He had felt badly, leaving Pa and Aaron with all the work, but they needed answers as to why this boy had been left with the family.

Ambrose reined in the horse and stopped beside Pa, who was leaning on the knob of his ax, beside one of the largest trees on the property.

"See this tree Ambrose?" Pa patted the tree he was standing beside, on the hill just above the cabin.

"You do love your trees, Pa."

The tiny boy jerked awake. For a moment he looked around, seeming to try to make sense of where he was.

"It's a blackjack oak. The mightiest I've seen on our land. I hate to take it down to make a barn out of it, so instead let's keep it right here. Then, when the good Lord decides my days are over, I want you to bury me and your ma here."

Ambrose took off his cap, wiping the sweat from off his forehead. "I hope that day is a long way off, Pa."

"Me too!" Pa smiled. "But of all the trees I've either cut down or blazed here, I've never seen a tree quite like this majestic one."

Pa had long been known to love trees almost as much as going on an adventure. He declared them to be the mighty works of God, especially the larger ones in the forest. Pa was right about this one; it was the largest of the majestic oaks gracing their new property.

"Okay, Pa. I'll try and remember that when it's time."

"What did you find out about the boy?" Pa laid the ax down and leaned against the large oak.

"Whitmore didn't know much, but said he's seen the lad with a tribe of Indians to the north of here. He'd often wondered who he was. The only thing he could remember was, several years before, a family was heading north up the river in a canoe. They'd stopped at the trading post for needed supplies, and he remembers seeing a tiny baby in a basket at the woman's feet. He didn't know if it was a boy or girl, but the next time he talked to the trader at the post north of here, the man mentioned they'd never arrived. He thought perhaps they'd gone in a different direction, until one afternoon he found their canoe along the riverbank just north of here. The man and wife had been killed, by the looks of it, but the baby was nowhere to be found. He wonders if this is the child from that canoe."

"They were white?"

"Said so. Felt bad for the family, but knew they were headed into some dangerous territory, down river from his post. He tried to warn them, but they didn't want to listen. He said it was about five years ago when this happened, but that's all he remembers."

The small boy looked up at Ambrose, and then back at Pa.

"Said their last name was Stevens. He'd tried to pass word along the trail south, to alert any family who might be looking for the dead couple. He buried them beside the river, about four miles north of here."

"What are we going to do with the young lad?"

"First, the little urchin needs a bath, but after that...looks to me like you finally got that second son you've always wanted."

Pa approached the horse Ambrose was still sitting on, took the boy off and slid him to the ground. "Well son, I guess you're a member of the Baker family now. The Lord giveth and the Lord taketh away." Patting the boy on his head, he handed him an ax. "Might as well get you busy earning your keep, but first let's teach you a few English words. This is an ax. Can you say that? Ax?"

The little boy looked at the ax, then at Pa, and smiled.

"Say it." Pa again pointed to the ax he held out to him. "Ax."

The young boy giggled.

Pa chuckled with him. "He seems happy enough, doesn't he?"

Ambrose slid off the horse. "That he does. You better give him a name soon. We can't just keep calling him, Boy."

"I'll take it up with Ma tonight at supper."

That afternoon, Ambrose watched as the little boy did his best to help haul branches of the trees deeper into the woods. He often searched the edge of the forest as if he were looking for someone, perhaps hoping the Indian woman would return for him.

Pa seemed to take to him right away, watching him, like he would one of Ambrose's younger sisters, especially when the men began to chop down trees for the barn. Ambrose knew that before long the boy would feel a part of the family, if Pa had anything to do with it.

Betsey couldn't help herself. She steered clear of the child all day, doing her best to just keep busy with chores. That is, until Ma asked if she could give the child a bath.

Caroline was busy by the fireplace, scraping up the remnants of the last few days' ashes.

171

Betsey rarely refused to take on a chore her ma asked of her, but she just couldn't get close to the child. It wasn't so much that the child himself brought her fear, but his smell made her heart race.

Caroline must have somehow sensed her hesitation. "I can do it, Ma," she offered. "I think the smell makes Betsey sick."

That wasn't the whole truth, but Betsey was grateful for her sister's intervention.

The child was washed thoroughly, and the bath removed most of the Indian smell which made Betsey jittery.

It didn't take long for his sweet smile to affect the entire family. Betsey began to realize that he was not someone to fear. He needed them to care for him and she needed to act like a grown woman. The child wasn't afraid of them why should she have a different reaction.

"Hey Pa, I forgot to tell you," Ambrose looked up from his plate. "Whitmore believes you might be the first farmer to settle in these parts. Only one other man has passed through the area, but he came a month after we did. Said if you want, he'll put us on his record books there at the post."

Pa sat up straighter in his chair. "The first, huh? Who would 'a thought?"

"There's another family just south of here a bit, but they came a little before your return this spring. You and I are the first in this area, by far, by coming out last year."

Pa smiled. "Well, I'll be. Did you hear that, Ma?"

Ma nodded but continued to spoon broth into Jillian's mouth. Jillian was smiling today, and a bit of pink brightened her cheeks. She still had a fever, but it seemed the worst was finally over. "I heard," Ma answered.

Pa looked around the table at his family. "Well, folks, looks as if we have another mouth to feed." Pa told the rest of them the story from Whitmore. Tears brimmed Ma's eyes. "He needs us, but I'll always wonder why the Indian woman didn't keep him."

"Me, too," Pa added. "But if he's to stay here, we need to give him a name, don't you think?"

Caroline jumped in faster than Ma could answer, "How about Alexander? I've always loved that name."

"Alexander Stevens. I think it's appropriate he keeps his pa's name, if he happens to be the little baby they say was in the canoe at the trading post that day. What do y'all think?"

"I'll put his name in the Bible in the morning." Ma patted the boy's head. "He's got blue eyes, just like Caroline."

"That he does, Ma. That he does."

Ma stooped down by the boy. "Alexander. That's your name." All she got was a big smile as he put a biscuit in his mouth.

"Hopefully we'll put some meat on his bones. 'The Lord preserveth the strangers; he relieveth the fatherless and widow...'" Pa added before smiling at the child now taking a place at their table.

CHAPTER FIFTEEN

May came without much notice as the family did their best to make their homestead more livable. Walls of the barn had gone up, and strips of bark would be placed on the roof to secure it and make it a sound animal shelter, from the predators of the night.

"We'll be able to sleep better, knowin' that roof is intact over the oxen," Pa said as he put rocks and sticks between the logs on one wall. "We'll need to get some moss, straw, and ashes and mix them with some of that thick clay, down by the river. It works great to chink the walls. It'll make all the walls solid against the winter winds."

"I'll go fetch a bucket of water to mix it up," Ambrose added.

"Tomorrow you two can put on the roof. I'm goin' to head out and get some furrows dug. If we're to stay here long, we need some crops, don't you think, boys? 'A time to be born, and a time to die; a time to plant, and a time to pluck up that which is planted.'" Pa had a knack for quoting scripture that coincided with the happenings of the day. "But today, we need 'a time to cast away stones, and a time to gather stones together.' I can't wait to taste fresh potatoes from the garden."

Pa picked up a stone from a nearby trail and handed it to Alexander, who now followed Pa wherever he went. The young boy put the stone on his shoulder and followed close behind Pa as they made their way over to the ground Pa had designated as the place to plant their first crops.

Ambrose whispered to Aaron, "There's a farmer just south of the trading post whose name is Lathrop. The other day, while at the Whitmore's trading post, I asked if the man was available to help plow Pa's fields. He should be here any day. I didn't want to tell Pa, so it would be a surprise." Ambrose stuffed more of the moist clay mixture between the logs. "That should do it for this side. How're you coming on that side, Aaron?"

The women had created a much more manageable kitchen than from the earlier days at the new farm. The girls had arranged items they needed close to the hearth, and Ambrose had chiseled some carved wooden spikes to insert in the log walls, to hold various cooking utensils and pots.

Daily chores became routine, each day having specific tasks all its own. Betsey had never felt such exhaustion. She struggled to get through each day without collapsing into a chair. At night, she always tried to beat Aaron to sleep before his snoring could snatch away her own slumber. Getting up each morning before dawn seemed to make each night mere minutes long.

The baby's movements increased daily, tumbling about as if he were looking for a way out. Pokes brought her laughter, until the child moved, creating pressure just above her bladder, she had to head to the outhouse. Ma recalled her own pregnancies with Ambrose, herself, and the girls. She'd always whisper to Betsey when she returned from the outhouse, "Your bladder will never be the same." Betsey cringed at the thought.

The worst part of her new life was the lack of one-on-one time Betsey could have with Aaron. They hadn't talked privately in days. Before leaving in the morning, Aaron would plant a kiss on her head as he headed out the door with Ambrose and Pa. Once home in the evening, he'd eat his supper and work until dusk.

During the late-night hours, he might be on watch until daybreak. Being so tired herself, she'd rarely stay awake after he'd leave the cabin for his turn. She missed him. In Pennsylvania, they'd talk long into the night about Aaron's job duties, their future, the recent happenings in town, and more recently, about the baby. Betsey missed his smile and their intimate moments together as a couple. As the busy days wore on, she realized they were miles apart in many ways.

Pa came in before noon one day and called to them all, "Come out here, girls. See what's happening on our property."

Everyone rushed out the door to see what was exciting Pa to the point that he didn't stop to snatch a taste of dinner. They followed him to the designated area where he would soon be planting crops. There they found a visitor. He'd brought a wagon and on it was a large piece of metal, gleaming in the late-morning sun.

Pa went to greet the man and introduce Ma to him. "Sally, this is Isaiah Lathrup. He's here to help me till up the ground for our crops."

"Nice to meet you." she smiled.

"He's come from down south of here a'ways, but thought he can help me, by using his new plow." Pa pointed to the plow Ambrose and Aaron were unloading from the man's wagon.

"That's very kind of you, Mr. Lathrup."

Lathrup was older than Pa by quite a few years, but he seemed spry and anxious to get his plow working.

"I'm gonna head to the barn for the oxen team. Be right back." Pa nearly sprinted to the partially-finished barn toward the back of the property.

Ma turned back to their new friend. "Have you eaten any dinner yet?"

The man took off his hat and slapped his knee. "Yes ma'am, but it was just cold fish and a few stiff pieces of dried meat."

"Please join us," Ma offered with a smile.

"I'd be obliged, ma'am, thank you."

Everyone watched Pa steer the oxen team to the far side of the field, dragging the gleaming, silver plow behind them. Crops would soon be planted if Pa stayed on schedule. Hopefully, the frost for the year had passed and things would grow well for their first season in the Michigan Territory.

Pa's traveling days were over. He was a farmer again. Betsey wasn't sure which gleamed brighter, the new plow or the large grin on Pa's face.

Betsey headed out of the cabin after dinner to check on the seedlings she and Ma had planted along the west side of the cabin. As she did, she rounded the back corner of the cabin and caught a glimpse of someone at the edge of the woods. Before Betsey could focus on who it was, the person ran out of sight. She wasn't sure, but she thought it was the same Indian woman who had brought Alexander to them.

Her reason for going outside was forgotten and she raced back to the door. Whoever it was, they had disappeared as quickly as they'd come. She again scolded herself for her persistent fear. *Would she ever feel comfortable venturing outside alone?*

Betsey thought about Alexander and how God had brought the little boy into their lives. He was a smiling, happy child, and seemed oblivious to the fact that he was new under their roof. He seemed to enjoy sleeping by the fire each night. Not once did he seem lonesome for anyone or cry like he was missing the people from whence he came. Betsey felt that was odd for such a small child. He loved Pa the most and followed close at his heels throughout the day.

Ma had been trying hard to teach him words, but he didn't seem to have a voice. If he'd ever been taught words, he didn't seem to know how to pronounce, or how to say them. He went about his day in silence, but listened intently to whatever Pa told him.

Ma asked Pa about the boy's non-speaking the next night. "He doesn't speak. Have you noticed that?"

"Yes, but perhaps he doesn't know the English language well enough yet."

"I don't think he *can* speak. Maybe he's mute."

Pa nodded. "You might be right. Ambrose has been trying to teach him words as well, but the boy just smiles back. He seems to understand, but he won't say them back."

"It disturbs me," Ma poured more cold water into Pa's cup.

"Thank you." Pa tapped her arm, "It'll be fine. Perhaps when Betsey starts up lessons with the girls this winter, she'll be able to start him off with a bit of schooling as well. He doesn't seem unhappy living with us."

Aaron stopped chewing for a moment and added, "We had a young boy back home who was deaf. Couldn't hear a thing. He didn't speak either."

"I never thought of that, Aaron. Perhaps he is."

The entire family stopped eating and looked at Alexander. He happily stuck another large piece of fish into his mouth. Pa said something to him, and he looked in Pa's direction.

"I'm pretty sure he can hear. He looks at you when you speak to him." Pa smiled back at the boy.

"He's such a happy little guy." Ambrose tousled the boy's hair.

Pa sipped a bit of his water. "Nothing to worry about. He'll be fine, but everyone do your best to talk with him. He'll start talking when he's good and ready."

The next morning, Betsey went out to find out how Pa was doing getting the soil prepared for planting. She stood at the edge of the field watching him meticulously dig holes for the seeds he would soon plant. As he made a turn, he looked up to see her watching him.

He stopped and motioned for her to join him. Betsey picked up her skirts and tried her best not to stumble over the large upturned clods of dirt, to reach Pa. She felt safer knowing he was watching her walk toward him.

"I have something for you, Pa. I wanted to give them to you now so you can make them a part of the new farm." Betsey smiled as she pulled a leather pouch out of the pocket of her skirt. "Hold out your hand."

Pa wiped his dirty hands on his pants. "What do you have for me, Bit?"

Betsey opened the drawstring of the small pouch and poured the contents into Pa's hand.

"Betsey, where did you get these?"

"I brought them. From Pennsylvania. Aaron and I were going to plant them on our land back home this spring, but now—they can grow on your land here."

"Are they fruit tree seeds?" Pa looked up with twinkles in his gray eyes.

Betsey giggled, "Yes. Apple and pear. I harvested them last fall from Aaron's folks' house. I hope they are okay from all they've been through to get here."

"That leather pouch probably kept them nice and dry. How wonderful!"

Betsey handed the pouch to Pa. "It will take some time, but perhaps soon I can send your grandchildren to your property to get me some apples for pies."

Pa hooted, "Betsey! You made my day. I'll get them planted soon. We'll have trees before you know it." He put the seeds back in the pouch and dropped it into a pocket. He kissed Betsey's cheeks. "Thank you, Bit."

"You're welcome, Pa."

Betsey turned back to the cabin.

"Bit, before you go back inside, can I ask you something?"

Turning around, she answered, "Of course."

Pa leaned on the hoe he'd made to work the ground, "Do you think your ma likes it here?"

Betsey didn't know what to say. She knew her ma had been struggling with being in the new territory. She'd never been able to tell an untruth to her pa. "I do believe this move has been hard on her, Pa."

"Do you think it's getting easier or harder for her?"

Betsey looked at the ground. "It hasn't been getting easier, Pa. She works awful hard every day. And many things worry her."

Pa dug at a small mound of dirt at his feet with the hoe. "How can I help her? I'm so tired each night, we don't get much time alone to, you know, talk it out much."

"It hasn't helped that Jilly is so sick. She worries about things, Pa."

"I know." Pa adjusted the tip of the hoe to dig a deeper hole. "I need to get back to work. If you ever think of how I can help her better, would you mind sharing it with your ol'e Pa?"

Betsey smiled. "You know I will."

Betsey turned to leave.

"Bit, do you like it here?"

"I am glad we came to be with you. I think Aaron feels the same way. It's just new. We'll all settle in soon."

As Betsey walked back to the cabin, she thought about her pa. He seemed content in this new land. More content than Betsey had seen him for quite some time. He'd shown her all the trees on the property, pointing out which ones were the grandfathers of the younger trees. Sometimes she wondered if his love of trees surpassed his love of adventure. Or maybe they just went hand-in-hand. Maybe a part of it was a chance to begin life in a new land. To farm in fresh soil.

She silently thanked God that she was here to watch her pa's face glow in the spring sunshine, knowing he was right where God would have him. And God was allowing her a glimpse into why they were there, together. A baby's kick sent her hand to her right side. She smiled. All was well.

In her heart, she had a feeling her ma would settle in soon. She hoped her fears would diminish in much the same way.

CHAPTER SIXTEEN

Betsey pushed a scoop into the large flour bag Ambrose bought while at the trading post a few weeks before while asking about Alexander. She felt happy to finally have some fresh supplies from which to make meals. The men were working hard, it became difficult to keep them nourished and fed well on the mere staple goods they had left after the Indian theft.

Pa had shot a wild turkey. It seemed it was something he did to try and appease Ma. After plucking it, they'd put it on a spit to roast over the fire. The splatters and sizzles from the cooking meat filled the cabin with delicious aromas. The cooking fire brought warmth. It had been a long time since they'd had such a feast.

Betsey was kneading dough to make fresh bread. She put a bit more flour on the table and worked the large, yellowish-gray blob into a good ball. The day had started off cool, but with the fire blazing and the meat cooking, the cabin began to heat-up, until drops of sweat nearly dripped off her forehead. She used her sleeve to wipe it, keeping it from spoiling the dough.

Ma came from her sleeping area, with a pale face, after giving Jillian her breakfast. Betsey knew she hadn't been feeling well through the night and now it showed in her tired face, and moist red eyes.

"Ma, sit down for a bit. You've been working so hard to care for Jillian. I think it's beginning to take its toll."

Her mother plopped down in a chair at the table. "I am tired, that's for sure."

"You look like you don't feel well." Betsey turned the large ball of dough over and poked her fist into the middle, to start the kneading motion over again. Flour dotted the front of her apron.

"I have been feeling a bit poorly this morning." She looked over at the meat. "It will be so good to enjoy a turkey feast tonight. Maybe I'll get some bread made from the cornmeal Ambrose brought us from the trading post. How does that sound?"

Betsey's stomach growled at that exact moment and both women laughed. "The baby seems to think that's a good idea too, Grandmother."

Betsey's mother sighed. "Grandmother. Hard to believe someone will be calling me that soon. I hope and pray you don't come down with this illness that has been plaguing us since we arrived. Whatever it is."

Betsey nodded. "Me, too. My only problem these days is how many trips I need to make to the outhouse."

Her mother wiped her forehead. "That never ends, even after the baby arrives, although it isn't quite as often."

"This child is so active at night. While now, working like this seems to lull him to sleep."

Ma patted the belly now bulging under Betsey's skirt. "'Wonderfully made.'" Ma winced as she rose from her chair, as if her joints were stiff. She wiped her hands on her apron and went to turn the turkey on its spit.

"What else shall we have—"

Before Betsey could turn, Ma cried out. A log had rolled off the large fire burning under the turkey, and slid onto Ma's foot. Wincing with each step, she shuffled to the table. As she sat down, her face contorted in pain. She patted her smoldering stocking, to stop further burns. Smoke from the rolled log filled the cabin.

"Oh, Betsey," Ma cried out as she stood, pulled up her skirt and untied the band at her thigh which held her stocking up. She peeled the stocking off, as blisters began to develop on the top of her foot. "This is not what I needed today!"

Betsey slapped her hands free of flour and ran to the open barrel of cold water by the door. She dipped a cloth in the barrel and wrung it out. She ran back to Ma and carefully placed it across the now beet-red, blistered foot. Ma cringed and cried out again.

"Oh Ma, it must be so painful. I'm sorry."

"Oh dear," Ma sighed. "How will I ever keep working with this kind of injury?"

Betsey went back to the hearth and pushed the stray log back into place with a stick.

"Careful, Bit. I don't want it to roll back on you, too."

Betsey nodded and did her best to get it back up and into place, beneath the still-sizzling turkey.

"Caroline, prop open the door. It's getting awful hazy in here."

As Caroline propped open the door, fresh air and bright light cut through the smoky room.

"We need to be more careful as we stack the wood for a fire. This could easily happen again."

"I'll tell your pa. He's been stacking it higher so we don't need to mess with it until he returns at noon. His thoughtfulness has backfired."

Betsey brought another chair to the side of the table where her ma sat and placed the sore foot on it. "Put it up here for a while to alleviate the swelling. Let me get you a fresh rag." Ma handed her the damp rag back for a second dip.

"Good thing the water is so cold from the spring. It was wise of Pa to build our cabin so close." Betsey wrung out the rag and handed it back to her ma.

Ma placed the cool rag over her foot. "Oh, that takes the sting away. Perhaps the burn won't fester so."

Betsey nodded, washing her hands in the cool water and returning to her dough. "You sit. I can manage. Caroline, run out and get Etta. Tell her we need her in the cabin now."

Ma looked up, tears filling her eyes. "I never imagined us having to work so hard here. Land, I don't remember so many bad things happening so fast or so often. I guess it was inevitable, coming to a new land with no one else around." Her ma sighed and wiped her tears with her hand. "I'm sorry to be such a blubbering mess."

"Ma, it's fine. I'm here to help."

"I'm thankful you and Aaron decided to come with us. I don't know what I'd do without you."

Betsey felt it was time to ask her ma, "Are you sorry you came, Ma?"

Her ma took a deep breath. "I don't know, Betsey. I keep reliving my memories of Meadville and I know I need to move on, and make this new place our home, but for some reason I just want to take it all out on your pa. He gets something new in his head and he assumes if I don't say anything, that it's okay for him to plunge ahead with little thought of the others around him. As I've always said, it's his only sin." With that comment, she smiled at Betsey. "The man can drive me crazy at times."

"But it is a great place to live, Ma. I didn't know it would take so much to live from day-to-day, but I do know why Pa believed it would be a good thing for us. I've been to the field with Pa—the soil is rich and black. The trees are magnificent and there will always be an abundance of water due to the spring and the river. I think," Betsey wasn't sure if she should say anything more, but she did, "I think Pa meant well when he decided to bring us here. He's been trying awful hard to make it a home."

Ma nodded. "I know. I know." Ma folded her arms and leaned back into her chair. "I guess I hate it that I'm not young like you. I've worked hard to be a good wife and raise Ambrose, you, and the other girls God has blessed us with. I guess," Ma looked down at the floor, "I didn't realize that as I did all that, I got old. I can't do as much as I'd always been able to do. My, when you children were little, I worked circles around my own ma. And now, here I am. You working, doing the same to me."

"But isn't that how life works, Ma? Each season of life opens to new opportunities, but new challenges, too."

"You're right, but that doesn't make my tired heart feel any better. Are you sad you followed us here?"

"As hard as it has been," Betsey said with confidence, "I'm thankful we came. I'm here to help you. We'll do it. Together."

Betsey's ma gazed at her, as if she were seeing her differently for the first time. "You've grown into a remarkable young woman, Betsey. I'm proud to be your ma."

"We'll soon get better established. By the way Ambrose talks, we'll soon even have neighbors. Close by."

"I hope so. Not just for our sakes, but for the sake of your sisters. They need friends, too."

"Ma?" Betsey turned the dough over and continued kneading it. "Have you noticed the Indian woman coming close to the property?"

187

Ma raised her head, her eyebrows giving Betsey a questionable look. "You've seen her, too?"

Betsey floured her working board, turning the dough. "I wasn't sure if it was an animal or another Indian, but I'm pretty sure it was her."

"I wonder how she came to have Alexander? The whole thing is such a mystery. Perhaps her people had something to do with his parents' death and she felt obligated to care for the infant herself."

"That's what I've been thinking. It would be hard to raise him to this age and then have to let him go, though."

Ma pulled off the cloth and looked at her foot. "So hard. I can't imagine. Maybe she just wants to be sure he's okay. Maybe that's why she's been coming close each day. Seems to me she loves him, too. By the way she's acting."

Nodding, Betsey finally had the dough ready to separate into tins. "What if she wants him back?"

"I don't know. Maybe she thought it better for him to be among people like us, instead of having to be raised by her own people."

As Betsey separated the dough, she added, "I'm glad she was kind enough to entrust him to us."

"Have you seen your pa? He adores him, just like a son."

Betsey's pa always loved being around children, but with Alexander, they seemed to have a special connection.

"If nothing else, it brings your pa joy. I've never seen him as happy as he is here."

"I hope you begin to enjoy it as much as Pa." Betsey wanted to tell her ma about Pa's worries but felt Pa wouldn't want her to voice his concerns to her ma. That was his job. She prayed they'd work it out, just as they always did, in their own time.

By noon, the outside of the turkey was roasted enough to begin slicing off portions for the men's dinner. Everyone said they couldn't get over how delicious the meat tasted. Ma limped back-and-forth from the hearth and to the table. Her foot would be extra-sore for a few days. Betsey wished the labors of their days would stop long enough for her ma to get rest, but out here, it was difficult to take any time from the necessary chores.

"Ambrose, how much seed did you purchase at the trading post when you went?" Pa sliced off a large piece of turkey and devoured it in a few bites.

"Enough seed potatoes for a whole field. Whitmore had turnip, carrot, pea seeds, and even a few onion sets, so I got a bit of everything." Ambrose consumed an entire portion of Betsey's fresh bread. The men's hunger seemed insatiable.

"Probably best to get the potatoes in first. Can you and Ma come to the field this afternoon and help us cut up the potatoes for planting?" Pa looked at Betsey, who had just sat down to eat her meal.

"I think so, Pa, but I think Ma needs to stay in this afternoon and rest her foot. Can Caroline and I do the cutting for you?"

"Surely." Pa acted surprised. "Bring the sharp knives from my whittling box, above the hearth. We'll plant as many as we can this afternoon."

After helping Ma clean-up after the meal, Caroline and Betsey set off to the field behind the house to help Pa and Ambrose plant potatoes. They'd helped Ma prop her foot up and encouraged her to rest while they were gone, even though Betsey was pretty sure she wouldn't listen.

Aaron was finishing up the roof on the oxen barn. Betsey felt disappointed she couldn't spend the afternoon helping him. It had been such a long time since they'd been able to spend daytimes together.

"Sit down here at the side of the field," Pa motioned for them. He set two large bags of potatoes beside each of them. "Cut them so there is a sprout on each wedge. Like this." Pa split a potato to show them. "We'll get to planting them as soon as you get them cut."

Betsey sat down on a stump that Ambrose provided for her, and Caroline sat on the ground nearby. She handed Caroline a sharp knife and soon they were dropping the ready-to-plant potatoes into the buckets Pa had provided them.

Pa headed to the far edge of the field and began digging a long trench. Ambrose set to digging at the opposite end of the row Pa had started. Pa yelled for Etta to come out to help plant the potato wedges into the dark, black dirt.

Pa stopped for a moment, leaned on his hoe and laughed right out loud. Everyone stopped what they were doing to look at him. "Look at us, family. We're officially farming."

Ambrose shouted from across the field. "Before long, we'll reap a harvest."

Pa took off his hat and slapped his knee, "Who'd have thought? 'He will supply our every need.'"

Betsey stopped her cutting for a few moments to glance around at her family who were pulling together to make this land their own. She loved the sight of Pa and Ambrose digging the trenches, and Etta placing the potatoes into rows. She glanced over at Aaron pounding the last of the birch bark onto the roof. Hard to believe that this was now, their life. Before she went back to cutting, a glimmer of shiny beads caught her eye, off to one side of the property. There she was again. The Indian woman.

Watching her, Betsey noticed she wasn't looking at her or the others in the field, but at Alexander, who was helping Aaron by the barn. The boy was handing Aaron bark strips.

Betsey was thankful that she was near the others as she watched the woman. The woman stared for a moment, and then, she seemed to catch Betsey watching her, and darted back into the woods. She was indeed looking at the result of her decision to bring the young boy to them. Betsey felt sorry that it was their gain, but the Indian woman's loss. She couldn't imagine what had led to her decision nor how hard that choice must have been.

Betsey's fear lessened as she grew empathetic toward the woman, but it still didn't stop her legs from trembling every time the reflection of beads flashed off the sun.

Ma's limp grew worse by evening. She'd scrubbed the floors of the cabin and had even aired some of the bedding out on the bushes beside the river. Betsey hated to think that she'd had to prepare the evening meal with just Etta and Jillian's help, but she, Pa, Ambrose and Caroline had been working endlessly that afternoon, getting all the potatoes planted. She hoped the vital, new leaves would soon emerge from the Michigan soil, and yield potatoes necessary to sustain them throughout the coming months, and into winter. Oh, how good it would be to devour a fresh potato again.

She urged Ma to sit down. Even Betsey's shoulders slumped from another long day, but her mother's red foot and determination to keep working, helped to encourage her to continue until all her work was done.

The men had gone out to claim the last few hours of daylight to help Aaron finish the roof on the barn. What Betsey wouldn't give to sit down beside the fire and stitch up a new baby nappy. She longed to sit, but Jillian needed a sponge bath, and Ma was waddling in from outside with the bedding they'd need to put back on all the beds.

How would they keep this pace up? Ma sat down for a moment and grimaced with pain. Carefully peeling off her shoe, she removed her stocking, to find her skin, raw and bleeding.

Betsey went to find a few strips of cloth she'd saved from an old petticoat, and stooped beside her mother. "Let me wrap that for you, Ma. It has to be so painful."

Her ma nodded. "Thank you, Betsey. It feels like it's still burning."

Betsey soaked the strips of cloth in the cool water and placed them carefully on her mother's foot. She wrapped the strips around the foot and then helped her mother put her stocking back on. "You need to sit and rest. Why don't I get your knitting?"

Without much hesitation, Betsey's mother gave in and nodded. "I'm so tired."

"I saw the Indian woman again today."

"I did, too. When I was out airing the bedding."

"She was watching Alexander. She doesn't seem all that curious about what we're doing." Betsey placed her mother's current knitting project into her lap and then went about putting the bedding on each of the beds.

Ambrose had secured another bed frame to the opposite wall of the house for Aaron and Betsey's bed. From the wall, he'd stretched ropes he'd purchased from Whitmore's trading post to a support log about four feet from the outside wall. It made a nice bedstead for Aaron and Betsey. They'd used linen bags and filled them with grasses from down by the river to make mattresses for the beds. The grasses made Betsey sneeze as she plumped the stuffed bags up and added blankets, now with an airy and fresh scent, over the beds.

Caroline and Etta were finishing the evening meal's dishes, singing a new song that Betsey hadn't heard them sing before. Jillian, back to helping but not her usual chipper self yet, was knitting in the corner.

If she hadn't been so tired, Betsey would have happily taken in the whole scene of the family, busy and ready to take on the worst of circumstances in the new territory, but exhaustion made her stomach queasy.

She also longed for time alone with Aaron, but it was only Friday. On Sundays, Pa often allowed everyone a chance to rest a bit after they ate their dinner and before he began to read the Bible. All Betsey wanted to do was walk the property for awhile with Aaron. Spend time holding his hand, resting.

Perhaps she could ask Aaron to do that this Sunday. Pa wouldn't question them. They could go in search of a place to build their home, which they hadn't been able to do yet.

A wolf's long cry caused Betsey to stand up straight after bending over to check the knitting stitches on Jillian's scarf. The men were out working on the barn. As darkness descended on the cabin, Betsey went to light a candle. Each family member worked as long as they could before darkness made it too difficult. Just because the sun went down, didn't mean an end to their work.

The days were growing longer. Soon summer would be upon them, but that could mean their chores would mount even higher. There was so much to be done when the weather grew warm.

Betsey slapped at a bug buzzing around her ears. Lately, as soon as she lit a candle in the evening and placed it on the table, the bugs got bad. The mosquitoes that Ambrose and Whitmore had warned them about were beginning to hatch. This particular one had managed to find his way into the cabin.

Summer would bring new and different challenges; Betsey was sure of it. With summer came the thought that she'd be soon giving birth to this baby who now kicked her instead of merely fluttering in her womb. A sense of fear rose in her heart. She would deliver the baby alone, with Ma's help. Ma had told her that the pain of childbirth was hard. She'd never had to experience excruciating pain. What would it feel like? What if she wasn't strong enough to push her child from her womb and into the world? What if something bad were to happen?

Another howl interrupted her thoughts. She couldn't concentrate on her fears. It would drive her crazy. She needed to cling to hope. To life. If only she could talk to Aaron about it all. Betsey found him to be a comforting balm to her troublesome thoughts.

It seemed to take forever for the men to get back to the cabin that night. They were hot and thirsty when they came in, way past dark.

"Nibi came out to see us tonight," Ambrose told them. "He's seen us planting and wants to help tomorrow."

"Really?" Ma placed her sore foot back up on a chair. "Why would he want to help?"

Ambrose shrugged. "I don't know, but he taught me so many things this winter about catching fish and keeping the cabin warm. I imagine he knows even more than Pa about the best way to plant crops here. Perhaps he can give us some wisdom."

"Awful kind of him. You know," Pa wiped his face with a cool cloth from the barrel. "We probably can benefit from the natives' help. Maybe they know the seasons better here than we do. Let's see what he has to tell us. Be right proper to listen."

"Where's Aaron?" Betsey asked the other men.

"I thought he was right behind us." Ambrose opened the door, searching the area around the cabin for him. Aaron wasn't there.

Beginning of June ~ Michigan Territory

CHAPTER SEVENTEEN

A few minutes later, Aaron came running into the cabin. As he did, the door slammed behind him. He grabbed the rifle off the shelf above the hearth and headed out into the night again before anyone had a chance to ask him what he was doing. Ambrose and Pa followed him.

The wolves were close, as howls rose into the dark night. Betsey longed to have Aaron and the other men back in the cabin. She needed to sit down for awhile. Just as she lowered herself into a chair, she heard a shot ring out from the direction of the barn.

Ma stood and nearly dropped her knitting onto the floor. These howls resembled the ones they'd heard on the journey here.

Everyone stopped what they were doing and listened. Soon they heard the men's voices. Alexander came running through the door first. He went to Betsey and wrapped his arms around her waist. Betsey hugged the little boy back.

Aaron was the next one through the door, his face white, fear in his eyes. Pa and Ambrose followed close behind.

"Hosea? What is all the commotion?"

"Wolves. Pretty close tonight. We wanted to stay out and work on the barn for as long as we could, but they were getting mighty close. We could hear them circling us as we got the oxen into the barn."

Ma sat back down, "Did you shoot one?"

Aaron shook his head and placed the rifle back on its place over the hearth. "He was close, but not near enough for me to get a clear shot. I wish we had."

"Whitmore said he'd pay me thirty dollars a pelt for any wolves that I kill." Ambrose dipped a ladle of water out of the barrel, taking a long drink.

Aaron came over to Betsey and kissed her cheek, "Too close for me." He pried Alexander from Betsey's waist and put him on his knee as he sat down. "Scared our little man here."

Pa laughed. "He made it back to the cabin faster than any of the rest of us."

Alexander placed his head on Aaron's shoulder.

"You've made quite the bond with him, haven't you, Aaron?"

Aaron loved children. He'd told Betsey many times how eager he was to have children of his own.

That night, the howling never stopped. Aaron whispered to Betsey that he thought the wolves were angry, because the oxen were now tied up snug and tight in the barn. The chances of them getting fresh meat was no longer viable. He was glad he'd finished the barn that evening.

"We'll all get better sleep tonight," Aaron had told her. "No more having to keep an eye out all night long. Now let's get some real sleep."

Just as he said that, the door to the cabin burst open. Betsey and Aaron sat straight up in their bed. Ambrose stood up by the hearth. Betsey couldn't see Ma and Pa due to the quilt they'd placed between the beds.

Ambrose was the first to speak, "What do you want?"

Aaron got out of bed and slowly pulled back an edge of the quilt so he and Betsey could see who'd come into the cabin. They both watched as an Indian came in and walked over to the hearth.

Betsey gasped. Aaron put a finger to his lips to encourage her to keep quiet. *What would he do to her sisters?*

Ambrose asked the man again, "What do you want?" The stranger brought a smell into the cabin that made all their eyes water.

Ambrose held out his hand, *"Miijin?"*

The Indian shook his head.

Then Ambrose said, *"Maajaa."*

The Indian shook his head.

He picked up Ambrose's blanket and placed it in front of the fire. Lying down, he pulled the blanket over himself and closed his eyes.

Ambrose seemed to resign himself to know what the Indian wanted and pulled down one of the quilts they used for a room partition. Ambrose used the blanket to cover himself, and the room grew quiet.

"What do you think he wants?" Betsey whispered to Aaron, who crawled back under the covers next to her.

"I don't know, but it looks to me like we have a visitor for the night."

Betsey wanted nothing more than to close her eyes and sleep, but the odor of their overnight guest overpowered her. Sleep eluded her, and fear gripped her heart. How could anyone sleep with this savage in their midst?

"I'm so afraid." Betsey murmured into Aaron's ear.

"Ambrose is out there, Bit. He's acquainted with Indian ways. If there were danger, he'd know."

Even with all the covers over her, and Aaron's arms wrapped tightly around her, Betsey couldn't stop shaking. *Would they be safe through the night? What if more Indians came into the cabin?* The rifle was above the hearth. Could Ambrose reach it, if he were to need it, in time? If they fell asleep, would any of them wake up in the morning? Her worries paralyzed her.

Betsey must have finally succumbed to her exhausted body's need for sleep. The Indian left before any of them woke the next morning. The only thing he left was a damp, musty smell that seemed to permeate the walls of the small cabin.

"What did he want?" Pa asked Ambrose before they headed out to fill the water barrel.

"I don't know. They did this to me this past winter. I think they're sometimes out hunting, or even traveling through, see a cabin and believe it to be adequate shelter. Not once have they bothered me for anything. They sleep and then leave quietly in the morning. I guess it's something we'll have to just get used to."

"Let's hope it stays that way. They do bring a mighty hefty aroma into a place, though." Pa waved the air.

"Funny thing happened though, as soon as everyone settled down, Alexander went to him and cuddled close to him. The Indian didn't reject him, but put his arm over him. It seems our little brother knew him."

Ambrose looked down at the boy who had picked up a bucket to follow Ambrose out to get water. He seemed oblivious to their conversation and only ready to help, with the morning chores.

Sunday finally arrived. The family woke to a bright, sunny day, after a night of heavy rain. Betsey was so happy to think that she and Aaron could spend a few hours together that afternoon scouting the property for a place to build their cabin.

Ma's foot was still raw and sore, so Betsey had been doing her best to relieve Ma from many of her responsibilities over the past few days. Her only consolation was the anticipation of spending Sunday afternoon with Aaron.

As dinner came to a close, Aaron must have been thinking about it too, because he stood up from the table and asked if he and Betsey could be excused.

Pa grinned. "Of course."

Heading out into the bright sunshine, Aaron took Betsey's hand and led her to a small trail beside the river, leading north. "Come with me, up here. I want you to see something I discovered this past week."

"How have you had time to find anything this past week?" Betsey teased him as she gripped his hand tighter and pulled up her skirt, to get through the tall grass by the river.

"I have my ways." he smiled back at her and winked.

They walked for some distance and then came to a large hill sloping up from the river. "Can you follow me this way?"

Betsey was tired, but she felt energized to finally be walking somewhere, alone with Aaron. She dropped his hand to hitch up her skirt, with both hands, to follow him.

Soon the trail grew steep. She had to stop a few times to catch her breath. Aaron tried to help by holding her hand, but she needed both of hers to hold up her heavy skirt.

They were surrounded by woods. Trees of magnificent size. The fully-opened leaves now bright-green and twirling in the warm breeze. Looking up, Betsey couldn't see the sky, what with the dense branches and leaves overhead.

Out of breath, Betsey asked, "Where in the world are you taking me, Aaron?"

He looked back. "You'll see. C'mon."

Betsey did her best to keep up, but she kept having to stop and catch her breath and to give her aching legs a break from all the climbing. Thinking they were close to the top, she soon realized they still had a bit further to go.

Betsey was out of breath and wondering if it would ever end when Aaron held out his hand.

"Just a few more steps, Bit."

Betsey let go of her skirt, grabbed Aaron's hand, and stepped up onto a ridge.

"Now turn around and look." Aaron spun her around and pointed to the view below them.

Betsey couldn't believe the sight. They were far enough above the river to see how it wound its way in front of Pa's property and then made a slight angle to the right. As she followed the river, her gaze saw that it turned and made a definite switch to the left. As it hit the bank, it again veered off to the right. It twisted like a snake, forming a letter S.

"Isn't that fascinating?" Aaron put his hands on his hips and looked beyond the ridge with her.

"It's even more beautiful than I imagined. Ma needs to see this."

Aaron folded his arms and stood tall. As if in triumph he said, "Yes, it is. I think this is where we should put our home."

Betsey wanted a better view, so she meandered farther inland from the edge of the ridge. "I'm not thinking the edge of this ridge is the best place to put a home where little ones will soon live. Let's walk a bit further beyond the ridge before we decide." Crossing another clearing similar to the one Pa had built his cabin on, Betsey turned to see the view that graced the high ridge above the river. The river could still be seen, twisting below them.

Aaron dropped his arms to follow her, "I didn't think of that."

"I'd hate for the baby to begin walking and toddle right off into the river below."

Aaron's shoulders slumped. "You're right."

Betsey kissed him. She hadn't had the luxury of showing him such open affection for weeks now. It just wasn't proper in front of Alexander and her youngest sisters. "But let's keep walking."

Aaron put his arm around her shoulders, pulling her close.

As amazing as the view was at the ridge, farther inland an opening in the woods revealed an even better location for a home. The trees still towered overhead, shielding the area from heavy wind. It was almost similar to Pa's property below them, only much smaller.

Betsey faced Aaron, "How about here?"

Aaron didn't answer, but pulled her around in front of him and kissed her with the passion of their wedding night. She succumbed to his kisses, melting in the moment, and soon they slid to the ground. Aaron pulled her onto his lap. It felt so good to share a moment just between them.

"Are you glad we moved out here, Aaron?"

"I'm glad I'm here with you," he answered.

"Perhaps I was a bit too hasty about wanting to travel all this way with my family. I didn't realize how much of our privacy would be lost by being here with them."

Aaron kissed her cheek. "I know. Me either. But we'll build our home here before winter and this is where we'll be able to enjoy each other again without three sisters, a brother, an adopted brother, and parents, all...in the same room."

As he said that, Betsey felt the baby tumble in her belly. "Oh Aaron, feel this." She took Aaron's hand and placed it over where she'd just felt the movement. He held his hand there for a few minutes, but as soon as he did, the baby stopped.

"I can't feel anything." Aaron brushed his whiskered face over her cheek. "But it's okay. I'll have plenty of time to feel the baby later. I just want to enjoy his momma for a bit."

Betsey giggled. She loved this man who had taken a chance and followed her family all the way to this strange, new place. She loved how hard he'd been working, and how strong his arms had grown since he'd been building the barn.

"Can we have more than just a one-room cabin?" Betsey knew the answer he'd probably give her, so she did her best not to get her hopes up too much.

"How many rooms does my beautiful wife need?"

"Two. Just two. One for us and one for the children."

Aaron laughed. "I will build you a house with three rooms. One for us, one for the children, and one big enough to invite your family over for supper."

He placed his mouth on hers and they fell back into the tall grasses that would soon surround their future home.

Aaron and Betsey spent most of the afternoon looking at property around the prospective site of their future home. They found black walnut, butternut, hickory, black cherry, maple, as well as white, blackjack, and burr oaks, surrounding them on all sides. Pa was a tree expert and he'd been showing Betsey the differences between the species since she could make out the shape of a leaf.

"Pa was right. There is nothing around here more wonderful than these trees." Betsey pulled back her hair and fastened her hairpins back into place.

"I think that's the best part of this place. The trees are magnificent."

"So how far north is Pa's property line? Do you know?"

Aaron shook his head. "We'll figure that out soon. I'm sure he won't mind us being up here on the ridge. We'll be able to see what's coming up the river." He pointed out a small assortment of sticks assembled in the river below that appeared to be a beaver dam. "A few of those beaver pelts might bring a fair bit of money as well. Ambrose said Whitmore pays for all kinds of pelts. He said the Indians trade for food with them, too."

"Ma said we should get some deer skins and make us shoes for the summer. She was examining the ones Alexander wore when he came to us and said they look comfortable and dry."

"So many new ways to live. So many new things to discover. This is a beautiful place to raise a family." Aaron plucked a small piece of grass and put it between his teeth. "I wish my father could see it here. We need a preacher. Do you think they would enjoy it as much as we do?"

Betsey shook her head. She didn't know if her in-laws would join them or what they're response would be about the territory, but for Aaron's sake, she hoped they did. Aaron's pa had been having all kinds of trouble with some of the residents back in Meadville, who felt he wasn't "the proper kind of minister," because he'd been married twice.

Aaron's mother had died when he was just a young man, and the wife his father chose wasn't quite the match Aaron and his brothers had expected their father to marry. She was rude, unkind to Aaron and his brothers, and not a woman suitable to be a minister's wife. She talked behind everyone's backs and wanted nothing more than to find out the gossip of the town and spread it to those who'd listen.

After marrying Betsey, Aaron had been able to keep his distance, but he did love his father. Betsey and Aaron thought that if John brought her to Michigan Territory, she might not be as tempted to cause problems. There would be no one to gossip to.

"Perhaps they'll join us next spring. What do you think?" Betsey asked as they made their way down the hill and back to her parents' cabin. Darkness was beginning to descend.

"Maybe. I worry about Father. We were someone he could come and visit without worrying about being gossiped about later. I wish he would have chosen more wisely when he remarried." Aaron sighed. "Perhaps we'll have a letter from him soon."

Before they could completely descend the hill back to the cabin, it seemed as if a barrel of trapped mosquitoes was released. They began attacking Betsey's face and hands. Aaron did his best to slap them off his own face, but the battle was useless, and the effort near-futile.

Betsey couldn't keep them off her hands. They bit her everywhere. She felt each bite grow warm and itchy as she did her best to slap the mosquitoes away. In her haste to walk with Aaron that afternoon, she'd forgotten her shawl.

Aaron motioned for her to run. "We need to get back to the cabin. These bugs are tormenting menaces."

As they rushed toward the cabin, they found no one outside. Getting to the door, they opened it quickly.

Pa hollered. "Hurry and shut that door! The mosquitoes have hatched."

Slamming the door behind them, Betsey did her best to swat the rest of the insects off her dress, as she felt another one bite her cheek. She slapped her cheek and the blood-filled mosquito fell to the floor, but left a stain on her hand. "They are horrible."

Ambrose leaned back in his chair, smoking his pipe. "Hang on, family! For the rest of the season, these thirsty critters won't give us a moment of peace. Not until the winter frost hits again."

The thought of that made Betsey's newly-formed, red welts itch even more.

June, Near the Shiawassee River

CHAPTER EIGHTEEN

Once back in the cabin, Betsey and Aaron found the younger sisters gathered together in a corner. Caroline was reading to them.

"Have a good walk?" Jillian snickered.

Betsey was pleased that Jillian could participate in everyday activities with her sisters again. Her small frame revealed the ravages of her recent illness. She'd lost weight, but she was her silly self again. Poking fun at Betsey.

Betsey pleasantly answered, "Yes, we did."

The girls giggled together, Jillian continuing to poke fun. "What did you do?"

Betsey folded her arms and unflinchingly announced, "We found a place to build our cabin."

"Is that all?" Each girl burst out in laughter, complete with Caroline's snorts.

Ambrose guffawed.

The young girls could be silly about such things, but Ambrose knew better than to poke fun. "Go back to your reading." Betsey waved off her sisters and glared at Ambrose.

"What did I do?" Ambrose shrugged as if he was innocent of any wrongdoing.

Betsey knew the only way to get them all to stop, was to ignore their teasing.

"Have a good time?" Ma seemed to really want to know if they had, but the room again erupted into giggles. "Okay, you girls, that's enough." Ma's foot was propped up and it appeared she'd been reading, too. "Mercy, I need to get up and get supper started."

Before she could move, Betsey stopped her. "Sit down, Ma. I'll start supper. My sisters need something to distract them from their sinful teasing. C'mon girls. Get up and help me."

"I'm not an invalid," her ma scolded her.

Aaron spoke. "We know that, Ma. I think Betsey just wants to help. Why don't you stay there and we'll all pitch in?"

Ambrose looked up with that comment, stood, and put on his hat. "I need to go out and check on the oxen."

Betsey chided him with her eyes. He just winked and darted out the door.

While in Pennsylvania, most Sunday afternoons Betsey would find her ma reading the Bible. But since they'd moved, it was hard to find time to read at all. Betsey felt thankful they'd all taken the time to rest for the afternoon, including she and Aaron.

"How's your foot today, Ma?"

Her mother massaged the knee above the injured foot. "It feels better —propped up. It's not as tender to the touch."

Betsey wrapped her apron ties around her growing waist, "Shall we just cut up a bit more of the meat we had for dinner?"

"That was my thought."

"Why don't you sit there and finish your reading?"

Ma sighed, "I sure appreciate that I took the time to read today. I needed it."

Her sisters left the cabin to gather water for the barrel. Now Betsey felt more at ease to tell Ma about their walk. "We enjoyed our walk." Betsey turned so Ma couldn't see her if she did blush.

"That's good. So will the ridge be a good place to build?"

"It's so nice there, Ma." She went on to describe the plateau on the ridge and how they could see so much of the river from it. "I think it will be perfect."

"It will be perfect. Aaron will build you a perfect house. And best of all—you'll still be close by."

"Oh Ma, I'm so happy we had the opportunity to come with you."

Aaron asked if Betsey could fix he and Pa a cup of coffee. "I'll take it out to him and let him know supper will be ready soon."

"Thanks, Aaron." Betsey saw Aaron's face. He looked at her with eyes that made her want to kiss him even more, but she knew her sisters would be returning soon.

Once Aaron left, Betsey felt even more comfortable about talking. "We need to check with Pa first, but I think it will be a wonderful place to live." Betsey told her about the river and its twists and turns, clearly visible from the ridge.

"I can't imagine the river being that curvy so soon after our section. It's so straight out-front here."

"I know, I was surprised as well. I'm sure in the fall it will be even more beautiful. Especially with all the autumn colors."

"Being as busy as we are, it will be here before you know it. Pa said there's a blackjack oak tree near the north edge of the ridge that he'd one day like to be buried under."

Right after that comment, the girls came back into the cabin, singing a cheery tune, each carrying a bucket. Even Jillian carried one at least half-full.

Betsey continued to tell Ma about what they could see from the ridge; the beaver dam, the hill sloping up to it, and the curvy river, which turned straight north, just past the prominent curve. "Just like Whitmore told us, about how it moves directly north past the ridge. The name fits, just like Pa said."

"Shi-a-wassee." Ma smiled as if satisfied with her good memory of the pronunciation.

That evening, everyone seemed rested and ready to begin another week of hard work. Ambrose had shot a large buck the previous afternoon and had brought in a large slice of the back straps for Sunday's meals. He and Aaron would be heading to the barn that evening to cut up and portion out the rest of the meat, in preparation of smoking it the next day.

After Betsey and Aaron told Pa about their thoughts of building on the ridge, Ambrose shared that he'd found property directly south of them for a house of his own. "I think this cabin has had enough of all of us together. As soon as we get the crops planted and harvested, I think I'll head south to purchase my section."

"I'll go with you, son. I think we shouldn't wait too long to purchase the sections we want. By the looks of the crowds in Pontiac and on the steamboat, we'll have neighbors real soon."

"We'll help you girdle the trees you want for your cabin soon, Aaron." Ambrose lit his pipe and took a long draw on it.

"We'll have our own little community here soon. Just as I imagined it during my first weeks here last year. We'll figure out how to hire a doctor, and start a church and school. My girls need schooling." Pa took a slice of cornbread and wiped his plate clean. "Have you seen the section just south of here, on the river, Ambrose?"

Ambrose nodded that he had.

"I think I'll start a grist mill there. It's a few years away, but as soon as we can gather enough crops and have a need for a grist mill, I think it will be a great place to build a mill. What do you think?"

"Sounds perfect, Pa. Maybe I can help you build it and help earn a living from it."

"That's what I was hoping you'd say, son." Pa's chest puffed out, and he straightened his back. "What are your plans, Aaron?"

Betsey was curious as well. She hadn't had a chance to ask him herself.

"I do think we need enforcement officers in the new settlement. As soon as we get the cabin up, I think I'll ask Whitmore about it the next time I head past the trading post. Maybe there are law enforcement officers that do work in these parts, but if not, perhaps I can be one of the first."

Pa concurred with that thought. "Sounds good, son. I think we'll soon have a nice little settlement here."

Betsey couldn't help but be proud of her family. They were not only settling in a new part of the country that had once been desolate, but they were also making a community. A community with hopeful visions and exciting possibilities. No wonder Pa thought it a good idea to move them all here. She glanced at her ma. She hoped Ma saw the potential of good things for their future, too.

The next morning Betsey awoke to torrential rains beating on the roof. Thunder had startled her awake in the night and now the rain pounded so hard it seemed the roof might cave in.

As she got up, she realized that getting washing done today would be a challenge. Perhaps she should start Tuesday's chores instead. Baking would probably take up most of the day. They could also help Aaron and Ambrose smoke the meat.

Ma was still limping but resting her foot the day before had helped it heal more quickly. When she removed the strips of cloth that morning, bright pink skin covered the raw parts from the week before.

"No planting today. Let's get out and see what we can do to get some nets ready to catch us some fish," Pa told Ambrose and Aaron as they headed out into the rain, to go to the barn. "If we have to get that venison preserved, we might as well get some fish smoked as well."

"Girls, get your shawls. I need you to gather some hickory chips to fuel the fire. We'll be smokin' meat today."

As the men headed out to the barn, a flicker of movement at the southern end of their property caught Pa's attention. An oxen team was heading into the tall, wild grass just south of the cabin. A man sat on the wagon bench, shoulders hunched, grasping the reins of a weary-looking oxen team.

Pa pointed out, the man and the wagon, to Ambrose and Aaron. All three set out to greet the unexpected visitor. Except the Indians, Whitmore, and the man who did their plowing, they hadn't seen another man since they'd arrived.

The man pulled his team up next to the barn, and as he jumped off, Pa could see he had a family in the wagon. Three little ones stuck their heads out from behind the canvas.

The man waved to them. "Hello. Name is Henry Leach."

As Pa got to the wagon, he stuck up his hand to shake that of the stranger, "Hosea Baker. Nice to meet you."

"Nice to meet you, as well." After leaning down to shake Pa's hand, he slapped his hands together. His hair was matted and damp, and his clothes looked like you could wring out enough water to fill a bucket.

"Family?" Pa asked, pointing to the back of the wagon.

"Yes, my wife and three children. We're wondering if you could provide us with a warm place to stay for a bit. We're wet and the children are mighty cold."

Pa smiled. Now his family could be the hospitable ones to others needing shelter or assistance. "Of course. Come to the cabin. We just finished breakfast, and I'm sure Ma has a bit left, and can give y'all a bite to eat. The Lord says, 'come all who are heavy laden and I will give you rest.'"

"Much obliged." The man lowered his three children off the back of the wagon and reached up to take his wife's hand, to help her down, too. They weren't as wet as the man, but they all shivered in the morning air.

"Come, come inside. This is my son, Ambrose, and son-in-law, Aaron. Let us help you with your team."

Pa escorted the family to the cabin while Aaron and Ambrose headed to the barn, leading the oxen team. "Right this way."

The griddle took a few minutes to heat back up, but soon more pancakes sizzled. Betsey watched the three children devour pancakes like they hadn't eaten in months. Pa had stayed in the cabin to help get the family fed, warm, and acquainted with Ma, Betsey, and the girls.

"Welcome to our little refuge in the middle of this new territory," Pa announced. "We're more than happy to welcome some new neighbors. Pa handed Henry a cup of steaming coffee.

"We've been traveling from Ohio for about ten weeks now, coming through some mighty swampy land. Seems good to finally find a place to consider home, although everyone has been very good to us along the way." Henry Leach seemed as hungry as his children as he finished up the last pancake on his plate. Betsey was glad she'd mixed up a double batch.

"Do you think you'll stay?" Ma asked as she offered the woman a hot cup of tea.

"I hope we can stop soon. Traveling is awful hard." The woman smiled at Ma. "Especially with the children and all."

Ma sat down beside the woman. "My name's Sally."

The woman wiped her mouth with a napkin Ma had placed beside her plate. She held out her hand. "Claire."

Ma smiled. "What a beautiful name."

"These are my children." The children seemed enamored with Alexander. He seemed excited to see a boy nearly his age. He couldn't stop staring back, showing them his slate.

Ma proceeded to tell them about all the things they'd discovered since they'd arrived on the property.

"How long have you been here?" the man asked Pa. When Pa told him, he commented, "I'm amazed that you have a house and a barn up already."

Pa folded his arms. "By God's grace, we've done well. We have a crop of potatoes now planted up in the field. We planned to plant a few vegetables this week but, as you can see, the weather isn't cooperating."

"Have you had lots of rain?" the man asked.

Pa held out his cup for Betsey to refill. "This is the first big storm we've had so far. Mighty thankful we didn't get other things planted yet or we might've lost them." Pa then picked up Henry's cup and had Betsey refill that as well.

Mr. Leach thanked Betsey. "It has rained almost the entire trip. Perhaps it's our fault that it's here now. It seems to have followed us all along the way."

"Only God is that powerful. Our local fur trader says, not much good comes from Ohio, but looks like he wasn't accurate with that statement. We're happy you're here. But let's hope this hard rain eases up a bit and we get gentle showers from this point forward."

Pa's longing for gentle showers never came. The Leach family pulled their wagon up close to the cabin that night. Ma made up beds for the children, next to Alexander and the girls by the hearth. Being small, they snuggled in tight to Etta and Caroline, who welcomed them with warm blankets and kisses.

Henry and Claire would sleep outside in their wagon. Both Ma and Betsey hated sending them back outside, but the cabin wasn't large enough for another couple. The rain continued to pelt the roof. With the addition of the Leach children, the cabin grew stuffy and crowded. Pa kept tripping over the younger children, before they settled down to sleep.

The next morning, they had to eat in shifts to get everyone fed. There weren't enough plates for everyone to eat at the same time. The rain hadn't let up at all.

If nothing else, it was good to have another woman to help with the cooking and cleaning. Claire proved to be a good worker, and she and Ma became fast friends. Betsey took time to be with the children, helping them pass the day by reading and playing with them. She'd always wanted to be a teacher, and with a cabin full of children, perhaps now was a good time to start. The youngest child was two, the next one up was three-and-a-half and the oldest was a boy about Alexander's age.

Ma had wanted the girls to keep up with their studies, but the work to set up a household left little time for such things. Ma set out slates and stubs of chalk so they could practice writing their letters, and Betsey helped the younger children with letter sounds. Betsey enjoyed holding the little ones on her lap as they sounded out letter after letter.

"Your daughter is a natural teacher," Claire told Ma as they finished up the dishes from breakfast.

"She does well. If you decide to live close, perhaps she'll be hired as the first teacher here." Ma smiled brightly at the thought.

"I agree. I think we'll find property nearby. I've been encouraging Henry to start looking for property."

Ma hugged her new friend. "I hope so. I think we'll make great friends. And, hopefully, neighbors."

"I'd like that and thank you for being so kind to us."

Although the days were filled with visiting, cooking, and learning—being crammed into the tiny cabin proved hard. Betsey prayed for the hard rain to stop, so they could send the younger ones out to play.

But the rain didn't stop, nor did it let up. It rained continually, for five seemingly endless days.

Cooking for everyone created a need for more food. Betsey and Claire were continuously bumping into each other. Claire was kind and apologized many times, but soon everyone grew tired of so many people in the tight, cramped space.

Caroline had been so good to help with the little ones, but they were beginning to wear her out as well. She was having a hard time creating things to occupy their time. Betsey couldn't seem to hold their attention either. The tension was getting the best of everyone.

Each day, as the rain continued, Pa would go to the riverbank to check on the roaring water. Ambrose had said that he had not seen the river rise to a dangerous level, but as the torrential rain continued, Pa wondered if there would be a moment when everyone would have to abandon the cabin and move to higher ground. He was also worried about the newly-planted potato field.

Henry had taken on many duties, in an attempt to help. He'd taken his oxen and tied them to the barn, keeping watch over them as best as he could throughout the night. Wolves had gotten close one night, but with Ambrose's help he'd been able to scare them off each time with a rifle shot into the air.

"The first thing I'm going to do is build us a barn." Pa, Ambrose and Aaron agreed to help him, but even before a barn, the Leach family needed shelter.

On Saturday morning, they woke to a silent cabin for the first time in days. As noon came and went, it was clear that the rain had finally stopped, and the storm clouds had given way to blue skies. For the first time in days everyone ventured outside, and while out they assessed what, if any, damage had happened to the property.

Pa came in that afternoon to tell Ma that many of the potatoes were strewn across the field. Only a few remained underground. As soon as the mud dried, he and Ambrose would replant.

The river had risen to a dangerously high level. The wild grass that ran along the banks was halfway submerged in the roaring water, and nearby logs had been swept away, no longer visible from shore.

Pa talked about it at supper. "I don't know if maybe we should move farther inland from the river."

Ma's determination came out in a harsh tone. "This is my home now. I don't plan on leaving it over a few days of heavy rain."

Pa abruptly stopped suggesting they leave for higher ground.

After supper Henry announced, "I think we'll head back south a bit. Find a piece of land on which to build. Ambrose, if you could point out the section where you've decided to build, I'll build in another place."

"That would be fine, sir. Thank you for considering my selection of property before you chose your own." Ambrose patted Henry on the shoulder.

"You've been more than kind to me, my wife, and family. It's the least I can do. Perhaps if we look around a bit, we'll find our own section. I'd be pleased to have such kind folks as neighbors."

Just after the Leach family moved on another family joined their ranks, but stayed with the Bakers for just one night. Each family brought stability to the new settlement springing up in the area just west of the Shiawassee River.

Ambrose proved himself a good neighbor, too. He and Aaron often left Pa to help someone fell some trees to build a home or even just a barn. Each neighbor set out to make it easier for the next one who came into the growing settlement.

They weren't alone anymore. Even though Pa and Ambrose had been the first in the area, with no one but Nibi to help Ambrose when he was all alone, Pa did his best to help others in their endeavor to start a new community or just build a homestead within their settlement. He was proud of the fact that others were choosing this good land to settle. Indeed, a new village was springing up faster than the crops which now failed to burst forth from the ground in his fields.

The new neighbors were a blessing, but what followed was a whole different menace. The heavy rains were followed by another burst of newly hatched, hungry, Michigan mosquitoes. They began to torment everyone. The option of leaving the door open during the day for fresh air, deemed impossible.

Trying to work outside toward the evening brought nothing but torment from the annoying, buzzing bugs. Ambrose's predicament of how to keep them out of the water supply now became clear to everyone else. Their hands and faces became swollen from the bites. The mosquitoes would buzz around their heads at night, making it nearly impossible to get a good night's sleep.

If they weren't slapping at the insect, they were picking them out of their food. After swallowing a few, everyone began to check their water before drinking it. Pa scolded anyone who forgot to put the cover back on the water barrel stored by the front door. If left ajar, the mosquitoes infiltrated the entire barrel quicker than flies to a lantern. Not only were they being bitten, they were swallowing them. Kneading dough proved almost impossible, as the tiny insects seemed to invade the dough with every flip. It was impossible to keep them out of the food, especially during cooking.

If they weren't swatting them away from their heads, they were scratching the welts on their skin, till their flesh became raw and bleeding.

As evening drew near, the fight of the insects seemed that much worse. The family literally felt their lives being sucked away by the pesky insects. Everyone's hands were swollen from the bites. Everyone felt lethargic and sickly.

Nighttime didn't give any relief. Unless they were completely covered with blankets, the insects attacked any exposed skin. They would awaken with swollen eyes, lips, and fingers. Betsey woke up several times with a buzzing sound close to her ears. She'd never experienced such an annoyance.

Nothing brought them respite. After a week or two of enduring the suffering, the family could barely leave the cabin, and each time the door opened, a cloud of the buzzing menaces flew into the dark, stuffy, one-room home. It became impossible to get anything done. Outside or inside.

Ambrose was out one afternoon, doing his best to dig up weeds from the rows and rows of potatoes now replanted in Pa's field. He couldn't stand still. His focus was split between weeding or warding off mosquitoes. He knew if he stopped moving, he'd be eaten alive, but the potato plants now needed to be mounded up around the budding greens coming up.

Something cool and wet touched his neck. Startled, he found Nibi behind him, applying the strong-smelling Indian ointment on the back of Ambrose's neck. He hadn't even seen Nibi approach him. The odor of it caused Ambrose to scramble away from Nibi.

"What in tarnation are you trying to do to me, Nibi? That stuff smells awful." The smell brought tears.

Nibi lifted his arm and pointed to a swollen mosquito bite rising on Ambrose's elbow. Dipping his fingers in a small leather pouch, Nibi picked up Ambrose's arm and smeared the ointment on and up Ambrose's arm. Soon it was being slathered on not only his arms, but his neck and ankles. The smell nearly killed Ambrose, but it brought him not only relief from the bugs biting him, but the ointment soothed his itchy sores. The smell repelled the mosquitoes.

That night, though, the family smelled Ambrose long before he came into the house.

"Ambrose, what in the world?" Ma said that evening when he came in to eat.

"Ma—" Everyone stared at him with wide eyes and disgust, covering their faces with their napkins. They all refused to sit by him. "Nibi wiped it on me, but I have to tell you—"

Betsey stood up. Her face looked as if she were seeing a ghost instead of Ambrose and ran for the door.

As the door slammed behind Betsey, Ma stood. "Out!" she shouted.

Ambrose dropped his spoon, which he'd just picked up to begin eating. "What?"

"Get out!" Ma removed her apron and began snapping it at him.

Ambrose screamed in protest. "But Ma, it helps. I haven't been bit all afternoon."

"I don't care, get out of my cabin."

Before he reached the door, Ma threw him a blanket and handed him his plate of food. "Not in my house!" She swished the air with her towel.

Ma slammed the door behind him. "I will not have that smell in my house." Then added, "Ever!"

Ambrose leaned against the door and hollered from outside, "I guess that means no one else wants to use the Indian lotion, huh?"

Ma sat down, shifted her napkin in her lap and shouted back, "Not if they want to sleep in my house!"

Caroline did her best not to burst into laughter, but Pa didn't hold back. Everyone else followed with muffled snickers and giggles. The younger girls glanced at Ma, and soon even she began to smirk.

"But Ma," Jillian asked, "What if it helps? These bugs are driving us all crazy."

At that moment, Alexander slapped a mosquito on his arm. Picking up his plate, he went for his blanket, opened the door, and left.

"I think he's going out with Ambrose. He knows what will work, but he knows you won't stand for it." Pa looked at Ma with a twinkle in his eyes.

Ma folded her arms. "Oh my. I don't know what to do."

"Maybe," Caroline stood and scratched at a new welt on her arm, "If we all use the lotion, we'll all smell the same."

Ma folded her arms and shook her head. "I can't. I just can't. And what about poor Betsey. She won't be able to deal with the smell. Especially in her condition."

Ambrose found Betsey retching near the corner edge of the cabin. He wanted to approach her, but he knew he was the reason she was bent over and miserable.

"I'm sorry, Bit. I know how sensitive you are to smells right now."

Betsey held out her hand to him as a warning to stay away from her. She gasped, "It's not what you think."

Ambrose still stood a few feet behind her. "It's not the smell making you sick?"

Betsey stood up and turned to him. She had a kerchief over her mouth and nose. "Yes, it's the smell, but Ambrose..."

Ambrose was confused. "I can't have these bugs eating me alive and this lotion really does help." He held out the pouch. "Try some. It not only wards off the pests, but brings a bit of relief to your skin."

Tears now filled his sister's eyes. "I can't. That smell brings back the vivid memory of the Indian who pinned me against the wagon wheel."

"What?" Ambrose was confused.

"On our trip here. Remember when the Indians stopped us and stole our food?"

Ambrose nodded.

"This smell makes me relive that moment. He must have been wearing this lotion." Betsey moved closer to him, but kept her kerchief over her mouth. "Each time I smell it, it takes me back to that moment of fear when he pressed his body so close to mine and—"

"Bit, I'm so sorry. I didn't realize." Ambrose reached out to her. He wanted to take her into his arms and hold her close, but how could he do it, smelling as he did.

"It's silly." Betsey lowered the kerchief. "I'm safe. He didn't do anything to me but put the fear of God into my heart. I need to get over it. I need to stop letting the smell cause me to panic so." But even as she spoke of the real reason she didn't want to use the ointment, Ambrose could see mosquitoes biting her cheeks and face. She slapped her cheeks to ward them off.

Ambrose folded his arms. "Bit. I need you to trust me when I say that Nibi has been a good friend to me. If it wasn't for him, I might not be here to have this conversation with you. I know the Indians can be scary and you have a reason for some of your fear. Your first encounter wasn't at all a pleasant one. But, Nibi especially, has been good to me. He means well."

Betsey nodded, wiping her nose. "I know. I need to try harder, but I will never forget the eyes of that man. He put a fear into my heart that I've not been able to shake. And when I smell this lotion, it makes me sick."

Ambrose scuffed his toe in the dirt. "And for that I'm sorry. Perhaps if you smell the lotion on me, Alexander, and hopefully the rest of the family, you'll realize it is just a smell and not something that always reminds you of danger."

Betsey nodded again, and smiled at him. "Maybe." She shook her head, "But Ambrose—"

"What?"

"You really do stink!"

Alexander handed the lotion pouch back to Ambrose, after he'd used it on himself, and stood grinning at both of them.

The next day, the lotion bottle left by Nibi, was passed around the family.

At first, they couldn't get over how well it worked. The smell made their eyes water and occasionally sent Betsey running for a bucket, but it made such a difference in their fight with something smaller than a fly. They'd battled mud, cold, a large boat ride, wolves, coyotes, and even Indians, but nothing was as tormenting as the Michigan mosquito.

Summer, Mid-July

CHAPTER NINETEEN

Aaron was getting anxious to build the house he and Betsey had been planning during their now-regular walks each Sunday. One July afternoon, as the sun bore down on him while tugging on the weeds in his father-in-law's field, he realized that it was getting past time to get their house started. He shouldn't be wasting time pulling weeds.

He'd girdled several trees to begin the process, but at that moment he realized he didn't want to wait any longer. He'd been chatting with Henry Leach, who'd recently gone to Waterford to purchase lumber. He'd told Hosea that the prices at a sawmill located there were good, and he'd even been able to purchase a window for their home. Why couldn't he do the same? If they were to have a house built before winter, he'd need to do the same.

But could he convince Betsey that leaving her now was best? Between the pregnancy and what seemed to be an ever-growing fear of the Indians, he wondered if she'd allow him to leave her.

One morning, only a few days later, Aaron set off with their wagon and oxen team to get the wood they needed to build. They'd made the decision together.

"I promise to return as soon as I can. Will you be okay?"

Tears filled Betsey's eyes, but she nodded. Even though she'd agree Aaron was right, it didn't make him leaving any easier. Her condition didn't help. She wanted to tell him they'd be fine, but worry for him tore at her confidence. How would he do on the long trip? Alone? The territory was still a dangerous place.

Aaron patted her now-round belly. "I'll be back soon, little one. Take care of your momma till I get back." Aaron looked at her as if it might be the last time he'd see her. "I wish I could take you with me, but I think it best that you stay here. All that jostling won't do you or the baby any good."

All Betsey could do was nod. Her throat tightened with sadness. How would she be without him for so many weeks? She knew it was good he was going. He'd return with lumber for their house, but why did it have to take so long? They'd talked about it long into the night. He worried if he didn't go now he might never finish their cabin before the winter winds blew or the snow would fall. By going now, perhaps they could be in their new home right after the baby arrived.

Kissing her firmly, he backed away, climbed up on the wagon, and headed south. She felt so alone, staying behind as the wagon pulled away. Yet when the little squirming soul in her belly delivered a swift kick, it solidified her decision to stay at home. She covered the spot with her hand, rubbing it for relief. She began to miss Aaron even before he was completely out of sight.

The summer days grew longer, and the sun gave the new settlers more time to work, but less energy to do it. Betsey didn't think tired could describe how she felt. The only disturbance of her sleep now was the active little body growing strong in her belly. Caroline was now her bedmate, with Aaron gone. They'd slept together for years before Betsey had gotten married, so it felt natural to have Caroline sleep with her again.

The crops needed constant weeding and hoeing. The potato mounds needed constant daily attention in keeping the dirt mounded well around the growing plants. Bean blossoms erupted into vines thick with vegetables to harvest. They'd snipped beans until their fingers were raw, and ate them at every meal. The greens supplied a delicious and fresh addition to the family's diet.

They'd discovered wild berries growing close to the river, among the briars and weeds. Actually finding them took almost as much work as picking them. They were mixed in with the riverbank grasses. Ma needed at least two cups for a pie and the only motivation to find berries was the thought of having pie for dessert.

The heat of the day made Betsey's ankles swell, and her growing belly made it hard to bend over to pick the berries. The only help was the sound of her sisters' voices in the woods. Their songs penetrated her lonely heart with words of joy and hope.

Ambrose had started to build his own home close to the Leach farm, just south of the Baker property. Pa now handled many of the outdoor chores alone. The added chores, due to Ambrose and Aaron's absence, took a toll on everyone.

Ma had come down with a somewhat different ailment than what Jillian had suffered a few months before. She struggled with a fever and cold fits for days, leaving Betsey and Caroline to do the washing, cooking, canning, harvesting, and housecleaning.

"Betsey what are you doing?" Ma had been delirious for quite a few days with a very high fever. She'd been talking in her sleep, and with the heat, it was hard to keep her cool inside the tiny, stuffy cabin. The medicine to bring her relief had run out.

Betsey moistened a cloth and placed it over her ma's forehead. If there were only a way to get a message to Aaron to bring back more medicine.

"Just trying to keep you cool, Ma."

Ma had grown worse through the night. Her eyes looked glazed and red. Betsey had never taken care of her mother before and it wasn't an easy chore, what with so many other things needing done. She called out to Caroline who was grabbing a large ladle hanging beside the hearth. "Caroline, come see this." Caroline hurried to Betsey, seated beside her ma's bed. "Look at her eyes."

Caroline got closer to her mother's face. The cabin was dark, as the door was closed in an attempt to keep the mosquitoes out.

"Do they look odd to you?"

"Scary." Caroline looked back at Betsey.

"I hope she can get through this. The medicine is gone." Most of the family had suffered, in varying degrees, with the fever during the past month. Pa and Ambrose struggled for a few days. Caroline and Etta also had the symptoms, but they had all continued functioning throughout. Betsey had been spared.

Caroline seemed preoccupied, seeming to want to get back outside. "I have to go stir the jam. It will burn and stick to the bottom of the kettle if I don't. Keep putting the cool cloth on her forehead, Betsey."

Betsey had noticed how much more mature Caroline had been acting these days. She'd picked up so much of the work since Ma had taken ill. But something seemed to be bothering her.

"I'll be there in a moment." Betsey put another cold compress on her mother's forehead and patted her hand. "Go to sleep, Ma. Rest."

Ma slowly shut her eyes.

Betsey went outside, into the hot sun of July. In the last few days, Betsey felt like she could wring the air out like a newly washed sheet.

Sweat trickled down Jillian's cheeks as she took turns with Caroline stirring the hot strawberry mixture hanging over the fire. "I wish we could cook this jam on a cooler day."

"The berries would have gone bad, Caroline." Betsey moved around the fire and took her turn at stirring the mixture, waiting for the pot to bubble. "You know what Ma says, 'A watched pot never boils.'"

A comment like that almost always brought a smile to at least one face, but not today.

Caroline wiped the sweat off her brow with her apron. "Was it ever this hot in Pennsylvania?"

Betsey nodded. "Of course. We just forgot, from one summer to the next."

"Are you alright?"

Caroline gave her an almost-guilty look. "I miss Billie."

So that was it. Betsey tried to not scold. "I know. I miss my friends from church."

"That's different, Betsey." Caroline gave her a disgusted look. "I think he'll forget all about me."

Betsey knew not to contradict Caroline's anxiety. "Why would he do that?"

"I don't know. I'm sure he's moved on to another girl. Why wouldn't he?"

"Because," Betsey now wiped the sweat from her cheeks, "you and he have been friends for years. You just don't forget someone that quickly."

"That's just it. We were just friends."

Betsey could see it wasn't sweat Caroline now wiped from her eyes. "If it is a relationship God wants you to continue, Billie will come find you."

"That's easy for you to say. You have Aaron."

Betsey knew she was right. She remembered feeling so alone before they'd become engaged. She knew the pain her sister was feeling. "Why don't you write him a letter?"

Caroline looked up as Jillian, who'd gone to get a bucket of water for the barrel, came toward them. Betsey knew a conversation like this would not be something Caroline would want Jillian hearing.

She handed the stirring stick to Caroline. "Jillian, let's you and I go down to the river and wash out these crocks. We'll need to put the jam in them when we finish. It might be a hot job but this winter, we'll love this jam."

"If anyone doesn't, I'll be telling them off. Finding and even picking these berries is hard work." Jillian picked up the crock next to the one Betsey had chosen.

As they approached the river, they found Pa knee-deep with the fishing nets. Alexander was there with him, doing his utmost to catch something himself, but with all his splashing around, probably scared more fish off than Pa would have liked.

"Catch anything, Pa?" Jillian called out.

Pa waved but didn't answer.

"I don't think he heard you."

As they put the crocks in the water, Pa stood up, holding a large fish. As he did, he stepped back a little too far and fell backwards into the water, losing the fish as it flopped out of his grasp. Alexander jumped right into the water and soon came up holding a small-mouthed bass.

Jillian and Betsey couldn't help but laugh. Pa had looked so surprised as he fell backwards, but when he saw Alexander holding the fish, he laughed.

As he stood up, soaked from head-to-foot, he patted Alexander's head. "Good job, my boy. If nothing else, that cold water feels good."

Betsey bent over as best as she could, to wash the crock in the lukewarm water near the shore. "It's so hot, even the shallower parts of the river are warm."

Jillian pulled off her shoes and stockings, to wade up to her knees. "Oh Betsey, you need to get in deeper. It's cooler out here."

It was tempting. Betsey was so warm. Which would be easier, standing here and allowing her hands to feel cooler, or sitting on the riverbank, taking off her shoes and trying to bend over to wash the crock in the water? Her oversized middle was a significant hindrance.

Before she could make up her mind, Jillian splashed her with water from her cupped hands. Betsey protested, as Jillian laughed. Though she didn't admit it, Betsey thought the water felt refreshing and cool.

"Jillian! What are you doing?" Before Jillian answered, she scooped up more water, again tossing it toward Betsey.

"Oh, little girl, if this baby wasn't keeping me from moving quickly, I'd be out there dunking you."

Pa plopped his backside back down into the water. "This is too tempting to not take advantage of."

Alexander brought the fish to shore and threw it in a bucket Pa had on shore. He then went back out into the water, and mimicking Pa, sat right down next to him.

Betsey wiped her crock off with her apron and headed back to Caroline, who would need a break from stirring the hot berry sauce. Reaching her, Betsey took over the stirring and told Caroline to get down to the river and give Jillian a good splash for her.

Without hesitation, Caroline rushed to the river and jumped in with Jillian. Laughter erupted from the river as the girls, Alexander, and Pa cooled off from the hot day.

Betsey hoped the fun would replace Caroline's anxious thoughts about the boy back in Pennsylvania.

That afternoon, Pa came in early from his chores. He seemed solemn and tired but determined to say something. Ma's fever had soared throughout the day and she lay shivering in bed. Betsey had just put a cool cloth on her forehead and another across her chest.

"Bit. Come sit down with me." Pa patted the chair next to him. "The girls can finish the dishes."

Betsey handed Etta her towel and sat down next to Pa.

"I have to ask you something."

Betsey had no clue what her pa would be asking, but it didn't take long for him to get to the point.

"I need to get to Jackson. The county is filling up fast. We have two more new neighbors since June. I need to go and officially purchase our property."

Pa's intense stare seemed one of concern. Perhaps he was waiting for a reaction or wondering what his next words should be.

"What, Pa?" She couldn't handle the suspense.

"We need to go now."

Realization struck Betsey. It was as if Pa was speaking a different language and she'd just deciphered the meaning. She'd be alone with a sick ma, three younger siblings, and a young boy. "Can Ambrose stay with us?"

"He needs to go, too. To purchase his land. You have to sign the documents in person."

Betsey's eyes must have shown her reaction clearly. Pa patted her hand. "It will be okay. Henry Leach has agreed to check on you from time to time. The crops will be fine until we get back. You may have to pick a few more green beans and keep the potatoes mounded, but other than that, nothing will be ready until we return."

"But what about—" Betsey's mind went blank. Thoughts of managing the house by herself scared her. *What if something happened to Ma or she got worse? What if they ran out of food?*

As if reading her mind, Pa grabbed her hand. "We will get a deer before we leave and butcher it. The girls will be a big help to you. They're old enough to work together and help."

Betsey looked up at her sisters who stood wide-eyed and looked as frightened as she felt inside.

Etta was the first to speak. "We'll help, Pa. All of us." All three girls nodded.

"What about Ma? What if she doesn't get any better?"

"We're going to see if we can find us a doctor, too. Someone who will come live close by. But your ma is strong. She'll be fine."

Betsey sighed and tried hard to fight back tears, now ready to spill down her cheeks.

Pa patted her hand. "I know this isn't the best timing, but God will protect you. He'll give you a peace about it all. Aaron should be back soon as well."

"But we don't know when. It could be a month from now."

Pa's face grew even more serious. Betsey hated when he did that, because she knew he wasn't going to change his mind. Just as his sense of adventure was strong, so was his word.

"For any other reason, I would never leave all my girls like this, if I didn't feel confident that they'd be fine. God will protect you. He didn't bring us out here to this wilderness to not sustain us in His care. 'They who wait for the Lord shall renew their strength; they shall mount up with wings like eagles, they shall run and not be weary; they shall walk and not faint.'"

Betsey had no ammunition against the Bible, or God's promises. She knew that. But deep in her heart, her soul began to tremble. A fear like she'd seldom known before began creeping into her being. The baby was motionless.

"What...in the world?"

Hosea sat beside his wife for a few moments, and now Sally did her best to speak.

"What do you need, Sally May? What can I get you?"

His wife's red, sore eyes glared at him with a fiery look. He was familiar with that look, but more so since they'd moved to the new territory.

"What are," she gasped, "you doing?"

Hosea knew what she meant now. She'd overheard his conversation with Betsey.

"I have to go. We need to purchase the land."

Sally grew rigid on the bed. Hosea knew to be thankful she couldn't give him a real taste of the anger showing in her eyes.

"We won't be long. You'll be fine. Betsey, the girls—"

"You've brought us out here," another gasp, "to die."

Sally wasn't mincing words. She meant business and Hosea knew it. Struggling to breathe, she was telling him exactly what she was feeling in her heart.

He lifted her hand to kiss it, but before he could put his lips on it, Sally pulled it away.

"I've obeyed. I've followed you." Gasp. "Done my best. But this." Sally rolled over, turning her back to him. "You're selfish."

Hosea finally understood what had been bothering his wife for months, but even if he decided to stay, he'd not appease her. So, he did what he knew to do. He pulled the blanket over her shoulder, gently patted it, and left to make preparations to leave.

Ma moaned in her sleep that night. Betsey heard Pa get out of bed several times and get water from the barrel.

Betsey wondered how she'd be able to care for Ma properly, as well as keep the farm running. They'd dealt with this fever before, but with Pa now expecting her and Ma to do everything to keep things going, how would she do it without her ma's help. She rarely said she didn't feel well, but this fever hit her fiercely, and hard. What would happen if she got it, too? She was the only one who hadn't gotten it yet.

Betsey slept restlessly that night. Fear began to take hold of her thoughts. It gripped her heart like little else ever had, almost consuming her. She thought through Pa's plans over and over until she had every conceivable scenario sketched out and how she'd fix it if, or when, it happened. But it all weighed so heavily on her, that she could barely move when it was time to get out of bed the next morning.

Their plan for today was to get Pa and Ambrose prepared to leave for the land office. They'd gone out hunting way before dawn. Pa was also paying a visit to Henry Leach at his cabin a mile or two south, to inform him of their plans. Pa returned to tell Betsey that she could send one of the girls or Alexander to the Leach farm if an emergency arose. Instead of giving Betsey encouragement, it brought yet another fear. What if they couldn't reach Henry in time? She also felt nervous about sending one of the girls, or even Alexander, out alone.

The scariest scenario among those rippling through Betsey's imagination, of course, was dealing with the Indians. She wasn't sure of their motivations nor if they were planning on harm or just simple curiosity, as Ambrose often knew. How would she be able to tell the difference?

It was the middle of July. Aaron should be back in a few weeks. That would still leave two months or so before the baby was due, but Betsey had so many other things yet to do. Could she make the needed preparations and continue to keep the farm going at the same time? Plus, her size was impeding house and outdoor chores more every day.

Her head hurt from thinking about it all. She knew God wasn't the originator of her fears. She'd heard Pa quote one particular verse so many times which addressed fear. *"Fearness and trembling are come upon me,"* but Pa quoted the next verses to appease the first, *"Cast thy burden on the Lord, and He shall sustain thee."* Why was this scripture not soothing her spirit now? How would she cast all her fears on God to sustain her, without taking it all back when the worries set in?

Betsey set to work gathering ideas on how to run the household without Pa and Ambrose, but she had to also consider doing it without Ma's help. She conferred with Caroline that morning, and together they'd divided up all the work between the four young women. Jillian was now stronger after being sick. She could help in bigger ways, too.

Caroline disagreed with the division of duties. "Why does it seem as though you have all the heavy duties? You have to give me some of the harder chores now."

Caroline was still such a small girl. She'd never been one to take on the heavier chores, but what choice did Betsey have? Caroline was right. All the men's chores, like mounding of the potato plants, hoeing and watering the garden, and hauling firewood would all become their responsibility now in addition to their daily household chores.

There was one other thing Betsey hated to think about, but she'd decided in the middle of the night to speak with Caroline about it the next morning.

"Caroline, go to Ambrose and have him show you how to load and shoot the rifle."

She'd practiced what she'd say if Caroline refused. But she didn't. Caroline nodded, dressed, went to the hearth, and took the large gun down. Tucking it under her arm, she headed out to find Ambrose.

"Are you gonna let her shoot that thing?" Jillian looked up at Betsey with round eyes.

"We have no choice. I can shoot it, but we need someone else to know how, too." Betsey gathered Jillian to her and gave her a hug. "We'll be fine. We just need to be prepared." The words came out of her mouth, but her heart didn't really believe them. She needed to cement it in her own heart. Maybe by saying it out loud enough, it would stick. "God will protect us."

Along with dinner, Betsey prepared food that Pa and Ambrose could take with them on their trip. She put Jillian in charge of Ma's care. She wasn't as likely to catch Ma's illness because she'd already had something similar, and almost as severe as what Ma had now.

What Betsey had packed for Pa and Ambose would hold them until they got far enough south to find more food. Also, if need be, other settlers along the way would likely take them in and feed them.

Betsey then thought of those who might also enter the territory. What if the travelers were men? Would it be safe for the women to house men, while there alone? This was yet another scenario Betsey had to consider. It was summertime, though, so the barn loft would be comfortable enough for travelers. Betsey tucked the solution into her barrel of ideas, now overflowing.

Staying busy helped a bit in keeping her anxious thoughts at bay. She needed to be strong for herself, but also as a good example for the girls.

Ma was delirious that day. Betsey could hear her utter nonsensical things. Jillian did her best to answer her, but her responses often didn't match the questions coming out of Ma's mouth. Ma would ask questions about what they'd have for Christmas dinner or why Aaron hadn't come for Betsey's hand in marriage. They all baffled poor Jillian.

Betsey whispered a prayer that Ma would soon be well. They needed her. Betsey longed for her strong mother's admonition and advice. She still couldn't believe she'd be the one handling everything, for now at least. As if to add to her fear, the baby gave her a swift kick, which made her wince a bit. She patted her belly, "I know, I know. Settle down."

If only she could encourage her thoughts to do the same.

Pa and Ambrose were going to leave that afternoon, but with preparing meat for the girls, they'd be getting a late start. During the early evening hours it began to rain, so they decided to wait it out until morning.

Pa sat Betsey down again that night and explained to her what to do if a large animal came onto the property. They'd seen the wolves, coyotes, and deer, but had yet to see a bear edge its way that close to the cabin. He told her how they were all very scared of people, and if it got bad, to keep a fire lit outside and all night, if she could.

Ambrose had done nothing but praise Caroline on her use of the rifle that afternoon. "She's a pretty good shot. I'm thinking she'll be able to hit something as large as a bear if she needs to."

All these discussions added to Betsey's fears. So much could happen. So many bad scenarios could unfold. As Betsey lay down that night, she imagined even more.

She was exhausted. She hadn't slept well the night before, but tonight, she could only do one thing to help her close her eyes and go to sleep: pray that Aaron would return to the cabin soon.

Pa had told her that he and Aaron talked about the property on the ridge before he'd left. In part of their conversation that night, Betsey had brought up Aaron and his intent to purchase their property as well.

Pa then told her, "You and Aaron can have the ridge property. I can't grow any crops there and it will keep you close. I'm going to purchase that section too, while I'm in Jackson, too. For you and Aaron."

Oh, how she wished she were there now, in the new house, with a baby in her arms. By that time, Aaron would have returned as well as Pa and Ambrose. For without a doubt, Pa wasn't going to change his mind. Ambrose and he would be leaving in the morning.

The next morning, Ambrose did the morning chores while Pa fastened the yoke on the oxen, which would then be hitched to the wagon now standing in front of the barn. Betsey and Caroline made extra for breakfast, so Pa and Ambrose could have leftovers for their next few meals.

As she placed the food under the wagon seat, Betsey's heart felt like it could beat right out of her chest. Perspiration dripped off her forehead and she had to keep wiping it with her apron. Her skirt had been getting tighter and tighter, and this morning she realized she needed to sew another button to widen her skirt to fit more loosely around her bulging midsection. *When would she have time for such a simple, yet time-consuming, task?* She sighed.

Pa kissed her cheek and Ambrose hugged her. "We'll be back as soon as we can. Keep letting Alexander sleep in the barn. He's fine out there and can keep an eye on things until we return."

Betsey pulled a small bottle out of her pocket and handed it to Pa, "We need more quinine, Pa. Can you get us more?"

Caroline stepped up to Pa and handed him what looked like a letter. "Pa, would you mail this for me?"

"I'm not sure, Caroline, that we'll find a place to do this. But if we do, I'll try."

Caroline kissed his cheek. "Thanks, Pa."

Her pa nodded. He bent over the reins a moment and prayed for their trip, as well as the safekeeping of Betsey, Ma, Alexander, and the girls. "Oh Lord. We beg for your protection, as we venture south to acquire our land. May you grant us safety as we travel, but more importantly, grant Betsey and the womenfolk protection from harm. Keep Betsey strong and able to do the work. Give Sally healing and restored health. We ask you in Christ's beloved name."

The whole family added their own *amens* to Pa's requests to God.

"Be good." Pa gave her a wink, and urged the oxen to move, with a stern command. Betsey, Caroline, and Etta waved as they watched the forest south of the cabin swallow the oxen, men, and wagon. Alexander seemed lost as he watched Pa go off into the woods without him. He came back to stand beside Betsey. He was small, but he seemed to know that he was now the only male left.

Standing tall, he looked up at Betsey as if to tell her he was there if she needed him.

Hosea's heart grew heavy. *Was he doing the right thing leaving Sally and his girls alone like this?* He hadn't slept a wink all night and his head hurt. Sally's words had cut deep into his heart, but he still knew they needed to purchase the property sooner than later.

"Who's Caroline's letter to?" Ambrose snapped the reins to push the oxen to move faster.

Hosea glanced down at the scribbles on the makeshift envelope Caroline had glued shut at the edges. "It's for Billie."

Ambrose grinned. "Why didn't you tell her that it would cost twenty-five cents for a stamp?"

Hosea looked up at the trees now surrounding them on all sides. "I couldn't. I just couldn't disappoint another one of my girls today."

CHAPTER TWENTY

That night, Betsey could feel Caroline shivering next to her in bed. It was too hot for that. They only had a thin blanket over them, to ward off the mosquitoes threatening their sound sleep. They'd continued to use the ointment Nibi had brought to them, but it was running low. Somehow the smell had grown tolerable since everyone was using it. Betsey reached over and pressed her hand to Caroline's back. It felt cool. Caroline rolled over in her direction.

"Are you sick?" Betsey asked her in a whisper. The darkness of the cabin helped a little, in keeping the mosquitoes at bay.

"No. Just feeling awful alone in the cabin tonight."

Betsey pulled her little sister closer to her. For being almost sixteen, she was tiny and small. "We'll be okay."

Caroline sighed. "What if something happens to Ma? What if Pa never comes back? What if—"

Before Caroline could add another thought that hadn't already gone through Betsey's fretful imagination, she stopped her. "Caroline. God will care for us. We're not alone. He is here with us." She hoped Caroline didn't hear fear in her statements.

Caroline pulled Betsey's arm over her shoulder and cuddled closer.

To ease the fear now assailing them both, Betsey knew she needed to be more convincing. "And now that you know how to shoot a rifle, we'll be fine."

Betsey began to giggle. It was small. A tiny laugh. But soon they couldn't help themselves.

"The rifle is longer than I am," Caroline snorted, and then they laughed even harder.

"What's so funny?" Etta called out from the floor, near the end of their bed. She'd moved her bed there because Jillian was sleeping beside their mother.

Betsey called out to Etta. "Caroline shooting a rifle. Can you believe she can do that?"

"Did it kick when you shot it?" Etta asked.

"Felt like that ole mule, Gus."

The girls laughed even harder. Their neighbor back in Pennsylvania was always coming to Pa and complaining about Gus, the stubborn ass he owned.

This made all the girls laugh even harder.

Once they calmed down, Etta called out, "We are going to be fine, aren't we Betsey?"

With as much courage as Betsey could muster, she told her younger sister, "Of course we'll be. Someday, you'll be able to tell your children and your grandchildren about what we experienced out here in Michigan Territory. Let's make Pa proud of us."

They all agreed that it was a good idea, and with that, remarkably, they all fell fast asleep. As Betsey listened to the others' soft snoring, she knew the only thing to do was to join them. Tonight anyway, exhaustion and laughter were a great cure for her insomnia.

The next morning the sun brightened the cabin walls before any of the girls stirred. They didn't have any men to feed, just themselves, so they'd allowed themselves to sleep in a bit. If Jillian had been up most of the night with Ma, no one had heard her. She now slept soundly at the foot of Ma's bed.

Betsey got up and slipped into her clothes. It took her three tries to get her skirt to button around her waist. If only she had time to move that one button. After getting dressed, she went to check on Ma, who felt warm, but was sound asleep.

She got herself washed up and started for the outhouse. She also wanted to check on the barn before she started breakfast.

A rising, blazing-red sun illuminated the eastern clouds causing them to appear on fire. Betsey remembered the familiar warning Pa often quoted when he'd see such a morning sky, *Red sky in morning, heed the warning; red sky at night, sailor's delight.* The sky forecast was seldom wrong.

Out at the barn she checked on Alexander, who was putting fresh slough grass in the stalls where the oxen used to be housed. Pa had given him daily chores to do. She smiled at him, and he waved to her.

As she came up the path back toward the cabin, she watched Caroline emerge with a bucket. They used water from the river to wash dishes and their hands throughout the day. After filling up a few buckets for that purpose, Caroline set out for the spring for their drinking water. She called out a greeting to Betsey as she made her way back into the cabin.

Jillian was washing up, using water from the first bucket Caroline had brought in. "This water isn't much cooler than how I feel." The recent warm days now made for murky, lukewarm water, even in the deeper parts of the river. "Can we start using the spring water to bathe in now?" Betsey knew Jillian was testing her authority. Pa never allowed them to use the good water to bathe, unless it was Saturday night.

"No, the river water will do just fine for a daily sponge bath. Keep the cool, spring water for Ma. She needs it to keep her fever down." Betsey said this in the best scolding voice she could muster.

Jillian stomped off. "I don't know why I have to be the one to keep taking care of Ma. Can't Etta take a turn?"

Betsey realized Etta was still sound asleep at the end of her bed. She went over and nudged her with her foot, "Estelle, get up. It's way past sunrise."

Etta muttered a response, but just rolled over and went back to sleep.

In Pa's absence, her two youngest sisters challenged Betsey's authority, which tried her patience. "Okay Etta," Betsey put her hands on her hips. "Get up and ready. Now."

Etta did move then. Sitting up, she stretched, and then folded her blanket to store under Betsey's bed.

"We've slept way too late. We have much to do." Betsey took a wet rag and began wiping off the table. She'd done it the night before, but mosquitoes and other insects always found ways inside, and swarmed the places where even just a speck of food had been left over from a meal.

Jillian motioned for Betsey. "Come check Ma."

Betsey dropped her rag right where she'd left off and went to Ma's bed. "Is her fever higher?"

Jillian nodded. "I think so. What do you think?"

Before Betsey could feel her mother's forehead, the door swung open. Caroline came into the cabin in a flurry, water spilling from her half-filled bucket, with a look of fear in her eyes. She slammed the door shut and then put the wooden latch in place, which was usually only done at night.

"What?" Betsey turned to see her sister's eyes. "Caroline, what's wrong?"

"Indians."

Betsey couldn't move. All she could do was ask with a stutter, "What, what—what Indians?"

"By the edge of the woods. Two men and a woman. They were watching me as I got water."

"Did they come after you?" Betsey felt the flush of fear start at her toes and rise to her face. "Did they talk to you?"

"No."

"Is it the same woman we've seen by the edge of the woods before?"

"I don't know. The woman who brought us Alexander? I don't know, I've only seen her once."

"Don't you remember what she looked like?" Betsey whispered. "But she's usually alone."

Someone tugged on the door, startling them all.

Jillian covered her mouth with her hand and mumbled, "What are we going to do?"

Betsey took a deep breath, even though she wanted to run for a bucket to vomit. "Pa told us not to ignore them. Remember?" She exhaled. She wanted to brace the door with the table, but thought nothing would hold back an Indian, intent on getting into the cabin.

Caroline shook her head, her eyes wide. "We can't let them in."

The girls heard Ma's bed squeak. In a whispered voice, Ma spoke, "Let them in. We will not bar the door just because your pa is not home." She reached for a blanket and wrapped herself up. "Feed them."

Caroline nodded, pushed Betsey aside, and opened the door.

Fear of the three natives standing at the door nearly made Betsey run to a nearby bucket. Their scent was much more intense than Nibi's mosquito ointment that they'd been using. She couldn't swallow, let alone talk.

Carloline stepped forward. "What do you want?"

The two male Indians pushed past the female Indian standing between them. They glanced around the cabin.

Betsey pulled her younger sisters closer to her and they stood on the hearth of the cold fireplace.

The two Indians mumbled something and looked around the room. As they did, Alexander came into the cabin and up behind the woman. He must have heard or seen them approach the cabin. As Betsey watched the men rummage through their food, Alexander came around the woman, as quiet as a fawn in the forest. When he did, the woman bent down and hugged him.

She, in fact, was the same woman they'd seen at the edge of the woods since Alexander had come to live with them. Alexander hugged her, and she patted his head. She mumbled a few Indian words to him.

Suddenly, the woman stood erect and uttered what seemed to be an order to the men rummaging through the flour bin with just their hands. They answered her with sharp, commanding words.

Alexander stood in front of them, and for the first time since he'd joined their home, he began to communicate to the men with hand motions. The men came toward him, shoved him aside, and walked out the door.

Ma, having managed to get out of bed, came and took Alexander by the hand, as she tightened the blanket around her shoulders with her free hand.

The woman looked back at Alexander with a smile and left with the men, following behind them, disappearing into the woods.

They had only taken a loaf of bread and a few handfuls of berries.

"Alexander, what did you do?" Jillian came up to him, kneeling down to his level.

Alexander smiled at Jillian and then up at Ma. Standing tall and with his chin held high, he seemed satisfied with himself.

"Whatever Alexander did, it worked." Caroline wiped the sweat off her forehead and went over to the hearth. She got the rifle down and started to load it. "I think we should keep this loaded. We need it ready to shoot."

Alexander went to Caroline and took the rifle out of her hands.

"Alexander, don't do that," Caroline scolded, but Ma stopped her.

"Caroline. Let it be. Seems to me that Alexander doesn't think it's necessary. Whatever he said to the men, they listened to him. Now can someone get some breakfast going? I'm hungry." With that comment, Ma limped back to her bed and crawled beneath the covers again.

"I wish he could talk," Etta said as the small boy picked up some plates and began setting the table.

"Me, too. I'm certain now that woman used to be someone very special to him." Caroline placed the rifle back over the hearth. "Perhaps she was trying to protect all of us, too."

251

Betsey still couldn't move. In fact, she felt a trickle of urine run down her leg. Thankfully, she was able to control the rest before she emptied her whole bladder. The last time she'd been this afraid was on the journey here. Her body trembled in fear. Caroline noticed and urged her to sit down.

"Betsey! It's okay. We're all fine."

As Betsey lowered herself onto a chair she pointed to the door, "Latch the door, Caroline."

Before Caroline could do it, Etta did.

How in the world would she be able to take care of her younger sisters and Ma with such fear in her heart?

It took courage for everyone to leave the cabin that afternoon. Caroline was the first to head outside, and seeing nothing threatening, urged her sisters to do the same.

As the girls worked on making candles that afternoon, Jillian brought up the subject of Alexander's communication with the Indians. "I wonder why he won't talk to us, even just with hand motions."

"Perhaps he doesn't believe we will understand him." Caroline hung up the last of the candles they'd made.

Etta gathered up the candle-making supplies, putting them away in a nearby barrel. Out of the blue, Etta said. "I wish we had a pig.

Betsey sometimes wondered how Etta's young mind worked.

"Wouldn't bacon or some pork chops taste good for dinner?"

Everyone nodded.

Betsey knew she needed to stop fretting about the Indians. Yet whenever she tried to walk out of the cabin, fear constricted her heart. The closed cabin was stifling and her ma needed more air circulation. When she finally got the courage to walk outside to check the fire, not a leaf on a nearby tree moved. She propped open the door again.

The sun was relentless. Since the heat of the summer had started, a fire had been set up on a pit just outside the door, but having to keep that fueled with logs was tiresome. A shift in the wind or dampness would threaten to put it out almost every day. If it wasn't their only means of cooking, Betsey would have given up on the fire immediately after Pa left. They could cook again on the fireplace, except now a fire there would make the cabin stifling hot.

But the outside fire wasn't just for cooking. They used it to light candles as well as a lantern and as Pa had told her, it could ward off more vicious animals like bears and wolves. If they didn't keep this fire lit, they'd have to create a new fire and that was harder than just fueling it to keep it going.

As she moved past the fire to the door of the cabin, a small breeze shifted the smoke of the fire in the opposite direction. It was so abrupt, the only way she knew it had happened was from the redirection of the smoke. Looking up and toward the woods, she heard a faraway rumble of thunder.

Heading into the cabin, she set a log down at Caroline's feet. "Looks like we might be getting a storm this afternoon. Better start a fire inside."

Everyone sighed. They'd had rain before, but seldom did thunder accompany the rain.

Within a few minutes, the approaching thunder grew louder.

Betsey had gone to Ma to check on her. Since morning, her fever had spiked and Jillian was doing her best to keep her head cool with a damp cloth. She put some water in a spoon and raised her ma's head, so she could sip it. "This will make you feel better, Ma."

Her ma swallowed and then whispered in a raspy voice, "I wish it was colder."

As they prepared supper, the thunder grew worse, often shaking the ground.

Betsey went outside to check the sky as she'd seen Pa and Ambrose do a dozen times. It was hard, among the tall trees, to catch a glimpse of any storm approaching. The only indication was the forest behind the cabin grew even darker, the sun hidden behind purplish thunderclouds. The mosquitoes were thicker than ever and not a blade of grass twitched. The air was still. She scanned the edge of the woods again for any sign of the Indians.

Coming back into the cabin, she placed the fish left over from the day before on the table, with some bread and a few peas from the garden. Everyone was in agreement, the fresh peas from the garden tasted as sweet as candy, when they'd eaten them the night before.

As they sat down, the whole cabin rumbled from the thunder. Betsey was the oldest at the table, so praying now was up to her. She prayed for a cool breeze, for the men's safety as well as their own, and thanked the Lord for the food. As they began to eat, Jillian attempted to show Alexander hand motions that might help him communicate with them.

She placed a spoon in front of him. Pointing to it, she said, "Hungry," then pretended to bring it to her mouth.

Alexander just smiled.

He nodded and put more food into his mouth.

Jillian sighed. "Do you think he'll understand soon?"

"I don't know," Betsey had more things to worry about than communicating with Alexander.

Thunder rolled loudly in the distance. A breeze stirred the fire to life outside.

Someone said, "Oh, did you feel that?"

Each one nodded. The still air that had surrounded them all day was replaced by a cool breeze that circulated into the cabin through the open door.

Betsey could hear the leaves on the trees outside begin to stir. "I think we're going to get some relief." She stood up and went to the door to look out at the sky again. This time she could see what was coming and rushed back into the house. "Alexander, are the doors closed on the barn?"

Alexander smiled back at her and continued to eat.

"I'll go see," Caroline said, and she stood up to go out. As soon as she did, the wind caught the front door and slammed it shut. A large rumble of thunder shook the ground beneath them.

"Hurry," Betsey said, as Caroline headed out into the evening to check on the barn doors. She left the door open for now; they needed a little light to fetch candles and to get them burning. Angry, dark clouds had taken over the sky.

Everyone began picking up their dishes from the table. As they did, they heard the barn doors slam, followed by silence.

Just as they were placing dishes into the wash pan, they heard Caroline yelling to them from outside.

Betsey wiped her hands on her apron and headed for the door. As she got closer, she felt a cooler-than-normal wall of air slam into her from outside. Turning and holding onto the outside logs of the cabin, she edged her way to the corner, and found Caroline fighting with all she had to get to the door and back inside. A bright streak of lightning lit up the sky. A bolt of lightning struck the forest, just past the barn. The thunder that followed made Betsey and Caroline cover their ears, and scream.

"Hurry, Caroline!"

Caroline did her best to push through the strong wind that now blew her apron up over her face. Yanking it down so she could see, she stumbled, and Betsey realized Caroline wasn't going to make it back to the cabin without help.

Betsey screamed back toward the cabin, "Shut the door and get under the beds!" She wasn't sure anyone heard her, but she shouted again, "Take cover!"

Then she did what any sister would do for another—she headed in the direction of the barn to help her sister get back to the cabin. Fighting the wind took all she had. Leaves and small branches were whirling all around them. One hit Caroline in the head. She winced and held her hand to her face.

Betsey finally made it to her, and together they fought their way back to the cabin. Another bolt of lightning lit the sky. By this time, the wind was strong enough that Betsey watched a small piece of the roof begin to peel off like a scrap from a potato. Larger branches hit the top of the cabin as the women neared the front and rushed into the small shelter. Betsey then realized they needed more protection in case the branches crashed through the roof.

"Get under the bed!" Betsey maneuvered Caroline toward the others as she looked up to see a small section of the roof blow off. *Were they going to die?* Betsey joined the others.

They'd feared the Indians and being alone, but this scenario hadn't even entered Betsey's mind. As the wind swirled and howled around outside, peals of thunder shook the ground underneath them, Betsey thought of Aaron. She crouched as close as she could get to Alexander, and wrapped her arms around him. He didn't seem as frightened, but he obliged, and then stared at them with his deep, dark eyes, the whites of which were all they could see in the darkness around them.

Betsey had gotten the door shut, but not latched. The wind kept opening and slamming it shut with each gust. They shook with fear as they heard a loud groan, followed by splintering wood, and then the sound of a large tree crashing to the ground.

As fast as the intense storm had come, it left. The door squeaked open and stopped slamming. All that was left was distant thunder and heavy rain. As refreshing as it sounded hitting the ground, water now streamed through small openings in the roof, left behind after the wind had torn away strips of bark. Betsey hollered for Caroline and Etta to get the buckets by the door.

They obeyed and placed the buckets under the water now pouring through the holes in the roof. The wind had stopped, but the rain fell in sheets as they gazed out the now open door.

Jillian was helping Ma up and out from under the bed. As she sat on the edge, water began to drip just above her. She hollered for Jillian to empty the dish pan and set it beside her on the bed.

She wrapped her blanket tighter, as the cabin began to cool off almost as quickly as the storm had come in.

The buckets filled up quickly. Betsey knew if they didn't dump them outside, they'd have a huge mess inside. Despite their attempts, the floor of the small cabin grew wet.

Jillian broke the silence of the moment, "If today would have been floor-washing day, it would have made a great rinse."

Looking around at each one huddled around the table, the women began to chuckle. Their giggles seemed odd due to their predicament, but if they didn't make light of it, they'd probably all resort to sobbing. The area they were in was the only part of the room that didn't have water dripping on it from above.

Soon the rains subsided. Betsey made her way to the door and saw that the latch on the door had been ripped off. Once outside, Betsey couldn't believe what she saw.

Everywhere she looked, large and small branches covered the ground, as well as leaves of all shapes and sizes. The river roared to life, as the rain had caused it to overflow its banks. A huge branch had fallen into the stream, rushing water parting around it. The barn roof had been stripped clean and one side wall had completely collapsed.

Moving closer for a better look, Betsey saw that a large tree had fallen just a few feet past the barn and the trunk, complete with branches, now consumed the fresh pea plants. The plants were smothered and already starting to wilt from the heavy rain.

Looking over Pa's crops, she could see that the corn had been completely flattened to the ground. Several stalks were a twisted mess. Betsey wondered if anything was salvageable.

"What just happened?" Caroline now stood beside her, seeming to take in her own view of the property damage. Jillian crept close to Betsey's side.

"I don't know; I've never seen such a wind."

Jillian's eyes grew wide. "I wish Pa were here."

Betsey nodded and began picking up a few of the larger branches as she headed back toward the cabin. Caroline did the same, but they soon realized it would take much longer than a few minutes to clean up.

Ma came stumbling out of the cabin to see the barn roof, and when she saw the damage, she collapsed. The girls rushed to her side as she mumbled, "Oh no. What are we going to do?"

Betsey and Caroline helped her up and back into the cabin. They dumped all the buckets, and Etta and Jillian began wiping the floor.

They pulled their ticks and mats to the center of the room just as the evening light began to grow dim.

"I'm so glad Pa and Aaron have the oxen. They probably would have died in the barn," Caroline said, as they did their best to make the room livable again.

"Well we can't do much more of anything tonight. Let's get Ma warm. Tomorrow we'll get out and see what we can do for the crops and buildings, and clean up the clearing," Betsey announced, as she pushed her bed tick to the center of the room, near Ma's.

What would they do now? It had been just twenty-four hours since Pa and Ambrose had left, and this disaster wasn't anything like what Betsey had imagined she'd have to endure while being alone and in charge. She made Alexander a small bed and got a fire lit again, even though it was difficult due to nothing but wet wood. The temperature had dropped significantly, everyone shivered in the cold. She sent Etta out for some wood and for the first time since they'd arrived, they started a fire with flint and a stone.

As she lay in bed that night, listening to the wolves howl in the forest beyond their cabin, she began to cry. *What now? What else could go wrong? How would they ever repair a roof?* Pa hadn't anticipated them needing to do such a thing, and had not told them how they could fix it. She couldn't get up on the roof in her condition. Neither could Ma. How would they ever be able to keep going without a roof over their heads?

Everything was wet. Mosquitoes buzzed in their ears all night. They used almost all of the Indian's stinking lotion to get through the night.

Betsey kept getting up and checking the door, which they'd barred shut with the table, to keep it from opening. Sleep eluded her and she prayed like she'd never prayed before for strength, courage, and answers as to how to keep the cabin safe and sound again. Even her fear of the Indians paled in comparison to what they'd experienced on this day.

The baby seemed to sense this, because she felt three good, sharp kicks causing her to cry that much harder.

Day After the Storm

CHAPTER TWENTY-ONE

They awoke to a cool, fresh morning. The sun shown through the holes in the roof, waking them early. Betsey had slept fitfully. *Would she ever get a full night's sleep without the men home?* Everyone roused, sitting up on their mattresses, looking at each other on bedding merged together to form one, large bed.

"Get up, girls," Betsey said as she twisted her tangled hair into a bun for the day. "We've got a long, busy day ahead."

Caroline had started a fresh fire outside and that's where they decided to eat their breakfast. It was warmer and less damp there. Hard biscuits with jam, was the morning's bounty.

"Caroline and Etta, you start picking up branches. Bring them to that side." Betsey pointed to the northern section. "Pa can split them when he returns."

They worked all morning, dragging various sizes of tree branches and heavy limbs to the north side of the property. After dinner, they'd tackle the garden to try to fix as much as possible around the fallen tree. The large trunk of the tree would have to wait until Pa or Aaron returned. It was too heavy for any of them to lift.

Jillian and Betsey began picking up branches around the barn. Betsey kept glancing at the barn, trying to make a plan. What could they do? The house was more important, but none of them knew how to patch or fix a roof.

Before rising that morning, Betsey had told God her problems, even though she was confident He knew them already. She asked for help in deciding what they could do to fix them. The barn could wait, but the cabin's roof was another thing. They needed to fix it before the weather turned rainy again. Sleepless nights stretched before her if they didn't secure it against the wolves or even the woodland creatures around the farm. She shook herself from her nightmare stupor.

Betsey watched Alexander gathering the necessary bark strips for the roof. He piled what he found near the cabin. "Alexander, what are you doing? I can't fix the roof. I don't know how."

Alexander just looked up for a bit and nodded at Betsey.

"What is he doing?" Caroline asked, as she watched the little lad head off into the woods. "Where is he going?"

After an hour later, Alexander returned, carrying an armful of bark strips.

"He has been working with Aaron. Perhaps he knows a way to repair the roof. But it scares me to think of him up there by himself." Betsey patted his back as he dropped his load. She pointed to the roof. "Fix?"

Alexander took off again.

"Let him go," Betsey told the girls. "Perhaps he has a plan that we aren't understanding."

They were hungry by midday, frustrated into the afternoon, and exhausted by evening. Just as they were ready to sit down for supper, they heard the soft rumble of a wagon making its way toward them, through the backwoods. Betsey stood up from the table and headed outside to look. Could it be Aaron back from getting the lumber for their house? Rounding the front corner of the cabin, she shielded her eyes from the sun. She saw a wagon, but it wasn't their oxen.

"Who is it, Betsey?" Caroline called out to her. "And come back and shut the door, the mosquitoes will eat our food before we get the chance."

Betsey swatted one on her neck. "I'm not sure, but it's someone we know. They're waving at me."

Betsey walked towards the wagon, which approached their property from the southwest. She then recognized their neighbors.

Claire called to her from the wagon's bench. "Betsey!" Waving, she shouted, "Are you all okay?"

"We're all fine!" Betsey yelled back. "We have a mess to clean up, but we're all well." Her sisters now joined her.

As the wagon drew close, Henry hollered to her, "Praise God! We've been so worried about you." Henry pulled back on the oxen team, stopping them as they grunted and snorted in protest. "Looks like your barn got hit pretty bad."

Betsey nodded. "Parts of the cabin roof are gone. Strips of elm bark are missing."

Henry jumped off the wagon. Claire held a basket out to him before she climbed down. "We have some food for your supper. Henry brought his tools. He can get up and fix the roof."

Relief filled Betsey's soul. How wonderful it was to have gracious, caring neighbors.

Henry was soon on the roof, patching it as best he could. Alexander was right there to help, handing him the necessary materials.

Claire began telling them about their property damage. "We knew you might have had it worse. Those winds shifted right in this direction. I'm so happy you are all well. We would have been here sooner, but there were too many logs in the road on our way here."

The noise of hammering and repairs made Betsey's heart soar. Just thinking of having a safe roof, for the night, made her count her blessings. She smiled at Alexander, who stood at the top of the ladder passing the gathered strips of bark to Henry. It was as if the child knew exactly how many to remedy the damage. God had sent him as a trusty helper.

As Henry viewed the crops, he shook his head. "I think the corn will be fine. It usually does this in a storm, but it can pop back up after a few good days of sunshine. It will still produce, but I think you lost about a third of the stalks when the tree fell. But the peas...that's one big tree."

Betsey nodded. "We'll get the potatoes mounded again. The peas were just now coming up, and it will be sad to not have any stored for winter."

"But praise God you're all safe. We worried for your lives." Henry patted Betsey's shoulder.

She acknowledged the sentiment with an *"amen."*

Jillian played with the Leach children while they finished eating that night.

It was growing dark outside when Henry finally hammered the last pieces of bark in place. "Thankfully, Alexander gathered every bit of strips needed. He's a handy fellow to have around." He tousled the hair of the boy standing next to him.

"I'm sure Pa will repay you when he returns."

Henry put up his hand in protest. "All is well. God provides."

"Thank you so much for coming so quickly."

"We were worried," Claire noted. "Staying away wasn't an option. I am worried about your ma. She seems awful feverish today."

Alexander scooted closer to Betsey, but seemed to be listening closely to the conversation.

"If you need anything more. Send Alexander. But we need to head home before dark."

Betsey nodded. She wished they didn't have to leave so soon, but knew it was selfish on her part to keep them away from their own home and chores.

"Let me take a look at that door and then we'll be on our way." Henry looked at the door quickly and hammered a bit of strap on it to repair it. "This should hold until your pa or Aaron returns."

"Are you sure you'd not rather spend the night?" Caroline asked.

"We've plenty of lantern light to make it home. I think your space inside is still damp. Get a fire going and that should help with drying out the inside of the cabin more," Henry advised them.

"Again, Henry, Claire...we appreciate your kindness." Betsey couldn't help but repeat her thanks over and over again.

Henry tipped his hat and motioned for Claire and the children to climb into the wagon. "Sorry about your barn, but it needs more than just one man to fix it. When your men return, they'll be able to fix that, too. Hopefully before winter comes."

Betsey nodded. Again she was grateful that the oxen were out of the barn and with the men.

As darkness fell over the small cabin in the woods, Betsey felt so relieved that their neighbors had come out to check on them. She relaxed in the better protected cabin, as wolves howled in the distance. The cabin was warm and dry, with a small fire burning off the dampness.

They'd been able to clean up most of the branches. Only large tree trunks remained.

Jillian came into the main room from checking on Ma. "Betsey, Ma seems to be spiking a fever again. She's shivering."

Betsey went to her mother's bedside.

Caroline and Betsey sat beside their ma's bed almost the entire night. Her body shook with tremors. The meager blanket covering her was damp with sweat, and she was delirious as the disease ravaged her body. Ma kept mumbling something to Pa. It was as if she were talking to him and he wasn't listening. She grew agitated and upset.

Several times Caroline tried her best to calm her by telling her Pa wasn't there, but her effort deemed futile.

Ma was convinced he was in the bed with her and he wasn't paying any attention. Slapping the bed beside her, she kept shaking her head in frustration.

"Why won't she listen to me?" Caroline's voice quivered as she again told Ma that Pa wasn't home.

"She's delirious. She doesn't know what she's saying." Betsey wiped off her ma's forehead and then her arms. They did their best to spoon water into her mouth. Betsey wished she had medicine for her. The damp cabin, after the storm, didn't help Ma's condition.

Alexander watched from the end of Ma's bed the next morning. He loved Ma and kept touching the blanket covering her feet. Picking up the empty bottle of medicine, he ran out the door. Etta tried to chase after him, calling out his name.

"Where is he going?"

Etta came back to the bedside. "I don't know where he went. He disappeared into the woods."

Betsey shook her head. "I can't take the time to chase after him."

At least one of Betsey's sisters stood by their ma's bed continuously throughout the day. By evening, her fever was high again.

"Do you want me to take the rifle and go look for Alexander?" Caroline asked, as she finished up the last of the dishes.

"He seems adept in the woods. He'll return. I need you here." Betsey got up from the table and went to stand in the doorway. "Where could that boy have gone?" What would she do if he didn't come back? Sending anyone out alone in the woods to find him was too dangerous.

Ma moaned from her bed.

"I think she's getting hotter," Jillian called to them from her bedside.

Now what could they do? Betsey sighed, folded her arms and leaned on the table. Just as she did, the door to the cabin flung open. Alexander came in. He held out something to her. It was a medicine bottle, just half-full.

Betsey pulled off the cork of the medicine bottle, putting her finger over the opening. She allowed a drop of it to moisten her finger, then touched the liquid to the tip of her tongue. It was quinine.

Caroline pulled Alexander to her. "Where did you get this medicine?"

The little boy just smiled at her and pointed to Ma.

Jillian stood close to Ma, holding her hand. "Where did he get that?"

Alexander left the cabin again. The girls knew it was useless to follow him, or even try to guess where he might be going.

Betsey went to the bedside and watched Caroline give their ma the medicine. Ma lay shivering in bed. Her nightgown was damp and clung to her frail body, the outline of which was easily seen through it. Her feet bare.

Soon Alexander came back into the cabin and added more wood to the fire. As the room grew warmer, he took his blanket from its hook on the wall, lay down in front of the hearth, and soon fell fast asleep.

Betsey watched hour after hour go by as they attended to Ma's needs. The night wore on. She and her sisters were now having a hard time keeping their eyes open, and not falling asleep. Betsey told each one to head to bed. She'd stay up with Ma, despite needing sleep herself. Last night's lack of sleep and the day's work had exhausted her. She sat in a chair she'd placed by Ma's bed, trying hard to stay alert and awake.

Soon her ma grew more peaceful, and stopped shivering. It seemed that the medicine was starting to work. Pulling the blanket back over Ma, Betsey sat back down beside in the chair. Soon, though, her efforts to stay awake failed.

The next morning, Betsey stirred awake to find the girls in the kitchen. Each tiptoed around the room as they seemed to be preparing breakfast as quietly as they could. Betsey's bladder was about to burst, so she took a quick peek at her ma, who was still sleeping soundly.

Rising up from the chair, she heard Jillian comment about Alexander and the medicine. "I wonder where he found it."

Caroline shrugged. "Maybe we'll never know."

After the last few harrowing days, Betsey wasn't sure what this day would bring. She hoped and prayed her ma was over the worst of the fever illness.

She meandered outside into the warmth of a beautiful morning. Sleeping all night in a chair had caused for stiff joints, as

Betsey pressed into her back with her fingers, massaging the ache there. She moved slow, probably as a result of the previous day's chores.

The sun was rising and adorning their little piece of land with light. As Betsey made her way to the outhouse, a small fawn, still with spots, darted between the garden and the cabin. A doe stood to the far side of the woods watching it. Betsey smiled at the scene.

When she got back to the cabin, the girls had breakfast ready and on the table. They pointed to Ma's bed and Betsey saw Ma propped up on pillows, smiling at her. "Good morning."

Betsey rushed to her ma's bed.

"Have I been sick for awhile?"

Betsey nodded. "Yes, but look—you're sitting up! Are you feeling better?"

"I think I will feel much better once I get some of that food."

Ma hadn't eaten in days. Betsey retrieved a biscuit from a plate on the table and spread fresh strawberry preserves over it. Bringing it back to Ma, she also handed her a cup of water. "Can you drink this first?"

Ma nodded, took the cup, and drank down a deep, long swallow. She smiled and nodded. "I don't know what you did Betsey, but I believe the worst has passed. I don't think I can get out of bed or stand yet, but my stomach has stopped twisting like I was on a boat."

Betsey told her about Alexander.

Ma listened. "What did you give me?"

"I think it's quinine. It's what it tasted like."

Ma took another lengthy sip of water.

"Where do you think Alexander went?"

Alexander recognized his name, and when Ma said it, he scooted out of his chair and came to her bedside. Ma patted his hand and he went back to his chair.

"This child has done nothing but bless us since his arrival."

Betsey told her ma about how he worked so hard gathering the necessary roof strips before Henry arrived to help.

Gazing at the little boy now gulping down his breakfast pancakes, Betsey realized they might have given this small child a warm home, food to eat, and a new name, but he was providing them with much more. She saw explicitly God's hand at work in providing for their every need, in part and through the actions of a boy who couldn't speak.

CHAPTER TWENTY-TWO

A few days later, Ma rose from her bed and began helping with the chores. She didn't remember much of what happened after the storm, but she hadn't forgotten that Pa had left them all alone to go to Jackson to purchase the land.

"One night you grumbled to Pa about all kinds of things," Betsey told her one afternoon while they were busy canning a few of the beans now ripening on the vines.

"I did what?" Ma stopped in mid-snap to gaze at Betsey oddly. "Oh dear, what did I say?"

"It isn't important, but you were mighty upset with him."

Ma grew quiet.

"Well, if nothing else, I realized how much of your feelings about Pa you keep hidden. If you were to really share with us how often you must get perturbed with him—" Betsey passed a few more beans to her mother, who had stopped snapping them.

Her eyes squeezed tightly shut, but a single tear slid down her cheek.

"Oh Betsey, I hope I didn't..."

Betsey dropped the beans she'd been handing to her ma back into her own bowl. "Ma, it's fine. None of us took it to heart. Most of it didn't make all that much sense anyway. But you were in one scolding mood."

Ma shuddered. "Betsey I'm so sorry you had to see that side of me."

Betsey didn't understand why, but her ma stood up, placed her bowl on her chair, and walked outside.

Betsey followed her.

Her ma stood away from the cabin, gazing out over the river, now back to normal after the storm.

Betsey approached her quietly. She could hear her crying, even with her handkerchief over her face. Betsey wrapped her arm around her. "Ma, what's wrong? What did I say to upset you?"

Ma blew her nose into her handkerchief. "I've been such a fool."

Betsey squeezed her shoulders. "How? What do you mean?"

"Let's go down by the river. I don't want the girls to hear."

As they neared the river, her ma turned toward her. "Betsey, I've had to repent several times lately. Mostly," Ma sighed, "I've needed to come to grips with how I've treated your pa, but also about my attitude. I've been harboring horrible bitterness in my heart against him."

Betsey folded her arms, questioning her ma's confession.

"I didn't want to come here. I felt your pa was on another one of his wild adventures." Ma wiped her face with her handkerchief. "And now, not only had he dragged me and your sisters into it, but you and Aaron as well. I felt he'd made a selfish decision, to leave Pennsylvania and come here. Ambrose wanted to come. It was time for him to leave us and set out on his own. But Hosea? Why? And why in such a hurry? I've been angry at him since we left Pennsylvania."

So that was it. Pa had sensed it and that's what he was asking Betsey to tell him, if she knew.

"I've not only been bitter against your pa, but I believe I've made things miserable for everyone with my actions. God had to get my attention with the fever and I believe He did. I know now that my behavior not only hurt your pa, but poisoned everyone I love the most in this world. I'd begun to see it when I met Claire. She had gone through so much to get here. When they came to us, they were cold, and so hungry. We didn't go through nearly as much as she and Henry did trying to move here, yet she was happy and thankful they were all together, and excited to begin a new adventure." Ma blew her nose again. "I'm not sure if it's my age, or just the phase of life God is putting me through right now, but I didn't want any part of this moving business. I'd forgotten one important thing, though."

Betsey listened as best as she could, but having her ma confess to her was something she'd never had to experience before.

"Your pa and his faith. His trust in God's ways has always been so much stronger than mine. The God he worships is a big God who will do not only what He promises, but will also guide us even through the worst of trouble. He truly believes God is with us in, and through, everything. So much so, that it often seems like your pa doesn't care about others in the process. But after thirty-seven years with him, I know that isn't true." Ma became more emotional, the tears flowing down her face.

"Betsey, please forgive me for my bitterness and how you and the girls have had to put up with me all these months. I know now this is where God has, and wants us. He's still with us in this new, seemingly forsaken land, and He's still taking such good care of us. Your pa is right. This is where we should be. Instead of resenting him for bringing us here, I want to ask his forgiveness, but now—" Ma looked out over the river as if its flow brought her comfort.

"He'll come back soon, Ma. He'll be here and you'll be able to tell him yourself."

Her ma nodded. "May God allow me the chance."

That afternoon, Henry Leach came by for a visit. He rode atop a large horse with a squirming old seed sack hanging on the right of his saddle. "I'm here to pay my debt," he called out to the women.

Caroline rushed to the horse to rub its nose. They hadn't seen a horse since they'd left Pontiac months before.

Henry got off his horse and handed the bag to Ma. "Looks like you're up and about now. Are you feeling well?"

Ma nodded. "Yes. I am."

"So good to hear. Claire urged me to come and find out after she gave Alexander the medicine he needed."

"Claire gave Alexander the medicine?"

"That little guy was so out of breath when he arrived at our house. It was hard to understand what he needed until he held up the empty medicine bottle."

Betsey and Ma exchanged a glance and smiles.

"What's in the bag, Mr. Leach?" Etta asked.

Henry placed the burlap bag on the ground. It seemed to come alive as peeps sounded from within. "Take a look."

Etta bent down and untied the end of the burlap bag, and little fluffballs of feathers scooted out, while tweeting...a disagreeable lament on being cooped up in a bag.

Etta cooed, "Aww."

"Your pa paid me in a few slabs on his lumber, and I agreed to bring him a few pullets from our first hatch. They're ready now to be delivered."

The girls opened the bag completely and about ten chickens fluttered out and began inspecting the ground around the women's skirts.

"They can graze pretty much on anything around your cabin. I'd see if you can make a bit of a coop out in the barn. I know it doesn't have a complete roof anymore, but perhaps under the section where it does. Make a protective place for them. During the day, let them roam. They'll eat grass, any table scraps, a few berries."

Ma clapped her hands together. "Eggs. I can't wait for a wonderful egg."

Betsey's younger sisters began chasing the feathered creatures around the yard. The pullets seemed to find places to pick at the grass and soon seemed right at home.

"Thank you so much, Henry. We appreciate your kindness. Yet with all the help you gave us after the storm, I'm sure your debt has long been repaid."

Betsey knew Pa would be pleased to have chickens housed and possibly even producing eggs, by the time he got home, but she also realized their care would be more work. For all of them. But as she saw the smiles on her sister's faces, she knew it wouldn't be a burden for them.

That afternoon, Betsey's younger sisters went to the barn to prepare one corner as a coop for the chickens. It was still protected somewhat by the edge of the roof and secure enough to keep the chickens in, and the predators out. Etta and Caroline took over all their care. They even found a bit of leftover wood from a barrel Pa had busted up and began making them places to roost and nest. They were too young yet to produce eggs, but it wouldn't be long.

As Betsey watched Etta and Caroline care for the chickens in the yard, she had a feeling the young birds would be in good hands. The girls were enamored with them. She hadn't seen them this happy in such a long time. Who would have thought a few chickens could bring such joy back into the lives of her hard-working sisters?

Watching them brought her an odd sense of calm. What a joy it would be to soon have eggs and chickens to eat.

"Aaron should be returning shortly," Ma noted as she kneaded bread dough on the table.

Betsey nodded, but before she could answer, a large knot formed in her throat. She took a deep breath, to prevent tears from trickling down her cheeks. She couldn't answer confidently, so she just smiled at her ma.

"Betsey, he will return soon." It was just like Ma to remind her that he wouldn't be gone forever.

It seemed like he'd been gone for years, not weeks. She longed for the warmth of his body beside her at night, to kiss her belly, and tell her he couldn't wait for their new baby to enter the world.

After all the hardships and struggles this year had brought, hopefully the blessing of a baby would restore their courage to build a community here. Hard to believe a small baby could bring such hope. She prayed nothing bad would happen to the baby before it could bring the family much needed joy.

Ma punched down the loaf with more force than Betsey had seen her have, as of late. She still struggled to keep up, but every day brought their hard-working ma back to help them.

"I'm just so afraid with Aaron and the men gone."

"That's Satan talking, Betsey. He instills that fear in our heart, so we doubt God's goodness and protection over those we love." Since their talk at the river, her ma's spiritual perspective seemed renewed.

Betsey sat down and let the tears fall. "I hate my fear. I know God will care for him, but on days like this when I miss him so, it's hard to stay confident. It's been over four, long weeks."

"As the days pass, and we still see no sight of his wagon, we do doubt that he will return safe and sound. I know this fear. I've felt it more times than I want to admit." Ma brushed the sweat off her forehead, leaving a smudge of flour. "I remember when we first moved to Pennsylvania. We'd had to rush out of New York, and I wasn't sure that heading south was our best option. For goodness sake, after Pa lost his shirt in New York, the only thing we owned was an ax.

"But your pa was insistent that Pennsylvania was the place to raise our small, growing family. Just as he is now." Ma again thrust her hand into the spongy dough ball. "I wanted to fight him. I wanted to stay where we were. I had to leave my parents. Run from the very place that I knew to be home. I didn't want to take my little ones to an unknown village to raise them." Ma shook her head. "You'd think I would have learned my lesson the first time."

Betsey thought back to the time before they'd ventured to the Michigan Territory. She hadn't considered how hard it would be. She just wanted to follow her parents. Her heart ached to think of living without them, Ambrose, and her sisters. They were her world, despite the love she felt for Aaron. "When life gets hard here, I realize how much my desire to be here influenced Aaron's choice, too. I often feel guilty about it. Do you think I have Pa's adventurous spirit?"

Ma winked, "I wonder the same thing. Pa can get awful determined when he wants to go somewhere. I've told you before, it's his only sin." Ma turned the dough and hit it again. "Most times, I do believe it's just the Lord directing him."

Betsey looked up at her mother's small figure. She'd lost so much weight that summer. Gray tendrils now edged her scarf. Her hands were rough and wrinkled, bulging veins replaced her once-smooth, soft skin. Dark circles shadowed her eyes that once sparkled with hope and happiness.

"Aaron came because he knew it would make me happy." Betsey swallowed hard as she admitted to her mother why they'd followed them to this new homestead. "But I don't believe we would have come, otherwise."

"We do that sometimes. We want things that we don't even realize might bring us more pain than good." Ma tipped her head back and looked up, "Oh I wish I could have taught you better, but indeed, you are your mother's daughter, too."

Betsey knew without asking that her ma had often wanted things that Pa wasn't keen on.

Ma laughed. "For some reason, I believe that my way is the best and sometimes even the only way. It's my sin. It's what I cling to yet when I give in or give up, as Pa says, in my deepest struggle with him...it's then when he considers my point of view and does his best to match it with his own. He either gives in or tells me no. From that point on, I have to deal with his decision and make it my own."

"I've rarely seen you pout or make a fuss," Betsey acknowledged as she used her hand to push a bit of the flour to the middle of the table so it wouldn't spill off the side.

Betsey's ma laughed, "That you know of. I've struggled with many things. You saw it clearly before we came here. I usually get busy and push myself to do what he's suggested and sometimes I feel his desire and reason to do something and it begins to grow. And then, I start to understand.

"It was good we left New York. We needed a new start. Pa was destined to be a farmer, like he's always desired. He got his wish there. But this place," Betsey's mother stepped back and wiped her floured hands down her apron. "I never envisioned this as one of his desires." Ma picked a small bug from the dough now sitting on the table.

"I wonder how many bugs we've eaten since arriving?" Betsey picked another dark insect spot from the other side before her mother could cover the dough with a cloth.

Her mother laughed again. "Probably more than we want to know."

Betsey wasn't sure she could get the courage to ask her mother, but the horror she envisioned when thinking that Aaron might never return, haunted her. "What if he never comes back?"

"Aaron?" Ma placed the cloth over the dough. "Child, he'll return. Maybe not when we expect it, but he will. He's good with a gun, he's smart, and he won't allow himself to get into trouble." Ma patted her hand. "Don't worry. We're all here for you. You aren't alone."

"So, do you think it was a good thing that we followed you, Ma?"

Ma sighed, "I can't say, for I don't know God's ways, but I'm so very thankful I have you here. Think of all the women in places like these who don't have a single person to count on when they're sick, tired, or just need a friend. I have you." Tears filled Ma's eyes. "And I will always be thankful for that."

Betsey nodded as her eyes welled up with tears.

Digging her handkerchief out of her pocket, Ma handed it to her.

That night, Betsey woke to a wolf howl close to the cabin. Caroline stirred, and as the second wolf cry echoed off the cabin's outer wall, she got out of bed. Betsey rose on her elbows, "Caroline, what are you doing?"

Caroline put on her stockings and shoes. "I can't just lie here. I'm determined that those wolves don't get into the barn where our chickens are."

Betsey pulled back the light blanket covering her. "But where are you going?" Getting out of bed took her longer with the baby now bulging beneath her nightgown.

"To the barn," Caroline whispered back to her.

Betsey grabbed her sister's arm. "Oh no you're not!"

"Yes, I am. There is no one here to watch out for our chickens. I want eggs, don't you, Betsey?"

Betsey held onto Caroline's arm, whispering back, "Of course, but you can't go out there. They'd much rather eat you than a fluff of chicken feathers."

"I know how to shoot the rifle. I'll just go out and scare them away with one shot. That's all it will take. Ambrose does it, all the time."

Caroline was right. The men had done it numerous times. The gun shot would scare the wolves back into the woods every time.

"Let me go with you." Betsey sat down to pull up her stockings and put on shoes.

"No. You stay here."

Before Betsey could find her stockings, her sister had gone to the hearth and took the rifle down from its pegs. Whether Betsey wanted her to go or not, she seemed awful determined.

As she opened the door to leave, a cool breeze woke Etta, who was closest to the door. "Who's here?" She sat up straight and glanced at Betsey as the door shut behind Caroline.

Betsey hushed her. "It's me, Etta."

"What are you doing?"

Betsey knelt beside her on the floor but continued to whisper. "Caroline has gone out to shoot the gun. Wolves must be after the chickens."

Etta tugged her light blanket off. "Our chickens! They can't have them."

"Sit here with me. We'll pray for Caroline's protection together."

"Why didn't you go with her?"

"She wouldn't let me," Betsey whispered back.

Betsey sat down beside Etta on the floor, offering to cover her with the blanket she'd placed back over her own feet. The girls clung to each other there on the floor. A small remnant of a fire took the chill off the room, yet Betsey shivered in the darkness.

The wolves howled again.

"Poor Caroline. Outside all alone." Etta clung tighter to Betsey. "I hope she can scare them off with one shot."

A shot rang out into the night. It woke Ma.

"What was that?"

"It's Caroline, Ma. She went out to scare the wolves away from the barn."

Ma sat up now. "She did what?"

The first shot must have worked, because the howls heard in response to the shot, seemed farther from the barn.

The three women watched the door in anticipation. When would Caroline return? Just when they thought it was time she was back, another shot pierced the air.

Everyone jumped this time.

Ma then climbed out of her bed and wrapped her shawl around her shoulders. "I need to go out."

Betsey rolled herself to a dog-like position on the floor and then grabbed a chair to help pull herself up. "No, I'll go."

"You are not going out there, too." Ma came closer. The small glow from the fire illuminated her face in the darkness. Fear shown in her eyes.

"I have to. Why did she have to shoot twice?"

Betsey grabbed her mother's arm.

"I can't imagine."

Before they could decide what to do next, Caroline burst through the door. She slammed it shut and pushed the leather strap back into place.

Leaning the gun against the wall, she fell against the door, slid to the floor and wept. Betsey and Ma moved toward her.

"Caroline? Are you all right? What happened?" Questions rose from everyone now awake in the room. Jillian now stirred under her own blanket. Alexander was still sleeping.

Everyone rushed to Caroline. Her small frame shook. Etta picked up her blanket and wrapped it around Caroline's shuddering shoulders, hugging her from behind. Everyone else followed with their own arms of comfort.

Caroline's sobs soon turned to heavy, shuddering gasps.

Betsey asked again, "Caroline? Tell us what happened."

Caroline turned toward the huddle as they all stepped back, "I think I killed one."

Etta's hand flew to her mouth. "A chicken?"

Caroline shook her head. "No. A wolf."

Everyone did their best to go back to sleep after Caroline returned to the cabin, but the excitement of the night wouldn't allow it.

Betsey held-on tight to Caroline, who now shook like a shivering frightened pup, as Betsey did her best to whisper words of affirmation into her ear as they huddled back in bed. "You did well. It's okay now. You're safe."

"I've never been so frightened in all my life," Caroline whispered back.

Betsey stroked the sides of her face, where perspiration had dampened her hair.

"What did you see?"

Caroline shivered some more.

"Can you tell me?"

Etta had crawled into bed with them and Jillian had slipped in beside their mother in the other bed. The only one left on the floor, was Alexander, still sound asleep.

"I couldn't see as much as I hoped. After leaving the cabin, I headed slowly around the corner of the cabin. My eyes adjusted to the darkness quickly, as a full moon lit up the area around the barn. Three large wolves were doing their best to dig under the barn wall to get to the chickens. I wanted to get as close as I could to scare them." Caroline shivered again and Etta wrapped her arms around her back.

"Did they see you?" Betsey asked.

"I don't know, but I crept as close as I could around the back cabin wall. For a better shot. As soon as I was close, I raised the gun and shot directly at the barn. The kick from the gun caused me to fall back and nearly hit my head against the cabin. I stood quickly, but the smoke from my gun prevented me from seeing well." Caroline trembled. "When my eyes finally focused—I saw him."

"A wolf?" Etta's tone made even Betsey fight back a shiver of her own.

"Yes. I hadn't only scared off the pack that had surrounded the barn, I actually hit one."

"You did?" Betsey asked, in awe.

Before she could ask another question, Etta spoke up.

"What did the others do?" Etta moved in closer to Caroline.

"They all scattered—I think. All I could see was the shadow of one of them, lying on the ground."

"What did you do next?" Betsey couldn't believe what Caroline had experienced.

"I wasn't sure what to do," Caroline gulped. "I knew that if the wolf was just injured, he'd probably still want to get to the chickens, so I knelt beside the back of the cabin and reloaded. Just like Ambrose had shown me. I've never done something so fast in all my life. What if the wolf was able to get up and come at me? I also thought about giving up and running back into the cabin, but I knew that if I didn't do something, there wasn't anyone else to do it. I didn't want a lame wolf out there to greet anyone in the morning."

"Then what did you do?" Etta's small, excited voice seemed to echo off the walls. It almost made Betsey laugh right out loud, but she also knew that poor Caroline was still shivering from the ordeal and didn't want to make light of her frightening experience.

"I forced myself to look over at the wolf. He wasn't moving, but I needed to be sure I'd shot him dead. I walked up as close as I could and when I did—" Caroline choked.

Betsey pulled her closer. "Don't tell us if it makes you more afraid."

"I shot again, just as I saw the wolf's head pop up. I thought he was dead, but he must not have been. I prayed I hit him again, but when I looked back, the body was gone."

"Oh, my." Etta began to whimper.

"That's when I ran back into the cabin. I just wasn't sure if the second shot had hit him or not."

All the girls clung to each other under the small blanket. Betsey pulled a larger cover from the foot of the bed and placed it over both sisters' shoulders, and then around her own. "It's over now. You're safe here. With us."

"All I could hear after I shot was Ambrose repeating, "Caroline whatever you do, don't miss."

"What did he tell you to do if you missed?"

"Exactly what I did. Run! Back into the cabin. But if I killed a wolf, Betsey, do you know what that means?"

"That you're a very, very brave sister."

"No. It means we'll have to skin that thing and hold onto the pelt. Ambrose told me that Whitmore is giving thirty dollars a pelt to anyone who shoots a wolf. Pa will be able to purchase us lots of flour and sugar with a price like that."

Betsey laughed. "I hope that's what you've done. Pa will be so proud of you. As will Ambrose."

"I hope so," Caroline added. "If not, we may have a very angry, injured wolf on our hands, come morning."

Venturing out of the cabin the next morning was quite an adventure of bravery. Everyone was eager to see what had happened to the wolf that Caroline said she'd shot. What if it was just outside the door waiting to pounce on them?

Ma wouldn't let Betsey go out alone. They'd all used the indoor chamber pots instead of heading out to the outhouse. Ma wanted to check out the area first. Caroline refused to let her do it alone.

"I'm going with you, Ma." Ma looked on as her second-oldest daughter loaded the rifle with the skill of a sharp-shooter.

"Now, let's go slow. We'll make our way around the front of the cabin like I did last night. Surely an injured wolf wouldn't have made it this close to the cabin." Caroline positioned the gun. "Let's go, Ma."

Betsey couldn't believe how brave Caroline was acting after what she'd gone through the night before. Instead of fear, the young woman exhibited bravery, but also caution.

Ma had made Betsey promise her that she'd latch the door shut as soon as they were outside. Betsey held it shut but didn't latch it. She kept peeking out to see what was happening with Ma and Caroline. She reported what she saw to the little sisters clutching her skirt from behind. Alexander seemed oblivious to the commotion and continued eating his breakfast.

She could hear Ma and Caroline whispering as they made their way around one wall. Betsey shushed her sisters, so she could hear what was going on.

Soon she heard Caroline call to them, "It's okay to come out."

Betsey opened the door. It squeaked, making the sisters still cowering behind her jump.

They went out into the sunshiny morning. Caroline called to them from behind the cabin, "Come see, girls. Everything is okay."

Walking around the front wall, they saw Ma and Caroline back behind the cabin, staring at the dead wolf lying at their feet.

Betsey shivered to think of what had happened. Her sister could easily have been killed. Thank goodness she'd gotten the rifle loaded in time to kill the now dead wolf at her feet. Another bullet hole was at the back of one of the wolf's hind legs.

"I have a pelt for Pa," Caroline proudly announced.

Ma looked up at Betsey with worry in her eyes. She knew exactly what she was thinking.

Late August

CHAPTER TWENTY-THREE

Caroline was determined to gut and skin the wolf herself. If it weren't for Alexander's help, it would have been too difficult for her.

Caroline kept the rifle loaded and leaned it against the front of the cabin for the rest of the day. *Would the wolves come back?* Etta kept reminding them that they might. They even kept the chickens in the barn the rest of the day, feeding them crumbs of bread and berries instead of letting them rummage for food outside.

They were all skittish, and every time a twig snapped, Caroline went for the rifle and scoured the area.

The girls had stayed close together all day, while doing their chores. No one wanted to stray too far from the cabin, for fear the wolves might return. Ma did her best to assure them the wolves were long-gone by now, but no one wanted to venture into the woods or out to the garden without having someone else with them. Alexander didn't seem at all worried and went about his daily chores, as if it were just another day.

Ma got Betsey off to the side one moment that afternoon and whispered, "Do you realize how close that child came to being attacked last night?"

Tears filled Betsey's eyes. "Yes, but let's not talk about it, Ma. Caroline has to have realized that, too, if she has put pieces of the night all together."

Ma exclaimed, her hand covering her heart. "Lord have mercy! Scares the livin' daylights out of me to even think about it. As Pa would say, 'Stand firm, let nothing move you,' but this—most certainly moves me!"

Betsey still felt weak as she imagined what could have happened to her younger sister. "Me, too, but let's not say anymore. Just talking about it makes me shake in my shoes."

A rustle from the edge of the woods made them both jump. Ma called to the girls standing out by the fire, "Girls, get Alexander's attention and head for the cabin." Caroline motioned for Alexander who was down by the river.

Betsey glanced again, to see what moved at the edge of the woods. She saw a wagon coming onto the property. She focused, and suddenly realized who it was headed toward her. She would know that smile anywhere.

Aaron couldn't believe that Betsey was finally in his sights and making her way to him. It had been a little over a month since he'd seen her, and he couldn't believe the difference. She radiated motherhood with her sweet face, and the bump under her skirt. Oh, how he'd missed her.

He got within six feet of her and couldn't help himself. He pulled back on the oxen, set the brake, and jumped off the wagon, to get close enough to smell her scent and embrace her. He'd hope kisses would be her welcome. She came into his arms with a tight hug and kissed his cheek whispering, "Oh Aaron, I missed you so."

He hugged her as tightly as he could, and when he did, he could feel the tightness of her belly against his own. He couldn't let her go. He'd longed for this moment. He wanted nothing else but to feel her touch. Speechless, he kissed her hair, face, and then her tender lips. "Oh Betsey!"

Betsey stepped away from him and lifted his hand to her large belly. "Feel."

The baby inside his wife's body kicked him in response. "Someone else is happy you're home."

Aaron laughed as he tried again to feel the tiny thump against his hand.

"Come here." He took Betsey's hand and pulled her around the edge of the wagon. "Look what I've brought you."

Aaron had done his best to fit as much lumber as he could in the wagon, but the larger pieces hung out past the back edge. He was pretty sure he had enough to build them a nice one-room home to get them through the winter. If more lumber was needed later, he could go for another load.

Betsey looked overjoyed to see the bright-white, freshly cut lumber, "Oh Aaron."

"I think it will be enough to make a good start on a new home for us, but this is what I wanted you to see the most. I can't believe I found one." Lifting the canvas cover off the lumber, a small window with real glass leaned against the side of the wagon's bed.

Betsey clapped her hands. "A window?"

Aaron nodded. "There was only one, but I knew it would be so nice to see outside especially in the coldest parts of winter."

"It's beautiful." Betsey's hands moved over the frame. "Thank you."

Betsey's younger sisters now surrounded Aaron with giggles and excitement. They seemed as eager to see Aaron as Betsey.

When Aaron caught sight of Betsey's mother though, he looked to Betsey for help in understanding what he was seeing.

Betsey must have understood his concerned look, for she whispered, "She's been ill."

He turned to gather up all the girls in a big hug. Oh, how he loved these younger sisters. They all seemed to have grown taller, too. As Betsey's mother came closer, he held out his arms for her as well. "So nice to see you, Ma Baker."

She embraced him.

"So happy to have you home, Aaron."

Etta was the first to speak. "Aaron, guess what Caroline did last night?"

Aaron looked to Caroline, who smiled. "What did you do last night, Caroline?"

Before Caroline could answer, Jillian spoke for her, "She shot a wolf."

Aaron scowled. "What?"

Looking at Caroline, she nodded.

Aaron then looked at Betsey, who nodded, "She was very brave."

Aaron looked around, "Where's your pa? Ambrose?"

Betsey's ma was the first to answer, "They've gone to purchase our land. They're getting yours and Betsey's, too."

Aaron eyed Betsey, "You're all alone?"

Everyone said, "Yes."

Betsey grabbed his arm and began leading him toward the cabin. "We've been alone for about a month now. But Pa couldn't help it. He needed to go. More and more people are coming into the territory and he didn't want to miss getting a chance to purchase this property for all of us."

Anger began to build in Aaron's soul. *How could they have left Betsey and the other women alone? Why hadn't they consulted him?* He wouldn't have gone for the lumber if he'd known. Betsey's pa had said he might go, but Aaron assumed it wouldn't be until he returned with the lumber. *Why would he do such a thing?*

By the look on Betsey's face and the excitement of the girls now singing around him, he realized it was true. They were alone, but the younger girls seemed oblivious to their plight. *Why would Hosea leave his wife, baby, Alexander, and the women alone and put them in possible danger?* He pulled Betsey closer and kissed her head again. Deep down, he thanked the Lord for protecting them, but he only felt contempt for the man who'd dragged them out to this wilderness in the first place.

Aaron wasn't eager to see the wolf Caroline had shot. After examining it, he agreed with Caroline that she would be able to get a good amount for the pelt that they now had drying in the sun. More anger filled his being as Caroline related her story to him. What if Betsey had gone out to do the job? He wanted to scold Caroline for even thinking it had been a good idea. They could replace chickens, but not human souls.

Not to disappoint Caroline, he praised her for a job well-done, but discouraged her of ever doing it again. "Wolves are dangerous out here, Caroline. You could have been—"

Betsey stopped him before he could finish. "Walk with me to see the barn, Aaron."

He grabbed her hand and held it tight as they walked away from Betsey's sisters and Ma. "Does she realize—?"

"Aaron," Betsey hushed him. "Please don't. We all know it could have been so much worse, but I don't think Caroline realized the danger she was in."

"She needs to," Aaron demanded.

"She does know. It scared her terribly. It took me almost all night to stop from shaking. But God protected her. It's over. She won't have to do it again, Lord willing. You're here now. Pa and Ambrose will be back soon, too. We're all safe."

Aaron looked up, and toward the barn. "Betsey, what happened to the barn?"

Betsey relayed the story of the storm and how they'd pieced together a portion of the remaining structure to house the baby chicks. "It's sturdy now. We just need to rebuild this section." Betsey pointed to the far right of the barn. "It's been a job trying to just keep up with the chores. Fixing the barn wasn't one for a bunch of women."

Aaron felt around the logs that jutted from the frame. They stuck out in varying angles past the barn wall. "When did this happen?"

Betsey told him it had been just after her pa and Ambrose had left. "Then Ma's fever grew worse. If it wasn't for Alexander going for medicine, she might not be with us now."

Aaron kicked a piece of log jutting from the side of the barn. He glared at her. "I can't believe—" He turned away, and when he looked back at her again, tears were welling up in his eyes and his face was red.

Betsey asked, "Aaron, what's wrong?"

"I'm furious!"

She inched closer to him and touched his arm. "Whatever about?"

"What would possess your pa and Ambrose to leave you all alone? I know other settlers are moving into the area, but he could have waited for me. One month. That's all it took me to get the lumber. I had no idea he would leave while I was gone. He might have left you for a few days, but over a month? Why did he do that?"

Angry words came out of his heart and then his mouth without thinking of the effect they could have on Betsey.

"Indians, sickness...What if you'd gotten sick, too? The little girls and Alexander would have been left all alone." Aaron strode away from her and over to the barn. "And look at this! Looks like some kind of wind to blow down a barn like this. What if—?" Aaron turned his back on Betsey. His hand went to his face.

Betsey stepped closer to her husband and turned him around. He was crying. She lowered his hand and moved closer to him. "Aaron, we're all fine. God protected us. Nothing has happened to us."

Aaron could barely choke out the words, "I wouldn't have been fit to be a civil man anymore if something had happened to you. I would have killed your pa when he returned."

At those words, Betsey froze. She shook her head. "Pa must have had his reasons, Aaron. I don't understand much of what he decides to do. He's just my pa, but I know he was anxious to get the property in our names."

"Pshaw!" Aaron remarked. "He would have had plenty of time. I'm sure of it. I can't believe he left you all like this. This country is too primitive. Too remote. He never should have left you alone so long."

"Henry Leach came to check on us. We weren't completely alone. He would have stayed if we would have needed him."

Aaron nodded, and tried to take this into consideration. "But look at you. With child. How dare he?"

Betsey hushed him again. "Aaron. I'm fine. The baby is fine. We're all fine. Please stop. Don't blame Pa."

Aaron shook his head. "I do. And when he returns, we'll have this out."

Aaron stomped off and went into the woods. Betsey didn't follow him.

Ma cooked a fine meal for Aaron that night. She'd taken meat from the dead wolf and chopped it up into a stew. There were fresh garden carrots, and she'd even dug up a hill of new potatoes to add to the meal. Betsey baked up some fresh biscuits, too. They hadn't had such a feast in a long time. Etta had gone out for more wild berries, and Ma had even made a pie.

Each one voiced their thoughts about the adventures they'd had while Aaron had been gone. Betsey watched to see his expressions. He seemed to be simmering below the surface for her ma and sisters' benefit.

His walk into the woods seemed to have relieved some of his anxiety. Everyone chatted and wanted to hear of his expedition, too. Traveling through the new country wasn't easy, and just getting to the closest lumber mill had been trying. The storm had also hit Aaron as he traveled, but not as heavily or with as much wind damage as it had them.

"I found myself under the wagon for most of it," Aaron told them. "Tree limbs littered the ground around my wagon. I worried mostly about the oxen not having the ability to seek shelter, but we all survived."

The whole ordeal reminded him of their trip to Erie to catch the steamboat. "Remember the mud? That's what I endured for the next two days. Mud. Getting stuck almost every other hour in some way or another. Thankfully, the oxen were tried-and-true and got me through the worst parts of the trail. They would lean and heave until the mud would release the wagon wheels and we could be on our way. It helped that the wagon was empty and not loaded yet with heavy lumber."

Aaron laughed when he spoke of the help he'd received along his journey. "Once, close to the mill, I'd been blocked by an overflowing stream. Crossing it seemed not the best idea. I waited for an afternoon until another traveler came along the trail, and together we helped each other get across. He was a fur trader from the upper Michigan Territory and had traveled worse roads and forded more dangerous streams than I. He knew the best way to get across. The only bad thing about the man was, he had a thick Irish accent and I had a horrible time making sense of what he was saying. But I do have a new friend. Together, we made it work."

Soon everyone grew tired. The sun had gone down and Aaron wanted to be sure to get the oxen into a safe part of the barn after hearing of the experiences of the night before.

Perhaps Caroline's kill would deter other wolves for at least a night or two. Scaring off the wolves might have worked. Aaron placed his gun next to the front door.

As Betsey and Aaron climbed into bed that night, Caroline returned to a bed on the floor, in front of the hearth, Betsey felt a bit timid at first, sharing a bed again with Aaron. Soon his arms circled around her and she remembered the comfort he brought with his presence. He patted her belly, even telling the baby it was time to rest. Almost as if the tiny child could understand, he also grew quiet and Betsey knew that, for at least tonight, she was safe in the arms of Aaron again. She fell fast asleep.

The next day, Aaron was out of bed before Betsey even realized he was gone. She stirred to hear Ma frying up something for breakfast. As she approached her ma, she realized she was frying up some of the leftover potatoes from last night's meal. They probably shouldn't have dug up the new potatoes, but having them last night helped welcome Aaron home. Now smelling them sizzling in grease made Betsey's stomach growl. Smells weren't bothering her as much as they had been in the early months of her condition. Now all she wanted to do was eat.

She scolded her mother and sisters for letting her sleep. "I should have been up an hour ago. Why didn't anyone wake me?"

They all laughed.

Ma handed her a bucket. "Go get us some cool water, Betsey. Your husband needs some strong coffee this morning."

"Why?" Betsey asked as she pulled her shawl high and picked up the bucket from beside the hearth.

"He's been up since before the crack of dawn checking on the oxen. If I'm guessing right, that man will fix the barn soon. Getting the oxen and chickens in safe and secure will be the only thing on his mind over the next few days."

As Betsey made her way to the outhouse, she could see Aaron perched on a ladder against the side of the barn most needing repair. Alexander stood on a bottom rung, holding onto a long strip of bark. He seemed ready to hand it up to Aaron when he needed it. Betsey went to tell them good morning before returning to the cabin.

"Ma's fixing us breakfast, Aaron. Did you sleep well?"

Aaron crawled down the ladder to her and kissed her on the lips. "Beside you, my darling, the best night ever...although I still had to get up on a regular basis to check the oxen."

"Come in soon. Breakfast will be on the table."

Aaron nodded and smiled. He seemed in better spirits than yesterday. Perhaps, over time, he'd understand her pa's decision to leave them, to go claim their property. She hoped he would, before Ambrose and Pa returned.

Just then, Betsey caught sight of the Indian woman staring at her from the edge of the woods again. It startled her, but Aaron was close by. As soon as Betsey spied her, the woman disappeared.

Aaron had to keep watch over the barn and the oxen for the next few days, but they'd not heard a single wolf howl since Caroline's kill. Aaron was convinced they'd return, but he didn't know when.

The next Sunday, Betsey and Aaron took their time on their afternoon walk, checking on their property. Aaron had reported on his last trip to the ridge that a few trees had come down since the last time they'd been there. It must have been from the windstorm. Aaron worked hard and soon had the area clear for them to bring their lumber up and unload.

Betsey struggled to get up the hill to their land. Carrying the heavy weight of a child caused her to stumble and she had to stop often to catch her breath.

Aaron helped her as best as he could. "Let's go a bit off to the west here, where the climb to our property isn't so steep."

Betsey was grateful for the gradual slope, instead of the sharp incline they usually took.

That afternoon, they sat on the ridge. A fresh breeze blew through the area, heralding the change of seasons. The sun cast long shadows across the cliff.

She pulled her shawl tighter on her shoulders. "Feeling a bit brisk today," she noted to Aaron, who nodded. "It won't be long now."

Betsey lay back, then raised up enough to rest on her elbows. The baby seemed to only be able to poke at her instead of doing the usual flips in her belly. Aaron placed his head on her belly and soon felt a good swift kick against his cheek. He sat up and laughed. "That was a good one."

Betsey felt like she could sit all afternoon feeling her baby move and sharing it with Aaron. "He'll be here soon," Betsey assured Aaron.

"Are you ready?"

Betsey shrugged, "I don't know. I like it just being the two of us but not having to go to the outhouse so often would be a blessing." The heavier the baby got, the more Betsey needed use the outhouse, but more lately, the scramble had turned into something more like a waddle. Yet in the past few weeks, the trips had been growing closer together.

"I am a bit afraid of the whole thing." Betsey looked at her husband who expressed sympathy with his dark, kind eyes.

"Your ma will be close, just like you wanted."

"I know. I shouldn't be afraid," Betsey sighed. "But I am."

"I wish you didn't have to go through it all alone. I wish I could ease the burden and take a bit of the pain, too."

"That's my job, as a wife and mother." Betsey rubbed the large mound of her belly. "When can we start on the house?"

Aaron sat up. "This week. I can't wait to start. I want, more than anything, to have it finished before the snow flies, and by the look of things, I better hurry."

"Are you still angry?" Betsey hated to bring up Aaron's anger at her pa, but she needed to know.

"Yes. I will have a few words with your pa when he returns. I don't understand why he couldn't have waited."

"He should be home soon," Betsey assured him.

"I hope so. I need help finishing up that barn. Alexander is a big help, but he isn't strong enough to get some of the top logs back into place. I can't do that alone."

Betsey nodded. "How long will it take you to finish our home?"

"A few weeks to possibly a month. If your pa and Ambrose return soon, they will be a big help. But then, the crops will be ready to harvest. They'll need my help with that, too."

"I never imagined it would be this hard. Did you?" Betsey pushed his hair off his forehead.

"Never. This has been quite the year for us. Can you imagine what it would have been like if Ambrose hadn't arrived before us? We'd just be finished building the cabin. We'd probably still be working on getting trees cut for the barn. Pa was wise in coming ahead of time and getting the cabin ready before we arrived."

"Yes, he was."

Betsey heard frustration in Aaron's voice. He needed to talk to Pa. All of her assurances regarding her pa's wisdom were no match for Aaron's anger. It didn't matter what she said.

"Please pray about how you approach Pa. Will you do that for me?"

Her husband chucked her chin up. "I will." He then leaned back and pulled her down on himself. They kissed for a long time. They couldn't get enough of each other since he'd been back. If nothing else, the desire for their own home increased with every kiss.

Early September

CHAPTER TWENTY-FOUR

As the girls were finishing up the laundry that next week, Betsey stood on the riverbank and wrung out the last drops of water from a work skirt. Kneeling over to wash clothes was impossible for her now, so her sisters did the heavy work. Each item of clothing needed to be scrubbed, then rinsed. Betsey's job was to squeeze as much water out as she could before spreading the clothes out on the nearby grasses to dry.

The last of Aaron's clothes were now being laid out. The girls were disturbed by the sound of voices in the distance. Betsey looked up to see Indians approaching in canoes. They'd seen Indians on the river in canoes before, but this time there were three males in each canoe, their faces and arms painted in an array of earthy tones. Betsey's sisters left the water to allow them to pass.

Eyeing Betsey, one particular warrior let out a whoop, like she'd never heard before. She gathered the girls closer to her. Jillian clung to her right arm.

"Be still," Betsey told them all.

"Where are they going?" Caroline looked down the river after the canoes passed.

"I don't know. Perhaps to the Indian camp just north of here. The one Ambrose told us about."

That afternoon more canoes floated by. They'd never seen so many in one day. Only male Indians were paddling the canoes, each one adorned in elaborate, feathered headbands, which fluttered in the breeze. Excitement and wildness seemed to fill their eyes.

"What do you think is happening?" Betsey asked Aaron that afternoon when she went to the barn to take him a cold drink of water.

"I don't know, but it worries me." Aaron took a long swig of the cool water. Some of it dribbled down his chin. He wiped it off with his sleeve. "Tell the girls to get the laundry in sooner than later. I think we need to make it an early night."

As Betsey headed to the cabin, three more canoes with painted men floated past. Their long paddles making the only motion in the somewhat still water.

"Ma, Aaron says we need to bring the laundry in early tonight. Do you need anything from the garden for supper?"

Ma was chopping up more carrots for their evening meal. "Bring me in a squash to cook tonight. If I roast it over the hearth fire, it will be ready in the morning." They no longer needed the fire outside the cabin, a hearth fire brought needed warmth back to the cabin for the now cool nights.

Betsey headed toward the garden.

Aaron could hear a distant rumble coming from north of their property. He wasn't sure what it was, but he kept his eye on the edge of the woods surrounding the property. Something was up, in regards to the Indians. He just wasn't sure what it was.

The rumble grew louder the longer he worked, and by evening, he could make out Indian calls and what he thought might be drums. The wind had picked up considerably, sending dry leaves swirling in different directions around the barn.

He looked to Alexander. "You know what that means, Alexander?"

Alexander had stopped smiling. He looked to the edge of the woods just like Aaron had been doing all afternoon. Close to dusk, without much hesitation, the boy directed Aaron to get off the ladder, as he first pointed down the river, and then to the cabin.

That night at supper, Aaron remarked on the odd way Alexander was acting. "I'm not sure what he was telling me, but it seems we are better off being close to the cabin tonight."

The loud rumble from the drums echoed through the cabin walls. Ma and Etta seemed greatly upset by the sound.

"What are they doing, Alexander?" Ma would ask the young boy, who would stop, listen a moment, and then continue to eat. "He doesn't seem afraid, just cautious."

Once they had the dishes washed, there was nothing more they needed to do, so everyone decided to head to bed early. Instead of lying down that night near the younger girls, Alexander lay right across the door's threshold. If anyone were to come in the door, they would step directly on him.

Aaron tried to encourage Alexander to move closer to the hearth, but the boy shook his head and lay back down. It was if he wanted to guard the door.

Aaron left the rifle by the door that night. Everyone was on edge. As the night went on, the drums and Indian yelps grew louder.

"What do you think they're doing?" Betsey asked Aaron.

"I don't know. The sound doesn't seem to be moving, but the drums are definitely just north of here. The sounds seem to be reverberating off the riverbanks north of here, perhaps making it sound louder than it really is."

Betsey shivered despite Aaron's presence right next to her.

He snuggled close. "Are you cold, Bit?"

Betsey answered, "No." Her shivering had nothing to do with the temperature.

Aaron squeezed her tighter. "I'm right here. We'll be fine."

Aaron glanced toward the door where Alexander slept peacefully.

"Why do you think Alexander isn't moving away from the door?"

"He seems to want to protect us."

The rhythm of the drums grew faster. Only one thing kept everyone calm. Ma sang quietly, and kept it up until Caroline and Etta joined her. *"All hail the power of Jesus' name, let angels prostrate fall. Bring forth the royal diadem, and crown Him Lord of all."*

Everyone joined in the words of the third verse, *"Let every tongue and every tribe responsive to his call, to Him all majesty ascribe, and crown Him Lord of all."*

Ma then began to pray for peace. Pray for their protection. Everyone said, *amen* as she finished.

The cabin grew silent, but for the distant beat of the Indian drums.

Betsey awoke to Aaron leaving the bed again, as he'd done at various times throughout the night. She wondered if he'd slept at all. For now—silence reigned. The only sounds were the soft snores of her sisters and a strong wind buffeting the north wall. Each time Aaron opened the door, the wind circled in, stirring the fire awake as he stepped over Alexander to leave. Betsey wasn't sure why he left, but soon he'd return to snuggle back with her again.

Now a soft glow brightened the room. She sat up in bed to watch Aaron leave, once again, to go outside and then return. This time he put all his clothes on, instead of just his trousers.

"What's going on? Can you see anything?"

"Whatever they were doing, it seems to have stopped. I can see the sun brightening the eastern sky, over the river."

Betsey threw back the covers on the bed. Easing out of bed was her only option. Moving now took great effort.

"You don't have to get up. It's early. I just want to be prepared for what the day might hold and check on the animals."

"It's okay. I need to prepare breakfast."

Betsey asked Aaron if she could go outside.

He nodded. "I'll go with you."

Alexander had moved himself closer to the fire now, away from the doorway.

The morning air was cool. The gray, dark clouds overhead moved as quickly as the wind, which now blew Betsey's shawl up, and nearly off her shoulders. Aaron tugged it back down, hugging her tight as he escorted her to the outhouse. He waited outside for her and then took her back to the cabin. Once inside, he grabbed Ambrose's rifle and headed outside again.

Ma was rousing from bed. "Oh, what a night. I'm not sure I slept at all."

Betsey wished her mother a morning greeting and began preparing some leftover venison to go with their biscuits. "I don't think Aaron, nor I, slept either. I think the drums just stopped a few minutes ago."

"I've never been so frightened," Ma whispered as she tied on her apron. "What is it like outside?"

"Colder, but silent. The wind has picked up considerably since yesterday."

"What do you suppose is happening?"

Betsey shook her head. "Perhaps it was some kind of ceremony or something."

As each of the girls rose, Aaron escorted them outside, bringing them back to the cabin. Alexander finally woke up, folded his blanket, and sat down at the table. He'd begun to use hand gestures now to communicate with the family.

Etta was the best one to get something out of him or understand what he was trying to tell them. This morning she sat down at the table and asked him, "What were the Indians doing last night, Alexander?"

Alexander pounded on the table. The beat sounded similar to what they'd been hearing all night.

Etta nodded. "Yes, drums. But why?"

The young boy pointed to the wolf pelt now drying near the fireplace.

"Wolf?" Etta acknowledged.

He then pointed to the Bible on the table beside Ma's chair.

"Bible?"

The boy nodded, chewing on a dry piece of meat.

Etta squinted at Ma. "What do you think the connection is with the Bible and all that noise?"

Ma shook her head. "I don't know, but I hope they don't start up again tonight."

Alexander shook his head.

Etta delivered his message. "He says no."

Her comment made the boy smile.

"Well, praise be to God for that." Ma put a biscuit on the boy's plate.

The girls told Aaron what Alexander had been trying to communicate with them.

"He says they won't start up again tonight." Betsey placed Aaron's plate in front of him.

"I hope he's right. I'm exhausted."

"But the Bible, Aaron, what do you suppose he means by pointing to the Bible?"

Aaron shrugged. "I have no idea."

Ma read from the Bible each morning. On this morning she read about protection, from the book of Psalms. "'The Lord is my rock, my fortress, and my deliverer, my God, my mountain where I seek refuge, my shield and the horn of my salvation, my stronghold.'"

After she finished, Aaron took up the gun leaning against the door. "I want everyone to stay close to the cabin today. If you need to run to the garden, have Alexander come and get me and we'll go get it for you. It would make me feel better knowing no one is out and about. I'll be working on the barn again today."

"Are you about finished?" Ma asked him.

Aaron placed the gun over his shoulder. "Just about. When Ambrose returns, I'll be able to use the oxen to shore up the worst wall and patch the roof above that. It will be secure soon. I'll have

Alexander pile wood up by the front door. No washing today. Do you have some baking to do?"

Ma nodded. "We always have baking that can be done. Thank you, Aaron."

Aaron tipped his hat to her, with Alexander following right at his heels.

"I wish we could get Alexander to speak. What do you think it will take?"

Ma began gathering the plates off the table. "I don't know. I wonder if it is some kind of birth defect. But it would be so helpful to understand some of the Indian ways, if he could just tell us."

It wasn't but a few minutes later, when shouting could be heard from outside. Betsey and Ma wiped off their hands and to go see what was happening. Caroline took down Pa's rifle.

"Just in case," she added as everyone followed her to the door. Ma took hold of Caroline's arm, pulling her behind her. Ma peered out first.

Everyone could hear someone shout from the southern part of their land. Ma's hand flew to her face. She hadn't allowed anyone else to look. Caroline pushed past Ma to see. When she did, she turned to the girls, as Ma took off in the direction of the shout.

"Pa's home!"

Betsey pushed past the other girls and looked south. Pa and Ambrose were waving to them from the bench of their oxen wagon. They were home.

Betsey turned and went around the front of the cabin, toward the barn, shouting, "Aaron, Alexander...Pa and Ambrose are home!"

They must have seen them come onto the property, for Alexander was halfway across the yard, waving emphatically to Pa, who was waving back and laughing at the boy.

He beat Ma to Pa and Ambrose, but not by much. Pa had gotten off the wagon and opened his arms to Alexander, who nearly tackled Pa to the ground. Ma followed close behind and as Pa let Alexander climb onto the wagon, he embraced Ma with a hug and a long kiss.

Ambrose was hugging Alexander and giggling. "Boy, did you miss us?"

Alexander nodded, causing Ambrose to laugh even harder. He then bent down to receive a kiss on his cheek from Ma.

The girls gathered around Pa, giving him hugs and kisses. It took Betsey much longer to get to the welcoming party. Aaron had waved to her to go ahead of him as he was doing his best to get down off the ladder which leaned against the barn.

"Oh, my girls!" Pa said, as Betsey finally reached him. He smiled at her. "My grandchild looks just about ready to enter the world. You look radiant." Pa was never cheap with his compliments, especially for his girls.

Betsey thanked him.

"My, we're glad to be home. I'm dying for some of your cooking, Sally. My innards haven't had a decent meal since we left."

Ambrose let all his little sisters join Alexander on the wagon seat as he clicked the reins, encouraging the oxen toward the barn.

Pa again held out his arms to Ma. "You've been starving yourself, woman. You need me home to put meat on those tiny bones of yours, don't you?"

Ma was wiping the tears off her face with her apron. "We had a bit of a rough night last night."

Ambrose called back over his shoulder, "We heard. Pa can tell you all about what happened."

Betsey asked, "What was it, Pa? What do you know?"

As Betsey, Pa, and Ma made their way toward the cabin, Aaron met them halfway. "Welcome home, sir." He held out his hand to Pa who shook it whole-heartedly.

"Aaron. Good to see you home, too. How long have you been here?"

"Just over a week."

"Fine, fine. Did you get the lumber you needed?"

"Yes, sir."

"Good, good. Well I have something in my pocket just for you." Pa reached into his overcoat and pulled out an envelope. "You'll find three deeds in there. One for me, one for Ambrose, and the last one is for you. You're a property owner again."

Aaron took the envelope and looked inside. Pulling out an assortment of folded papers, Aaron looked through each one and peeled off the last sheet.

"That's the one. Congratulations and welcome to Michigan." Pa laughed. "That's what they told us at the land contract office."

Everyone laughed. Betsey went to Aaron to look over his shoulder, at the paper he was holding. Sure enough, both their names topped the paper that was the deed to their land.

"You're in section twelve. Ambrose has section twenty-three, and we have sections twenty-four, thirteen, and fourteen. It's official now. I signed for all the land, but I cajoled the officials to add your name to the deeds." Pa grinned as though it was the Fourth of July and he'd just won the bareback horse competition. "Got it for just one dollar and twenty-five cents an acre. What a steal."

That night after supper, the girls shared their harrowing stories of what had happened during the weeks Pa and Ambrose were gone. Ambrose couldn't get over Caroline shooting the wolf. No one spoke about how close it had been to being a tragedy. Ma would probably tell Pa about it later.

"They are getting thirty dollars for pelts. That's what Whitmore told us while we were at the trading post, before heading home. He said that many of the new settlers are living off the profits of pelts until they can get their crops in and established," Ambrose relayed to them.

Pa quoted Song of Solomon, "'Catch for us the foxes, the little foxes that ruin the vineyards.'" Everyone laughed.

"So, what happened last night?" Pa asked Aaron, as he took a long sip of his coffee. He'd brought a whole load of supplies from the trader, including coffee beans. Ma was delighted to serve the men a cup.

Aaron told Pa of the long night they'd just endured. "What do you know about it?"

Pa took another long sip of his coffee. "It's an Indian sacrifice they do every year."

"Sacrifice?" Ma's eyes widened. "What do they sacrifice?"

"A dog," Pa exclaimed.

"Wait, a dog?" Etta motioned to Alexander. "So maybe Alexander was telling us that when he pointed to the wolf pelt on the wall."

"And the Bible must have been the sacrifice part." Betsey ruffled the hair of the boy sitting next to her. "That makes sense now. But what does it mean, Pa?"

"A long time ago, there were Indians who lived in these parts called the Sauk Indians. They were a cruel and mean bunch. So mean, that many of the Chippewa and other nearby tribes hated them. They dominated the land right here, where we're living. They wouldn't allow the other tribes surrounding them to hunt or live in the area. If they found them, they mistreated, or even killed them." Pa pointed. "Down river here, there's supposedly a deep hole. If anyone or anything goes into the river at that spot, it disappears. Never to be seen again."

Caroline shivered, "Where is it?"

"I don't rightly know." Pa added, "But Whitmore says that every fall the Indians living here now have to appease their gods by sacrificing a dog to them. Have you been seeing more Indians on the river these past few days?"

Betsey nodded, as did the other girls. "There were lots of canoes heading that way," Betsey told him.

"But why do they have to do that?" Ma asked him. "And why a dog?"

"Tales be told...the Indians at the north and the far south decided they'd had enough of these Sauk Indians and their vicious ways. They banded together and one night came upon the Sauk village undetected and killed every last member of the tribe.

Slaughtered every one of them. Male, female, and even the children."

The girls all groaned. "Oh Pa, that's horrible."

"Well now, the Indians feel they did something wrong. They caught the Sauk tribe completely off guard and destroyed the entire village. In the Indians' eyes, it wasn't a fair fight. Then, because of the evilness of the tribe, they didn't give any of the tribe a designated place of burial. They just killed them all," Pa waved his hand, "left them where they died. For the Indians, that's not a good thing. If an Indian doesn't have a proper burial, they feel their spirits or souls can haunt others." Pa took another sip of his coffee. "I'm so glad we brought these beans to your ma, Ambrose. This coffee is delicious."

Ambrose filled his pipe, "Whitmore says that now the Indians feel haunted by the tribe of those their ancestors killed. They are deeply afraid of their spirits, that they claim now haunt this part of the territory. Because of this, they're even afraid to hunt, live, or travel through here. The myths and superstitions cause them great fear."

Pa continued, "For many, many years, they have chosen a night in the fall when Indians gather together to try and appease their gods for the lives of those their ancestors killed. They do that by having a special ceremony where they paint up a dog and throw him in the river as atonement for their past sins of killing off the Sauk tribe."

"Last night," Aaron asked, "was their ceremony night?"

Pa nodded and took a long sip of his coffee. "According to Whitmore. He told me knowing full well that we'd probably hear the ceremony from our cabin. We were going to spend one last night just south of here, but instead, Ambrose and I pushed through the night to get to you, hoping to be here to explain what was happening, but I guess, we were too late."

"We're all exhausted from lack of sleep." Ma sat close to Pa. "The drums alone were horrible. Aaron stood watch most of the night."

"Well everything is okay now. Whitmore said the day after the ceremony is pretty quiet. He says the Indians love their drink on that night and take most of the next few days to sleep it off."

"But oh," Etta exclaimed, "the poor dog."

"What would cause a spot in the river to be so deep?" Aaron inquired.

"Whitmore doesn't know. Knowing the area well, he figures it must be just a pocket of some kind, causing a bit of an undertow. But he says, they usually never see the dog again, so that's why they believe their gods accept it as a sacrifice."

"They do it every year?" Betsey asked.

"Yes. Every fall."

"Well wonderful," Ma folded her arms in exasperation. "What a grand thing to look forward to each year."

"Indians are very superstitious. Whitmore said there's a tale going around by the other fur traders. They say the Indians get spooked by simple things, like even the snap of a tree branch. He says that traders know the legend of the Sauk Indian massacre and know full well the Indians' fear. While they are out harvesting sap, some of these traders will spook them by either breaking twigs or climbing trees or making funny sounds. It spooks the Indians and they all run, abandoning their stations and cooking vessels used to harvest it. Then the traders go in and steal their things."

Pa leaned back in his chair and folded his arms. "Whitmore doesn't tell that tale to many of the traders coming through. Too many would use it to take advantage of the Indians." Pa shook his head. "One time, Whitmore asked a Chippewa chief why the Indians run, and the Indian told him they're afraid even though the massacre happened many, many years ago."

"Huh, that's awful wicked of those traders to take advantage of them like that." Aaron held out his cup for more coffee. Ma poured him another cupful.

"It is. We need to be careful not to spread that story too broadly ourselves. The settlers here need to know the reason why the ceremony takes place, so they know not to be afraid, but other than that, we should follow Whitmore's advice and keep it to ourselves."

Pa continued, "One thing about it, Whitmore said that's why we aren't really bothered by the Indians in this part of the territory as much as other areas, they still feel guilty their ancestors took part in such a horrible slaughter."

"It's almost like we've settled in a good place. Indians might keep to themselves more," Ambrose added.

"Although," Ma acknowledged, "There have been times when we've needed them."

"You're right, Sally May." Pa put his hand on Ma's shoulder. "God does help in mysterious ways."

Everyone agreed.

"Seems like all of us could use a good night's sleep. We should call it a day. We have much to do in the morning. Ambrose and I can help Aaron with rebuilding the barn, and then we need to get started on Betsey's house. Doesn't look like that baby is going to wait much longer."

Betsey rubbed her belly and knew Pa's prediction was probably right.

CHAPTER TWENTY-FIVE

Hosea cuddled with his wife in bed that night. "Not much here to hug anymore, Sally. I feel so badly that you didn't get better as fast as you usually do."

"I don't remember much. Betsey said the only thing that saved me was Alexander. He went and got more medicine from Claire."

"That boy. He's continuing to earn his keep." Hosea snuggled closer, kissing her ear.

Hosea sighed. "Whitmore and I talked about Alexander. He's fairly sure it is the baby he once saw a few years back with that white-skinned couple. He thinks perhaps the Indians might have clipped his tongue. That's why he can't speak. They didn't want him speaking English in a camp full of Indians. Perhaps the Indian woman realized we were more his kind than she. That's why she's brought him to us."

"Clipped his tongue? Do you think?"

"Could very well be. He hasn't talked yet, has he?"

Sally shook her head. "No, but Hosea, the child has been like an angel of mercy to us. He knows when we need someone to help us. He guards the door with bravery, like David facing Goliath. He's isn't afraid. The Lord has been good to bring us just the right people to help us with our adversaries and hardships."

"You are right about that. He's a hard-working, good boy. I'm proud to care for him."

Sally murmured. "Yes. Etta seems to be making headway with communicating with him. Somehow she's gotten through to him better than any of us."

"My Etta," Hosea whispered. "Oh, how I love that child."

The faint glow from the fireplace made it almost impossible to see faces in the dim light. Sally reached over and cupped her husband's cheek, "Hosea. I need to ask your forgiveness."

Hosea was taken aback by that comment. "Whatever for?"

"I've been harboring bitterness in my heart over coming to Michigan."

"Oh, Sally." Hosea kissed her forehead. "It's not necessary—"

"It most certainly is." Sally rubbed his chin. "I was wrong and didn't realize that a great bitterness had filled my heart. Please forgive me."

Hosea hugged her close. "It's you who needs the apology. God pushed this impetuous man into your life. But while I was away, I began thinking about what you've had to give up because of my adventuresome nature, and I want to give you this assurance before I nod off to sleep."

"Hmm." Sally snuggled closer.

"This will be the last time. I won't make you move. Ever again. I promise."

"Are you sure?"

"This ol'e body can't take much more of startin' over. I'm done. The next home I move to will have golden streets, pearly gates, and the One I love more than even you."

"Thank you, Hosea."

"One more thing. How long do you think it will be before we get to meet that grandbaby?"

"Hosea. That's none of your concern."

Hosea giggled into his wife's neck. "Maybe not, but she's becoming quite great with child. I was just wondering if you know for sure."

His wife snickered, "She is growing large. I'm expecting our first grandbaby will arrive as all our children did."

"I know, I know...in their own good time." Hosea could barely keep his eyes open. "So—within the month?"

"I expect so, but God ordains the day to be born. Not us."

"Yes, he does." Hosea felt himself drifting off to sleep. "'Thou hast covered me in my mother's womb. I will praise thee; for I am fearfully and wonderfully made: marvelous are they works; and that my soul knoweth right well. My substance was not hid from thee, when I was made in secret, and curiously wrought in the lowest parts of the earth. Thine eyes did see my substance, yet being unperfect; and in thy book all my members were written.'"

Pa began harvesting some of the potatoes and squash the next day. He seemed eager to be about the job of bringing into the cabin what the Lord had allowed him to grow in his first year in the Michigan Territory. Alexander and the girls helped him carry all the produce to the newly-restored barn. Much of the crops were put into barrels, amidst slough grass from the riverbanks.

Within a week of Pa's return, the barn had been completely fixed, and Ambrose had built a lean-to just behind the cabin, where some of the harvest could be stored.

One morning, Etta ran to the house after checking on her chickens. Meeting Betsey along the path to the cabin, she smiled as she ran past, while cradling a treasure in her apron. "Come see what I have for Ma," she said with a grin.

Betsey had a hard time following anyone who was running, but she made her way to the cabin behind her little sister. As she reached the door, she watched Etta hold up a perfectly oblong, brown egg.

"Look Ma," she squealed.

Ma laughed and clapped her hands. "Etta. This is wonderful. Don't tell your pa. We'll surprise him at dinner."

Etta said, "We'll have more soon. I saw the other hens making nests of their own this morning."

The now full-grown chickens could be heard clucking and announcing the morning sunrise. The girls let them out each morning and pushed them back into their shelter at night. Etta took charge of them as though they were her children and she was their ma. They would have eggs, thanks to her care and Caroline's determination to keep them safe each night while the men were gone.

As Etta walked outside to get back to her chores, Ma whispered to Betsey, who was standing just inside the door, "I will prepare this egg for Etta and Caroline. I do believe they have earned the right to eat it themselves. What do you think?"

Betsey thought it would be a wonderful surprise for her hardworking sisters.

Late September

CHAPTER TWENTY-SIX

Everyone had a hard time distinguishing one day from another. Each day seemed to merge into the next and before they knew it, another week created a piece of the Baker's first year story. The family did their best on Sundays to keep it holy and to avoid work. That's also when Betsey and Aaron would sneak off to see their property and make plans for their home.

One afternoon, Aaron approached Betsey. "Let's go to the property."

"But it's not Sunday. I have to help Ma bake this afternoon." Chores seemed endless. One lost afternoon might not seem such a big thing, but it would postpone chores to another day, and halt the progress of getting everything done before winter.

Etta came up from behind Betsey, singing, and must have overheard Betsey. "Do you need to take the afternoon off? I can help Ma."

Betsey looked to Aaron. "I guess we can. Let's pack a dinner and go." Betsey was so proud of how hard her little sisters worked each day. They were becoming quite efficient and handy helpers...growing into women.

Betsey thanked Etta for her kindness.

They knew not to climb the ridge anymore. Betsey had a hard enough time walking these days. The baby had grown in such proportions that even sitting was uncomfortable. Aaron had made a path to their property, along the gradual slope, to avoid having to climb the steep ridge by the river. Aaron held Betsey's hand to steady her as she made her way up the hill.

"Why did you want to come up here today, Aaron?" Her breathing grew heavier the higher they climbed.

Aaron gave her an 'I-have-a-surprise' look. "Time to plan the house. I need your help with a few decisions."

Betsey tipped her head. "Is that the only reason?"

Aaron's shoulders sagged. "Do I need another?"

Betsey shrugged and smiled. "Maybe."

The dry leaves crunched under their feet as they walked. August and September days had been particularly dry compared to the earlier months. Betsey loved seeing the varying colors of leaves starting to emerge. She knew, before long, their hues would be bright-yellow as the sun, others bright orange like a pumpkin, the red ones would blaze like a roaring fire in summer. Looking farther up the trail, she saw the hardwoods that made up their property. As much as Pa loved the grandeur of the forest surrounding their home, Betsey was beginning to love it almost as much. Each tree creating a canopy of protection over their new homes and land.

"Hard to believe that these beautiful trees could make traveling here such a hardship. Look at how tall and majestic they are." Betsey pointed to a line of bushes, "Look at these bushes. They look like they're burning."

"We've been looking forward to this time of year for such a long time and now that it's here, it's hard to believe you'll soon be giving birth to our first child."

Betsey patted her swollen belly. "I can't even see my feet anymore," she laughed.

As they stepped onto the ridge, Aaron led Betsey to a certain spot of land where the ground had been leveled and tamped down, into a perfect, dirt square.

"This is it. You're in the main part of our new home. I'll be hauling up the rest of the lumber tomorrow. Tell me where you'd like the hearth, our bedroom, and a good place to install a pantry."

Thoughts of all of this were overwhelming for Betsey. They'd had a nice home in Pennsylvania, but from what Aaron had been sharing with her, this house would be even nicer. She twirled around, and started dreaming of setting up a home. "Let's put the hearth here and the front door looking toward the river."

Aaron agreed. "How about the window?"

Betsey put a finger to her mouth and thought a moment. "Let's put the window beside the front door, so we can look out over the river. I will be able to sit here during the winter months and gaze out over the Shiawassee which passes not only my parents' home, but also winds north into Indian Territory. I can also see if anyone is coming from that way to visit us."

Aaron led her back toward the woods. "How about putting our bedroom here? I'll make a wall here," Aaron motioned with both hands, "with a door, so it can be shut to give you some privacy."

Betsey knew her sisters would be visiting often and a door on their bedroom would be perfect when she needed to nurse the baby. She smiled, and nodded her approval.

"I think I have enough wood for a good, sound floor. It will be easier for you to sweep than a dry, earthen one."

"A window and a wood floor!" Betsey rested her arms on her husband's shoulders and clasp her hands behind his neck. "What more could a wife want?" She kissed Aaron full on the lips. "I'm very happy."

He took her hand and led her to the back portion of their property. The mosquitoes weren't as bad now, yet one still managed to bite Betsey on her hand. When she swatted it, a bit of blood soiled her arm. She wiped it off with her other hand.

"Next summer we'll build a barn here. Your pa will appreciate having our oxen out of his barn."

Betsey pulled Aaron close. "Have you talked to Pa yet about leaving us?" She knew he needed to have a talk with him, but she was afraid of Pa's reaction.

"He relies so much on God, that sometimes it's common sense he forgets." Aaron gave her an annoyed look.

Betsey found a close tree stump to sit on. "God is our refuge and strength. We need to fully believe that in our lives. Especially here, in this newly-settled environment."

Aaron sat down beside her. "I know that Betsey, but leaving you alone was not an option I would have chosen. If I would have known he was heading to Jackson so soon, I would have waited until he returned, before going for the lumber."

Betsey kissed the back of his hand. "I know, but Pa's been through many trials in his life. He knows when he can depend on God to care for his family." She picked up his chin and looked into his eyes. "You need to remember to do the same. There will be times when you'll have to leave the baby and me."

"I won't do that unless I know your pa is close."

Betsey searched his dark eyes. "What if Pa isn't around? Will you be able to completely trust the Lord for our care?"

Aaron turned his face away. "I don't know. You're so special to me...and this baby," Aaron leaned down and put his head on her belly. "You're my everything."

Betsey smiled at the thought of being so important to her husband, but she also knew to caution him. "Aaron, childbirth is hard. There are dangers in giving birth. We have no doctor. We knew that when we came. I need to know that if something were to happen to me—"

Aaron interrupted her with pain in his eyes. "No. Nothing is going to happen!"

"It might. I need you to know that I love you and always will. As much as we want this baby to be strong and healthy, we need to prepare ourselves in case something bad were to happen."

Aaron's head fell. He didn't look at her.

"If something were to happen, I want you to tell me you'll still build this home. You build it just as we've planned. And," Betsey blinked back tears, "I want you to find another woman to love. You deserve a full life and children. Promise me you'll do that."

Aaron shook his head. "You'll be fine. God will protect you."

"Promise me you'll believe that. With your whole heart. Even if...," Betsey now fought her own tears, "it's releasing me into His kingdom."

Betsey looked off to the left of where they were sitting. She pointed to a tree. "See that huge tree over there?"

Aaron looked in the direction she was pointing. "That oak?"

"Yes. But it's not just an oak. It's a blackjack oak. Pa brought me up here to show it to me when we first moved here. Its leaves are three-lobed and bell-shaped. Pa said he never saw anything like it in Pennsylvania, but he found one once, by a river in New York. His father pointed it out to him and told Pa they like to grow in sandy soil. Pa says it's very rare to see a blackjack oak in this part of the country." Betsey squeezed Aaron's hand, "that's where he wants to be buried someday."

Aaron's head snapped back up, and looked at Betsey. Tears now threatening to roll down his cheeks.

"If something happens to the baby or me, bury us there, too."

"Why do we have to talk about this?" Aaron's eyes now filled with hurt with what appeared to be frustration at her words.

Betsey cupped his cheek with her hand. "Because we're never guaranteed tomorrow, but we will cling to God's promise to see each other again. Remember that."

That night while finishing up the dishes, Betsey began to feel extremely weary. She knew these last few weeks would be hard, but tonight she felt more than just a normal, busy day tired. Standing beside the hearth, she felt particularly warm, too. Perhaps it hadn't been a good idea to venture to the ridge.

"I think I need to sit for a bit." She handed Jillian her towel. "Could you finish up the dishes for me?"

Jillian took the towel. Her sisters all knew her time was drawing near and Betsey had overhead Ma instructing them to help Betsey more and to take on some of her chores.

Ma must have seen Betsey heading for a chair, because she went over to pull up the rocker. During their travels to Jackson, Pa and Ambrose had found it in an abandoned wagon and brought it home to Ma. "Here Betsey, sit here."

"That's your chair, Ma. I'll be fine in a regular chair."

Ma took her hand and led her to the chair. "Sit." Ma's stern warning made her feel as if she were a five-year-old again.

Betsey smiled and sat. The baby had been more than active that day and after walking up to the property that afternoon, she'd grown weary faster. Sitting down brought relief to her swollen and tired feet.

Ma got down on her knees and began to untie Betsey's shoes, "You look too tired tonight. You need to stop doing so much."

"I'm fine," Betsey argued.

"Your time is coming soon, Betsey Anne Baker."

"Baker-Swain, Ma."

Her ma finished untying her shoes. "Mrs. Swain, you need to keep up your strength. Birthing a baby isn't for the weak."

Betsey leaned her head back against Ma's chair and closed her eyes. She knew Ma was right, but by keeping busy, it kept her mind off what would happen soon.

CHAPTER TWENTY-SEVEN

Betsey did her best to open her eyes. She could hear people talking, but she couldn't make out what they were saying. She wanted to tell them to speak up, talk in words she could understand, but a heavy weight on her chest kept her from catching a deep enough breath to ask them.

"She's burning up." Ma placed a cool washcloth on her eldest daughter's forehead.

Caroline took another cloth from the stack Ma had given her that morning and placed it in the cool water Etta had brought fresh from the spring. Betsey lay motionless on the bed. "Is it the fever?"

"Seems to be. It came on awful quick though. She was so tired last night. I assumed it was only because of her delicate condition." Ma wiped at a tear, now trickling down her cheek with her sleeve. "This seems worse than when I had it."

Caroline patted her mother's arm, "You were this sick too, Ma. You just don't remember it."

Ma took the washcloth off Betsey's pink face. "Wring out that new cloth." Ma pointed to the bowl.

Caroline did exactly what she was told. "Let me sit with her for a bit, Ma. You've been here all morning. I can do it."

Ma looked at her with wide, tear-filled eyes. "This isn't good. The baby should be here soon. A fever at this point might take the child."

Caroline nodded. "But look, Ma." She pointed down to the movement in her sister's belly, seen through her thin nightgown. "The baby is fine."

"But will it live through this illness?" Ma wiped her eyes as she stood. "Let's pray so."

As her ma walked out to begin her daily chores, Caroline sat down beside her sister's bed. Tears began welling in her own eyes. What if something were to happen to her sister? Placing her hand on Betsey's large belly, she prayed for them both.

Aaron came in throughout the day to check on Betsey. He'd found her that morning burning up with fever. She'd vomited several times in the night. Each time, he'd gotten up to help clean her up and settle her back to bed. They assumed that perhaps childbirth had started, but by morning, Betsey was incoherent and burning up.

He was haunted from her words the previous day to bury her by the blackjack oak tree. What had made her tell him that? Aaron shivered even in the warmth of the day. What would he do if something were to happen to Betsey or even his unborn child?

He sat down on a fresh log cut for the floor of his house and wept. A voice disturbed his grief.

Betsey's pa touched his shoulder. "Son."

Aaron jerked his head up and wiped his face with his hands. "Hosea, I didn't see you there."

Hosea sat down beside him on the ground. "This fever is the demon of our new home. I can't get over how much it affected Sally. When I returned from our trip, I almost didn't recognize her. She was so thin and pale."

Aaron turned his face away from his father-in-law. The ache of how Hosea had left the women to go purchase the land still felt raw and made him edgy toward the man.

"What can I do to help you?"

Aaron sighed. "There isn't anything I can do to make it go away. She has to suffer through it. All alone. I just feel so helpless."

The men sat quietly for a moment. The leaves rustled in the wind. The beauty of the season evident in every leaf which fluttered to the ground.

Hosea was the first to speak.

"I love this place. I know I'm being selfish by saying that, but I do. I've always been attracted to trees and here," Hosea pointed to the woods behind the cabin, "I've never seen such beauty."

Aaron didn't know what to say. He was losing the battle to fight back tears threatening to spill down his face. "I love her, sir. More than this, or anything else in this world."

Hosea patted his shoulder. "I do, too. Bit is my firstborn daughter." He sighed, "You know how she got her nickname."

Aaron shook his head.

"Betsey is named after her grandmother, but I chose Bit as her nickname. When she was little, she was fierce. She came into the world a tiny thing. Ambrose was just two. He looked so big compared to her. I could fit her head in my hand," Hosea opened his hand, held out his arm and turned it palm-side up. "Her little feet barely went down half my arm." Hosea pointed to a spot just before his elbow. "Sally had a hard time getting her into the world. I will never understand why God gave such a burden to a woman; bringing life into the world is so painful. Life is such a miracle. I have five reasons to believe that with my whole heart. I also have two waiting for me in heaven someday. I don't know what's worse, wanting to take their pain while you sit back and watch them suffer, or wondering if they'll survive the ordeal to see the fruit of their labor."

Aaron's head was down. He watched Hosea's foot push dirt forward with the toe of his shoe.

"Every single time I look at my children, I realize how gracious and loving my God is. He allowed me the opportunity to help create them, and God gave me a wife with a love great enough to almost sacrifice her life to bring them into the world. It's the most miraculous thing I've ever witnessed, and I love them all more than even these trees that surround us."

"Why did you leave them?" Aaron blurted out his frustration without thinking of how it might be perceived by his father-in-law.

"What?"

Aaron raised his head and looked him in the eyes.

Hosea sat up straighter, with a quizzical look in his eyes.

"Why didn't you wait for me to get back from purchasing the lumber?"

Hosea took off his hat and looked away. "So that's why you've been cold to me since I came back."

"I still can't believe you left them. And all alone! We aren't in Pennsylvania anymore, Hosea. The closest neighbor," Aaron pointed to the south of the property, "is too far away to know if there were any problems."

Hosea took a deep breath and slowly let it back out. "I know it seemed like a hasty decision but it really wasn't. I thought long and hard about it and even argued with God for a time, but then God prompted me to get going. If I didn't go then, I might have had to leave too close to the time when Betsey would be giving birth. I felt that I needed to get it done and back before that."

Aaron shook his head, but didn't know what else to say.

"I alerted Leach and Whitmore to check on them from time to time, but I knew that if I left and got back before Betsey's baby arrived, I'd be better equipped to help you two when you might need it the most. If I would have waited, I wouldn't be here now."

Aaron's jaw hurt. Without realizing it, he'd been clenching it. He forced himself to relax. "I wish you'd have waited."

Hosea nodded. "You have a right to protect your wife. I have a duty to protect my own. I had no idea there would be a windstorm and that Sally would grow sicker. I never imagined that Caroline would take on wolves with a gun to protect chickens or that you'd be gone as long as you were. I weighed the dangers that this new land might hold for my family while I was gone. But God knew they'd be fine. His mercy was evident the entire time I was gone."

Aaron still didn't understand.

Hosea added, "And now that Betsey is near to giving birth, I won't have to leave, freeing Sally and the girls from their chores to help her. I'll be able to prepare food for winter and even help you build your home. Somehow God knew I would be needed here now and He'd protect the womenfolk while I was away. I'm sorry you feel it was the wrong decision."

Aaron knew he had no control over Hosea's decisions.

"Trusting God when things are out of our control is when He shines the brightest. Look at all He did while I was gone. He healed my wife, protected the womenfolk during a pretty bad windstorm, he brought a kind neighbor to check on them, he was with Caroline when she picked up a rifle to shoot a wolf, and even got you back in time to be with them during the Indian incident. He was here. Doing His job, while I was off doing mine.

"Now. I'm here to help you. We have a baby coming and I've found the best thing to do when you're worried or afraid is to beg God to keep you strong. I do it often. I've relied on God to protect my family, but most of all," Hosea pointed toward the sky, "I've relied on Him to take away the fear that often creeps into my heart. I pray while I pound nails, harvest a crop, or drive the oxen. That's what works for me. So why don't we grab Ambrose and head up to the ridge. You have a house to build. But before we go, let us sit here for a moment and pray for my daughter and your wife. She needs all the power God can give her to not only get over this illness, but to bring this new life into the world to join our family."

Aaron bowed his head as Hosea put his arm around him and prayed for health, strength, and the ability to trust God in the worst of circumstances.

When he was finished, he stood and put his hat back on his head. "Aaron, do you know who Betsey's baby will be?"

Aaron now stood, choking back new tears threatening to overtake him. "No, sir."

"Whitmore told me on our trip back. Betsey's baby will be the first baby to be born in this area. Someday, if all goes well, people...fifty, a hundred, or even two hundred years from now, will find Aaron and Betsey Swain's baby was the first child born in these here parts of Michigan Territory. God has always known that. But now, so do we."

Hosea took a few steps toward the barn. "Just think of that. The first baby to be born here, along this bank of the Shiawassee. As soon as we get a fit name for the place, the baby's name will go down in the history books, too. Ain't that excitin'."

His father-in-law's promising words gave Aaron the courage to keep moving, keep working toward that hopeful celebration. He also hoped that one day, he'd have the same kind of confident trust in God that Hosea seemed to have. It might give him an easier, more confident life, too.

That evening, Betsey awoke to find Aaron beside her. He'd just placed a cold rag on her forehead. She could feel the dampness cool her warm brow.

He spoke, "Betsey, can you hear me?"

She did her best to nod. Her eyes wanted to open but she couldn't garner enough strength to do it.

"You have the fever, like your ma. We're doing our best to keep you cool. Can I get you something?"

Betsey's mouth felt dry. She was able to mouth the word, "water."

Soon a spoon was in her mouth and she felt the cool water on her tongue. Trying to swallow, she felt a drop run down her chin. She opened her mouth again, hoping it would signal Aaron to give her more. Another spoonful came and she relished in the coolness it brought to her throat. Her stomach raged for food, but she also knew she hadn't done very well in keeping food down over the past few hours. Lifting her head from the pillow was almost impossible, the feat too strenuous.

After a few more spoonfuls of water, Betsey sighed. Reaching down and placing her hand on her enlarged belly, she felt the swift, strong kicks of her baby. She whispered a prayer in her heart. *Protect our little one, God. He's been so strong and active. Give me strength. Don't take him before I can hold him and kiss his cheek.* With that prayer, Betsey fell back asleep.

"It's been a whole week." Aaron twisted his hat with his hands as he stood at the foot of his and Betsey's bed. "Shouldn't she be waking up more now?"

Caroline stood and came to stand beside him. "Ma was just about the same. We just kept cool cloths on her forehead and kept spooning her water whenever she woke up. It took Ma almost three weeks before she began to feel better, and—" Caroline folded her arms.

"What?" Aaron pleaded. "And what?"

"Alexander went for the medicine."

"Can we give it to Betsey?"

Caroline got a clean rag moist from a cool pan of water on the table. "Ma is scared to give Betsey any quinine. Midwives, back in Pennsylvania, told her it could be dangerous for a woman carrying a child." Caroline sighed. "I don't know what else to do."

Aaron placed his hat back on his head. "I'm heading up to the ridge. If there is any change, or you need me, send Alexander. I'll make him stay close to the cabin today."

Aaron left the cabin and found Alexander ready to head to the ridge with him. He motioned for him and explained the best he could to him to stay close by the cabin. The young boy nodded, seeming to understand.

Ambrose had a wagon ready to head up to the ridge. He shouted to Aaron to climb aboard as he snapped the reins.

As Aaron scrambled aboard, Ambrose patted his shoulder, "How is she?"

"The same." Aaron slapped some dirt off his pant leg. "I feel so helpless."

Ambrose clicked to the oxen to move faster toward Aaron and Betsey's property. "Does it help to keep busy?"

Aaron hated to admit it but Hosea was right about keeping busy. It did keep his mind occupied. He just wished he could figure out a way to be by Betsey's side and also finish building their house.

"What do you think about adding a loft before we roof the house? Ambrose had been a great help to Aaron and his suggestion made sense.

"Do you think we'll have enough time? We have to get the roof on soon."

"I don't see why not. That will give you good storage for food, but also room to add more children to the family."

Aaron slapped Ambrose's leg, "Let's get this one here first, Ambrose."

Ambrose grinned. "Okay."

Aaron liked Ambrose. He had a gentle nature, and he was a hard worker. Aaron often kept things to himself, but lately his emotions were so on edge, he'd been chatting more than ever with Ambrose, while they worked.

"I feel bad that you have to spend so much time working with me, that you can't get your cabin finished."

Ambrose patted Aaron's knee. "Your turn will come to help me, but for now, I feel better helping you. It's almost like I'm doing something to help Betsey get better, by building her new home. Besides, if you haven't noticed, there aren't that many women wandering around to distract me."

"You don't need a wife as a reason to build a cabin."

Ambrose nodded. "I know, but it does give a man a bit of hope that someday he'll have the same opportunity to start a family, like you and Betsey are doing." Ambrose turned the wagon up onto the slope heading toward Aaron's work in progress. "And," Ambrose coughed from the dust being stirred up by the oxen, "I love building things. I'd rather be doing that than farming, like Pa."

"I hope you get to do that more then, Ambrose. I appreciate your help."

"Let's work on the second floor today. We'll have to leave gaps between the floorboards on the second floor. It will help heat from below reach the loft in the winter."

A loft hadn't been part of Aaron's house plan. He definitely hadn't purchased enough lumber for one. Before he could ask about the lumber shortage, Ambrose added.

"Henry Leach stopped by. He had extra lumber and Pa bought it from him. It'd be awful nice to surprise Betsey with it, don't you think?"

Aaron smiled at the thought. "She'll love it."

Ma and her girls worked every day to preserve and store the vegetables harvested from the garden, in between taking turns watching over Betsey. Pa and Ambrose shot game and caught fish, smoking and salting the meat to preserve for the upcoming winter. The cabin nearly burst with the delicious smells of fresh food being gathered and preserved.

Betsey was missing it all. She'd been bedridden now for almost three weeks, with a fever which sometimes rose then cooled, just as Ma's had done earlier that summer.

"If only we knew what caused this illness. Perhaps then we could have some kind of treatment for it," Ma voiced to Caroline one evening." Ma wiped her hands down her apron. "I wonder if the Indians know better how to treat it?"

"Ma, you can't mean you want an Indian to come here and help us?"

"I know. It sounds crazy, but they've been here longer than us. They use many natural remedies to treat illnesses. There aren't doctors in the tribes to help them. I wonder if they could help us?" Ma sighed, and headed toward the hearth to start a meal. "Well, all we can do is what we've done for the past weeks. It's almost time for the baby to arrive. Have you seen him moving lately?"

Caroline shook her head, "I'll try and pay more attention today. I did see a kick a few days ago."

"She needs to eat. That baby needs nourishment soon." Ma sighed. "That's my biggest worry now."

Late October

CHAPTER TWENTY-EIGHT

Betsey woke to heavy pressure in her abdomen and a pain like she'd never felt before gripping her exhausted body. The pain was so intense; it seemed to wake her out of the stupor she'd been in for weeks. She touched Aaron who was lying beside her. He stirred, but didn't move. Another pain seized her middle. She nudged Aaron harder. "Aaron."

He finally stirred. "Betsey?"

"Get Ma." Betsey rolled onto her side, gripping the edge of the bed with all her might as fluid spilled from her body, onto the blanket beneath her.

Ma soon rushed to her side. Still in her nightgown, she grabbed Betsey's shawl and wrapped it around herself. "Go get Caroline up," she told Aaron, who was now fumbling with his pants, pulling his suspenders over his shoulders.

The room came awake as, one by one, each family member came to Betsey's side. Pa asked Ma what she needed him to do.

"We'll need water and clean blankets."

Pa snapped his suspenders in place and then motioned for Betsey's sisters to follow him.

Alexander finally seemed to understand the urgency of the situation. He stood at the head of Betsey's bed and wiped her forehead with his hand. He looked up at Ma with wide, bright eyes.

"Betsey's having a baby, Alexander." The little boy came near her, patted Ma's arm and then turned away. Sitting on the floor, he laced up his leather shoes, grabbed his jacket, and left the cabin.

"Where is he going?" Aaron asked Ma.

Ma was busy getting a dry blanket under Betsey, "I don't know, but I have other things to worry about here."

Aaron nodded. "What can I do?"

Ma stood up straight. "Caroline and I will need hot water and a small piece of thread. Etta and Jillian can start making everyone breakfast." She motioned to Pa, "Can you figure out how to get another blanket up here for a bit more privacy?"

Pa answered, "Yes. Let me head out for some rope." Aaron followed close behind.

Betsey began to yell, "Ma, this hurts so bad."

Ma stroked Betsey's cheeks. "Today will not be without pain, Betsey. You need to be strong. Try and breathe normally after each pain. I believe today, your baby wants a birthday."

Hosea and Aaron put up blankets to block the view of Betsey's bed from the rest of the cabin. Aaron was shaking so badly that Ambrose had to take over the job of pounding a wooden peg into the wall, to affix the rope from. Caroline helped layer blankets over the rope to create more privacy for Betsey.

Betsey cried out in anguish. Aaron's face grew white and Hosea knew the best thing to do was to get him outside and into some fresh air. He gripped his shoulder and encouraged him out the front door.

The sun was rising, casting long shadows over the rippling river water and onto the eastern portion of the homestead. A deep frost coated the ground. Hosea breathed in deeply. "Smell the land, Aaron. Fresh and new. Today, my boy, you'll be a pa...just like me. It will be a day you'll never forget."

Aaron seemed even more nervous once outside and away from Betsey's bedside. "Can't I just be with her?"

Hosea shook his head. "This, my boy, is women's work. She's in good hands. Sally will do her best to help get this baby into the world."

"Hosea, I'm glad she has her ma by her side today. I'm glad we followed your advice to come here."

Hosea patted his shoulder. "I'm sure Sally feels the exact same way. They know best how to get these babies into the world." Hosea breathed in deeply again, with his hands on his hips. "'Yea, the darkness hideth not from thee, but the night shineth as the day: the darkness and the light are both alike to thee. For thou hast possessed my reins: thou has covered me in my mother's womb. I will praise thee; for I am fearfully and wonderfully made: marvelous are thy works; and that my soul knoweth right well. My substance was not hid from thee, when I was made in secret, and curiously wrought in the lowest parts of the earth. Thine eyes did see my substance, yet being unperfect; and in thy book all my members were written, which in continuance were fashioned, when as yet there was none of them. How precious also are thy thoughts unto me, O God! How great is the sum of them! That I should count them, they are more in number than the sand.'" Taking in another breath, he added, "Praise be to God, the giver of life and breath." Hosea gazed up into the trees at the traces of colored leaves which would soon be covering the ground.

Aaron declared, "'Blessed be the name of the Lord.'"

As the pair walked toward the barn to begin the morning chores and get another day started, Aaron asked, "How are you able to quote so much scripture, Hosea?"

Hosea laughed right out loud. "That's how I learned to read. Back in my day," he chuckled, "we didn't have primers or books to learn from. All we had was a Bible, and it was read daily and often. Ma taught me to read by using it. Some of the words I read over and over again, and you know what—"

Aaron plunged his hands into his pockets to keep the morning chill off of them.

"I've never regretted having it as my primer. You never forget the first words you can read by yourself."

Hosea patted his son-in-law's back. "Time to keep ourselves busy. We'll have something to be thankful for as soon as this day is done."

The men had dug out their winter coats to work the morning before and on this day, it felt good to wear them. The leaves had begun to fall forming a deep, soft, multi-colored carpet over the now hard ground. The bare trees permitted a far-reaching view than during the spring and summer months, the sky bright-blue in color. The river gushed downstream, sprinkled with leaves.

"We'll have snow soon," Pa called from atop a ladder. "Hand me up some more of that bark, Ambrose."

Ambrose gathered the strips he'd been cutting and partially climbed the ladder below Pa. "Let's get this roof sealed up today and then we'll be able to work inside a bit and get out of this wind. Looks like we're in for a cold night."

"It turns cold fast." Ambrose got down from the ladder. "I can get busy on the hearth today, Aaron." Ambrose couldn't hear Aaron on the other side of the cabin. He'd been working to add strips of bark to the opposite side of the roof. He walked over to see if he was okay. "Aaron?"

Surprised, Aaron nearly fell off the ladder. "Ambrose! You scared me. Is Betsey okay?"

Ambrose put his hands on his hips. "I don't know. I've been up on the ridge with you all day, remember?"

Aaron sighed, "Sorry. I was deep in thought."

Ambrose chuckled, rubbing his nose. "The hearth? Do you want me to start mixing mud to get it started?"

"Is Pa almost done on the other side of the roof?"

"Yes. How're you coming?"

"I have another whole section yet to go."

The trio had worked hard throughout the day. It did seem to make the current situation at the cabin seem less weary, but Ambrose knew Aaron's mind wasn't all that much on his work. "I'll mix up the mud. We can get at least a few stones in place before evening."

Aaron descended the ladder. "I wish I knew what was taking so long. Will one of the girls come up here to tell us when the baby arrives?"

Ambrose shrugged. "I assume so. We've not had a baby in some time."

Aaron rubbed his whiskered face. "I wish giving birth to a baby didn't take so long."

Caroline worked hard coaching Betsey through the worst of the pain throughout the afternoon.

"This poor girl isn't well enough to give birth in a hurry. We just need to encourage her to continue to fight." Betsey felt her ma wipe off her forehead with a cool cloth.

Caroline urged her sister. "You heard Ma, Betsey. You can do this."

The effort to talk was strenuous, so Betsey only mumbled answers to Ma and Caroline throughout the day. Enduring the pains of childbirth took all her energy. She felt like a rag doll. It was even an effort to raise her hand off the bed. "I'm not sure—"

"I want to hear none of that. You're a strong woman, Betsey Baker-Swain. This baby is going to come soon."

Betsey did her best to smile for her ma, but even that took incredible effort. "Water?" Her mouth felt parched.

Caroline hollered for Etta, who had been bringing her water through the day. The young girl's hands shook as she brought in a ladleful of cool water. "Is this enough?"

Caroline took the ladle. "It's a start. Why don't you heat up some of that broth from the turkey Ma cooked last night?"

"Good idea. A bit of nourishment might do her some good. Give her body strength."

Caroline leaned toward her ma, "Alexander has been gone all day. Do you think seeing Betsey in pain scared him? Maybe one of us should go looking for him."

Ma shook her head. "No. I need you here. She doesn't seem to be delivering as fast as I hoped."

Betsey could hear the conversations of her ma and sisters. The concern etched on her ma's face gave Betsey determination to try harder. Another hard pain took her breath away. Caroline grabbed her hand as Ma took a look to see if any progress was being made.

"I don't see the head. It's just a waiting game now, but I don't know how much longer Betsey can fight. She's so weak."

It exasperated Betsey that Ma and Caroline were talking about her and she didn't have the strength to join in, nor answer them. She knew she needed to try harder to bring this baby into the world. She did her best to rest between each hard pain. She'd close her eyes and gripped Caroline's hand. The pain was so strong that it often left her breathless and exhausted after each one. Just when she thought she couldn't get through one more, her belly tightened, as if it didn't care whether she could handle another spasm or not.

"Aaron?"

"He's working up on the ridge. He needs to keep busy, Betsey. Menfolk get awful upset to see their wives in so much pain."

Betsey took in another deep breath as another excruciating pain hit again.

"Try to relax after each one. Close your eyes and breathe in deep." But before Betsey even had the chance to breathe deeply, another pain gripped her middle section.

"Oh Ma, I can't do this."

"Yes, you can, Betsey. Yes, you can."

Her body felt spent. She wasn't sure how much she could take. So, she did the only thing she knew to do. She asked for divine strength to bring life into the world.

Aaron, Ambrose, and Pa made their way down the slope to the cabin. They'd worked long and hard all day to keep their minds off Betsey and the impending birth.

As they came closer to the back edge of the property, Aaron saw Alexander leading an Indian woman by the hand toward the cabin. He jumped off the wagon and ran toward the cabin. *What was happening? Why was Alexander rushing to the cabin? And with an Indian woman?*

By the time they got close, Jillian was sitting just outside the door. She had tears in her eyes, and when she saw Pa she jumped into his arms.

"Honey, what's wrong? What's happening?"

Jillian gulped. "I don't know. I've been outside all day. All I've done is go get water from the spring whenever I'm asked."

Pa announced to Aaron and Ambrose. "Let me find out how things are progressing."

Aaron attempted to follow. "Let *me* go see what's happening. I promise to come back out to let you know how she's doing." He ducked inside the cabin.

Alexander got closer. The Indian woman followed behind him.

"What's she doing here? Betsey is petrified of Indians!"

Ambrose gripped his shoulder and squeezed. "I know. Pa will know what to do. You gotta trust him."

Aaron pushed his fingers through his hair as he watched Alexander lead the Indian woman through the door behind Hosea.

It seemed forever before Pa came back out. "Betsey's had a hard day, but Sally thinks the baby is almost here. The child is struggling to be born."

Aaron leaned against the cabin and skidded down to the ground. "Oh God. Help my wife."

Betsey watched as the Indian woman approached her bed. Alexander was pulling her by the hand. Betsey squeezed Caroline's hand tighter. "What's she doing here?"

Ma turned to the woman, who removed a colorful blanket covering her shoulders and dropped it onto the floor. She looked at all of them, nodded, seeming to access the situation. Mumbling words to Alexander, he scooted back outside.

"My daughter is in labor. I can see the head, but during the past hour or so, she isn't making any further progress. She's very weak, I'm not sure she can push the baby into the world." Ma used hand motions to communicate to the woman, but she seemed to assess the situation by just looking at Betsey.

Acting as if she wanted to help, Betsey glanced at Caroline and her ma. "Don't let her touch me. What is she going to do to me?"

"Betsey. Calm yourself. I think she wants to help."

Betsey felt more pain crescendo in her belly. She grimaced. Whether she wanted it to happen or not, the Indian woman came toward her. Bringing out a mortar and pestle from a wrapped cloth, she pulled herb stems out of her pocket. Handing the tools to

Caroline, she motioned for her to start grinding the leaves. Caroline did what she asked.

The pain Betsey now felt made her want to push with all her might, but the Indian woman gently pushed her hair back from off her forehead and smiled at her.

Pointing to herself, the woman spoke, "Waussinoodae."

As fearful as she was of the Indian woman, she began to relax as she felt her gentle hands and what seemed to be a kind gesture.

Caroline broke everyone's stares by pointing to herself. "Caroline." Then she pointed to Betsey, "Betsey."

The Indian woman nodded, but then began pushing Betsey to roll to her side.

Ma stood back a bit, biting her lip and watching the Indian woman work. She motioned to Betsey, "Do as she says, honey."

Waussinoodae then motioned to Caroline to help Betsey into a dog-like position on the bed. Betsey moaned as Caroline did her best to help her into the position. With gentle hands, Waussinoodae began rubbing Betsey's belly. The extreme pressure Betsey had been feeling began to dissipate the more the woman massaged her belly.

Soon Alexander came back into the room and handed the woman, what appeared to be, plant roots. Waussinoodae nodded at him and gave them to Caroline, motioning her to grind them.

She then pointed Alexander toward the door. Said a few words, and he left.

Other instructions were given, by the Indian woman, by hand motions. She pointed to the pot over the water, then wiggled her fingers. *Boil some water.* She picked up a cup off the table and pointed into it. *Put it in a cup.* She pointed to Betsey, then lifted the cup to her own mouth. *Give it to Betsey to drink.*

349

Betsey felt a large movement from the baby in her womb. Waussinoodae gently patted her back and motioned for her to lie down on her back again. Betsey had just seconds to swallow the hot mixture before more pain seized her body.

Whatever medicine was in the water, Betsey began to feel more relaxed despite the intense pain. Soon after drinking it, she felt even a bit more energy to push, as the Indian woman now instructed her, with a grimace expression on her face and tight fists.

A sense of relief filled her soul. She wasn't sure if it was because of the medicine or the massages from Waussinoodae's soft hands, but Betsey could feel things progressing much easier. The woman was gentle, and even her words that no one could understand, seemed kind and supportive.

As Betsey thanked God for a bit of relief from the day's labor, she thought it odd that God was answering her prayers in the most ironic way. He was using one of her greatest fears, in the form of this Indian woman, to help her. And in the process, her fear gradually gave way to respect and admiration.

Ambrose looked up to see Nibi approaching the group gathered outside the cabin. The Indian stood off to one side until Ambrose motioned for him to join them. Ambrose picked up the lantern they'd just lit as the day was growing darker. "Pa, this is Nibi. The Indian friend I've been telling you about."

Pa held out his hand. Nibi didn't seem to know what he was trying to do, but held his arm up against his chest. Pa did the same.

To Aaron it seemed as if this meant some kind of greeting.

"Do you know the woman in the cabin with my sister, Nibi?" Ambrose pointed to the cabin.

Nibi seemed again to understand. He spoke, "Waussinoodae." He then pointed to himself, "Nibi."

"Waussinoodae?" Ambrose repeated. "That must be her name."

The Indian nodded. He then waved his hand off to the north as if telling them a direction. Pa seemed to pick up on it right away. "North?"

Nibi smiled. Then he pointed to the lantern.

"Light." Aaron guessed.

Nibi smiled again. He then pointed to the horizon toward the north.

"Northern Lights." Ambrose said.

Nibi nodded and then spoke softly, "North..ern light..s."

"Is that what Waussinoodae means?" Ambrose responded.

Nibi nodded. He then motioned to his mid-section, using his hands in an outward motion to define a pregnant belly. Then pointed back to the cabin.

"Waussinoodae must be an Indian midwife." Pa announced. Pa then pointed to Alexander. "Mother?"

Nibi put up a finger and shook his head. "Waussinoodae." Then put three fingers up behind his head.

Ambrose guessed, "Does she belong to the chief?"

Nibi nodded. "Waussinoodae!"

"She must be the chief's wife." Ambrose patted Nibi on the shoulder. "Thank you, friend."

Nibi smiled. He then waved to the family and disappeared back into the woods.

"Do you think it's safe the woman is in with Betsey?" Aaron wiped the sweat off his forehead, despite the frigid temperature of the coming night.

Ambrose nodded. "She's not dangerous. Nibi and his chief have been nothing but a help to me. Alexander must have known that this is the kind of help Betsey needs right now."

Pa stooped to Alexander's level and gave him a bear hug.

The boy grinned and hugged Pa's neck to return the thankful gesture.

About an hour later, Aaron, Ambrose, Alexander and Jillian heard a loud blustery cry come from inside the cabin. It sounded as if Betsey had cried out for Aaron. Aaron stood, heading for the door. Ambrose stopped him. "Wait Aaron. Listen."

Aaron stopped long enough to listen as he heard a baby's cry follow Betsey's wail.

"Let me go check. Wait here." Hosea left them on the doorstep. He soon returned. "She's here!" he announced.

"She?" Aaron's eyes grew moist, but he managed to smile.

"It's a girl. Sally said she's crying well. She'll be fine."

Aaron needed to know, but he couldn't seem to get the courage to ask about Betsey. Before Aaron could muster up enough courage to speak, Ambrose asked.

"How's Betsey?"

Pa lowered his head, but looked up again. "Sally said she's very weak and exhausted. Time will tell."

Aaron felt arms going around him. He buried his head in Ambrose's shoulder and wept.

CHAPTER TWENTY-NINE

"How much longer do we have to wait?" Aaron had been pacing out in front of the cabin since Pa announced his daughter's arrival. "I want to see Betsey."

The door to the cabin opened and the Indian woman came out. She looked up at the men now staring at her, bowed her head, then scooted off, disappearing into the woods beyond the barn.

Before any of them could react, Sally came out. She smiled at the men standing guard at the door. "Aaron, you can go in and see Betsey now."

Aaron hesitated a moment.

"Go ahead, son. Go see your family." Pa nudged him into the cabin.

Caroline appeared at the door. "She's so tiny." She looked as tired as Sally.

Etta stood behind Caroline, clapping her hands. "Wait 'til you see her, Pa. She's beautiful."

Sally went into her husband's arms and he squeezed her tight, "So I guess we're grandparents now."

Sally stood on her tiptoes and kissed his chin.

Tears glimmered in her eyes. "Yes, we are. She's was so strong, Hosea. Our Betsey is a new momma."

"Hey," Ambrose pounded his chest. "That makes me an Uncle. Right?"

Everyone laughed.

The family huddled in a small circle and Hosea gave thanks to the Lord for His utmost care and protection over their family in the new land. He also prayed for Waussinoodae who seemed to have been sent from God to get them through their most trying trial yet.

Aaron went into the cabin to find his wife propped up in bed. Her eyes were closed and in the crook of her arm was a tiny infant. Betsey didn't seem to know he was there. Aaron approached the bed. He could see the baby's bright, dark eyes gazing up at him. He bent down to get a closer look, peeling the soft blanket down below her chin. The fire in the hearth cast shadows on the wall behind him.

"Betsey?" he whispered.

Betsey didn't respond. He dug his hands under the tiny bundle and gently lifted the child's face to his own. They were cheek to cheek, and the baby turned its head and began to suckle his face. The soft tickle made him laugh.

As he did, Betsey woke. She smiled.

"Betsey, she's beautiful!"

"I'm so tired." She closed her eyes again.

Aaron repositioned the child a bit and settled her into the crook of his arm. He sat down and stared at the round, chubby cheeks of his baby girl. "Hello, sweet girl. I thought you were gonna be a boy."

The baby drew her fist to her mouth and began sucking on it. Aaron wanted to laugh right out loud, but instead he just smiled. "Momma will be ready to help you with that hunger real soon."

"I can't even lift my arms," Betsey murmured.

Aaron bent down and kissed Betsey's cheek, finally cool to the touch. "It's okay, Bit. But this little one seems to want to eat. Can you manage it?"

"Will you help me?" Betsey motioned for him to pull back the blanket she had over her.

Aaron pulled the blanket down, laying his new daughter against Betsey's chest. Before long, she found her source of food, and a soft, suckling noise announced a baby enjoying her first meal.

"Hold her there for me, Aaron."

Aaron placed his hand underneath the baby's bottom for support, and they both watched as the infant suckled. Aaron reached up his other hand, brushed Betsey's hair off her face and kissed her cheek. "You just rest. I'll keep watch."

Relief enveloped Aaron's soul. He felt useful again.

Soon the family had all been fed, and each one took turns cradling and holding the new baby.

"Have you decided on a name yet?" Ma asked Aaron as they gazed at the baby's tiny feet and toes.

"Were we this little once, Ma?" Jillian couldn't seem to get enough of the tiny child.

"Yes, believe it or not, but you didn't stay that way very long."

"We haven't really chosen a name yet," Aaron told the family. "As soon as Betsey regains her strength, we'll choose one." He chuckled. "She was supposed to be a boy. Theodore doesn't sound appropriate for a pretty, little girl."

Everyone chuckled while they admired the baby, the cabin door opened, and Ambrose and Alexander carried in a beautiful cradle. "I made this for Betsey. I was going to give it to her way before the baby arrived, but when she got sick, there never seemed a good time."

Aaron stood and took the cradle from Ambrose. "It's amazing. When? How?"

"I worked on it during the evenings. Pa and I had saved back a bit of leftover wood from your building materials. We've been working on it off and on."

Aaron rubbed his hand over the smooth boards. "It should work fine. Betsey will love it."

"I hope so," Ambrose rubbed his chin. "Now let me hold her." Ambrose opened his arms so Etta could place the new baby into them.

"Betsey ate tonight," Caroline announced as she came out from behind the curtain and took Betsey's plate into the kitchen to clean.

"How did Waussinoodae help Betsey?" Pa asked as he tickled the soft cheek of his granddaughter.

"She gave Betsey some kind of herb mixture. I don't know what it had in it, but it sure worked wonders. I also believe she did something to cause the baby to move in Betsey's womb because shortly after she did it, Betsey's labor progressed quickly." Caroline told her pa.

"Betsey was so tired, I wasn't sure how she would have any strength left to push the child into the world." Ma's eyes were droopy. He face was tired. "I think I'll head to bed now. It's been a long day. The baby will probably need to be fed every other hour or so tonight, Aaron."

Aaron nodded, "How will I know if she's hungry?"

Pa tipped his head back and roared in laughter. "Oh Aaron, she'll let you know."

"She will?" Aaron didn't understand the insinuation.

"She's already shown us her lungs are good." Pa laughed, patting Aaron's shoulder.

"Oh, yeah. Well that." Aaron finally caught on.

"Let's all try and get some sleep."

Aaron opened his arms for Ambrose to place the baby back in them. "Let's go see Momma, sweet girl."

Ambrose had managed to put her to sleep while he'd been holding her.

"Look at you, Ambrose. Soon you'll be able to hold your own."

"Let's not get ahead of ourselves, Aaron. I need to find a wife who wants to be a momma first."

Caroline brought Aaron some blankets she'd found inside Betsey's baby barrel. Betsey had been making clothing while Ma had stitched together a few blankets. "Let's use these blankets to put around her in the cradle."

Caroline and Aaron placed the cradle on the floor next to Betsey's side of the bed. "I think she'll be warm here. Betsey's much too weak to care for her in bed. Can you help her when the baby needs to be fed?"

Aaron was confident that he could and nodded.

"I'll be out by the fire. I'm pretty tired, too. I think I'll go find my own blanket."

"Thank you, Caroline, for all you did."

"I've never seen anything so wonderful as birth. I was glad to help my sister. Although, it wasn't me who did the most. That

Indian woman, I believe, saved the baby's life. Perhaps even Betsey's."

Aaron placed the baby in the cradle and covered her with a new blanket. She looked so tiny underneath it. He then crawled in beside Betsey and pulled her into his arms. She barely moved. He hoped the food she'd been able to eat would sustain her and give her body enough nourishment to help her gain her strength back.

If only he could transfer some of his own to his wife. He would do anything to help make her well and strong. How long could a wife, who hadn't eaten in weeks, nourish a tiny being? He knew only one thing: God did provide and sometimes in the most unusual ways. Aaron relaxed as he realized that his wife's grave wouldn't be the first plot on the hill. He'd do everything in his power to protect Betsey and the baby, but he also realized that God had a better handle on that than he would ever have. Today's experience gave Aaron insight into Hosea's strong reliance on God. He'd try hard to never forget it.

As he held his wife, he knew he couldn't be a good husband or father without God's guidance. Before he went to sleep he uttered a grateful prayer for all God had provided that day. Then with a needy heart, he asked God to help him trust Him more. As he fell asleep, he saw Hosea's faith now as an example, instead of a burden he'd been carrying for far too long.

CHAPTER THIRTY

The next day, everyone watched as Betsey conjured up enough strength to sit up and begin to care for her daughter. Aaron had been helpful all through the night. Before he left, he'd helped Betsey consume the first full breakfast she'd had in weeks. She ate well and he made sure she drank enough, too. He'd have to leave Betsey and the baby in Caroline's care so he could get back to building their home on the ridge.

"Do you think you could help me with a sponge bath today? Or brush my hair?" Betsey asked Caroline.

"I think we could manage that. Let me heat up some water." Caroline left and Betsey gazed down at the small body of the child in the cradle which Ambrose had made. She was thrilled when Aaron had finally showed it to her before he left.

Ma came in carrying a cup of tea. "Drink this. It has herbs in it from the Indian woman. I'm happy you seem to be feeling a bit stronger today."

Betsey's hands shook as she held the cup, but she managed to swallow the tea Ma prepared for her.

"I think we have a name." Aaron had asked her about it that morning, and together they believed they'd chosen the perfect name for their new daughter.

Ma looked at her with raised eyebrows. "Already? Well, what will our precious bundle be named?"

"We'll tell everyone tonight."

Ma winked. "I had a feeling I'd have to wait longer."

"Do you think I have enough milk to feed her, Ma? She seems to be eating something when I try and nurse her." Betsey took another bite of food.

"You need to drink, Betsey. You've lost so many fluids. If she gets too hungry, she'll let us know." Ma giggled again as she told Betsey about Aaron's comment the night before about how to know when the baby was hungry.

"Be gentle, Ma. He's never been a Pa before."

"I know." Ma took the cup from Betsey. "Now you get some more rest this morning."

Before her ma could leave, Betsey asked, "Do you know what the date is today?"

Ma shook her head. "Ask your pa. He'll know. I think it's close to the end of October."

"October! My, I've been sick way too long."

Her ma turned to leave. "Yes, Betsey, you have."

That night, Ma brought their family Bible to the table, as the family sat around it, and Pa dug out his calendar.

"Now let's see," Pa looked at the calendar he'd put into the Bible. "Looks to be the twenty-ninth of October. That makes our granddaughter born on Saturday, October twenty-eighth."

"I'll mark that in the Bible," Ma said, as she leafed through the thin paper pages to the section where new baby names were written. The last entry was Alexander. "I can put the date in here, but Aaron, we need to know a name for our new granddaughter."

Aaron asked Betsey with his eyes. They'd removed the curtain so Betsey could see everyone from her bed. "Go ahead, tell them."

Aaron announced, "Her name is Julia Swain."

The whole family cheered and clapped, causing baby Julia to whimper in protest.

"What a beautiful name for my new baby niece!" Etta clapped her hands and twirled in excitement.

Betsey laughed from her bed. She hadn't realized what a stir a new baby would bring to her family. They'd had quite the year at their new home. There'd been heartache and joy, laughter and tears, and frustrations and hardships, but they'd gone through it together. She was sure that, for years to come, she'd have stories to tell about their first-year adventures in the Michigan Territory.

It took Betsey nearly two weeks to gain enough strength to finally get out of bed. Caroline and Aaron had been able to help her care for Julia. Aaron had gotten up in the night to bring Julia to her when she was hungry. He felt useful and that brought him joy, too.

He was finishing up their home and said they could move there just before the New Year, if all went well. Betsey was thrilled to think of having a home again, but she'd miss waking up all together. All the activity of her ma and sisters brought her joy. Everyone had their chores and worked well together.

Ma managed to put up food for Aaron and Betsey, too. Betsey couldn't believe it had been nearly five weeks since she'd had the ability to get out of bed and help. The first morning she was at the table for breakfast brought her joy.

Ma told her more about how the Indian woman had helped deliver Julia. "I've never seen a woman work in such a gentle manner while delivering a child. Whenever I've participated in births where the infant was struggling to get into the world, the doctor uses force to help, but that's contrary to how she helped you." Ma hesitated before adding, "Caroline watched closely. I wonder if we have a midwife in the making. She did even more for you than I. After delivering the afterbirth, the Indian woman wrapped it in a cloth and packed it in her bundle before leaving."

"What will she do with it?"

"I don't know. It seemed as if it had great importance to her."

"Do you think Alexander knows her name?"

"It would be nice to call her by her real name. I tried to ask her about Alexander before she left that night after delivering Julia. She patted her throat and seemed to tell me the child had some kind of neck injury. She then pointed to the river. I do believe Whitmore's assumption about the baby in the canoe...is likely correct. We may never know."

They rarely saw Waussinoodae after that. It had taken Alexander such a long time to bring her home that day when Betsey delivered Julia, Hosea wondered if the tribe she lived in had moved on deeper into the territory. It surprised no one that this might be the case, for more and more settlers had been filtering into the budding community since Julia's arrival.

One afternoon Caroline was busy feeding the chickens. The day was brisk and cold, heralding the coming of winter.

While she sprinkled seeds for the hungry chickens, a horse with a rider approached the property from the south. No one else was outside at the time, so Caroline made her way toward him.

Approaching closer, Caroline realized it was Whitmore. He smiled at her as he got down off his horse.

"Hello!" he called out.

Caroline smiled. "Hello. What brings you here today?"

"Well, I don't often do this, but I've got a letter that arrived several weeks ago. I haven't seen Ambrose or your pa for weeks, so I thought I better bring it to you, before the snow flies."

Caroline took the letter from Whitmore. Glancing at the print, she realized immediately who it was for, but especially, who it was from. She clasped it to her chest. "Oh, thank you Whitmore!"

Whitmore laughed, "I guess, you're the one it is addressed to."

Caroline nodded. Tears began filling her eyes.

"Well I hope it brings you good news."

"Thank you so much."

Whitmore tipped his hat. "You're very welcome."

In her excitement, Caroline almost forgot her manners. "Will you come to the cabin for some coffee? Warm up before you leave?"

Whitmore nodded again. "I thank you. Yes, I will."

As they made their way back to the cabin, Whitmore added, "You know it costs twenty-five cents to mail a letter. At that price, mailed letters must bear very important news."

Caroline felt her face blush. She never knew the cost of mailing a letter from their new home.

Later that night, after reading the letter from Billie, she thought of her pa. He'd forced her to leave Billie, but he also must have known how important it was for Caroline to get word to him. He'd spent good money to mail her letter.

Caroline approached Pa as he sat at the table that night and, without saying anything, wrapped her arms around him and kissed his cheek.

"Well, Caroline! What's that for?"

"I got a letter from Billie today. He's planning on coming after he graduates. Next spring." Caroline gave him another squeeze. "Thanks Pa, for mailing my letter."

Her pa's eyes twinkled. "You're welcome, sweet girl." He planted a kiss on her cheek.

November 13, 1833

CHAPTER THIRTY-ONE

A tiny whimper stirred Hosea. Opening his eyes, he blinked a few times to distinguish the sound coming from the other side of the cabin.

It was rare that he was the first to hear the sound, but soon he could hear the baby grunting a bit of protest from her cradle. Hosea couldn't guess why Betsey wasn't gathering the baby up for her breakfast, as the soft stirring noises continued.

Sally didn't move as Hosea gently laid back the quilt covering them. He shifted himself out of bed, placing his feet on the cool floor. As he slipped into his trousers, a soft glow of light radiated from the hearth fire. Someone had been up and put the initial log on the fire for the day, the fresh flame devouring the log that reflected light off the cabin walls.

Tip-toeing across the cool floor, Hosea went to the cradle beside Betsey and Aaron's bed. He found their bed empty. Peering into the cradle, he could make out the contours of Julia's tiny face. She gazed up at him with dark, alert eyes.

Hosea smiled. It was rare that he had the chance to hold his granddaughter, what with all the women in the family. Julia had brought new joy to the tiny cabin by the river. He needed to take advantage of this moment and enjoy it. He went to the door, pulled on his boots and slipped into his coat.

Returning to the cradle, Hosea gathered up the blankets surrounding the infant, wrapped her tightly in a bundle, then lifted her from the tiny bed. Julia didn't take her eyes of his face as he carried her to the door.

A heavy blanket hung by the door. Hosea lifted it off the hook and wrapped it tightly around his granddaughter, for even more protection. He whispered to her, "Let's go outside, sweet thing."

No one stirred in the cabin as Hosea cuddled the infant tighter. He walked out into the early morning darkness, gently closing the door behind him.

Betsey and Aaron must be outside in the privy, Hosea thought as he walked down toward the gurgling water of the river. The chilly morning wasn't ice cold for an early November day. They'd had a day or two of warmer temperatures. He stood close to the river and opened a crack of the blanket, covering Julia, so he could see her tiny face.

She squirmed in the blanket, as if she wanted to see what he was seeing, but soon grew intent on watching his face as he smiled at her. Her mouth seeming to mimic Hosea's, as he talked to her.

"Well Julia, it's morning here in Michigan Territory. Do you know that you're the first baby born here in this new land?"

Julia didn't take her eyes off him. Her mouth opened wide in a yawn.

"Yes, it's early, but I haven't been able to talk to you much yet. And I wanted you to see the morning stars. It's my favorite time of the day. God and I do lots of talking on mornings like this. I share with Him my thankfulness for a good night's sleep, and ask Him about His plans for me on this new day. I thought perhaps," Hosea lifted the infant closer to get a better look at her face, "you'd like to join me today."

A sound of the outhouse door slamming startled Hosea. "That must be your momma and daddy. But let's just stand here a bit more and take in this morning together, shall we, sweet pea?"

Hosea loved coming out in the early morning air. Looking up at the stars, he wondered if he should introduce Julia to God, but he knew well that God knew Julia even better than her new family. A Creator knows His creation.

He planted a kiss on Julia's forehead. "I think you're going to love it here. Your new home. A place for you to grow up, with hopefully," Hosea chuckled, "new brothers and sisters to join you. You'll be able to play in the stream of this river. Catch crawdads, and get your feet cooled on a hot summer day. Even beyond that, you might have the chance to find a handsome young man some day, and together, you'll be able to bring your own children to this river, to say prayers with them as well."

If Hosea had the opportunity to rise before the sun, he often would come outside to gaze at the stars flickering in the late-night sky. It seemed that this morning a brighter-than-usual array caught his eye.

Looking back down at his granddaughter, Hosea shifted the blanket close around the baby's face, to be sure she wasn't getting too much cold air. Sally would surely scold him if the poor baby grew colicky after their morning excursion.

Julia continued to gaze up at him with her dark eyes.

"God often spoils me on mornings like this, with a sky filled with bright stars." For a moment, Hosea took his eyes off his granddaughter and looked up into the heavens. He couldn't believe what he was seeing. "Well, I'll be. Would you look at that?"

As he pulled the baby closer to his chest, he looked back up to see the show God seemed to have created for just that morning.

Not only did the stars seem to glow brighter, but shooting stars began to streak across the sky. Hosea had never seen anything like it.

"What do we have here?"

The shower of stars reminded him of the sky during a thick, nighttime snowstorm, when he'd hold up a lantern to brighten a path.

Hosea spoke in a hushed tone. "I wish you were old enough to see this, Julia. God's showin' off for us this morning." The stars seemed to explode in all different directions, like sparks when a log is thrown into the fire, only brighter. The spectacle before his eyes, reminded him of a firework's explosion he'd once seen at a Fourth of July celebration.

A voice came from behind Hosea. "Pa, are you seeing this?"

Betsey and Aaron approached him from behind.

"We were just coming from the outhouse. I can't believe what we're seeing, can you, Pa?" Betsey came closer.

The lantern Aaron was carrying brightened the area around Hosea. "Put that lantern up close to the cabin, Aaron. I want to see this clearly."

Aaron took the light away as Betsey edged closer to Hosea. "Pa, do you have Julia?" She chuckled at him.

Hosea nodded, but didn't take his eyes off the spectacle above him. "She's fine. I have her wrapped tight."

Hosea looked down long enough to see Betsey peel back the edge of the blanket to look at her daughter. "What do you think is happening?"

Hosea returned his gaze upward. "I haven't a clue. I've never seen anything like it." Stars left streaks across the sky as they swept across the dark background in a spectacular display before seeming to fall toward earth, but it wasn't just one or two stars, but hundreds.

Aaron returned.

"This is more magnificent as anything I've ever seen in a morning sky." Hosea looked down again into the face of his grandchild, who now had her eyes shut and appeared to have fallen back asleep. Hosea's gaze returned to the light show above them. "Never in my life."

"It's as if..." Betsey drew closer to Aaron as he wrapped his arm around her shoulders, "the stars are falling."

Hosea wasn't sure what was happening, but a sense of calm came over his heart. He didn't feel disturbed or frightened by the spectacle. In all his days, Hosea knew this sense of calm could only originate from God. The stars were falling in incredible numbers, but for some reason, it didn't frighten him, but rather made him praise the God of all creation.

"Pa, what do you think is happening?"

"I don't know," Hosea answered his daughter's awe-filled question. "But I don't think we need to fear it." Hosea counted off days with his fingers. "If I'm counting correctly, this is the morning of November thirteenth. I think we should remember this morning. Write it down so we are reminded about when we saw this amazing display. Perhaps—"

Hosea couldn't take his eyes off the sky as star after star streamed across his view. Words weren't enough to describe the morning show.

"Julia." Julia startled awake as Hosea peered down into the blankets surrounding his granddaughter. She gazed up at him. "We need to remember this morning. I'll tell you about it often. I'll write it down so one day you'll be able to tell my great-grandchildren all about it. Perhaps even my great-great grandchildren."

"Do you think we should go inside, Pa? The whole thing is scaring me." Betsey left Aaron's arms and pulled in close to Hosea.

"I don't think we need to be alarmed. I have a strange peace about this. What if this is God just telling us that what we've done here, in this territory, is a good thing? Like this star show is His approval or congratulations to us." Hosea hugged the bundle in his arms closer.

Betsey wrapped her arm around Julia still in Hosea's arms. "I wish she was old enough to see it."

"That's why we need to write it down. We need to remind her from time to time." Tears filled Hosea's eyes. "This is incredible."

Hosea knew only one way to commemorate the moment. He did what he always told his girls to do when they were uncertain or afraid. *"I sing the mighty power of God, that made the mountains rise. That spread the flowing seas abroad, and built the lofty skies. I sing the wisdom that ordained the sun to rule the day; The moon shines full at His command, and all the stars obey."*

Betsey's voice joined in. *"I sing the goodness of the Lord, that filled the earth with food. He formed the creatures with His word, and then pronounced them good. Lord, how thy wonders are displayed, where'er I turn my eye. If I survey the ground I tread, or gaze upon the sky."*

Aaron also joined in singing the song. *"There's not a plant or flower below, but makes thy glories known. And clouds arise and tempest blow, by order from Thy throne. Creatures that borrow life from Thee, are subject to Thy care. There's not a place where we can flee, our God isn't present there."*

Silence hung in the air on the bank of the Shiawassee River as they continued to watch the sky burst forth with falling stars.

Pa broke the silence. "Whatever is happening, it's all from God. I know He is here. With us. Just as He's been since the moment I stepped foot on this property. Just as I told Aaron why I left you and the girls here alone. He'll always be here protecting us. We have nothing to fear." As the stars continued to streak across the sky, Hosea continued. "'Surely, the darkness shall cover me; even the night shall be light about me. Yea, the darkness hideth not from thee; but the night shineth as the day: the darkness and the light are both alike to thee.'"

A sliver of light soon penetrated the darkness, as the sun began to rise on a new day.

Note from the Author

The research for *The Year the Stars Fell* started with a search for farmers living in the Durand, Michigan area. Soon excerpts regarding the Hosea Baker family began to emerge, and before long, I realized this particular family had a great part in the early history of Shiawassee County in Michigan.

My first search veered off track as the Baker family stories drew me in, like a beagle on a rabbit trail. Snippets of information emerged, followed by details of the small village of North Newburg.

How did this small, now extinct, village emerge? Who were the first settlers? How long did the village exist? The more inquisitive I became, it raised more questions than answers. I wondered why the small village no longer existed.

Accurate facts include - Hosea Baker was one of the first settler in the county to build a home, plant crops, harvest those crops, pass away in North Newburg, and buried in one of the first plots in the Newburg Cemetery. Before him, only fur traders and Indians existed in the county. Two brothers, named the Williams brothers, were said to be the first business men to enter the county and they eventually started a lumber mill in Owosso, just north of Hosea's property.

It was reported that Hosea and his son, Ambrose, came to the Michigan Territory in April of 1833. Hosea then blazed a trail back to Pontiac, on his way back to Crawford County, Pennsylvania to bring his family back to settle in North Newburg. His family consisted of his wife, Sally and several daughters, including Betsey, and Betsey's husband, Aaron. I know Hosea had several daughters, along with Betsey, so I took the liberty to give Betsey, three younger sisters.

Records show that Hosea headed back to Pennsylvania in August, but they must have returned quickly, for on October 28, 1833, his daughter, Betsey, gave birth to her first daughter, Julia Swain, who is listed as the first baby to be born in Shiawassee County.

Hosea initially purchased 600 acres in Shiawassee County. Not only did his family live here, but as a politician, Hosea played a major part in the beginnings of North Newburg, including starting a grist mill and sawmill, as well as the Newburg Cemetery. The blackjack oak tree mentioned in the book stood by his grave until 1984, when it blew down in a major windstorm. It fell across his grave, but did not harm the stone erected there in his honor.

Hosea lived a short life, to standards today, dying at the age of 53, and Sally followed him just two years later. Research showed that the experience of establishing a farm was difficult. Mosquitoes were a menacing threat for the settlers. The fever, talked about in this book was ague, and it was later determined that it was the mosquitoes that gave settlers the illness, which killed many.

Wolf pelts could be sold to the local fur traders for thirty dollars each. A stamp for a letter was twenty-five cents, making it hard to notify relatives that a settler had arrived, or whether or not they were well, after their journeys west.

Indians did like to come into settlers' cabins and sleep in front of the warm fires. Sometimes they would steal food, but mainly only wanted alcohol and firearms. They did have a yearly sacrifice near North Newburg, to appease the gods. Why they sacrificed a dog is unknown, but their reasoning was an effort, on their part, to atone for an earlier generation's massacre of the Sauk Indian tribe.

The Indians also used a salt lick close to Knaggs Bridge, because salt was a good meat preservative, during the winter. They often were known to bury their canoes close by the bridge, as well, so the canoes could endure the deep snow caused by Michigan winters.

The family could have traveled by land from Pennsylvania, but that was highly unlikely. Steamboats were a major means of transportation for pioneers heading west. Northern Ohio and southern points of Michigan were swampy and difficult for wagons to get through, so in lieu of wagons, parts of the journey were taken via steamboat or canal boat. The boats traveled down the Erie Canal from Buffalo, New York and on into Detroit, where settlers and their wagons then took the Grand River Road Trail through Michigan to Chicago, then further westward.

One specific tale of the Baker family included an emphasis regarding the singing daughters. Excerpts say that others could hear the Baker family daughters' singing before they could see them. Caroline did get three wolf pelts the first few years the family was in

North Newburg, but she trapped them instead of shooting them, as my story depicts. The family was reported to have a child with them and his name was actually Alexander Stevens. There is no record of who he was or why he was with the Baker family.

Some records indicate that the Baker family could have established a home closer to Knaggs Bridge first and then later moved to North Newburg.

You will find Hosea and Sally Baker's grave in the Newburg cemetery, but Betsey and Aaron Swain later moved to Newaygo, Michigan and that is where you will find their final resting places. Many children followed the famous Julia.

'The stars falling'—was a spectacular meteor shower, called the Leonid Meteor Shower of 1833. They said it was like no other, seen across the United States, and deemed, "the night the stars fell." Hundreds of thousands of meteors per hour were seen. Just before dawn, people threw on clothes and gathered in roads and fields to watch the 150,000 meteors (about 30 per second) dance in plain view during the storm's peak.

Some people thought it was the End of Days spoken about in the Bible verse in Mark 13:25, "and the stars of heaven shall fall." I didn't know about the shower until it was reported on a television show my husband and I were watching one night while I was writing this book. What struck me odd was its timing. 1833. When I heard the date, I knew my story had to include it and later the title was created.

The sequels of this story will include many others who literally risked their lives to come to the remote locations of the Michigan Territory. Each book will continue the stories of the Bakers, Swains, and the village visible only in the historic books of Shiawassee County. I hope you enjoyed this story and the series that, I pray, will follow.

~**Elizabeth**

About the Author

Elizabeth's first book titled *Under the Windowsill,* is a coming-of-age story about a young woman named Kenna who runs away to Mackinac Island in search of a better life.

Elizabeth's second book titled *Promise at Daybreak,* has a Durand, Michigan setting and is about two elderly sisters who are forced together due to illness. They meet again to fulfill a pact they made at their mother's grave.

Elizabeth's third book titled *Just a Train Ride,* highlights a love story from the 1940s. An elderly woman recalls her story for a frustrated fellow passenger on a train from Chicago to Michigan.

A sequel to Just a Train Ride is Elizabeth's fourth book, *Mere Reflection.* It is the continuing story of Blaine, the young girl on the train. What kind of life got Blaine to the place she is now and why is Callie's help so important?

For more information on where to find Wehman's books, check out her website at **www.elizabethwehman.com** or like her on Facebook at Elizabeth Wehman/Author for new and upcoming books.

Elizabeth lives in Owosso, Michigan with her husband. You may email her at elizabethwehman@yahoo.com.

Made in USA - North Chelmsford, MA
1108308_9781732652224
07.20.2022 1706